Gaha: Babes of the Abyss

JON FRANKEL

Whiskey Tit ● NYC & West of Nowhere

This book was produced using PressBooks.com, and PDF rendering was done by PrinceXML.

For Maja, Elizabeth, Catherine, Zofia, Jesse and Andrew

Acknowledgements

The author gratefully acknowledges the following people for their friendship, generosity and insight: Cara Hoffman, Michael Salwen, Nancy Moss, Eric Maroney, Billy Coté, John Fousek, Julia Kreutzman, Steven Adkins, Joel and Julie Copenhagen, Ubaldo Valli, Bob Stratton, John Newman, Oskar Eustis, Miette, and Maja Anderson.

For the story, and one felicitous phrase, I am indebted to Bernard O'Donnel, who wrote *The World's Worst Women* (of the twentieth century). In it you will find Chapter XI: The First Acid Bath Murders, about the sisters Katherine and Philomene Schmidt and the lawyer Alexander Serrat. They dissolved their victims in acid.

The title, as well as some names, come from *The Complete Enochian Dictionary*, "A dictionary of the Angelic language as revealed to Dr. John Dee and Edward Kelley...." *Gaha* is the Babe of the Abyss, an angel.

For language, I have been wayward, promiscuous and omnivorous, unapologetically. All errors are mine. Malaprop uses of languages other than English are not to be corrected.

Thank you Mike Salwen, for proofreading, yes, and enumerable, incalculable acts of love and friendship for 40 years.

Deep gratitude and love to Oskar Eustis, cousin, comrade, and friend, and the greatest analyst of narrative on the planet.

I owe a huge thanks to Cara Hoffman for everything.

I wish especially to acknowledge the unending loyalty, friendship, encouragement, intelligence, determination and kindness of Miette.

What lies beyond gratitude, beyond measure, my love for Maja Anderson, who makes all things possible, including the cover of the book.

"It's going to be a hard, dirty business."
– Philip K. Dick, *Game Players of Titan*

Chapter One

LA: 2540

She was seventeen and all leg, banging the hell out of a pinball machine. I watched her play, my back to the bar. There was a cigarette going in her left hand with a cone of ash hanging off the end. The muscles in her bare thighs tensed up every time she bumped her pelvis into the coin box. As the ball shot toward her flippers she turned her feet in and banged with the right and then the left hand, knocking the ash to the floor. The red light on top of the machine started to turn and a police siren went off. It barked, "Pull off to the side of the road!" and she slapped the flipper, sending the ball up into a thousand-point hole. While the lights flashed and sirens sang she took a long drag off the cigarette.

I should have known better. I was on the job for Junior. There were two kilos of cocaine in my briefcase. I had only stopped off for a shot before going home. It was not the time to be messing around with girls who play pinball. But I felt like one night with her would light the fuse to another big bang. So I hopped down off the stool and stood beside her. She waited for the ball to release, her head held back, still, poised as if about to strike. "What are you drinking?" I asked.

She eyed the ball, breathing through her nose. "Fuck you, I am shooting," she said, in some kind of an accent I didn't know.

"It's just a game," I said.

"Game? No." Thwock. The ball knocked around making bing-bing noises and then disappeared in a shade. Her neck tightened. She had short tufted hair in a jumble of mismatched dyes and cuts. Her skin was lit up in neon beer signs and pinball. She wore a green tank top and orange cotton shorts that rode up her butt and lime green jellies on her feet, toenails painted red. A black pearl on a gold chain bounced on her chest. The machine exploded to life and the ball shot down the center. She hit both flippers and missed. "Chinga tu madre," she muttered. "You did this. You owe me a drink. Oaschloch."

"I never heard that one before. What's it mean, Okschlott?

"Oaschloch. Asshole you would say." She made an 'o' with her thumb and forefinger and held it up to me. "Not the jerk, where the shit comes out."

"Let's sit," I said. We took our seats at the bar. I called Tony over. "Make it Mekong and bironga this time, and whatever the perrucha wants."

"Bironga and Mekong is good," she said. She had the high triangle face and eyes of an Egyptian cat and two little bumps on her chest.

Tony went about getting our drinks. He wore shabby pants and suspenders that seemed to drag his ass from one end of the bar to the other. His eyebrows were big salt and pepper tufts and his cheeks were pitted like old concrete.

"So what do you do?" I asked. I had her in the stool—so far so good—but she was bored, staring at the bottles with her chin propped up on her hands. Her eyes were the color of the room.

"Nothing. Why do you ask? Where's my drink?"

"Relax, it's coming."

"O.K." She scowled and stared at the bar and then at me. Tony put down the beers and poured the shots. She downed hers and drank some beer. I took a sip and watched her. She didn't sit still. She was like a long guitar lick. Every minute she pulled a new face on me, or the mirror, or she twisted back and forth on the stool, her eyes spiteful and narrow, her mouth about to spit.

"You don't go to school— "

She stared at her hand, trying to pick out a finger to gnaw to the bone and asked, "To what? School? No. Do you take me for an idiot?" She looked me in the eyes and said, "Why don't you tell me what you do?"

"Real estate, mostly. I'm a small business man." My old man always told me to go get a shingle, whenever he wrote from Alcatraz. Work your angle from inside the law, he said. Be a broker. Real estate, CPA, lawyer. Anyone who takes a cut. And that's what I did, mostly.

"Small business, right. Pimp?" She half smiled.

"What the fuck is it with you?" I asked. "Pimp. Is that how I seem?" I didn't like pimps much.

"Forty-year-old guy, seventeen-year-old girl. What do you call that?"

"Bad arithmetic. I'm 25. You're in range." I raised my glass to her and smiled, all 37 years of me. "I wouldn't expect no remuneration or nothing, for my greater maturity."

"You think I don't know those words? Because of my accent?"

I didn't know what to think. "It's a lawyer joke. I can do that. I'm a lawyer."

"That must come in handy." She rolled a thin cigarette up from a pouch of Kretek and lit it. The smell of cloves sweetened the air.

"Are you really seventeen?" She held her wrist up and showed me a scar code, an ugly patch of red welts. "Who gave you that?"

"*The roller of big cigars.* A Ruler on his giant horse."

"What the fuck are you doing here anyway?" I asked.

"What the fuck is *anyone* doing here?"

I wondered that all the time.

The clock above the cash register said ten-to-five. I had hours to kill. If I could get her into my car, I could get her into my bed and still get to the party in time to set up, and deliver the tributo to Carlos at midnight. "You wanna go for a drive? This place is dead."

She shrugged and it was like she wasn't there. She was a ghost, a sleepwalker. She had drifted. "Maybe. I'm waiting for someone."

"You tell me now? After all that? You break my heart?"

"You never asked. She will be here soon." Her face was flat and still.

"She. A bloody tortillera. My fucking luck."

The door outside opened, letting in a flood of sun that lit up her face. Her eyes flared like matches and then they were the dark unbroken blue of desert sky. In walked a woman, blinking. She shut the door and searched the room. The girl got off her stool and called, "Elma, over here, here." Elma looked a little older, longer in the face, and she was a bad dresser. She wore paisley pants like bags and her feet were filthy from walking in sandals. She had an expensive hair cut. It hung straight down to her shoulders, and it was all one color of blond, except the front left side of her head, which was of LuminEssence flashing in the dark.

"This is my sister Elma."

Elma nodded and tried to smile.

"Now I know who she is but who are you?" I asked.

Elma answered. "She's my little sister, who should not be talking to people like you."

"People like me? Now what is that?"

"I won't say. Irmela, are you done playing pinball?"

"Yes, I am all done."

I got down off the stool and faced Elma. "We were just having a drink. I hope you don't mind. In fact, I invited Irmela to go for a drive. Why don't you come too?" I figured, if it doesn't work out with the perrucha, maybe it will with the big sister. And that would give me time to work on the little one. Like my old man said, from the inside.

Elma examined my face like a plastic surgeon. She gulped and looked away. "This we cannot do."

"Now don't be so harsh." She smiled at the floor. The hook was set. "Irmela can sit in back. You sit up front with me. We'll go along the coast. I know a bar with great food looking right out over the ocean. We'll get steak and dance all night long." She pretended to grimace and now, for me, it was a matter of pride. "If you don't wanna do that, then I'll drive you wherever you're going."

"I have a car out front."

"Am I fishing in the wrong hole?"

"Why don't you buy me a drink here. Later I can decide about the roadhouse and all that stuff." A sarcastic smile lit across her face and her hair glowed. She laughed at me. And I laughed back.

I turned to Irmela with a big smile, thinking, now for you. But she wasn't there. I looked down the bar at the same three old people with wrinkled, tanned and tattooed arms who'd been there for the past 30 years. The ceiling brightened and as I turned around the door closed down the light and the bar was dark again. Footsteps crunched on the stones of the parking lot. "What the fuck—"

Elma said in a placid monotone, "Irmela does that a lot. She's very moody. I must go after her." She walked out the door and I sat down and took a sip of beer. Oh well, I thought. I really can't be chasing after crazy girls who play pinball. I had a delivery to make, a party to set up. Things to do. Carlos didn't like when a man was late.

I finished the shot. When I went to pick up the briefcase, my hand reached into empty air. It was gone. "Fuck!" I yelled. Tony looked up, his mouth hanging open. I ran out the door into the blasting sun. Elma was trotting across the parking lot, chasing my car on foot. I patted my pockets. Irmela had taken my keys and wallet too. "Goddamn it!" I screamed. I loved that car. I didn't love anything more, except maybe the house I was living in, but that wasn't mine. The car was mine.

Elma stopped running and turned towards me. "She drove off in someone's car. I tried to stop her, but...."

"Yeah, my car. And she stole my briefcase too." I was fucked. Two kilos of cocaine, gone! I never had to kill anyone before, never even thought about it and I'd only known her five minutes and all I could see in any direction was murder.

It was the hottest part of the afternoon. 160-degree waves of heat radiated off the crushed stone of the parking lot and baked my face. My eyes winced at the wind. I needed a silver snood and goggles but they were in the trunk. She looked around the parking lot and said, "There. That's where I parked. Come on."

I followed her to the car and my spirits fell as soon as I saw it. "Oh hell," I said. It was pathetic, a solar toy made of Litewood and rubber with two solarsails. Useless at night after a couple of hours. And a maximum speed of 40 mph. "This will never work. I must be nuts," I said and got in the car.

"She's always doing this, I'm sorry. What was in the briefcase?"

"Important documents. I'm totally screwed with my firm if I lose those things. Like dead screwed."

"Well she doesn't care about your documents!" Elma said, laughing. "You are like a child. She is only after money or drugs."

Chapter Two

Elma checked her rearview mirror. The car shook as the sails lifted taut and she spun us out of there. "Put on your seat belt. We'll go to her usual spots first."

I tightened the belt and tried to stretch my legs but there was little room on the floor and my stomach was in knots. The seats were like padded bowls. The car had a faint foul odor, of upholstery stained with sweat and glandular secretions. "She has a route when thieving? Where I come from that will get you a knife in the back of the head."

"You think she's very beautiful?" Elma asked, craning her neck as she drove. I didn't answer. Sure she was beautiful. That wasn't even the word for what she was. But I wasn't going to say so. Not to the sister. She looked in the rearview again. "Sometimes she follows me. I must drive around until she thinks she catches me, but I have really caught her; then I chase her around for a while. We learned that back home."

"Where would that be?"

"Tell me your name first."

"Bob Martin."

"So you are the man from Mars." Elma turned onto a dirt road that took us towards Beverly Hills. The small adobe domes on either side looked like igloos with kitchen gardens, grape arbors and orange trees. We raced along the ruts. Dust blew up around the windshield and rained rocks on the roof. She drove with one hand and put the other through her hair and said, "Montreal. Then New York, Vegas. We have a musical act."

We came to a fancier neighborhood with Spanish colonial houses behind stucco walls and gates and modern bungalows with fences. She pulled off the road and parked under a giant eucalyptus tree in front of a low, single story block building with a flat reflective roof. "Maybe she is getting a hair cut," Elma said.

"That's just what I would do in this situation."

"She is young. She has not learned." There were three unoccupied hair-drying units shaped like eggs against one wall and three sinks where three people were getting their hair washed by decrepit old men with long pink fingers. None of them was Irmela. We got back into the car. Midnight was creeping towards us.

Back in the car I was so twisted around on myself I couldn't stand it anymore. "Where does she drink?" I demanded.

"She doesn't drink. She plays pinball."

"She knocked the Mekong back today like they were old friends."

"We will go to streep mall next."

Elma kept her eye on her rear the whole way to streep mall. She got off the freeway and onto a local pitted road lined with shacks with goat and chicken pens and cactus hedges. The dust rolled up and engulfed the car. Up ahead three ceramic building ports shimmered in layers against brown dirt and dead grass. Horses and buggies, mule carts, cars and bikes were parked under the palm trees. At the turn off there was a sign that said, streep mall.

"So what's here?"

"The bar where she knows a girl. They all have big breasts. Irmela could not get a job in this bar. She has boy's body. The owner said, *this ain't some Ruler bar.* I have heard of Ruler bars only in ludicrous stories in the newspaper, the kind you get at the train station, for the toilet and the waiting room. Where they make those lies to keep you quiet while the train goes."

"I'm familiar with them."

We entered the first port. The stairwell down stank of piss and rotting fruit. The climate control clanked. Inside the air was cold and wet. It smelled like mildewed carpet. There was a long bar full of men with boob jobs. The bartender was a six foot blond dressed from the neck down in black. Elma spoke to her in what she later said was French, but I didn't know French from German.

"We'll look in back," Elma said, taking my hand to lead me through a curtain into a dark circular room with ten pinball machines and a red light in the ceiling. We stood by the curtain watching. Their faces were lit up yellow as they stared unblinking into the game and rocked their hips and pushed their knees into the machines. Smoke filled the dark red light. There was a girl with unruly hair at one of the machines that looked like Irmela for a moment, but it wasn't her.

We drove in light traffic towards Santa Monica, through Serra Springs. Elma was cool. Her lips were pursed like she was whistling. I was not. Sweat poured down my neck and soaked my shirt. The right thing to do at that point would have been to shoot them both when they handed over the drugs. But I didn't have a fusca. I never carried one.

The vents were clogged with dust. Dirty air spit out into the car. The engine had a weak heart and nearly lost power on turns.

We drove in widening circles into the dark until at best we had two hours of power left. I was hungry. It was late. I didn't just have the meeting with Carlos, I had a party to run, in a Malibu palace I was managing. I was going to be too late to meet the caterers and the band or check the liquor and roulette tables. My partner, the Priest would have to do everything. I didn't like that. "Just one more place," Elma said.

"Doesn't Irmela ever get hungry? I mean, what kind of a game is this? I'm starving." The blood was pounding in my ears. "I'm gonna lose what's left of my mind here." Maybe I would have to beat them to death.

"You cannot stand a little hunger to get what you desire? What kind of a weak man are you? If it were my briefcase I would not rest till I had it back again. I would not think of food."

"Must be I can think about two or three things at once."

"Where we are going is a restaurant with a good pinball room that serves sticky rice, in Hollywood."

"I am so fucking sick of sticky rice!"

"Everyone likes that. With the dried shrimps and chilies."

"Yeah, yeah, and fish sauce. Ten years I lived down the block from the Kathasaritsagara Nam Pla factory. You know I learned to sleep with that smell in my head? I was once so drunk I curled up with my dog and slept with my face in his ass and didn't even fucking know it, that's how bad it was."

"This is the place. Can you try to control yourself a little?"

"If it will get my briefcase back."

The restaurant was above ground on a desolate lot at the end of a block of one-story homes with all the windows broken out, live ammo rounds scattered on the ground. Inside was efficient, clean, with strong fans, but sweltering hot. There was a counter and three small tables against an opposite wall with a view of a compost dumpster and some stunted bougainvillea and jacaranda, lit a dim metallic green by the interior lights. The walls were white junk block, and the tables were boards screwed to metal stands. Out back, under a corrugated solar roof with screened-in sides and flickering orange whale oil lamps were five pinball machines with a line for each. There was a bar at the far end where a girl dispensed bottles of cheap bironga and boiled water.

A short man with bags under his eyes and a potbelly stood behind the counter leaning on his hands, staring glumly out into the empty dining room. There was a strong scent of toasted dried squid in the air. He looked at Elma and smiled. "Oh, Elma, long time you haven't been in."

She said in a low voice, looking at the floor, "I was not permitted to leave."

"Sit down, please. And your friend," he looked at me a little critically. I tried to get a line on whether he was her dad or not, but got nowhere with that. I looked at the clock. It was nearly nine. The knots in my stomach had tightened into bolts of fire. I said, "I'll take a toasted squid and rice and a cup of tea."

Elma said, flipping the menu over twice to check between two things, just to be sure, "Convolvulus, with tempeh."

"And brown rice?" he asked, looking up from his pad and smiling.

Elma's face cleared and she smiled at him. A warm light rose in her blue eyes and her hair glowed. "You remember. Thank you. And a mango juice with Keane's Cane."

"I don't really even like toasted squid, but it smelled so good," I said.

"Thaksin chars it. They all come here for the dried squid."

"Who?"

"Ruler Bikers, who else?"

I made a little air noise with my throat. "Is Irmela friends with them?"

She smiled again, only this time there was nothing kind about it. "Irmela is friends with everyone."

"Does she steal everyone's wallet and keys, and their briefcases?"

"No, not everyone. Everyone else though."

Thaksin brought our food and I sat silently eating balls of sticky rice and toasted squid, dipping it in a spicy dried shrimp sauce while she ate the convolvulus greens and brown rice with a spoon and fork. It was good and my stomach felt a little better. I said, "That car of yours hasn't got two hours left on it. I'm under a very serious deadline."

"What do you mean? The charge? I have two spare batteries. I can go all night."

"Well in that case, I'm belching, let's go."

I paid Thaksin and we took our food out in paper. As we headed into the parking lot, a pair of headlights came on. "That's my car," I said. It was beautiful. Long, thala green, with a tinted white roof. Irmela's face was a pale smudge in the distant windshield.

"You see? She is waiting. Now she is done chasing us and we have to chase her."

I ate the food out of my lap while Elma followed Irmela for block after block of boring shithouse homes. Lumps of clay in the desert. I could have been in the hills above Malibu sipping mock blue gel out of a martini glass and screwing an actress in the pool. The caterer would have the grilled prawns out. The band would be tuning up. The first guests would be spread out here and there.

The Priest ran whatever needed running. He treated my money like his own, so I had to be careful and know exactly what he was stealing. He had the ultimate shingles, MD and Priest. Or at least, he once did. He was defrocked in both professions, shorn of his titles and rights to practice; but not of his abilities. A medical man is invaluable in all kinds of business. And a priest knows how to win the trust of others.

The taillights were more or less in view for about an hour, and I was blowing aneurisms to find out if she even *had* the briefcase or if she'd turned it over to her Ruler biker friends.

Finally Irmela pulled onto the shoulder off the San Diego Freeway. Elma drove up alongside her and I rolled down the window. "Do you have his briefcase?" Elma shouted. "He says he needs it. There are men who will kill him if it is gone." Irmela bit her nails and stared with big unblinking eyes at us.

I yelled, "Look kid, I know you got the bag."

She shook her head and then her eyes dilated. "I gave it to David. Like he asked."

"Asked what? David who?" I screamed.

Elma yanked my sleeve and I turned on her. Her face was an inch from mine. I could smell her breath, shrimp and garlic and lime juice. "You want the briefcase back?"

"Yes I do want the briefcase back."

"Then shut up for a moment. Let me talk to her. Irmela, David has the briefcase? For how long?"

"While you were at the restaurant I brought it."

"Goddamnit, would he open the thing? What kind of a pendejo scumbag is this guy?" I asked.

"A real one," Elma said. "Much worse than you. He is a schwein. He makes me do mamar. Blowjobs." *Whores?*

"I'd make you do that too." Whores. I never would have figured them for that. And why not? It happens all the time.

"I hope you will not find out what a schwein he is."

"He said we owe him money," Irmela said.

"But it is a lie," Elma said. Then she began talking with her eyes, opening them wide, and screwing her lips up like an asshole. She flexed her nostrils. Irmela stared at her with her moon white face, blinking and raising her eyebrows, which didn't even wrinkle her forehead.

Irmela swallowed and said, "We have to pay. You know we have to pay. It is what you always tell me. Why would I not take it and give it to him? All that cocaine? You will never have to do mamar again. We don't even have to sing." She paused and said, softly, enunciating each syllable, "And he will forget we exist." Her face trembled as she spoke. The vapid childish stare was gone. Her eyes were dark and bright all at once. She was feral, inhuman. My heart knocked at my ribs.

There was business at hand! It was time to concentrate. "If you think I'm gonna let that whatever the fuck schwein is keep the briefcase, forget about it. I'm taking it back." Maybe I didn't have a weapon, but nobody else knew that.

Her head hit the roof of the car. "Shshs! Cocaine? Why didn't I know that? Am I so stupid? *Court documents*," she snarled, and shook her head from side to side and erupted, "Oaschgeign!"

"Oh, you took pity on a poor lawyer, but an *Oafsgrime*, that's another story then? It's my briefcase and your pinchita pendejita sister stole it and gave it to your pimp."

"Hijo de la puta madre, we are not whores. He pays us to *sing*," Elma said.

Irmela said, "We should go back before it is too late."

"I agree," I said.

We drove to Sunset Strip where there were 500-seat theaters running classical TV comedies—*Bewitched, The Honeymooners, Dragnet*—strip joints and destination restaurants. I used to screw a Samantha Stevens a couple of times a year around there, different ones in different seasons, and a Trixie understudy when I was starting out with Junior.

But David's joint wasn't on that block. It was off of Sunset Boulevard, on Disney Street, a toilet. David's end was the back

end. There was a dairy on the corner and a peyote shop that also
sold toilet paper and water and chocolate candy. There were three
clubs and a bunch of bars and whorehouses. The clubs were small
and unhealthy. The singers there were going down or nowhere.
The whorehouses weren't any better. What in the fuck were they
doing in this place? They could double the number of teeth on a
block just by walking down it.

David owned The Morrow, a nightclub with a loud pink neon
sign above the door, squeezed between a whorehouse and a bar.
There was a hot wind. Irmela yanked open the door. To the left
was a zinc-topped bar with a few old men eating pickled eggs and
toasted habaneras, and drinking shots of mescal. To the right was
a blacked-out room with a small stage with lights in the flies and
amps on the floor.

We walked to the end of the bar. There was a doorway with
a black curtain. Irmela drew it open, revealing an office with a
couch and a desk and a worn-out swivel chair that smelled like a
fat man's behind.

"He's not here," I said.

"Then he is in his room," Irmela said.

"Maybe," Elma said. "And maybe we don't want to know what
he's doing. Do you have a fusca, since you are a gangster now?"

Irmela looked at me. She was afraid. So was I. "Let's go," I
said.

"We will go up the front way. It is backstage."

We went up a stair behind the stage to a dented, unpainted
metal door. It smelled like goat piss. The stairs were soft under
foot. She opened the door and we entered a room where the
air was curdled. Reclining in an easy chair was a giant square
head separated from a mountain of belly fat by a couple of chins.
He hadn't shaved in days. He wore tinted glasses and breathed
through his mouth. Under his arm were big patches of sweat. He

had a remote control in his hand and he was watching two women fuck each other with a double dildo. On the floor by the chair was the briefcase, unopened. He turned the sound off. "Hello ladies," he said, without taking his eyes from the television. "And whoever the fuck you are." The air was warm and still and smelled of dirty laundry and unwashed scrotum.

"I would be the fuck who owns the goods in that bag."

He turned from the TV and stared at me, his little pig eyes pink behind the amber lenses. "I was expecting you to show up. No offense, I hope? I was trying to protect her is all. She's like a daughter to me. Ever since they came to audition. Have you caught their act? They play two electric guitars and sing Austrian folk songs." He smirked.

"Ech," Irmela said. "Futschas."

"I thought you said you came from Montreal?" I asked Elma.

"After Wiener we came from Montreal. Do you want a genealogy from me?"

"Hey," David said. "We aren't getting anywhere." He nodded at the briefcase.

"There's nowhere to get," I said.

"What's it worth to you? What's the finder's fee?" He leaned back in the chair and rubbed his balls with his left hand, and draped his right across the armrest, on the far side. I guessed that's where the gun was. He would have to reach for it, and then swing it up from the floor. There would be time, but there didn't seem to be a lot places to take cover. So even if the first shot missed, he'd hit me with the second and third. So I had to keep him from going for his gun.

I swallowed. "I'd be willing to consider not killing you if you give it back for free."

He sniffed the air and asked, "With what weapon?" His hand dropped off the armrest. He let it hang there, out of sight. The TV flashed on the walls. I was choking on his body odor. He was like a wheel of cheese.

David's arm tensed and he reached to the floor. There was only one thing left I could say and Junior wouldn't like it much. I said, "I don't need a fusca to take the bag. It doesn't belong to me. It belongs to Junior. Tributo. For a man connected to the Vizier of Tenocht. Comprendes? My fucking pimp friend."

His arm was still. He nodded. "That's about what I figured." He stopped scratching his balls and smelled his hand. Then he reached down behind the chair quickly and I searched for a place to dive. He brought up a bottle of Cerveza Norte and lifted it to his blistered swollen lips. "Go ahead, take it. Junior is my friend."

I stared into his glasses. He looked disappointed that he hadn't killed me. He sat upright in the chair and pushed the briefcase across the floor with his foot. I opened it and examined the package. It was intact. I stepped back away from him and looked at Irmela and Elma. Irmela's face was flat. She stared at no fixed point in the room. Elma bit her lip and watched David's arm.

David said, "That concludes our business. If you don't mind, I'm busy." He pointed towards the door behind me.

I hated pimps. Where I came from, everyone did. That was no way to make a buck. "That doesn't conclude it, no. These two," I pointed at them with my thumb. "They're coming with me."

"They're not going anywhere," he said to the girls. "You two got business with me. And that's the last time you steal my car! I'll have you whipped for it, in front of an audience. On camera!" He turned to me, his lips hanging open. "You, I told you to beat it. I didn't mean your dick."

"It's still their night off. Let's go girls."

Irmela and Elma faced each other and each searched the other's eye without blinking, or twitching. They didn't breathe. Elma said, "We can't, if he says no."

"Come on." I reached out and took her hand. It was warm. Her heart beat in her wrist.

He grunted and sighed and stood as if it pained him. His belly and chins fell into place. "They belong to me."

"Who the fuck do you think you are? They don't belong to anyone. Not anymore." I pulled Elma towards me. Irmela smiled at David. "You got a problem with that, bring it up with Junior. He's not just my boss. We're partners, OK? I'm not gonna fuck around with you anymore. You wanna shoot my ass, go ahead. Otherwise I'm walking out that door. With them."

He rubbed his index finger back and forth beneath his nostrils. "The Junior card plays both ways, amigo. And he's got many partners."

"Play whatever card you want."

His dead pink eyes gazed at me through the glasses. He ground his teeth and eased down into the chair, forcing all the pent up air of the seat cushion out into the room. Then he bent his massive ball of flesh forward and turned the sound up on the TV, where the number of women with bobbing dildoes had grown to four.

Elma's face was low and haggard. She budged towards me and mumbled to Irmela, "Let's go."

And Irmela waved at David and said, "Goodbye."

Chapter Three

"So, you want to go to a party?" I was in a good mood, now that I wasn't dead. The air outside was hot and dusty and dry but clean compared to the infected spoor leading to David's lair.

Elma stopped outside. She said in a low sad voice, "He will come after us. I think I would not like a party. Let's go to the steakhouse and have dinner and dance, like you said."

"Too late now. You can thank your sister for that."

Irmela was hanging back, near the door. There was no way to keep an eye on her. She was like one of those half-alive people that slip in and out of reality. I just kept patting my pockets down and checking the exits. She leaned back against the wall, crossed her arms and rocked herself in the shadow of the building. A horn blew in the distance. There were scattered gunshots and light flashes over the horizon. "What did I do?" Irmela asked. Her face was wild and angry.

It wasn't worth trying to answer that. I would only get tangled up in coils of logic. I said, "The party's in a mansion above Malibu. Better than any seaside steakhouse."

"Is there a view?" Elma asked. She must like a view, I thought.

"Sure there's a view. And a pool, gardens, gambling, food. You can eat and drink for free." I tried to imagine them at the party. Elma's face was long and disagreeable sometimes, but she was beautiful and her hair was hypnotic, pulsing slowly in the dark. The guests would let her slide on the ugly paisley harem pants. But her feet were hard to take. The nail on her right big toe was cracked and her heals were practically black. You might scream if you woke up at night and saw those feet in your face. And Irmela! She looked like a child. Sneering over a pinball machine must have aged her. Maybe it was the swagger of the game, because off the game she didn't even stand like a woman; her stature was that of a slightly retarded 12-year-old. Her tits weren't big enough to dent her shirt. I'm not an idiot. Just because nothing she did seemed deliberate, didn't make it so.

"I'm not dressed for a party," Elma said.

"Don't sweat it, you're with me. The food is excellent. Grilled prawns, flank steak, pork adobo. Fried yucca and frijoles negros."

"We already ate," Elma said.

"I didn't eat a thing. I sniffed some of the cocaine and it killed my appetite," Irmela said.

"You mean my load will be light?" I asked.

Irmela touched my elbow and looked into my eyes with eyes the color of water in moonlight. "It might perhaps be so anyway. But I did not give any to that pubic ass hair."

"Well, you must have been careful. The package looked intact when I checked it out."

"She has the fingers of a surgeon," Elma said.

"Yeah, I noticed."

Except for the lights of signs shining on the dirt it was dark. The moon was low in the sky. Overhead were smears of stars. We got in the car, Irmela in back, Elma in front. I settled into the leather seat and started it up. You won't catch me riding a fucking horse.

"Where did you get this car?" Irmela asked.

Elma looked into the back seat and cut her off. She asked, "How long is the drive?"

"It was a bonus for a million dollar home sale, right where we're going now. That's my territory. The canyons. There's a lot of money there if you know how to get it. We'll be there in no time."

I drove to Santa Monica and up the Pacific Coast Highway, hugging the ocean, which would rear into view and hang out as we went up Carbon Canyon and took back roads to a dirt track through a damp, tree-hung gully where there was a long driveway. I left the car to a valet. There was the woof of wings beating the air and then the brief squeak of a rodent being eaten. Whale oil lamps flickered along the gravel path up to the front door, which was fifteen feet high and painted black with a gold and copper handle in the shape of a lion set in the center. The air was heavy with the scent of night blooming jasmine. Fruit bats flew around the high trees overhead.

The mansion was modeled after a Minoan palace. The walls were plastered blocks three feet thick, surrounded by galleries with rose-colored pillars. Tree ferns grew in mounds along the paths, and on either side were groves of fig, orange and lemon, gardens of roses, oleander and hibiscus. Music drifted through the branches with the rumble of voices. People splashed in a pool with a mosaic of Cycladic dolphins on the bottom.

I said, "See if you can wash those feet in the bathroom."

"I think maybe that you are insane," Elma said. Beneath her petulant face there was a smile.

The hostess, Cervenka, a singer and a waitress at a luncheonette in Compton, greeted them. When she saw they were with me, she said, "I never knew you to go for a sister sandwich, Bob."

"There's been some moral backsliding."

"This is the place for decadence," she said, smiling. "Rome."

"Actually, it's Minoan," Elma said.

"Yeah, right, Minoan," Cervenka said.

In a room frescoed with monkeys people were dancing slow, cheek-to-cheek, hands resting gently on their waists. The guests were the usual mix of minor lords with Ruler connections, low level entertainment people and hustlers in the movie and theater business, plus a slew of climbing lawyers and realtors and people who listen up in dive nightclubs for where the party will be.

The Priest was busy checking the bottles in the bar and keeping an eye on the band. He wouldn't let them drink until after the third set, and he only fed them after the second. If they managed to remain upright through to the end they got a bonus of 25 bucks and a bottle of mescal. That is why musicians are so often the last ones standing.

Fredder blew into the sax and then the whole band started to play, slow and sultry, just how people like it. Irmela and Elma drifted towards a large square window that looked out east. The moon was rising over the hills and its light was reflected on a pool of lotuses below. Elma's face was lit partly by the moon and partly by the hair hanging against her cheek. Irmela leaned half way out into the night. The orange shorts rode high on her thighs and her heels were lifting out of the jellies. I left them like that and caught up with the Priest in the kitchen.

The Priest had a lean face. His eyes were dark and sad like a dog's, set in black rings. He looked like he was suffering from a slow-wasting, tropical disease, but he was not. Maybe if he didn't smoke so much he would have breathed a little better. He took out a pouch of Indian tobacco and rolled one up and lit it with a silver match. "Bob. I got everything under control here. General Carlos is in the den. Go down a flight and make for the back of the house, you'll find him. Where were you?" A man went by with a tray of grilled prawns. A lettuce leaf was dislodged and lemongrass and chili sauce was dripping off the edge. "Hey," the Priest said. "You with that tray, stop." He tucked the lettuce in place and said, "Go my son."

"This woman I met in the bar ripped my bag off," I said, in a very low voice.

He laughed. "Your problem is lust."

"You saw her, didn't you?"

"Yeah, she's hot, but look at those feet. They're biblical."

"There're lots of them around now."

"Barefoot women. That's why I got out of it."

"Nothing to do with lust, Priest?"

"They're related, of course."

"Enough," I said. "It's not her, it's the sister."

"The what? That piece of spring chicken, for you? Don't be cruel."

"She's the one that stole my bag. And she picked my pocket."

"You let that wild thing take your shit?" He laughed low. "That's good."

"She's good. Don't turn your back on her, that's all I can say."

"But you did."

"Learn from the error of my ways, Father."

"How'd you get it back then?"

"Elma, the big sister, drove me around. They have this game. While we were looking for her, she was looking for us. She found us first, and then we had to follow her. No. *Chase* her. Chase! Pinche chichis."

"Anything I should do?"

"Nah, go enjoy yourself. Take a swim."

The Priest laughed at the joke. It was hard to imagine him swimming.

General Carlos was square-built, stiff and serious. The glare in his eye was shaming. He was attached to the Vizier of Tenochtitlan. He was of the Aztlan faction at court. They were making a play for LA and he was their man in town, the Vizier's eyes and ears. He served on the general staff of the Mexican Consulate in Santa Barbara, and had diplomatic status, and immunity. He and Junior were made for each other. Junior hated the Rulers and wanted them out of LA. Together, they had plans. And in their plans, I was to get everything north of Santa Monica. Not just canyon mansions. Commercial properties in Malibu, Oxnard and Ventura.

General Carlos sat on the pine bench sipping a mock blue gel cocktail and nibbling a grilled prawn. "I was worried you were going to be late," he said.

"I did my best. Your package from Junior." I placed the briefcase on the floor before him and he took it. His hair was white, cut into an arrowhead flat top, and his face was lined and weathered, the color of brick. There were scars across his nose, on his forehead and intricate hatching on his chin, like someone had played tic-tac toe on it with a razor. "Stay and have another drink, on me."

He shook his head and smiled. "No thanks, Bob. I've got to drive back to Santa Barbara. Maybe next time." He stood and left. Tributo delivered. I sat in the quiet room for a while looking at the books in the bookcases and the pots of ivy growing by the window. It was a nice place, if you like Minoan palaces, but mine was nicer, less pretentious.

Irmela and Elma were at the bar chatting up the Priest. He nursed a dry martini, one rock, and appeared to be relaxed. But the man couldn't hide from his own eyes, and it showed. It's hard to explain, that's just the way he was, and how people are sometimes made. And you act it out then, how you were made, once you know. I knew what I was by the time I was twenty. I was my father's son. Enough said.

The Priest still dressed in black and kept his hair trim. A heavy shadow of beard showed on his face by late afternoon and it deepened throughout the night. I looked for Margaret but she wasn't around. He called her Peg, and he adored her. Margaret was smart and she could make you laugh but you didn't fuck with her. And when they were on the booze together it was desperate and dirty. One night, after he'd been drinking all day and could barely form words, he confessed, "Peg and I, we love each other so, it's a sin." Hugged himself. "We're like this, in Malebolge." And I asked him, "Where's that?" And he said, "Eighth circle of hell. Read *The Inferno.*"

So I read *The Inferno.* And then I knew where he was. Upside-down in fire or shit, under the flail. Where you turn into a reptile and demons tear you to pieces. I couldn't imagine loving anyone like that. I had never lived with a woman for more than a few days and counted myself lucky.

"Well, that was relaxing," I said, getting a handful of peanuts from the bowl. "Give me a blue one," I said to the kid behind the bar. He got to work right away with the crushed ice and the mock blue gel. It came up to the rim and he shaved off a curl of orange zest, which he placed in the center of the drink.

"Your friends were telling me about their act," the Priest said.

"What was it, Australian folk music?" The iced gel had a sweet, citrusy taste with an after burn of Keane's Cane liquor.

"Austrian," Elma said. Irmela turned up her nose.

"What's wrong?" I asked Irmela, standing closer and closer to her as she nudged towards Elma to escape me.

"It's what he says," Irmela said. "It is some bullshit of that dickeye. We do not sing Austrian folk songs. David made that up to get you off of his back. He is a fart from the cunt, an ass violin."

"You mean small talk, don't you?" I asked.

"No," Irmela said. "If I meant small talk I would have said it. He makes no small talk, he only does lies. And sex movies. All he wants is to watch girls licking the butt."

The Priest gave in to a dour laugh. "Watch only?"

She pumped her fist up and down and said, "Then he makes the paja. Sometimes mamar." She gagged and made a frog noise.

"How about we go out into the garden? I've been cooped up all day," I said.

The Priest looked around. The band was blowing a dirge; couples hung on to each other and circled the dance floor like dust devils, against the rhythm. The women's clothes were flouncy and red, with burgundy and plum scarves and the men wore long suits.

We went into the garden. There were a few couples in various states of disrepair sitting on a low stonewall, smoking and laughing. One of the women, with curls of cheap LuminEscent hair falling down her back, was doing a toreador dance and pausing to laugh.

I took out some cocaine and said, "The world could end tomorrow. Let's take drugs."

Elma drained her glass and said, "I'd like another drink." I passed around the little glass container with the cocaine and we each put some in our nostrils and sniffed. As my head lightened and I started to wing, I got refills for us all. The Priest left us; he didn't like drugs other than alcohol or peyote and the peyote was religious. When I handed her the drink she smiled. "These are very good cocktails. Not like the mierda we serve at the Morrow."

"Sock juice," Irmela said.

"Well if you stick around until we go to my place, I have real whiskey," I said.

The conversation became lively. They seemed to nod at what I had said, so I had some hope of bringing them back to my bed.

Irmela and Elma began to chatter, half in Austrian and half in Moron English, with all these Aztlanian curses thrown in. They looked sober, other than their pale skin becoming flushed and their eyes like blue zeros. Suddenly they'd cackle, or giggle, or snort-laugh, and turn to look at me. Elma touched my shoulder, drained her glass again and said, "Things are looking up. I will get myself another now; you don't need to serve me. What Irmela just told me is," she turned to Irmela. Irmela had horse fright in her eyes.

"Don't tell him!"

"Oh, but it is funny. Or else he will think we are laughing at him," Elma said.

"Then he will say we are a foitrottl."

I said, "I don't think you're a foitrottl, whatever that is."

"A complete idiot!" Elma said. "So she was saying to me just now, that the Priest is like your dog, and we remembered a dog we had that looked like him, with black fur around his big sad eyes."

"He had thick velvet wrinkles around his head and neck," Irmela said.

"The Priest runs the show for me is all."

"But you do love him?" Elma asked.

I laughed and gazed down at Irmela's feet. Even with green jellies they were clean, and she didn't have the black hair on the knuckles like Elma did. "You don't seem like dog types."

"It was in Paris," Irmela said.

"No, Montreal! You remember."

"I just remember it all happened in French."

They looked like they had swallowed glass. The mood crashed. I asked, "What happened in French?"

"This was not good," Elma said in a low, deep voice. "Our uncle made us eat the dog without telling us."

"We deserve to die."

"We were hungry!" Elma said, her scold-face back. "We did what we had to do."

I breathed in the sweaty tang of night-blooming flowers and oozing tree sap and waved at my neighbors, Frank Orsba, an entertainment lawyer, dressed in a white suit with a green knit tie, and his companion, Arphe Lux, the famous medium. She wore a vermillion ruffle and wrap with dyed eagle feathers and cultured pearls. They were business partners of a sort, steering clients my way and then working the parties I threw in the houses, for their own purposes. He knew movie stars and she knew how to predict their futures. They waved back and Arphe winked her jaded green eyes, under a heavy awning of lashes. I downed my drink and thought to slow down; I didn't want to be too high, not while the party was on, not before collecting the take. The Priest took me aside and I asked him for a door count.

"Two hundred so far tonight, 75 still here. We have two thousand on the bar, another two in cocaine sales, and twice that at the Black Jack table."

Ten percent of everything was mine. It would be a thousand dollar night, easy. Not bad. Enough to keep going, anyway.

Irmela trailed after the Priest. Elma, who was quite drunk, asked me to dance. We went inside. Her body, hidden under the soft paisley sacks, was strong and muscular, and she had a smooth step on the dance floor. I rested my head on her shoulder and her hair glowed in my eyes. Then they played a polka and I twirled her around. Her face got red and she started to smile. We were both sweating after that. I gave her some more cocaine and she held to me tightly. I craned my head around looking for Irmela but she was not in sight.

After a few more polkas and a waltz we were wiped out, drinking down water at the bar. Still half out of breath, she said in a slurred voice, "Now we should dance in the pool!" and ran off. I followed her out into the backyard, a formal garden with a rectangular pool of illuminated water and lotus ponds. Torches burned along the side, where naked and half-naked people sat around tables drinking and laughing, their cigarettes glowing in the dark. Mosquitoes zapped in the insect lights. Elma staggered out of her clothes and dove into the water. I don't like to swim much but I followed her in. We swam around with abandon. She wasn't the same person in the water. In the water she let it loose and I forgot where I was.

Normally I'm not going to show my ass to strangers at my own party. I'm not the boss anymore then. But it was late. I wasn't thinking about that. I was thinking about those beautiful white tits swaying in the water just a few feet away. Other couples dove in and soon there were a dozen people cavorting in the water. The band played a little louder. There were shrieks and the din of laughter as all the guests crowded the pool and expanded onto the lawn. The band set up outside one by one, each playing the part he came with and then going off. And the guests were dancing, and swimming, and the waitresses worked them for drinks.

"Should we look for Irmela?" I asked.

Elma had a frozen mock blue gel smile. "Oh no, not just yet. I'm sure she has found a friend." She put her pants back on and fastened her bra. I thought, what a fucking shame that is. She pulled her shirt down over her head and lost her balance. "Ha! Now you have to catch me." She fell back against me and her wet hair pressed in my face. I let her slide down and cradled her with my left arm and I gazed down at her half-open mouth. Then there erupted a tremendous, distorted electronic noise followed by a slow descending run of guitar notes. Elma shrieked, "You've found her!" She ran off into the crowd and I followed her. Standing with the band, an electric guitar slung across her chest, was Irmela. When the feedback and notes stopped reverberating, and the boys in the band were still chuckling, she strummed a few cords and started to sing in a voice so pure and perfect I couldn't imagine it coming from her frozen face. But there was no one else singing.

It was getting late. The sky was lightening. There weren't so many people there but those that were there were all done. They'd pass out where they stood and not wake up until the sun got too bright. A few might manage to crawl into the shadows till mid morning, but the Priest would take care of them. I edged away from the girls and headed in to wrap things up.

The caterers had packed and gone. The kitchen was spotless. The oven and fridge were exactly as before. There was no more alcohol in the house, other than what Margaret and the Priest sat consuming on folding chairs in front of frescoes of octopus tentacles. Margaret had on a red dress with a wide white collar, and white rubber shoes. Her face was shaped like a frog's, and her skin was pink. She had wavy red hair that made her look ten years older, and between the hair and the lipstick her complexion had a hot glow that grew more intense when she got angry. When she was angry she blushed crimson and her eyes swam in vindictive tears.

"I'll take that now, Peg," said the Priest.

"Don't Peg me unless you want to get busted one. Hey Bob. A good haul."

"If that's what the Priest says."

"You'll net twelve hundred, after my cut," he said.

"The bank?"

"Safe. Junior's bag took it."

"Why didn't you tell me he was here?"

"You were in the pool, Bob. I had a heart."

"I suppose that would have sucked." I laughed. They nodded their heads knowingly and laughed like a bladder losing air. She handed me the bottle and said, "Go on, sluggo, do your best before the Priest turns it into water."

I drank a little and handed it to the Priest. "We'll all turn it into water, of the Dead Sea," he said. He gazed at the bottle and smiled. "My sweet baby glass." He took two big glugs. "Here ya go Peg love, till we meet on the mountainside. I'll be rolling the boulder up while you chase yours down."

"I'll be rolling it up your arse, mate."

"I thought I might go," I said. "Can you wind it up? I'll take the twelve in silver and pearls now, keep anything else that comes in. The house is closed. Everyone out before the landscaper comes."

"My son," the Priest said. "It's done."

Now all I had to do was find the girls. They were walking around the shadows at the edge of the lawn, arm in arm, holding each other upright. "Party's over," I said, coming up alongside Irmela, who was in better shape than Elma.

"OK," said Irmela. "Elma, we have to walk this way now."

Elma lifted her head up and then let it flop forward. Irmela led her up to the house. At the car she let go of her and Elma leaned against the hood and groaned.

"I don't like that groan," I said. "You get in first, and see she pukes out the window." I stuffed Elma into the back seat, rolled down the window and shut the door.

I drove down to the coast highway and headed to Topanga Canyon. The house was a split-level bungalow with tiled roofs, built of wood and stone, perched on a bluff overlooking the Pacific. The driveway was lined with banana, mango and lemon trees, and there were stands of eucalyptus, pine and cottonwood around the property. A network of stairs and trails led down to a cove with a beach. I parked by the front door. The sun was up and it was starting to get hot. Elma had fallen asleep without throwing up. She wouldn't budge from the backseat. "What's with her? Can't she hold her drink?" I asked.

"She took a pill. She wanted to be asleep."

"Fuck. Help me then. Push her out and I'll take her in."

"OK, I will help you." Together we got her up to the front door. "This is your house?"

"Yeah it's my house." I held up the key and we were in.

In fact it was not actually my house, in the sense of ownership. That would be the de Marcoses. But I was the listing agent on the property and they were in Baguio. I was in no hurry to sell that home. I never even showed it.

I hit the light. "We'll put her on the couch upstairs. The covers are canvas so it's OK if she bludges in the night."

We carried her up the wide stairs through the French doors and into the living room, which had a view on three sides through floor to ceiling windows. And there was a deck off the back. We laid her down on the couch and I got a blanket out of the cedar chest in the corner and put it over her. Irmela stood at the west window gazing out at the pacific, beneath a sky brightening into violet. "Now what about you? A nightcap?"

"That is OK. You have whiskey?"

"You bet I do. I get it from New York. None of that Hong Kong shit." Elma snored softly and shifted on the couch. "You sure she took a pill?"

"What do you mean by *sure*?"

"I mean did you see her take it or did she just say she took it?"

"Said. But she does that when she takes cocaine. She drinks a lot and then, you know, she wants to take a pill to end it. But nothing ends."

"She's a restless sleeper."

"Yes. We have travelled to many places. Her feet were born in motion our mother said."

We went downstairs to the kitchen and I got the whiskey out. She stood next to the door staring out the casement windows at the inner courtyard garden. Bougainvillea overgrew the stone walls. There was a bench seat at a wrought iron table with a couple of chairs beneath an awning off the kitchen roof. I poured us each three fingers over one rock and nodded towards the door into the garden. "Do you want to sit out there, or on the deck upstairs?"

"Out there."

"Suit yourself."

She took the glass. "Soon there will be humming birds."

"Yeah, and a bunch of other stuff too."

"Like what, parrots you mean? They were all over New York. It was disgusting. They say they drove the pigeons out."

"A sure sign of decline, when parrots drive your pigeons out. I guess the West coast has it all over the East."

We sat down on the bench and sipped our drinks in a silence that was comfortable and familiar. We had made it to the next day. We could count toes and fingers and sit in the glow that damaged brain cells give to early morning light. She said, "I don't think this West coast has it all over the East one."

"Well, I haven't been to both places, so I won't say."

"Everywhere is the same."

The sun was up. Hummingbirds covered the flowers. It was getting hot. And she was looking good, ragged from the night, the cocaine and the drink. Her hair was frightful, sticking up this way and that. And there was something about her blank stare. Enchantment hovered over her, lit her from without and within. There was only one thing left to do. "So let's shake it up then," I said.

"Oh, you mean like, we could dance?" she asked in a dead voice.

"I think we're past that."

"You and Elma danced. You are pledged to her, no?"

"Pledged? No. Not pledged to anyone but you right now." She shrugged. "Look, there's one thing left to do here to make it a perfect night."

"No, my pussy hurts."

"Well, I'll fuck your ass then."

She laughed. "I don't think so. Not tonight."

"How about a little head then?"

"That one is small enough."

I drained the glass and rolled a Kretek cigarette up. "You want one?"

"Sure. I'm very tired, but I can't sleep. I will have more whiskey."

I tossed her the cigarette and a lighter and rolled another one up for me. The smell of cloves hung in the air, mixing with jasmine. "Yeah, me too. But this'll be the cheap stuff."

She shrugged and went *pffrr* with her mouth. I went into the kitchen and got an idea. There was bound to be some methaqualone around somewhere. I could offer her that for sleep. Then I could see how things went. I searched the kitchen cabinets till I found where the de Marcoses kept their drugs and there it was. One each should do it. I poured out two Mekong Whiskeys and put them on a tray with two glasses of water and the pills.

"Real service," she said.

I put the tray down. The glasses were beading up. "I've got some methaqualone if you want. It will help you sleep."

She laughed. "Foitrottl. I don't want that."

"You know what *that* is?"

"*Yes.*"

We finished our drinks and I'd had it. She was inert. My armpits started to sweat and then my head. I was fading, even as her body taunted me. The black pearl hung into the V-neck of her green tank top, dangling between her breasts. Her legs had no sign of sun on them. They were bluish purple in the shade, the veins and arteries faintly visible. A small scratch on her ankle was crusted over with blood. The orange shorts were so tight in the crotch I could see bumps. She sat there motionless until, suddenly and without apparent reason, she kicked her jellies off and vigorously scratched the top of her foot with her big toe. The nerves bucked around inside me and my throat burned. "You're driving me nuts here," I said. She looked away from the hummingbirds and narrowed her eyes. "What am I supposed to do?" I asked.

"Go and fuck my sister if you want, or beat off. I don't care."

Fine. "Where do you want to sleep then? There's the other couch in the living room, or the guest room downstairs. It has TV and radio."

"Couch with Elma."

"What are you, a package deal?"

Irmela looked at me strangely then, full of hatred, but also at a far away spot. She said, "You could have hurt David for us. But you had no gun. Now when we go back it will be much worse." Then she turned away and I followed her inside, feeling like I was in her house. She pulled the cuff of her shorts down and then the hem of her shirt. She filled a glass of water from the tap.

"How do you know you can drink that?" I asked.

Irmela faced me. "Because you are rich, and rich people have clean water, even when they don't drink it."

"How do you know so much about the rich?"

"I read somewhere that they don't drink the water on Mars."

I laughed. "I read somewhere that women like you play with men the way kittens play with a ball of twine."

Irmela nodded. "It is the way a cat plays with a mouse before she eats it." She drank down the water and put the glass in the sink. Then she walked up to me very close and kissed my cheek with wet lips. "Good night," she said, and walked away. I waited for my cheek to dry.

Chapter Four

I had just managed to fall asleep when the door opened and a pair of dirty feet approached the bed. "I can't sleep without a blanket," Elma said. "Will you make room for me?" I groaned and didn't open my eyes, pretending to be more asleep than I actually was. All I had wanted was a good fuck before the night was done, but now it was done and I did want to sleep. When I didn't reply she said, "Will you move over? I can't sleep next to a wall, I feel like I'm choking. Please." Her voice was strangely sad, so despite my not wanting to, I moved over against the wall and she got into bed. "Thank you."

"Good night, now," I said, and fell back into a clammy, fitful sleep. I felt like I had been ripped away from something warm, and that the something warm was lying next to me. So now this something became like a nothing, but it bugged me all the same. Gone or there I felt uncomfortable. I turned onto my back, but that was spinny. Not drunk spinny, but cast adrift spinny. The way I imagine they felt in 2210 when Ocba the Great tried to kill Iocle the 2nd in orbit above Mars, and Iocle, rather than retreat, cast his crew into space, where they drifted until their flight suits failed them. But Ocba and Iocle lived at a time when you could write the rules of space.

I tried facing away and facing towards her. Towards her was the only way I could lie without feeling wrong. So I curled up around her and fell asleep until about an hour later when the door creaked open again and I awoke to find Irmela whispering into Elma's ear, "I can't sleep down there alone. Please move over." My nose was pressed against the cold wall.

Elma woke up first, leaving Irmela two thirds of the bed and all but a handful of the blanket. The blanket was just there for comfort. The room was hot in the afternoon, the whole house was. Either it was too damp or too dry, too hot or too cold. In the wet there was mildew. The cisterns were placed wrong. But that's what you expect with a 500-year-old bungalow. With that view of the Pacific, hot nights were not a big deal. My real home was a Jeannie Bottle pod on Goyaałé Street in Puvungna. It was a pit. And I had no other plans, nowhere to go and no one to love, except my old mother out in Barstow. LA was like a big tree on one side of a path, and north of Santa Monica was another tree and I was a spider hanging in between, catching bugs as they go by.

It was late afternoon and the sun shined down through the sky tube and on the bed. Three bars of light advanced slowly but steadily towards my face. I could feel them warm my arms and then my chest and then they crept across my cheek and over my eyes where they merged and seemed to stay forever. Irmela yanked the remainder of the blanket away and I awoke violently. I pulled on some pajamas and went upstairs. The west facing windows were on fire and Elma was seated on the couch with her feet up, sipping coffee and staring at the light.

"I made you some eggs," she said. "And bacon."

"That was nice. Thank you." In the kitchen was a plate with two fried eggs and three pieces of bacon and some toast. I poured a cup of coffee and brought the cold food back up to the living room.

"There's also Bloody Mary if you want."

"Where did you find something to make that with?"

"You don't know what you have? Are you married or something?"

That was the funniest thing she had ever said. "No, not married."

"Well I made mix from the V8 cans and there was spice. You have Keane's Cane. If you want Bloody Mary I'll make it for you."

"Yeah I want Bloody Mary, thanks."

She came back with two Bloody Marys and we watched the sun together.

"Can you go swimming here?" she asked.

"In the pool. And there's the ocean. I use the pool."

"It's a beautiful kitchen," she sighed. "I have never seen one like it before, or a house like this. May we go swimming in the ocean today?"

"If you can take the cold water." I felt hollowed out and dizzy. My head ached.

Elma laughed and stretched her toes. Her feet were much cleaner, though the heels appeared to be tattooed black. "I told you you were weak. That water is not cold."

"I don't like sharks."

"I could have heated the eggs up."

"No, I prefer them cold and congealed."

She stood. "One more Bloody Mary and then we can go?"

"Let me get in the shower first and have another cup of coffee. Let me make it this time. I want an espresso." She followed me downstairs to the kitchen and watched as I filled the bottom of the pot with water and carefully spooned coffee into the capsule, tamping it down slightly with the spoon, brushing grains off the rim. Then I fitted it to the top and put it on the Sunfire 3. "There's milk, if you want."

"I'll have it like you."

"Black. You've been on the deck?"

She shook her head no.

"I thought you would do that first thing."

"I did not want to get in trouble so I sat here."

"But you found the eggs and everything."

"You would want me to do that. It is your house."

We went out on the deck, wearing sun goggles and snoods. There was a strong, gritty breeze. A couple of old pines remained rooted in the outcropping rock of the lower bluff and behind them was the ocean, at the bottom of the rift, white capped and blue, and the clear sky and the afternoon sun. We leaned on the rail and looked at the water and sipped the espresso.

She asked, "How do you walk down?"

"Well, the bluff is jagged, not sheer. You'll see. There's a stair."

"There is no other place like California."

"I guess. I've never been anywhere else. None of my people have been. Not for a long time. My people are aboriginal. We were created not far from here. You can drive there in a few hours. I didn't make it far. Just to South LA. Everyone else, you all people, had to come all the way from Africa."

"You are autochthons?"

"Awe tock thongs?" I had never heard of that one.

"Men of the soil. Like when Jason sows the dragon's teeth and skeletons rise up to fight with the swords. We heard these stories."

"I heard that one too, in school they told us. Well see, my old man's people came to be in the movies, or for the gold. That's what, 600 years ago? But my mother is one hundred percent Tejon Indian. She is Kawaiisu. And Kawaiisu are the ones who have always been in California. That's what she says anyway. All the old people do."

I showered and when I got out Irmela was sitting on the couch reading a book called Die Marquise von O by von Kleist and eating toast with butter and jelly. She had a pot of tea on the table and stared down into the book.

"Where'd you find a book?" I asked.

"In the guest room," she said, not looking up. "There is a whole library, did you not see? Spanish, German, French, Russian and English classics. And the English translations of the Greek and Latin authors and of the Middle Ages. There is philosophy and also some history."

"I guess I haven't been in there much. Why does the Marquise gotta die?"

Irmela looked confused. She twisted her face up and said, "That's the definite article in German. The book is about the Marquise of O, who is saved by Count F. from Russian soldiers, but who also possibly rapes her while she is unconscious. The father has turned her out because she is pregnant."

The gardens of the house spread out around it, tall trees merging into woods at the borders, citrus and banana in the yard, and garden beds of gardenias and hydrangea, a wisteria arbor, palms and yellow roses around the pool. The seaward side of the bluff was arid and the smell of sage and txaparil drifted in with the sea breeze. Elma and I took a path cut through the scrub. "Look out for snakes," I said. "The vipers in the canyons have flesh-eating venom."

"Philoktetes of Lemnos," she said, "suffered from a festering snake bite. I have been to Lemnos. I have seen his bow."

The steep, dusty path twisted down through boulders and cacti, and led to a wooden stair with a loose rail. This zigged and zagged a ways through sage, scrub oak and txaparil and then we stepped through some tall grass, and onto the Pacific Coast Highway, which we crossed to a path and another set of stairs, down the lower bluff and onto a beach sheltered by a rock cove. We were alone. The waves were up. We swam out into the surf and bobbed about, riding the high waves and letting them roll ahead. The water was cold, but I got a kick out of watching her swim back and forth.

The sun was low on the horizon and the sand was glowing. It was time to climb the stairs and go back up the path. By the time we got to the house we were hot and covered in dirt so we plunged in the pool and lay out drying off on the furniture.

"I'm hungry for some real food," I said. "Let's go get steaks at The DelBar. It's a short drive to Malibu."

"I have nothing to wear. Look at my clothes." They looked like a corpse had been buried in them.

"I'm sure we can a find a wrap, and I'll take you shopping first. I'll give you a hundred bucks. It's your cut for getting people into the pool."

I rooted around Mrs. de Marcos's closets and found a saffron silk wrap. That would do. Irmela and I watched her body disappear beneath the layers of silk. When she was done Irmela laughed and said, "You look like the giant cigar at the Hamburg carnival."

Elma put her hands on her chest and looked at them sadly, like she'd awakened with new ones and had no memory of where the old ones went. She said in a low voice, "I don't want to go out there. I just want to stay here."

I said, "Let's get a beat on then."

The fans were spinning and it was much cooler inside than out. I put on some music and we had cocktails in the living room.

"So what is the name of your act anyway?" I asked.

"We are Gaha: Babes of the Abyss," Elma said.

"*Gaha: Babes of the Abyss?*"

"What if David comes?" Irmela asked. "He said today we must be back. It is already late."

We fell silent. David? Who the fuck is David, I thought. "What's he got to do with anything?"

Elma asked. "Can we smoke something? I feel like smoking."

"We have to do that in the car, or outside."

"I can't go out looking like an old clown."

Irmela said, "But if he does come."

"What do you think that paisley thing looks like? You go out dressed in a sack. Those things make your ass look dumpy," I said. "And you have the finest ass I've ever seen."

She became indignant. "It's very William Morris. I am a Pre-Raphaelite."

"Is that why you got the LuminEssence?" I asked. Her hair wasn't just your usual implant. It responded to her moods. It was like she couldn't turn it on and off, it was something that happened. At times the light would pulse brighter and other times, when she was silent, it would brood. And it was just the left side of her head that would sometimes swing down across her eyes and light up.

"That was a gift. Back in Austria. Wiener."

"That was not a cheap gift. So let's go for a ride and smoke Kretek. We'll stop off at a clothing pod and get something cheap and paper."

We got in the car and drove down to Malibu where there was a subterranean, beach-themed clothing arcade. Elma got blue velvet sponge and a pocket book and Irmela, hissing at everything she looked at, walked barefoot, carrying her jellies in two fingers. She stared finally for a long time at a Top and Bottom rack. Sleep clothes. She said, "I never wear black. It's boring. Will you buy this for me?" She was holding up a black Top and Bottom.

I made like I had to think about it. "What's in it for me?"

"Some more boring transaction now. Man wants mamar. More boring than the black hose and the shirt."

"What a fucking pisser you are."

"What would you like for these, my chingar." She made a big sad face, like a clown, and almost barked the last word.

"Make the beds for a week my pinchemoyotita."

Irmela laughed. "Go hire a Moron for that."

"Hey man, I told you, my father was a Moron. That'll look good on you. Now, how about you get a wash and a cut?"

"You want to talk about hair? When do you plan on growing some?"

Elma said, "Let's get the clothes, I'm starving."

I said, "You heard her, let's go." Irmela took the clothes off the rack and I paid the bill.

The DelBar was built into a bluff. You parked above it, entered the pod and from there took a lift down to a huge dining room with a wall of curved glass looking out on the Pacific Ocean. It was like floating in the air above the water. There was a crowd but I knew the maitre d' and he got us a small table by the window. In back was the dance floor. The DelBar house band was the best around. We ordered martinis and steaks with baked potatoes and salad. Elma and I danced while Irmela ate breadsticks and mustard. We drank a bottle of red wine with the steak and then had apple pie and coffee. It was about the most perfect night out I'd ever had.

After a few more dances we split and flew along the back roads. I don't know how we got home. We drank all night and into the next day and then a day after that and after that. I lost count. We had a fire on the beach one night. Another night we were thrown out of The DelBar for laughing too hard. It was at the end of that night that the Priest woke me to say Junior was on his way over. I had 45 minutes to get cleaned up.

Chapter Five

My gums bled when I brushed my teeth. The beard on my cheek was tough and I bled from that too.

Junior didn't come to my place often, not unless he was out and about with his driver Jorge, a punk he freed from servitude to the Ruler Bard, Bard 4 now that he's dead, the American Ruler of LA at that time. Bard 3 was a great hero, a compassionate Ruler who died too young, but his clone was the boldest and baddest Ruler we had seen in a half century, and he didn't forgive Junior, but Junior wouldn't take the stick out of his eye and Bard 4, biding his time, planned on yanking Junior down. That never happened. A war got up in LA Yaanga. When Bard came down out of the hills to strut on that giant horse of his, pro-Mexican, Moron rebels blew up the convoy: the Ruler Bard, horse, and all. So like his father, he was killed in his prime. They sent in the Ruler Tobor Ocktomann after that. The Bards and Ocktomanns had ruled parts of LA for 80 years and before that all of Norte Califas. The Ocktomanns were nine-feet tall, freaks even for Rulers, and politicians who preferred the palace to the battlefield. Junior kept Jorge and Jorge was grateful not to have to put his ass out anymore.

I downed a quick espresso and put the black suit on. The girls were still in bed, curled up like a couple of cats. We were so drunk I didn't remember going to sleep.

Junior arrived and waited in the car so Jorge could suss out the security. We were close but he never went into a room first, he always sent his dogs ahead. Jorge was small. He kept his shirt clean and suit pressed. He had come up from Tenochtitlan looking for work when Bard 4 attacked San Diego, and got stuck on the gabacha side, which is how Bard's troops found him, doubled over in a bar, full of mescaline and pulque. He woke from a dream with Bard's bat in his can, one of a harem of prison boys. He treated them OK. He didn't make them kill for him and he didn't torture them for pleasure. Of course, things went in a different direction after the Ruler Tobor Ocktomann lost half of LA and they sent in some real brain to back the brick, but that's rushing ahead.

"So, is it safe for him to come in?" I asked Jorge.

He smiled. "If there aren't any other little hairy assholes around."

"Just your mother's. I haven't washed yet." I shook his hand and slapped his back. "Tell Junior I'll get a pot of coffee up for him."

"Tell him yourself. He's in the car."

Junior was a big man. No one would mistake him for a Ruler, but he was over six feet tall and wide, with a hard face and dark glaring eyes. He dressed well, always in a suit with zippers and a tie. He did not carry a gun. No one dared to touch him. I did not want to make him unhappy. No one did. He wielded great power over people.

Junior came into the foyer and smiled. "Bob, where've you been?"

I didn't like that smile. It almost always meant he was unhappy. "Just hanging out," I said.

"I got something for you."

"For me?"

"We haven't talked since Carlos."

"Did it go alright?"

Junior sighed and reached into the inside pocket of his suit. "He thought you were going to be late."

"I was there."

He drew out a sack with two fingers and held it up by its strings. "And the peruchas?" he asked.

"What about them?"

He focused his black eyes on me, like polished cufflinks, until I looked away. "Carlos was happy." He handed me the sack. I opened it. It was full of white pearls. Enough to keep going for a while. We went up the steps and through the French doors into the living room and looked at the ocean and the pines on the bluff. "Some place this is. When do the de Marcoses return?"

"They go to Canada next."

"You got anything else lined up?"

"Nope."

"How long can you hold out?"

"With this?" I held up the sack. "A while."

He shook his head. "I wish I were young like you."

"So what's next? Have a seat." I pointed to the couch with my head. We sat down, and he sent Jorge into the kitchen for ice water.

"I want you to show a property for me tomorrow. It's up in the Los Padres."

"The Los Padres? What are you doing up there?"

"I've got a seller, an old LA family. The buyer is the Ruler Tobor Ocktomann himself." He laughed slowly. "I know, I know, why am I doing business with them." He laughed some more, not gleefully, but ruefully, it didn't make him happy. "I know this guy, Charlie Gets Along. His boss works for a guy who manages the

Ruler Tobor Ocktomann's affairs in Sur Califas. He wants to buy a palace, and I've got a fortress to sell him. Charlie Gets Along will meet you up there. I also want you to check out a property outside of Needles, an abandoned subterranean Air Stream camper museum. I want to know what it would cost to put on a party there."

Jorge came in laughing to himself. He handed Junior the water and burst out, "Sorry boss, I can't breathe, she makes me laugh so hard. I can barely talk."

"Is she up already?" I asked.

"Goat, you can't fuck those tits they're so small," he said, handing me the water. "That's just what they say."

"We'll see about that, culeroita, my fucking friend," I said.

Irmela came in wearing her orange shorts and green tank top. They were wrinkled and stained. Her shoulders were rolled forward, and the hair was matted down on one side of her head and roaming about on the other. Her eyes were puffy and half closed and her mouth was slightly agape. "I did not know you had friends. Excuse me," she rasped.

"No, that's OK. Junior, Irmela. Irmela, Junior. Jorge you've met."

They gave each other a nod and we finished up our business. Junior was almost out the door when Elma came up the steps and through the French doors and stood next to Irmela. She wasn't in any better shape. Her make up was smudged, but she looked more put together, partly because of the blue foam, and partly because of the dim radiance of her hair. Junior paused. He was holding back, I could see it in his eyes. Elma surprised him, and he didn't want me to know. Her expression of whiskey-dazed sleep was fixed. Junior smiled. "Come into the office tomorrow morning and we'll go over the details. Be there at 8 sharp. And don't bring your flies." He and Jorge walked out the door.

"Fuck. We got a day to get normal," I said.

There was a knock at the door. It was the Priest. I made coffee and we sat down upstairs. "So what did he say?" the Priest asked. "He didn't sound happy on the phone."

"Oh, he was pissed. Smiling a lot. I gotta show some place up in the Los Padres tomorrow and be at the office by 8."

"He likes the way you show a place." The Priest put down the coffee and poured a shot of Keane's Cane in from a hip flask. "Ladies? Can I interest you in a snort of Cane? It goes well with coffee and the jitters."

"Sure," Elma said, holding out her mug. Irmela and I passed.

"When I show a place, I don't do a thing. All I do is walk around with them."

"Well you must do something."

"Beats me what it is. I mean if they ask something and I don't know it, I'm good at making shit up. That's something I suppose."

"Well now we're talking bricks and mortar."

"Yeah? Well, here's some bread and butter. An abandoned underground Air Stream camper museum. Outside of Needles. We have to estimate an event."

"The desert." He tapped his head.

"I'm worried about the water too."

He held up three fingers. "We need three guns."

"We can go to Barstow, or Long Beach."

"We still might lose water."

"Right. Insurance. That comes off the top then. I'll talk to Junior. Our end is OK. I wonder if we can set up tables?"

The Priest shook his head. "Not for a sit down. Not in campers you don't." He was angry. Campers made him angry.

"We all got some kind of reason to hate. You oughta know that, *Doc.*"

"Of theology and medicine. I'll drink to that. You know once I was called in to read the last rights over a man's body. The surgeon was so drunk that we were worried his breath would ignite when it hit the operating lights. They were certain the patient would die. In fact it was not a complicated procedure and the man stood a chance of living. So instead of reading him his last rites, I seized the scalpel and performed the operation myself. I faced the dilemma of saving his life or his soul. Naturally I chose to save his life, but unfortunately I wasn't successful, and likely that man went off to hell."

Chapter Six

It was our first sober day together and soon I started to tire of Irmela and Elma. All day I thought I should get rid of them and concentrate on business, but I couldn't quite figure out how to get them off the couch.

For some reason Irmela decided around three to join Elma in a few beers. I was in the office trying to figure out who to call for a party of two thousand. I had been at it for six hours and I was hungry. They were laughing loudly, loudly enough that I could hear them through the ceiling, even with the music on. I waited till it had gone quiet for a while. Elma would be napping and Irmela would be reading just as she had been at nine. I could go into the kitchen without getting caught up in it. They were like an undertow. Sometimes I would go into the living room for something, and sit down to say hi, and four hours later, get up.

I had to snap to. I needed a good man's sleep. I felt sick and haunted with after-images of nights I could barely remember. I know there were hours of nothing but hilarity, but it had no purpose. We just laughed at everything because we were so drunk. The Priest drank all day long without cease. But you would not know or imagine that he was drunk, till the very end of the night, when he and Margaret would hit the wall running and break their faces.

I went up the stairs. It was getting on five o'clock. I had made a bunch of phone calls and written up preliminary figures for the job. I was starting to calm the gnawing acid feeling in my stomach and the jumps in my nerves. I went into the kitchen and dining room. Irmela was splayed out in her favorite chair, reading. I had a clear view right up her shorts. The sunlight flashed on her pubic hair. It was killing me. I sighed and drank down black coffee and ate a hard roll with cheese and mustard.

I went down to take a nap and there was Elma, asleep, with a magazine lying on her bare chest. She was diagonal across the bed. I picked her feet up and dragged them over to one side, not against the wall, and she started to swim in her sleep. The magazine slid off. I looked at her breasts and lay down to sleep but it was impossible.

I sat up and watched her. Asleep she lost her troubles. Her face was smooth and young, beautiful and strong. I wondered why she was so relaxed. Surely even in sleep she had learned to be vigilant. They had been on their own for a long time, since Elma was 14, or so I thought. Their wanderings ended always in Wiener, which after a while I figured out was Vienna. Everyone's heard of Vienna. And there was always the wicked Uncle, never named, who fed them their dog.

Every day Irmela cornered me at some point and touched my chest, or grabbed my arm, and spoke to me intensely about something. I knew if I stuck to it I would sleep with her, but it was taking too long. Yet every time I gave up, there she was. The night before, when I was thinking that this perrucha is taking a walk tomorrow, she sat in my lap. It was agony in my diaper. Once she started drinking, you never knew. There was this couple of hours when anything could happen, so you hang around waiting for it, the explosion, the laughter. When Irmela drank she died to the world.

We did nothing, yet there wasn't enough time to do all we did. How many days had it been?

It was getting dark. I wanted to eat. I shook Elma. "Wake up," I said. "It's time to get going. I have to make it an early night."

"Get going where?"

I stared at her. She was still half asleep and vulnerable. It made her look sad. "I don't know," I said. She propped her head up with her hand and her hair started to glow against her fingertips. "I," I said, and said no more. I was transfixed and speechless. I kissed her. She kissed me. We kissed. That was it. I wanted it again, and I didn't want anything else.

Around seven I awoke, still curled up behind her. It was the first decent night of sleep I'd had in weeks. It felt warm and complete lying still, breathing in and out. I thought about this and that, drifted into a dream, and then, suddenly, I remembered that I had to be downtown by 8 o'clock. I jumped out of bed and pulled on a suit. There wasn't time to shave.

"What are you doing?" Elma asked.

"I got that meeting. I'll be back in 4 hours, 5 tops." I brushed my teeth and ran upstairs to the kitchen, where I grabbed a banana and made two espressos before heading out to the car. It would be close, but there was time.

The car wasn't there. I had nowhere to put the coffee and the banana. I looked around for someone to blame, but there was no one there but me and the trees and the xango motherfuckers chattering in the leaves and racing around throwing their shit. So I set them on the ground. Only then did I realize that the car was actually not there, that it was really gone. After that, I guess all I did was yell, "Elma!" until she came out wrapped in the blanket. "She took the fucking car!" I said. "Again."

"Don't yell at me, I didn't take it."

"But she is *your* sister. She keeps taking my shit. I gotta go to work. Where the fuck did she go?"

"Maybe to play pinball if she couldn't sleep. She likes to drive around all night going from bar to bar trying to find a game. She gets bored if she wins too much. She feels restless. That is how we were born. To keep moving."

"Yeah yeah, she told me about that. Or was it you? Like I give a fuck." I picked up the banana and peeled it and tossed the peel into woods. The only thing to do was to call the Priest. "I'm calling the Priest. I'll be late, but I'd rather lose my head than sit here losing my mind." I went inside and called him. He hadn't gone to sleep yet; he was hammered. "I'll come get you, my friend, don't you worry," he said, breathing heavily into the phone. The Priest's car was a giant black sedan. It comfortably sat five, and if you had to you could cram a few more in on top of that.

We drank coffee in the kitchen and waited for the Priest. Elma was looking good and I wanted nothing more than to get back into that bed with her. I loved to watch her from the other room as she drank her coffee and sat on the couch in the shadows staring at the sun motes, her hair glowing. She looked serene, thoughtless, like the fountain of the praying Indian in El Rodeo de las Aguas. But I couldn't take the idea of Irmela flashing her twat day after day on that couch, crawling into the bed at night and stealing the car.

I stared out the window thinking, I've had it, they've got to go. A car door slammed and we went out to the driveway to meet the Priest. It was Irmela. She looked at Elma first and then at me. It was like she was scanning us. She said, "I remembered you needed the car, so I came back. I hope it is not too late."

"I can't take this anymore," I said. "I'm taking you home." They said nothing. Elma's face hardened. Her eyes focused on the calculation. "Aren't you going to say anything?" I asked. She wouldn't look at me. She gazed at the ground. Her hair was dark.

"It's late enough. Get in the car. Go on, both of you. I'm taking you back."

"But she brought it back," Elma said.

"I don't care. She's been nothing but trouble."

"Twice! That is all," Elma said. "You!" she said then to Irmela. "Let's go."

"You got any stuff?" I asked.

"Not that I care about." She glared at me.

"Look, I need a few days to take care of business. It's not getting done with you around."

Elma stared out the window of the car, past me, at the house. Irmela got in back and pouted. We drove into town. On the way we met the Priest. He was weaving his tank up Topanga Canyon Road and we nearly collided going into a bottom. He honked his horn three times and I honked twice back and we made a cloud of road dust together.

"I don't have time to drive around, so I'm dropping you at David's. You don't like it there, steal his car and drive somewhere else. I hear Portland's nice, Vancouver is cool." We were heading towards West Hollywood and a truckload of Mexican soldiers came barreling along in the opposite direction. "Shit," I said, and turned down a side street. There was a whistling and an explosion followed by mortar rounds. They were landing near. I drove into a barrio, down single lane roads with adobe buildings falling into ruin. Chickens ran around the better-kept yards, where there were gates and fences. Humans and goats and donkeys swarmed like moyotis, in search of food and water, or trash. The gunfire stopped. I wasn't sure where we were. People were staring at us. We had reached a hinterland of shacks built from pallets and scrap metal. Around an overgrown park a few scrawny goats chewed on the grass. I drove hunched over the wheel, staring with red exhausted eyes out the windshield, my sphincter tighter than a mustard seed. After about an hour I was back in West Hollywood and dropped them off on Sunset Boulevard.

"Alright ladies, it's been nice."

Elma draped her arm across my seat back and said, "Do you think I would have made love to you, if I thought it would end like this?"

"It's not you, it's you two."

"But all you really want is to fuck my sister. Or maybe it is both of us you want."

"That's a thing that sounds better than it is. Like something you sell, not what you buy."

She got out of the car and slammed the door. Irmela looked back and waved at me, smiling.

The road to Junior's was totally fucked up. The Mexican army truck, the mortars, and now Ruler child soldiers on patrol on every block, shooting at shadows, and Bikers cruising in formation up the boulevards, or tearing after suspects like a swarm of wasps. I drove around a checkpoint and made it to Beverly Hills where he had his office, a small, gold and silver entrance pod with BrainFoam Lights. The lift lowered you through a SensiWeb interior and released you into the reception area.

Jorge sat in a neo-Modern faux steel chair with leather straps for the seat and arms, reading a paperback crime novel about an attempt to smuggle alien DNA to Earth from Mars in a baby. They made a musical about it a few years back. But it's an old story, at least two generations. My mother told me a version sitting by a greasewood fire, out in the Mojave, when I was a kid and we were drifting down from Tehachapi to LA Yaanga. Martian Curtain is what it was called. Or maybe it was the Nouse. That's what they called that little Martian baby.

Junior's wife Gildebrand manned the desk, making phone calls and keeping his schedule. She ran the business. He did the face to face. Gildebrand had been with Junior since she was a kid. She went where he went till they were both out of the toilet. Now he was landlord to half the city and that was just part of all he did.

She sat at a real stainless steel desk behind pictures of her children. One of them, Sean Patrice, poked his nose out from under desk. She must have kicked him because he made a face and disappeared. She was a 48-year-old blond with rings under her eyes and lines at the corners of her mouth. Her lips were full, set to the task of running the show.

She looked up and smiled. "He's really pissed," she said, and handed me a folder. "This is the Palace." It was ten past ten. I walked through the stone doors and into his office. He sat behind an empty glass desk in a mica chair. There was a giant plant behind him and a trickle of water flowing over jasper.

"Bob, you made it."

"I'm sorry, everything got all fucked up. The moyotis made off with my car."

He cleared his throat. "I hope you're done playing with flies. Stick to professionals, or get a wife, that's my advice. Because of cooz you kept me waiting two hours. I need dependable men around me, Bob. I've never lost a dime on you, but this is a bad sign."

"I earn."

"I need more than that from you, and you know it. General Carlos is our most important sponsor on the other side. When Mexico returns you won't find me up on a post with a blindfold. If I were you I'd stick with me, and General Carlos. Now, look here, you're showing this house to a guy I know on the buyer's side, Charlie Gets Along. His boss has the Ruler Tobor Ocktomann's ear and that's good for us. They don't know shit about money.

They don't carry it, they don't count it, they don't earn it. But they know how to spend it."

"All that land up there is Chumash."

"Not this place. It's an old family deed. They didn't become Rulers. They started to drink too much, go to seed. No one earning for the family, they sell land a parcel at a time. This is the last of the lot. It's over 200,000 acres. They've got it gated up. There's plenty of space for the Ruler Tobor Ocktomann's Summer Palace. They say he sneers at Bard 4's stupidity and that they laugh openly in the hall about his rule.

"Charlie wants to see the land, so drive him around the perimeter road and show him all the out buildings. It's all there in the folder, maps and pictures and descriptions. Be sure to mention underground chambers and reinforcements, the armory. All of its systems are self-contained and protected. There are five missile battery installations in shockproof, subterranean pods, and room for temporary barracks to be built. All the Ruler Tobor Ocktomann needs is a gold-plated toilet to puke in. And the owners, who stay anonymous, have completed all of my recommended upgrades. All you have to do is get to each of the points so he can verify and evaluate. Now, Charlie doesn't want to be snowed."

"Yeah, yeah. No problem."

"You don't look good, Bob. We've been together a long time. But I've been in business even longer and know the signs of man going down. I'm worried. Those two kept you up for the past week?"

I scratched my unshaved cheek and coughed a little. "They smoke too much tobacco. It makes me hoarse."

He stared at my face for a long time and said, "Your eyes are bloodshot."

"That would be the marijuana. And it was a drag having to go for a drive every time they wanted to smoke. The de Marcoses don't allow it, not even on the porches or grounds, but I had to bag that. Now it'll smell. They'll know."

"Just blame it on the plumber." He pushed a button on his desk and said, "Send in Jorge." He smiled broadly and folded his hands on his belly. "You're not going to like this, Bob."

I didn't feel good.

The door opened and in came Jorge, excited. "Where's your buddy?"

"The Priest is out on business," I said.

"I mean the sister with the glowing hair."

"All right, knock it off. Jorge, show him on the TV." The screen on the wall behind his desk turned blue. He swiveled around in his chair and leaned back, hands still crossed on his belly. There were no credits, just a shot of a dark hallway, and then of a bed in a tiny, filthy room. "Skip over this part," Junior said. Jorge fast-forwarded, and the images raced by, of a woman taking off her clothes and lying down, and then the camera moving up over her whole naked body. Then another girl raced in and undressed. "There." He slowed it down to normal speed and I could see that it was Irmela and Elma. But they were much younger. Irmela really did look 13.

Their faces were totally blank, like petroglyphs. Except for Irmela's eyes. They were uneasy. The more I looked into them, the harder she was to read. She wasn't scared and she wasn't jaded. They didn't move exactly, but there was something happening in them that would never make it out. She knew exactly what was happening to her, she just couldn't respond. They started to kiss and touch each other and then they got out the strap-ons. I didn't want to watch. "Turn it off, I've had enough."

"That's who you're hanging out with. You know what that was called?"

"Incest."

"Gaha: Babes of the Abyss."

"No, that's their band."

"No, that's their *act.*"

"They play Austrian or Australian folk music. I saw them. I heard them play guitar and sing."

He smiled and pulled forward into the desk. "You've been drunk for weeks. See, when a man goes down, it's everyone's concern, because when a man goes down, he takes out those above him, and below him. You bag out, there goes the Priest, and the six or seven maggots that depend on him. And I lose my man in the canyons. But I won't have you take me down. You are not alone in this world, Bob. I didn't bring you up to see you self destruct."

I opened the folder and started to go through it. "Can we get back to business?"

He shook his head. "This is business. Other people have businesses too. Like the man who gave me this film, who rents his theater from me. Who sells me things, and buys things. And pays me for my services. You took something of his. Lay off the booze and the cooz, that's my advice. And lay off those two moyotis. Send them back where they belong and all will be forgiven."

"It's done."

"Good. Now, the property's worth about two million in gold, but Charlie thinks he can get his boss to tap the Ruler Tobor Ocktomann for six. That'll cost us two. Two go to the owners. That leaves one for Charlie and one for me."

"That would be some party we could throw there."

"You should not even think that, much less say it. So Bob, do you want a copy of the movie, in case you miss them?"

"Alright, I got it, I got it."

"Do you want to take him with you?" He nodded towards Jorge. "He's got a gun and he drives. You'll be able to study the property that way. Get a little rest too."

"Let's go," I said.

Chapter Seven

Jorge drove and I studied the property. When we hit dirt I took the wheel and he snoozed against the door. The road climbed into the hills and soon we were in dense Douglas fir. The road was rutted, and the vegetation was lush. The turn off was coming up I thought. We were the right distance and it was the right elevation. But a turn off is easy to miss. I woke Jorge. "Get up," I said. "Keep an eye out for the turn off. It's not marked."

"Which side will it be on?"

"The right. I'll watch the left. It should be on the right though."

I started to think about Elma and Irmela. I wondered if what I did was for the best. Was I supposed to be able to drop anything for Junior? Yet, why not? He was right. They were just two girls I met one night. That had happened hundreds of times before. Thousands! What was the big deal then? Because I wanted to fuck them both? Who wouldn't? I'm not that good a man. But not at the same time! That was disgusting. Knowing they were sisters, and kids, what motherfucker would make them do that? Unless they did it on their own? It was twisted either way. I didn't know whether to put it past them or not; and if they did want to do it, so what? What would that mean? I couldn't fuck up my whole life just for screwing Elma and putting up with Irmela. It was crazy that I was even thinking about it. They kissed each other. They fucked each other's butts. I didn't want to think about that stuff. They ate a dog. Were they that hungry? And don't people eat dog all the time? They do in LA. It's very popular. I didn't know anything about it really. There was the Uncle. And vague things about New York and Vegas. That film was David's work. I could smell him on it. He liked to watch girls fuck. I owed it to them to get them out of there. I didn't care what Junior thought. Junior was wrong. And who was Junior to tell me what to do?

"That's it up there, see?" he said.

There was a circular clearing marking out four corners where the roads crossed. "It should be to the right. We'll go right."

"Yeah, whatever you say boss, it's your boat."

"I don't like boats."

The road narrowed rapidly and made a sharp turn and clung to the edge of a gorge for about a half-mile before turning in again. This would be the drive. And there it was, a broad brick drive a quarter mile long approaching iron gates set between two stone towers. The way in was webbed with sensors. Waves pulsed through my bowels and particles bounced around my brain. I hate being probed. You get too connected and start to disappear. Things don't end and begin the same.

The gate opened and a light passed over the car. It was now under house control and drove us slowly up to the next guard house, where a bald, middle aged man in a grey suit stood, briefcase in hand, his mud-spattered car parked off to the side. I stopped and Jorge held open the door. "Hello Charlie, sir," he said. "Junior asked that I should send you his fond regards."

"Tell him I say hi back," Charlie said solemnly. His breath was heavy and skin unhealthy, like wet sand. I cracked the window.

"Good idea, open the windows, turn off the air. These firs smell magnificent."

"Parts of this forest go back to the days before the conquest."

"You don't say? They'll love that. Big people need big air, and they love the hell out of Indians."

"It's over 200,000 acres."

"I drove it myself. Got here early just to do that. No offense Bob but I knew Junior would send someone slick in, so I wanted to get a first impression on my own. Hope you don't mind. I'm not trying to steal your thunder. Let's have a look around, shall we? I love seeing these old palaces before they move in."

The drive went on straight, lined with young redwoods, and ended at the front entrance, under a carved wooden portico in the style of a Minangkabau longhouse. Dated. But they could always tear it off and rebuild. The palace was built of stone and stucco, with a slate roof. There was a domed entrance 5 stories high, and the wings branched off behind that in the shape of an H. The front door was set at Ocktomann height. High off the ground was a brass ring knocker.

"Shit," Charlie said. "Junior said it had been modified, but I had no idea. They didn't fuck around, did they?"

"And neither does Junior. He advised them all the way, so you know what you're getting is by the book. Junior has an instinct for these things. He knows what the Ruler wants before the Ruler knows it. For instance, there's a stable out back. They reinforced it with cast iron. And they re-dug the pool to 18 feet. This place is move-in ready."

"You said it about the stables. Most of the time that isn't done. The client never thinks it's necessary!"

"Well yeah, cause nothing bad's ever going to happen to *them*."

"Until it does. I saw one of those things they call a horse get pissed off once and kick a stall to pieces."

"They're modified to eat meat."

"This sale goes through, I'll meet you up here one day and we can watch the Ruler Tobor Ocktomann's horse eat a small pig." I unlocked the door. It swung open into a marble reception hall. There was no furniture or decoration of any kind. We paused to gaze up into the rotunda. It was built of glass and copper and the pattern was repeated on the floor in black, white and red marble. We walked through the reception halls and rooms of the first floor, and upstairs to the bedrooms and then the servants' quarters, and nursery and Surrogate's suite. We looked into every closet, toured the armory in the basement, the control rooms, every inch of the joint, leaving only the indoor gardens. They were dormant and smelled like the woods at night, but cleaner, and silent. There was a dim light in the air, just bright enough to see by.

"Will ya look at that," Charlie said. "The East Coast doesn't have anything like this." He shook his head. "The boss is gonna love it. He'll get it right to the Ruler Tobor Ocktomann. Now, about those battery placements. On my circumnavigation I saw four. Where's the fifth? I'm not sure I like how easy they are to find."

"The battery points aren't visible from the road, I can promise you that."

"Well maybe someone cut back the vegetation."

"The launch tubes are underground. What you saw were the cutouts for the road. You could put in fast growing vegetation and have the perimeter filled to a uniform density in two years. Before that, shield it, wipe it out, whatever."

The deal seemed to be done. The place was perfect. We shook hands at the gate and Jorge and I drove back in silence. I wasn't bothered by thoughts of Elma and Irmela. The work had quieted my mind. Junior was happy when we got back and reported on what we had done. He didn't smile at all. We had a few shots of single malt and I drove home and got in the shower and then stretched out in front of the TV with a beer. The lights were down. I had eaten a steak and green beans in my shorts. I was starting to feel normal and I wanted to nurse it along. A slow recovery, a slow return. The sale had been just what I needed. A big deal, important to Junior, but a piece of cake, nothing to do but be there and don't fuck up.

Some time around midnight the Priest came, without Margaret. He sat down next to me and lit an Indian tobacco cigarette.

"I told you, you can't smoke anywhere on the property."

"I thought because you had smoked on the patio with the conechichihualli, I could take it a step further. Maybe we don't give a shit anymore."

"I'm not there yet. But we can go out on the deck."

It was still blazing hot, one of those nights that feels and smells like a tar pit. A troop of xangoes made a racket in the gum trees. The ocean was placid. We sat back in the chairs and he lit his cigarette and I rolled up a Kretek with some hashish and we smoked and looked at the stars. "Where's Margaret?"

"Out with some friends, bowling she says. I suppose they do bowl, but the bar tab is generally high. I don't mind the drinking, but the lying is certainly a sin."

"In small things as well as large?"

"I wouldn't know about small things. Without Peg I'm rudderless. Thought I'd catch your current. Did Junior show you the film?"

"You saw it too?"

"Sure, we all did. The slob David brought it over. He was pissed. They were his big act."

"Why would Junior take his side against me? He risks his life, his business, to save that piece of shit Jorge, but sucks that pendejo pimp motherfucker's dick with the girls. I don't ask for much. And I earn more than his theater, if you want to call it that, ever does. I'm sure of it. Men reconstituted out of crud, drinking Mexican piss while a girl waves her ass in their faces."

The priest sat thinking and said slowly, in his dark way, "Junior doesn't like you getting drunk with incestuous porn queens. He loves you like a son. In his eyes, he breathed life into you. And now, he sees a sign of weakness. You live for *them*, not for him. He's a purist; he wants your soul as well your heart. He needs you, but he needs you in a certain way. Don't ever underestimate a man's capacity for self-contradiction and hypocrisy. Scripture teaches that the only man to live without sin was nailed to the cross for it. And for that, they called him the son of god. To live without moral contradiction is to live either in pure sin or total sainthood. Without god's grace, we're all in hell."

"It's been peaceful here without them."

"It is certainly peaceful," he said, and for a minute we sat staring into the night, listening to the insects sing in the black shadows below. "Too bad you'll have to give it up."

"We'll see about that."

"And the property?"

"The Ruler Tobor Ocktomann wants it for his summer palace. That leaves what, eight months of the year?"

"You wouldn't dare."

"Wouldn't I though? Just one party. You'd have to charge admission."

"You know you would burn or drown for that." After a while he said, "Nevertheless, they were fun to have around. I found out both had worked as nurses aides when they first came to LA, at Metro, where I did rounds for over a dozen years. Irmela knew my old mentor there, Dr. Sloane. Dr. Sloane didn't object to rosaries in the OR. She said they were good anesthesia." He laughed from the gutter up and took a deep drink from a silver flask. "A sense of humor goes a long way in a hospital known as The Gallows."

"Do you believe them?"

"I see what you mean. What bothers me most is David. His name makes Irmela quite mad. It brings out her worst defensive posturing."

"She stole my car twice. Don't you think that's her true personality? Defensive posturing is what *you* gotta do around *her*."

"They've been on their own for a long time, those two. They are old for their age. My first ministry was among the poor in Hollywood, when it was Mexico. I sheltered a lot of girls like them. By thirty years old they're shot. They look a hundred. That's a thirteen-year-old girl in those movies, but it wasn't her first time. You just sent them back to the man who did that to them."

"But Junior! I told you, he said to get rid of them. Even if I wanted to take them back."

"They're afraid of him."

"How long have they been on their own? I can't keep it straight. They tie you up in knots and you give up and do whatever it is they want to do. I feel sorry for David! He's had them for 3 years, I *think*."

"And you haven't even slept with one yet. Excuse me, I'm going to get a bottle and some ice. It's bloody hot here."

"Yeah put fruit and sugar in mine, and a splash of water."

The surface of the ocean started to glow. The moon had risen high enough to wash some stars out. He returned with an ice bucket, two glasses and a bottle, along with a dish of kalamansi lime wedges and some sugar cubes on a tray. We fixed the drinks and lay back, now looking out over the ocean and the silhouette of the pines against the sky.

"So," I said to the Priest. "I did sleep with Elma."

"Elma!" he said, smiling. "Because I think, you know, for what it's worth, you should leave Irmela alone. She needs to get over what's been done to her, if she can."

"When I think how they're sisters, I think, I had a brother once. I wouldn't have done that with him."

"No, of course not. Even if you were starving and at risk of being raped constantly, and a man came and said, if you let me rape you and make you do appalling things to each other, I won't let anyone else touch you, and I will feed you and treat you otherwise kindly. You would have died first, you and your brother."

"Ask me when it happens."

"Nevertheless, you said yourself—"

"Yeah, David bothers me. And it bothers me how hard she looked when I told her to get lost, like I was the twentieth person in her life to kick her in the ass and tell her to go. And Irmela, she is impenetrable! She waved goodbye and smiled like an idiot." I sipped the drink and rolled up another smoke. "Junior may be right. I'm better off without them."

"Junior. Always Junior. We don't need him, Bob, if we have the girls. It's the right thing to do."

"I don't know. Junior gets what he wants. There's nothing I have that doesn't come from him."

"That's bullshit. He's a rich man, he isn't God. He rules a piece of LA, but he doesn't rule here. Ocktomann does. We can branch out with the girls. Peg and I've been thinking, she could marry a guy about to croak, some skid row loser, and then we take out a life insurance policy. I can fake the exam. He dies, we collect. Only problem is, they'd know something was up with Peg, if she was the beneficiary. She gives it off. You smell the jail and the guilt on her, like someone stealing water. But Elma? Even if they figure her for fraud, she will as you say, tie them up in knots. I believe she must have had a Jesuit education."

"Junior won't like that any more than a party at the Ruler Tobor Ocktomann's."

"We'll work out of Santa Monica and Santa Barbara. It's Tobor the Great who won't like it. And whatever possessed that line to go to nine bloody feet? Isn't seven five scary enough?"

"Some people have a crude idea of power."

"Like David for instance."

"He's a schmuck is all."

"Contemptible."

"A cockroach. He lives in filth. He's bad, and he stinks."

"He smothers them. He writes and directs the films. *Gaha: Babes of The Abyss* is everywhere."

I imagined David's fat ass rotting in that chair. "They acted like it was all a game."

"Whatever it was, they're like robots now."

"I don't want to think about it."

"They're playing tonight."

"Well, I'm not. Tonight I'm gonna getta good man's sleep." I couldn't tell if the sound he made was a sneer, a snicker or a laugh.

"I'll drink to a good man's sleep any day." He made the same sound. "Think about that insurance project. All you have to do is get a license to be an insurance broker, and write the policy." He laughed. "Hell. I'll read him the last rites if it comes to it. We've got the deal in hand, all we need is a sap."

"Like my old man used to say, play on the inside of the law."

"Let me know what you decide. If you take them back, I'll throw in with you. The south is hell now."

"He's not without influence up here. He's selling that palace, and the deed will be registered in Santa Barbara. And the de Marcoses, they aren't the only property we have."

"The de Marcoses are an exclusive contract though—"

"de Marcoses, yeah. I'm the listing agent. Junior can't get in there. But he can rat us out. He has channels everywhere."

"Think of that sweating fat man forcing himself on Elma."

"We all have to make a living."

He left and I went to bed. First I changed the sheets. They were crisp and cold. I pulled the light linen blanket up to my chin and tucked into it and fell asleep. I was in deep space, the way I always, since I was a kid, imagined the space between Earth and Mars to be. I guess every kid thinks about that. Every kid secretly wants to be a Martian Ruler and go anaerobic, like Ocba and his kin. Compared to that, LA is just like all the rest of it, only drier, hotter and dirtier.

Chapter Eight

Some time in the night I awoke with the stink of David in my nostrils. It was like the way phlegm tastes when you have an infection. I had the sensation that he was standing at the door and I was afraid. The breath went in and out of his mouth and I could imagine it hanging open. I lay there silently, hoping he would go away. Time slowed to a stop. Only when I knew it was morning did I dare move my eyes. The stench was, if anything, stronger than it had been and I expected to see him standing not in the doorway but at the foot of the bed, so I stared at the ceiling first. When nothing happened I turned my head. The smell was gone and there was nobody there. The door was shut. I had not slept at all. It would be another wasted day.

There was nothing to eat but I didn't feel like going anywhere. Down the drive there was a mango tree that I figured might have some fruit on it. I sat on the deck. Everything was in morning shadow except the far edge of the sea, which was bright blue, and the curl of the breakers colored pink and coral by the sun. The coffee was still too hot to drink. I rolled a Kretek up. I love the smell of cloves and tobacco on the morning air, it reminds me of the old village in Puvungna, Long Beach, where I grew up.

Not far from the room my mother and I lived in was one of the many lots where the food hawkers came with their pushcarts. Even now, when I smell Kreteks I hear the hiss of nasi goreng frying in a wok, and the soto ayam seller tolling a bowl with a spoon. At the other end of the street there was the taco maker, the tamale stand and a menudo truck. There was the sausage woman and Frank the Noodle Guy. A hundred other things for sale. Fruit, hunks of pineapple, watermelon and papaya, oranges, figs and grapes. You'd get off work on the docks and swarm in, morning, noon and night, whenever there was a shift change, and half-way through. Or between classes, or on your way to somewhere else.

My mother used to give me 50 centavos and send me out to get dinner, so I got to know them all. Then I started to make deliveries around the neighborhood. Sometimes there was some junk I could sell. Anything to stay out of the water. Only once did I dive off the boats for change.

All the time growing up it scared me that when I turned nine I'd have to dive off the boats to catch money, like the other kids did. The water was dirty. Ships came in and out dumping their bilge and their sewage and their trash and everything else, crocodiles and octopi and snakes and jellyfish, mutant bugs and bacteria. The Tongva down there are tough. Diving in didn't bother them at all. They remembered worse. Pestilence, plagues brought in by ships that seemed to kill everyone but them. But my mother never wanted me to be one of those boys. She acted like the water was out to get me. Maybe it was guilt or a dream she had but didn't tell.

When I was nine my friend Dave took me down to the ferryboats. I stared at the water and felt cold. Everything else receded from sight. Images seemed to float up to the surface and sink, but whether they were jellyfish or the faces of the dead or waterlogged junk I didn't know. I thought I saw someone floating ass up. The kids were shrieking and laughing. The sun was straight overhead and there were all these people getting on to go up the coast and out to Catalina. And they looked at us and called out, "Catch the centavo, and you can have it." The kids leapt up and down, so I did too.

When it was my turn, they packed in behind me, about six or seven naked boys, nudging me forward with cold wet arms. I stared out over the edge. We were in the bow and it was nearly ten feet off the water. A taut, thick rope with a beard of seaweed crossed the area we were diving into. To the right was the pier, with black truck tires bolted to the side and the well-dressed people, whistling and waving for the show of the jumping boys to go on. They tossed a 50-centavo piece and I dove in after it. The water was salty and full of grease and filth. I had no chance of finding it and only grabbed at the bubbles of air erupting out of me. I floundered around and blew out water till I could grab a tire and hang on. Then I climbed onto the pier and threw up all over the place. A passenger near me said, "Ew," and stepped away. I ran home.

I kept away from the docks then, till I was big enough to load the boats. Buying and selling became my racket. Because even on the docks I was trading what had fallen off with the agents. And some of those agents came from El Rodeo de las Aguas, Beverly Hills.

I put on my shorts and walked down to the beach. It took forever. By the time I reached the bottom I felt like a flagellant. Cactus and thistle had overgrown the path. And I couldn't tell if I had simply chosen the wrong way without knowing it. There were paths I hadn't noticed when I was following Elma, identical to the one I thought I was on. A cactus managed to sprout from every mound of dirt, even from the hollows of boulders. The barrel shaped Cocytus, a ball of pain, seemed to mark all the crossroads.

Then I didn't know one side from the other; the right way was wiped from my mind. The only thing to do was head down and hope to find the stairs.

At the beach I cast my clothes off and dove into the surf. It was low tide and the water was tepid and blue. A wave crashed in and it took me up and out. But now I panicked. I was out where the waves start to rise. I don't swim well. The ocean isn't like a pool. Elma made it safe, and she wasn't there. The swell was rising. My heart beat faster. I rose up over the beach and began to sink, and crash face first into a pile of sand, surf and foam. When I got my footing, after flipping over and falling down backwards, I ran for the high ground and sat panting and coughing up the sea.

The climb back wasn't easy, but I didn't care, I just wanted to get the fuck out of there. By the time I got home I was hallucinating rats and spiders. There was sand and water dribbling out of my ears and nose. I took a brief, harrowing shower, turned on all of the lights and the radio and lay down in bed, with the door locked shut. Eventually I fell asleep. When I awoke it was one in the morning. I was totally sober, and everything was clear to me. I was going to drive down to The Morrow and get Elma and Irmela. I went for the fusca strapped up under the bed but it was gone. Irmela. I laughed and grabbed a baseball bat.

I parked out in front of The Morrow. Mine was the only car. The rest were scooters and riders and bikes and sticks. A few horses and buggies clopped down the street. The air tasted like salt grass and dust and it smelled like dried horse dung. Grit blew into my eyes. There were a few other fleabag operations up the block and across the street. It was a sorry looking place. Dark and barely hanging on. The big pink sign flashed on the door. I hid the bat under my coat and handed silver over to the door guard.

In the nightclub side a dozen old men sat alone at tables with beers in front of them. On the stage were Irmela and Elma, completely naked, playing electric guitar and singing in Austrian accents. They sang *Eidelweisse* and *Gunther Goes A-Maying*. A guy called out, "Put on the hats and take off the guitar."

"Yeah, lose the guitar," yelled another. "They never used to have a guitar or sing or anything. They never used to. This is crap."

"Yeah, crap."

"Shut the fuck up will ya? I ain't paying to listen to you."

"Well I ain't fucking paying to listen to you either, bub."

"Take it outside fellas," the bouncer said.

"Now look what you done did. Fucker. I'm gonna get you."

"I said, take it outside," the bouncer said again. It was dark and he was talking from the shadows. All I could see of him was his hands. They weren't the kind of hands I'd want to be on the wrong end of. Two of the old men stood and exited. The girls continued to play. Elma gyrated her hips and Irmela got down on her hands and knees. I turned around and went to the bar, as there was the scattered raucous applause of dry, bony hands slapping together in the dark.

The bar was a zinc counter under dim lights with four bottles on the mirrored wall, rum, vodka, Mekong and mescal. I couldn't see the vermin, but I could sense it. Everywhere smelled like mouse and cat, and the mice outnumbered the cats. I ordered a beer from the bartender. She pulled it out of an enameled tub of ice, shook the water off her hand and dried it with a bar wipe.

They started to play a ballad about being lost on a Martian rover. I didn't turn around. I didn't drink the beer. I just sat there chewing the inside of my lip. The bartender was a woman in jeans and a T-shirt. She did her job the way someone who sweeps floors for a living sweeps a floor. There was another song and another and the men started to whoop. The longer I sat there the more I realized there was an indecent smell in the room. It started to feel like a crypt. They say in the mission days the mausoleums were full of rotting bodies. People lived among the dead.

The top of the bar was greasy and smudged with fingerprints and food spills. There were stains in the corner of the ceiling where the pipes ran down. Puddles on the floor reflected the lights. Someone lit up a cigarette, two stools down. He was talking to the bartender and she was ignoring him. I couldn't. His voice was indistinct but the noise was enough to keep me from thinking clearly. I stared at my hands and the beer and felt the muscles in my neck tighten. I tried not to watch what was going on.

I've seen women fuck on stage before. It wasn't that. I didn't want to see *them*. It was like they were my sisters. Or my mother. It was like watching my mother and my sister screw in public. Or it was like something worse than that, whatever that might be. I just knew I had to go kill David. My old man always said, whatever you do, don't kill anyone. They burn you for that.

I went down towards the stage, walking along the wall as if I were going to take a front table, and then ducked backstage. The screech of Irmela's guitar and Elma's somber voice, rising to a cry. I walked through the red and yellow and green lights, past a drum kit and behind a blue velvet curtain, where there were a couple of stage hands playing chess on a board resting on their knees and a lot of junk, lights, set pieces, boxes. There were three dressing rooms with dented metal doors covered in graffiti. Two were dark and locked. The third opened into a narrow room with a double bed crammed in the back, two grey flat pillows and a blanket. The lights were on.

Clothes were everywhere, in piles, hanging off the backs of two chairs and from hangers on a wheeled rack. There were dozens of shoes in a shoe bag hooked to a nail coming loose from the plaster wall. There were three fly shit spattered mirrors with makeup lights above a workbench where the other girls put on their makeup and hairspray and stuff. The air was hot and musty, like a locker room. And I could the smell bugs. They weren't far away. I turned the lights out and waited a few minutes. When I put them on again there they were, antennae bobbing, a dense pack scattering back into walls, as big as your thumb and lacquer-brown.

The only new thing in that room was the lock in the door. I remembered being a kid hearing about the twelve whores in San Berdoo who died in a brothel fire because they'd been chained to the beds. Everyone talked around it when they came by to drink coffee and schwank with my mother and her kin. As a kid, for a while, it was cool to brag about what you'd do to the man who killed the whores of San Berdoo, when you grew up. "Vengeance will be mine!" You think about all kinds of things as a kid. And then most people they grow up and they don't do shit. I never expected to.

I looked at the floor around the head and foot of the bed, and at either end was a coil of rope. It could be he was just tying them up for fun, but the door lock didn't have a kink in it. The bat came alive and poked me in the armpit. I grabbed a hold of it by the handle and smacked the palm of my hand three times, then headed up the stairs. It was like following a spoor. The man shed dandruff and hair. It stuck to the walls and was ground into the floor. He had fetishes. He collected his toenails and fingernails and kept them in a jar beneath his bed, to ward off demons.

Even the walls smelled like him. They radiated David. It didn't hang in the air; it pulsed. I held my breath and knocked on the door and waited. Then I knocked again.

"Go away."

"I'm not going anywhere. I want to talk to you."

There was a low growl. "Who the fuck are you, and why should I care?"

"We've met. I'm a friend of the girls."

There was another growl, this one more guttural than before, less staged. "Come in then. It's open." The door pinged and I opened it. He was overflowing his recliner and staring at the TV. His T-shirt looked like it was melting off of his body. His stink was sharp, acidic. He said, "Well, Bob Martin. I thought Junior took care of you."

"Junior takes care of himself. You make movies of the girls?"

He still looked at the screen. The light played across the black whiskers on his cheeks. He lifted the hat off and mopped the beaded grease off his brow with his sleeve. "Is that what you came here about?" He put the hat back on. "I gave you the bag back. Get lost."

"So I'm gonna take that as a yes."

He grunted and rubbed his nose and squinted at the TV. "Is there some reason why I should stop watching this to talk to you?" I took out the bat. "I see. You have a weapon. My security sucks for a reason." He hefted a large bore shotgun from beside his chair and pointed it at me. "I don't need it. Now my friend, I'm going to extend the same courtesy to you that you extended to me."

"I'm taking them home."

"I say they stay. Their vacation is over. I make money and I kick up and I ain't having some Moron come in here and tell me how to run my business. I'll tell you something you don't know. In Jerusalem they didn't go to private school while their mother went to University. Didn't happen. She was long dead. They were sold to pedophiles by one of their many uncles. They've been screwing their way across the world for a long time. That footage you saw? Shot in NY. Everyone says Vegas because the product has raunch and New York is slick. You're dealing with professionals, Bob. Why doncha go have a drink on me." I didn't move. He had the gun of course, and I must have been huffing ozone or something because

I was right *there*. I had total clarity of purpose. The gun didn't faze me, and I wasn't listening to that stuff about New York and Jerusalem. It didn't matter where they came from or what they had done. I didn't even care who they were.

I looked at his lips, the color of lunch meat and the little eyes, filtered by his glasses and the TV light reflected in them, at his drenched arm pits and the cap that said Master Head on a head with greasy hair sticking out, and at the roll that sat on top of his belt buckle. Resting on it, two short barrels with wide bores. The bat didn't stand a chance. Even if he couldn't see his own dick, he'd be able to pull a trigger without moving his eyes. Me, the bat and everything in our aura would be in pulpy threads. His nostrils twitched. The skin was pitted with acne scars and even in the dull light there was a visible sheen of grease and alcohol. He reached down to the floor with his other hand and brought up a beer. "Shall I have Irmela bring one up for you? Elma?"

"I don't want a drink."

David took a long pull off the bottle. He put it down and picked up the phone and said, "Send up the girls."

"I told you, I don't want a beer."

David wiped his mouth with the back of his hand. The hair soaked up the beer on his lips and moved around on the dense stubble of his chin. If he even once eased up on that trigger or looked away, I was going to smack him as hard as I could across the side of the head with the bat, and then do it from the other side. "Well I do. I'm thirsty."

Behind David's chair was a larger room with the lights off. There was a door, but the rest was in shadow. The girls came into the room from out of the darkness, dressed in baggy grey clothes. A metal door swung shut. David didn't take his eyes off of me. They stood behind his chair, six feet back. Irmela was staring at the TV screen and Elma watched the back of David's head. In her hand was a pint of beer. Our eyes met. Elma's hair flashed and she covered it with her hand.

"Well, what do you want, boss David," Irmela said. She faced me. "Why is he here?"

"Where's my beer?" Elma set it on the floor by his chair, next to the other one. "He won't be here long, if he don't leave now. I thought maybe you'd be able to persuade him." He sniffed. "This holding back of mine is in deference to our boss."

"Don't do me any fucking favors," I said. Irmela reached into her pocket and took out my fusca, her hand shaking. Well fuck, I thought. Now she's getting me killed for real. I couldn't tell if David knew she had the gun on him or not. Elma's face was like space on a clear night.

"Why does Junior put up with this shit? Bolillo motherfucker and two peruchas. I should waste this prick."

Irmela steadied her hand and pointed the pistol at the back of his head. She said, "David, stop. Let him go."

"Hear that?" he asked. "Let me tell you, they ain't worth it. You stupid fuck you. Standing with a bat, over what? You don't know one thing true about these two. And I've known them for years. Ever ask her about that hair?"

"Which one?" I asked.

"Shut up David," Elma said. "He's a liar."

"You hurt my feelings. I thought we were friends. Ask them about Azerbaijan. And ask them what—" David's eyes shifted slightly. I tightened the grip on the bat. Irmela looked at Elma. She closed one eye and pulled the trigger. The shot missed.

David swung around in her direction, and I let him have it, I smacked him across the side of the head with the bat. The shotgun went off with a roar that shook the room. It aerated the TV into a mist and all the plaster melted off the wall in long cheesy strings. I hit him from the other side and his head cracked. The glasses flew off his nose. His eyes were dazed but still operating, while the eyelids fluttered and his lips twitched. Then Irmela faced him, her face tight and furious, like she was about to flip a ball into a 10,000-point hole. She took aim, closed one eye and pulled the trigger. The bullet hit his chest and she pulled the trigger again, and again. Blood and wood splintered the air. It smelled of burning fat. He slumped back in the chair. We looked at each other and ran through the metal door in the dark and down the rancid stairs and out into the alley, where I gasped the dry hot air as if it were a spring of fresh water.

Chapter Nine

I knew Junior would be pissed, but I didn't know how pissed. I didn't sleep; I sat with a bowl of cocaine and the girls in the living room until the Priest showed up around ten one morning with contracts for the Air Stream Museum deal to sign. The morning sun was lighting a fire up Irmela's skirt. She was reading a giant insect book, Thomas Mann's *Der Zuberbug*. The Priest nodded at them and sat down on an ottoman.

"Where the fuck have you been?" he asked. "I thought we were working."

I couldn't reply. There was no brain left, just snarls of fear. "What."

"Contracts. For the caterer, for the water truck, the cleaning company. I thought we were going to check the space out."

I had forgotten that. "Where is it anyway?"

"Outside of Needles. Barstow's on the way." He was giving me the Priest eye now.

"My mother," I said. "My cousins."

He smiled and patted my knee. "It'll do you good my son."

That night we drove up to my mother's, over the mountains and through the desert. My hands and feet and eyes knew all the turns, bumps and washouts. The headlights played across the dirt and stars smothered the sky. The girls dozed in back under a blanket.

"I can't see at night anymore," the Priest said, flicking ash out the window. I drove between the ruts of truck tires, obscurely lit by the headlights. It was like searching for something in the dark with a flashlight when you're drunk. The tracks were just wide enough for the car, unless the side had caved in. Then I would lose the front tires to the wash and start to slide on the rocks and gravel, down the grade, the headlights swinging over the dark hills and into the sky. When that happens it's a race against spinning wheels and dirt and dust to get back on the road again.

The Priest, after a long silence said, "Well I heard about David. Did you think no one would notice?"

"I don't know what people notice, but they gossip like old ladies. What did Junior say?"

"What did you hope to gain by it?"

"Gain by it? I just did what you told me to do, Priest. Or was that a doctor's advice?"

"I never said to shoot the bastard. I said to get the girls out of there. But you had to go and beat the man to death and gun him down in his chair."

"I couldn't take it. Them being with him. You should understand. You threw it over, the biggest racket of all time, for a waitress."

"What did you think would happen?"

"Thinking didn't enter into it at all."

We were family now. Elma was strong and beautiful. When I was with her I felt this dark tide between us. We were raw and simple. And I chased after Irmela, through all her complications, which never seemed to end. It was like every little thing got sucked up into it. Like her hair. Every time it grew more than an inch she would panic and we would rush out to the store to buy hair dye. In the hair dye aisle she would say, "What did I get last time?" and puzzle it over, gazing at me as if I knew. She would grab at the ends of her hair and try to look at it. "I don't see the same color. I think it was henna something. Henna Gold. What do you think? Are they the same? Close?" And whatever color she happened to be looking at she would grab. Back home she'd run into the bathroom and dump it on her head. Then would come the wail of grief when the two colors didn't match and another layer was born.

I watched them sleep in the rearview mirror, Elma against the door, Irmela's head on her shoulder. "What is it about Junior and this culero motherfucker David? Fuck me, man. Fuck Junior. Fuck David." I shook my head. "Strunzo. It was self-defense. I've got witnesses."

"Junior won't try you."

"But would he kill me over a pimp? How much money could that fleabag earn? We own houses together! I do his legal shit!"

The Priest shook his head and looked at the girls. His skin was pale for him. His eyes swam in mescal. "I'm not sure about this job," he said.

"I'm not sure about it either. Let's get my cousins out there today to plan the security."

We approached Barstow as the sun was rising and drove into long purple shadows and a burning orange glob towards trailers and adobe domes and pods glowing in the first morning light. Elma cleared her throat and Irmela sat upright in the rearview. The blanket fell away from her chest. "Are we there yet?" she asked.

"It's not far ahead," I said.

My mother's pod was on a block of half-acre lots. Mailboxes stuck in the sand with a dirt drive up. The lots on either side were empty, and across the way there was an adobe dome with two shacks and a goat pen. The air was still and cool but you could feel that the sun was crouched on the horizon, about to pounce. We walked up to the door and I knocked and tried to see in through the porthole, where a light was on. Irmela and Elma looked back and forth at the desert and laughed.

"Coming," my mother said through the intercom, her face ballooning in the monitor.

"That's your mother?" Irmela asked.

"She's so beautiful," Elma said.

My mother is a lot of things, but beautiful ain't one of them.

"You're seeing into her soul," the Priest said.

"Give me a fucking break," I said. "She's OK for living out here in this shit hole. The water truck comes once a month. You don't want to be here on the 28th." The door opened. "Mom."

"Are you in trouble?" She laughed and gave me one of her big hugs and a kiss. "You lucked out, sweetie, I just got done fixing some scones. I must've known you was coming." She clapped her hands on either side of my cheek and we crowded down the spiral stairs into the living room. The plaster walls were painted like a desert sky at dusk. It smelled like quartz. There was a low stone table with a couch and two chairs facing. The Priest and the girls sat on the couch and I took a chair. She brought in a plate stacked with scones and a crock of lard. "Now Bob, the Priest I know, but who are your other friends?"

"Elma and Irmela. Should I get the coffee?" I asked.

"No, it's already on, it just it has to perc." My mother was 60. One shoulder was humped. Her knuckles were like knobs and her fingers were twisted like busted twine from carrying buckets and digging. She was missing her bottom front teeth and a couple of molars. Her hair was short and grey. She had a strong face, sun baked and wrinkled like an elephant.

It smelled like coffee. She put on her glasses and stood. "The milk's powdered, but the coffee's real. That new man down the way brings it in on his mules." She left and came back with a tray of coffee and scones, a bowl of sugar and a jar of milk powder and set them out on the table the way a waitress does. She went and got the mugs and spoons and set them out. Even busted up like she was she could handle plates. She could type too; transcribe, take shorthand. And she built roads for relief. There was nothing she hadn't done to make a living when we were growing up.

Elma laughed. "What is mules?"

My mother said, "That's the offspring of a horse and a donkey. What they call a sterile hybrid." She poured the coffee out and passed the mugs around.

Irmela took hers and said, "The mules is lucky," and Elma glared at her.

My mother sat down and crossed her feet out in front of her. "I don't suppose I ever thought the mule was lucky. They beat the hell out of them. Me, I never owned no horse, or no mule or no donkey." She shook her head. The coffee was good. "So what brings you out here?"

"A project," I said. "I need you to hire Rafael and some of the brothers to ride shotgun on a water truck delivery to Needles. And I need them to meet there later today. Can you swing that?"

"Needles? What kind of a project?" She looked Elma and Irmela over pretty hard.

"There's an abandoned underground Air Stream Camper museum there. Junior wants to throw a party in it," I explained.

"Priest? What's he talking about?"

The Priest explained, "Air Stream Campers are made of chrome steel. They're shinier than silver, precious. They're parked in underground chambers and the guests will wander from camper to camper. Each one will have a different theme."

My mother snorted. "I'll bet. How do you girls fit in? Let's have it, I know what goes on."

"Don't sweat it mom," I said. "They're with me."

"So where are you from then? It ain't LA."

Elma said, "We are Austrians."

Irmela said, "The mules are lucky because they can't fuck and make children. It ends with them."

My mother said, "What you bring into the world ain't yours." She sucked her teeth and shook her head. "Rafael's moved up to Tehachapi with his mom and his brothers are in the Seven Villages."

"Can you either get them or see who they know in Barstow? I'll pay well," I said.

She chuckled, and said, "You don't necessarily want those Barstow boys."

"If Rafael says they're OK, they're OK. I'll give you the address."

"Do I get a cut?"

"A fee. In pearls. Can I show them the tunnels while you make the calls?" I asked.

She nodded and headed off. We put on headlamps and walked in a stoop down a long stone tube and into a large chamber. Off of this were four more short spurs with terminal chambers. None of them were furnished and some were unlit, but they were all vented, and there were hatches to the surface. The headlamps played off of our faces and the domed ceilings and circular walls. There were flashes of Irmela and then of Elma, as if I were blinking them on and off with my eyes.

We left around noon. The walk to the car was dangerous. It was 125 degrees and getting hotter. You can feel your brain boiling at those temperatures. My mother smiled and waved from the door as we drove off. The car was cooler than outside but not much and the air conditioning was slow. The Priest and I sweated hard. Elma's hair was drenched. The car stank, and we fought for hours on Route 66. We blew two tires and were driving on autofill. The girls were useless, and even the Priest cursed god when the third one went.

"You bastard," he cried, pulling off the road into the desert. "I sometimes think God is a fucking lizard."

Irmela said, "In some places they believe god is a microbe."

"I'd like to know where that is," the Priest said. He climbed out of the car. We joined him. The sun burned the earth. There wasn't even a buzzard in the sky. I suppose we might have laid out there dead for six hours before anything came along to eat us, except for ants. "Man hasn't worshipped a grasshopper in 3 million years, never mind a microbe," said the Priest as he rummaged around the trunk. "Here," he said to Elma, handing her a silver snood. "It will keep you cooler."

Elma's face looked like it was going to ignite. Her eyes were the color of the sky. She said, "Irmela makes things up."

The Priest handed Irmela a silver snood. "No," Irmela said, indignant, not even wilting a little, but vigorous, as if she were hydrated by the sun. "I read this in a magazine about Mars. They have these there too."

Elma fastened the snood under her chin. It looked like a foil burka.

"I'll take Irmela's if she doesn't want it," I said.

"No one said anything about Mars," the Priest said. He stuck his head deep into the trunk. Stuff moved around. Out in the desert the light blasted the color out of things. It was a pale expanse of greasewood and stone, and outcrops of wolfberry and h'upivithorn, the road cutting into the hills.

Flies crawled around on my face. My nose hurt from breathing. "Chinga tu madre," I said.

"Calm down," he said. There was a gargling noise in the bowels of the car and then a rhythmic shudder shook its rear end. "Ah!" He removed his head and faced us. "Fixed." The flat tire started to hiss and slowly inflate. "We're lucky it's not a tear. Let's go."

We turned off the highway onto a narrow dirt track littered with boulders that ended at a parking area. There was a mule cart with a mule team tied up in a corral and an antique composite entrance pod with pole electronics. Spaced every few feet in the desert were low bell vents, like a bunch of eggbeaters turning together. We got out.

"What's this?" Irmela asked.

"The museum site," the Priest said. "Bob, you can see now what a pain in the ass this will be? This is the one entrance. There are a couple of hatches, but nothing with a lift or even decent stairs."

"Whatever the fuck," I said. The entrance was wide enough for two abreast, and there was a landing where you could stage to load the lift. "I don't see how Junior is going to get a thousand people down that hole, much less two. I don't care how wide a spread it is under ground."

We came out about five stories down. Spread out for acres was a fleet of Air Stream Campers, chrome shining and glinting in the light of naked light bulbs hanging by wires between each one. The pattern repeated in all directions for as far as I could see, except for the door to the lift.

"Where do we go?" I asked.

"I don't really know," the Priest said. He headed into it, maybe three campers deep, and we followed him. When I turned around it was as if the space had closed in behind us. In every direction now it looked exactly the same, there was no in or out.

We entered a camper and the Priest laid out the floor plan on the kitchen table. We got to work plotting out where things would go. We thought of it like tents in a carnival. There were food campers, sex campers, gambling campers, drug campers. There would be an animal camper, and of course, several bathroom campers, bathing campers, shopping campers, campers for mirrors, bravado campers and sadness campers. Campers for music and campers for silent prayer. When we were done we counted up the campers and knew how many people to hire, and what vendors for the water, the ice, the food, the animals, the prostitutes, the casino, the sanitation. Deliveries beginning the next day and continuing for 48 hours. Load out and clean up would take another 24.

"No one came from Barstow," I said, when we had finished.

"No," the Priest said. "We'll hook up with them tomorrow." He rubbed his darkened chin and mused, "This is quite a budget. Biggest ever."

"I'm glad it's not our nut that's in it, cause I think it could blow."

"It might could do."

Elma said, "Are you going to talk business all day? We have not had any fun yet. You said it would be fun."

"That's just what you say when you're going to go and do business and you want someone to come along. You say it will be fun. You say you won't be long."

"I hate when you look at me like that and use that tone of voice," Elma said.

"If you were me you'd hate him all the time then, and you wouldn't fuck him at all," Irmela said.

"Why, so you could?" I asked.

Elma looked at me strangely and said, "You are the first stupid man I have ever loved. I keep thinking that you are pretending."

"Yeah, so you see right through me. Let's go out for dinner."

"I won't eat rattlesnake," Elma said.

Irmela said, "Rattlesnake. I have not seen anything juicier than a biting ant."

"We saw that dead rat thing," Elma said.

The Priest led the way through the maze. "How do you know your way out of here?" I asked. "And don't tell me god leads you."

"What do you take me for, a heretic? I know where I stand with God, and it's not here. The trailers all look separate. But you know, there aren't so many of them. What you are seeing is a holographic mirror maze."

"They have those in Amsterdam. This whole place is very Amsterdam," Irmela said.

We got the lift up to the parking lot. After the cool deep rock the entranceway was suffocating. I gagged going in it. Not only had the sun been roasting it but people had added their gas to the walls over the years and it smelled of vaporized sweat and alcohol. The sky was white in the window and wind blew hard at the entrance. The Priest got ahead of me and said, "Let me go first."

"I gotta get out of here." I winced. The Priest went out. The air roared until the door sealed. I could barely see him through the porthole. He seemed to be waiving. I couldn't wait any longer. "I'm going out. Don't follow me. I'll come back for you, or the Priest will." It was almost a relief to walk out into the dry air, until I was blinded by the blowing dust. I couldn't see the Priest. And I didn't see the car parked next to mine either. I didn't see Junior standing right there in sun goggles, gila monster boots, a silver snood, and a blast vest.

"Bob," Junior said. The air cleared around him as the dust of his car settled. Jorge was standing there with a baseball bat, talking to the Priest.

"Junior." I started to tremble. Death by rods. When you would pray to burn.

"I warned you off them," he said.

"I didn't know you got to do that," I said. "I thought who I ran with on my off hours was my own business."

"David's business *was* my business."

"Am I supposed to know that?"

"You were told, it was clear."

"You don't know what that guy was doing."

"I showed you what that guy was doing. I trusted you. I consider you to be family, you know that Bob. This is business, but with us, business is in the heart. We're friends. I depend on your judgment. And you betrayed me. I can have Jorge beat you to death in this parking lot for that. And don't think I don't want to." As he spoke, over his shoulder, a cloud of road dust was rising. "So now, from this moment on, you and me, we're done. You don't work for me anymore. I don't know you." His eyes reddened and he turned away to go to his car but was stopped by the column of dust engulfing us as two large black armored cars pulled up.

The doors flew open and Junior backed away. Four armored guards stepped out in desert gear and aimed their batons at us. The one who was in charge said, "Which of you is Bob Martin?"

"That's me," I said. "You work for me. And the Priest's with me." The Priest smiled and nodded at the guards.

They aimed their batons at Junior and Jorge. The one covering Jorge said, "Put the bat down." Jorge lowered the bat to the ground and looked back and forth. "Now take out your gun very slowly. Lay it on the ground." Jorge didn't look to Junior. His eyes were on the guard. He reached behind his back and slowly drew the fusca from his holster and placed it on the ground. "Kick it away." He kicked it out of reach. "Now kneel with your hands behind your head."

"No, I won't. I won't do that."

"Jorge," yelled Junior. "Let's go." Jorge knelt and the guard put the baton against the back of his head.

Another walked behind Junior and commanded him to kneel. Junior smiled and sank slowly down on his knees. He placed his hands behind his head and thrust out his chin. The silver snood fluttered in the hot wind. The guards waited for my orders. And I let them wait. There were advantages to killing off Junior. For one thing, that would be one less guy on my ass. And I wasn't sure Junior wouldn't have ended up letting Jorge loose with the bat. Still, I liked Junior. I had no reason to kill him. Someone's gotta run the show. Kill a guy like Junior, what happens next? Could it be more fucked up than it already was? Yes. His backers would want revenge. I would bring the Mexican army down on our heads if did that. So I thought about it, and waited long enough to make Jorge and Junior sweat, but not so long that they would wet their pants. I said, "Let them go."

The guard with the baton on Junior said, without looking at me through his sun-starred goggles, "Are you sure boss?"

"Yes. It was a friendly disagreement. Let Jorge take his gun and the bat."

Jorge looked at the gun, just out of reach on the ground. The guards stepped back and stood at attention. Jorge scooted forward, scooped up his gun and stood shakily. Junior rose off the ground and glowered at me, his eyes dark and more baleful than usual. "This changes nothing," he said, and drove off with Jorge behind a tower of dust that drifted over us and settled slowly over everything.

Without Junior's protection I was an outlaw from Santa Monica to Torrance. From now on there'd be no past between us. Wherever our paths crossed, there'd be no heart in it. All there'd be was business.

I said to the head guard, through a haze settling on my eyelids, so that when I blinked I felt the dust fall from my eyelashes and onto my cheek, "The job's cancelled. I can give you some silver pesos now and get what else you need from my mother in Barstow."

He stared at me through the helmet, two black goggle-sized windows for eyes and a respirator. "That's fine, Bob. Sorry you lost the job." I counted out all my silver and they marched back to the two cars and rumbled off raising another wave of dust.

"Well," the Priest said. "What now?"

The pod door opened and Irmela and Elma stumbled out, blocking the light with their arms.

"Whatever the fuck," I said. "Won't someone think of something?" I laughed. "Let's get high in the car."

"At last," Elma said. "I thought it would never end. Stuck in that hallway."

"Oh, it just ended," the Priest said. We got in the car. "We can't blow too many more tires." He started up and I passed around a warm bottle of Mekong. "What do we have to smoke?" I asked.

Irmela said, "Give me your Kretek. I have hashish and opium all mixed up."

"Who'd you blow for that?"

"No one. I played pinball. I do not have to do mamar to make the money."

"Well that's a good thing," I said. "Cause we're going to have to go out and make the money." I handed her the pouch of Kretek and she rolled cigarettes with opium and hashish.

"What do you mean?" Elma said. "You are a lawyer, a real estate agent. You are rich."

"See, a guy like me doesn't save anything. I live on my earnings. *We* do. So now you gotta help bring it in. But I won't put you out to work like that greasy-headed dick David."

Irmela said, "Your shoulder has chip."

"I just got fired. So let's get our asses going. We gotta pack up the house."

Elma said, "You're going to lose your house?"

"Who said it was my house?"

The Priest rumbled into a laugh.

Irmela said, "You said it was yours. Why would we not think it was yours?"

"Gee I don't know why. Maybe because I wouldn't believe what anyone told me about themselves? Like when you said you were from Montreal."

"We didn't say that."

"Well, whatever. The fuck. Azerbaijan. I don't even know where that is. It might as well be Mars. Jerusalem."

"You lied," Elma said, pronouncing her verdict to her shoe. The roof of the car started to thunder as the road deteriorated. Gravel washed beneath us. The front grill sucked in the dirt cloud and dust started to come in through the vents.

Irmela said. "He did help us with David."

"Yeah, I didn't have to do that. And look where it landed me. You should feel bad about that. It's all your fault. You're why I'm here!"

"So if we are garbage get rid of us," Irmela said.

"I tried that. Didn't work out, did it?"

"When do we have to leave? Where will we go?" Elma asked.

"It depends on how much money we have. It ain't exactly a rental. It's more like a borrow, until the owners come back or it sells, see? I just live in the place in between. But with Junior against us, it won't last. All I own is a Jeannie Bottle on Goyaałé St., in Puvungna."

"Puvungna? Where is that?"

"It's a Tongva village in Long Beach. Junior doesn't reach that far south."

They nodded and stared out the window. No one talked for several hours. The Priest said, "If it's money we need I think I know a way."

"What," I said. "Your insurance scheme?"

"What if it is?" he asked. "So what. It will work. I have the patsy, all I need is the girl."

Elma said, "I knew this would happen. Every man is a pimp, the priest most of all, because he makes a whore of the Virgin. You can only sell a virgin once. He sells her many times." She spat.

The Priest's voice dropped. "There's a man, a sailor, a patient I know. They're treating him for TB and AIDS. He won't last long. I believe if we paid him he'd marry you. We tell him it's a marriage for papers. You guys are Austrian. It's perfect. We take out a life insurance policy on him. He makes you the beneficiary. When he dies, we split the pay out."

"I don't know," I said. It was a shade too close for me. But we were desperate. "Who's gonna insure a guy like that?"

"I work at the Gallows when they have need of an extra knife. I'm clean, you see." He held up his hand to display the clean nails. It trembled. "I'll sit in a doctor's office while he's at lunch and I'll examine you, and put the guy's name to it. His name is Detreuil."

"What happens when he dies? The cause of death, TB or whatever, that's gonna show up. No adjuster's gonna buy that. He'll know the doctor was in on it with the wife."

"Don't worry, when he dies I'll do the same thing, with a different doctor. They don't want to care for these cases. They're happy if I do. The cause of death will be acute pneumonia, or maybe intestinal parasites. No one wants to get near a bowel full worms. He'll go straight to the incinerator."

"And who writes the policy? Does Detreuil have to sign?"

"You'll write the policy. Go to Santa Barbara for the underwriter. Detreuil will sign anything I tell him to. He knows me as a Priest and a doctor."

Elma asked, "I would have to marry him?"

"That's the idea," I said.

She looked out the window and we drove on silence.

Chapter Ten

Junior sold every house we had behind my back. He deputized an agent and sent him up to Santa Barbara to close on all the properties with Jake Hernandez, who owned everything else up to Monterey. I had a few freelance properties rented out in Malibu and I was still the ink on one or two contracts in the canyons. But that didn't last long. The Rulers condemned my Malibu houses and one by one the properties I represented fell to other agents after the owners got a call from Gildebrand. Without rent, we could scrape by on the jewels I had. What we needed was time to ripen the plan. Detreuil could die on us and we'd have to wait for the Priest to dig up another half-dead patsy.

The Priest and Margaret and all the piglets hanging off of them were running out of money. The piglets dropped off and they holed up in the house and let rip for a few months. We nested in it. We smoked and drank and hustled through the day and night until late in the year, during the wet, I got the word from my neighbor Hank Orsba that the owners were coming back to California to pack up everything and ship it north to Canada.

We were in our familiar stations, Irmela with her leg draped over the arm of the chair, reading Der Grune Heinrich by the author Keller and drinking tea, Elma sitting up and staring into the middle distance, me looking out the window and flipping through a magazine. And we were having what was by now a tired argument. I said, "We have to get out of here. Will you marry Detreuil?"

Elma said, "You lied."

I snorted. "Like it's the first time!"

"What is that supposed to mean?" As she became more and more indignant, Elma's face winched tighter. "You cannot twist out of your own dishonest—"

"Dishonest!"

"Do you deny that you lied to us about this house?"

"And your age," Irmela said. "You said you were in your twenties."

"I am, I am," I pleaded.

They laughed. Elma said, "Until that day you never said you did not own this house."

"It was implied." I got up. The sky was grey but the room was bright. There was no ice. "There's no ice."

"So make it yourself."

"I'll just pour it into coffee."

Going to the kitchen I could hear them snickering. I poured Mekong into the coffee and sat back down. The Priest and Margaret came in with a case of wine. The Priest opened a bottle of red and poured out two glasses.

"We don't have much shit," I said. "We can stay at my pod in Puvungna. Long Beach is safe." I turned to the Priest and Margaret. "You two head down to Pedro. We'll meet in Long Beach and do the deal."

Irmela and Elma looked at each other. "Goyaałé Street."

Clouds were unbroken out across the Pacific. They looked worn out. I was spent. By three in the afternoon I couldn't take the light anymore and started drinking wine with the Priest and Margaret. I felt like I hadn't pissed one out in weeks. Every day the sweat got worse and the view didn't mean a thing. "What are you holding on to?" I asked Irmela and Elma. They didn't even look at me. When I was in bed with Elma now, we fucked because there was nothing else to do.

Irmela stretched her legs. "Does it smell in your pod?"

"It's clean. There's a shower and toilet."

Elma said, "I've gotten used to fresh water."

"No money at all?" Irmela asked.

"No, do not worry," Elma said to her quietly. "I will not do it."

They stopped talking. Irmela widened her eyes and stretched her head like an alarmed bird, to which Elma made a pinch face, with narrowed eyes. Irmela shook her head and refused to look away. Elma made her lips look like an asshole. There was some breathing then, until finally Elma turned to me and said, "She thinks you are asking me to be a whore."

"I didn't kill that fucker because I approved of his profession."

"I pulled the trigger first," Irmela boasted.

"And missed!" I said.

"It distracted him."

"It did do that. The wall looked like melting beeswax wax. That could have been me."

"But you gave him 20 whacks," Elma said

"And then you gave him 20 more!" They squealed so hard they looked ten years younger.

I went down to the kitchen and got a glass of water. It was late now, after dark, and we hadn't eaten. I poked around the freezer for steaks but there was nothing but lime juice mix and chocolate ice cream. "There's nothing to eat. It's your night to cook, Elma."

Elma stared at me with dark blue eyes, light beating in her hair, and said nothing.

"You'd never never have to go to bed with him. We'll hole up in my pod, and he'll wander Long Beach till he drops. The Priest will be at the Gallows, or in San Pedro. We go on about our business."

Elma said, "I don't know. I don't like it." She shrugged. "But if it must be done. And I will care for him, if he needs it."

"We can take care of people," Irmela said. "In Montreal I was candy stick in an old age home. They had sling cases and ambulatory. I read to everybody the same. And we worked here, at the Metropole."

The Priest had a coughing fit. His whole body went into action. He contorted with every hack, and the hacks got deeper, till it was like he was coughing up his guts. Margaret stared at him with disgust, her nostrils pulsing like fish gills. The coughs subsided. He panted and cleared his throat.

I said, "Priest, when can we meet this guy?"

"Tonight. He's always at a bar on Haudenosaunee Street in Long Beach, by the docks. I'll arrange a meeting."

The bar was in a three story pink stucco building flanked by kuwavibi cacti, with a big sign that said Come In Lounge, *Come* and *Lounge* painted on the saloon doors. It was a narrow place without much light. Overhead beer signs flashed and to the sides were dozens of shouting people crowding the bar and tables. Towards the back were booths jammed with loud young drunks with big teeth laughing too hard, and a couple of guys in white T-shirts with beards. One booth was empty, but the sconce was on and there was an ashtray with a lit cigarette.

Detreuil was seated in the corner, nursing a glass of Keane's Cane on the rocks. There was a dish of orange wedges, half of them eaten, gnawed down to the zest. "Hello doc," he said to the Priest.

"Marseille. I've brought my friends."

Detreuil lit up a Gauloises and said, "Sit. The waitress will come. She's slow."

His voice was faint and the noise in the bar was deafening. He was a harmless looking man. Tight, transparent skin gripped his bones and his unlit eyes lay at the bottom of deep sockets. He took a sip of Cane and stuffed an orange wedge into his mouth, grinding the pulp out, slurping and sucking and gnawing at the pith until all that remained was a skin like his own. This he lowered onto the plate. "I'd like another." He took a breath and coughed into a handkerchief, checking the result before pocketing it.

"Have you been taking your pills?" the Priest asked.

"I sold them, doc. Couldn't be helped. A man has to eat, even when he's dying."

The Priest's five o'clock shadow deepened. "I want to help you with that. Could you use some ready cash and a place to stay? Someone to take care of you?"

Detreuil stared into the Priest's eye and weighed him. "What do you mean, doc? I thought I could trust you."

"No, Marseille, hear me out."

"Sell my organs? I'm not a strunzo, they aren't worth shit. You want to rip my DNA."

"No," the Priest said. "Nothing like that. My friend Elma has a problem with her citizenship. We would pay you to marry her. And she and her sister here, Irmela, will care for you while you are ill."

"Care for me?"

"Your pills, your food."

The waitress squeezed through the overflowing booths. I ordered mescal all around, except for Detreuil, who got another Keane's Cane on the rocks. Detreuil stared at his hands. He was mostly bald and the skin on his head was webbed with blood vessels. He had a dairy smell, like a barn full of dirty cows. "You can get me food and pills?"

"Yes, we can get you back on your feet again," the Priest said.

"How much?"

"480 silver pesos," I said. "We keep this arrangement between us. I have a form for you to sign, if you want, stating the terms of the marriage. And a consent form, and a nondisclosure agreement."

He shook his head to the music and took a shallow puff of the cigarette. "I have a navy pension. That goes to my mother. You ain't getting it if that's what you're after."

"All we want is the citizenship papers. We'll get you to the hearings."

"480 silver pesos and there are hearings?"

The Priest said, "Marseille, do you want the job or not?"

"Va te faire foutre! Plotte! Hijo de la puta madre. Pendejo motherfucker. Bironga!" He got rat-like and scratched at us with his fingers. "I spit on your 480 silver pesos. Schmuck."

The waitress came with our drinks. The Priest raised his glass to Detreuil and said, "My son, lechaim. Don't say I didn't try. And no hard feelings among amigos. Let us drink to something cheerful."

"The wedding stockings," Irmela suggested.

We drank to the wedding stockings, whatever they were.

"Waitress," the Priest called. She was halfway to the bar, swallowed by noise and bodies. She turned around and he tossed a silver coin in the air. She pushed her way back to the table. The Priest said, "Make it a double round, please. And keep the silver for yourself." He turned on Detreuil and asked, "What is your plan then?"

"The shelter's got a bed. I can sell my pills for a while, until I'm a little better and can ship out. I want to go to Java." The effort of talking made him lie back against the booth with his eyes closed. He picked up an orange and eviscerated it. "In Java, they've got green oranges, mandarin's. And the food stalls! A man can eat for nothing there. People aren't savages."

"My son, who would take you on?"

Detreuil's ears drooped and his eyes sagged. "Would you be cruel then fadder? Putz. Farang motherfucker. Ngentot lu. Memek basuk!" He stared at the last orange segment on his plate, at the booze, and then looked around for a waitress. "At the bar I never have to wait."

Elma sipped at her drink and winced. She was used to Mekong. "Would you rather drink somewhere else? We will go for a ride up to the hills, to our place, if you like. I can draw a bath. We will eat some meat."

He looked at her like he was looking at old fish. "I don't like women," he said.

"I don't either," said Elma. "Except for my sister."

The Priest raised his glass and said, "To Marseille."

"Marseille!" we toasted.

Detreuil laid his head on the table and looked up at Elma. "If I had to have a wife, you wouldn't be so bad." He drank down the rest of the Cane. "I have nothing, you know."

"That's why I suggest," the Priest said.

The tables nearest us became loud and a guy pulled another guy up and threw him on the floor.

"Let's go," Detreuil said. "These are longshoremen here. Soon half of them will be dead on the floor. I'll go with you."

I said, "All right then, it's off to Topanga. Drink up."

We piled into the Priest's car and headed home through heavy traffic, slumming Tenochtitlanian millionaires up for a little Moron poon. In the living room Detreuil stretched out on his chair and dozed in and out, swigging from a bottle of Cane. I put out heated snacks we had bought on the way home, beef samosas smothered in gado-gado sauce, prawn chips, hotdog dumplings with Chinese mustard and fried nuts, along with a jug of Mekong.

"Detreuil," I said. He sat upright and looked at me with pale pickled eyes. "Aren't you going to eat? Look at all this food we got." I picked up a paper platter of dumplings, the hot dog tip poking out of the dumpling skin. "These are right up your alley," I said. "They're all pork, no filler."

"You think I give a shit about that?" he asked. "It's like that rotten pussy sitting on the couch."

"My friend," Margaret said. "You can walk home if you like. If not, I'll thank you not to speak that way of Elma." She stretched her lips down in a smile and bulged her eyes out until they were pink.

He took a dumpling, squeezed mustard on it and wolfed it down. "I was a fruitarian, until now."

The Priest laughed. Elma said, "That is a very healthy diet."

"That's what the doc told me, right doc? In cases like mine, a diet of fruit is often the best. But my gorge is empty."

"Well eat up, my son," the Priest said. "Ignore all prior advice."

Detreuil tucked into the dumplings and then demolished what remained of the samosas, after the girls had had at it. His skin, already just a blush shy of powder blue, blanched. He said, head resting back against the chair, to the ceiling, "I've over done it." His eyes fluttered and he passed out.

"Scheisse," Elma said and the Priest raised his hand to silence her. He lowered his ear slowly towards Detreuil's nose and lips.

Detreuil didn't move. His chest was still. But the vein in his neck was throbbing. The Priest nodded.

"Detreuil," he said. "Are you OK?"

"Fuck, si. Let me sleep, I'm desolated."

A shudder ran through him and his throat bulged out like a water balloon. He started to cough. Gargles made their way up from deep within his intestines and erupted from his throat. Irmela shouted, "No!" and bolted towards him. It was too late. Lightning followed thunder and he vomited undigested food and Cane up all over himself. Elma kneeled down beside him and held his hand. "Come, Marseille," she said quietly, into his ear. He staggered to his feet and a couple of echoes from the big bang came up his throat. Elma led him through the French doors and down two flights to the bathroom with the hinoki ofuro.

Irmela asked, "Is he going to die?"

"Not tonight," the Priest said.

Margaret took in a deep breath and seemed to hold it. She opened her red frog lips and said, "We better hope not. Irmela, go down and check on them in a minute."

"I was going to go," I said.

"You keep out of there. He's no idiot. He knows he's being played but he's having a good time. Let's see where that goes. Irmela, go and ask if she needs help, dear."

Irmela got up as slowly as she possibly could and made a cat face. Margaret laughed and coughed and lit up a Kretek. "Maybe we should head out tonight, not tempt fate. The de Marcoses could come home any minute."

The Priest scratched the beard forming on his throat. "You may be right."

"Will the girls go for it?" Margaret asked.

"They're along for the ride, they ain't driving the car," I said.

"That may be," Margaret said. "But they're in for a cut, are they not? Is it coming out of your end?"

"It ain't coming out of my end. We split five ways."

"Then the pain and the risk and all the rest of it is a five way split too. They've got to be in. And we're agreed, we've got to go."

"And then there's Detreuil," I said. "We promised him a bed for the night."

"That's a promise you may not be able to keep."

Irmela returned looking more alive than I'd ever seen her. Her skin was rosy and full. The steam had relaxed her hair from its peaks and valleys and there were no stray locks sticking straight out off of her head. "You should go down. It is like Pieta," she said.

"Go on," Margaret said. "But don't say anything stupid, Bob." And then she gave me this look, this look that she had that was both like an interrogation and like she was laughing at me.

"What can I say? I love her."

The Priest looked me in the eye and nodded his head as if he were tipping a hat. I went through the French doors and down to the bathroom on the lower level, a large cedar planked room with slate floors and sky tubes. There was the hinoki tub, a shower deck and a Lie-N-drY. Detreuil's nasty clothes were piled up in the corner. He was seated in the ofuro, water up to his neck. His pale, fleshless arms rested on the cedar rim, and his fingers touched the water. Elma, in a white robe, sponged his face and shoulders, pouring water from a cup to rinse him. She washed his scalp. He reclined there, eyes half closed, a small smile on his lips. She wiped his brow and hummed a song in his ear. She cradled his head and talked to him.

Elma knew I was there. I wanted her to take her hands off of him. I said, "Is everything alright?"

"That is what Irmela asked," Elma said. "I told her to go too."

There was nothing left to it. I went upstairs, seething. "She won't let me talk," I said, staring out the windows into the black. "It's useless."

"Aren't they beautiful?" Irmela asked. "As if Marat had his lover with him."

"Are you just trying to piss me off?" I snarled.

"Bob," Margaret said.

"We've got to blow," I said.

"Do you mean vamoose?" Irmela asked

"Yeah, like, tip ass, only quickly."

Irmela said, "In this you are correct. She will not leave or do anything now. We cannot talk to her, she is impenetrable."

"She better hope so," I said.

"In that case," said the Priest, "Let's have some more mescal." He poured out shots all around. There was a sound down by the front door.

"Did you hear that?" I asked. No one else had heard it. "Well I thought I heard something."

"Maybe they're coming up," Irmela said.

"Maybe." I walked away from the windows and down to the kitchen. There were headlights shining in the windows of the front door. Fuck. I ran up to the living room. "There are headlights in the driveway."

Chapter Eleven

We didn't panic, not really. The Priest sat paralyzed in his chair, his eyes like those of semi-extinct pachyderms in zoos.

"Who is it?" Margaret asked.

"I don't know."

Irmela said, "We have only one fusca."

"We have a tire iron and a bat too," I said. "I always keep them around just in case."

The Priest spoke. "Take out the weapons, but don't use them."

"I say we go out the fire ladder and take them in the driveway. Or we drive out as they come in," I said.

"What about Elma? And Detreuil?" he asked.

I said, "We can ditch Detreuil if we have to, but not Elma."

"They're opening the door, it's too late," Margaret said.

The door closed and there came a scream.

"It's them," I said. "The de Marcoses."

"Not Rulers," the Priest said. The blood returned to his face. He sat forward in his chair. "The gun."

"I have it," said Irmela.

They were shouting in the kitchen. The woman at the man, the man at the woman.

"You know they're still here?" said the woman. "There are cars in the driveway. The garbage is warm. You can smell them. Look at this place. It's disgusting." They came up the stairs.

"Give me the fusca," I said.

"Why, you don't trust me?" Irmela asked. "Did I not save your life once?"

"Bob's right," the Priest said.

"I agree," Margaret said.

Irmela handed it over. I faced the entrance. They opened the French doors and at first didn't see us. They were still bickering. I held the gun behind me, in the shadow. "Who are you?" I asked. "What are you doing here?"

It was dark. Her silhouette was long and her hair stood a foot off the back of her head, in the shape of a hatchet. The man was even taller than she was. He had natural fibre optic hair, the real stuff, cut into a grass green flat top that bathed his forehead in light. "We're the de Marcoses. This is our house," the woman said.

"Yes, what are you doing here? Does Bob Martin know you're here?" Mr. de Marcos demanded. They were in the room and could see us clearly now. "A Priest?"

The Priest stood. "Emeritus. And a medical doctor too, if you ever have need." He reached his hand out. "We've just put the people who did this to your house out. We were, if you'll forgive us, celebrating our victory and enjoying the view, over a glass. It's been a long week. We're only half done with the clean-up I'm afraid."

They had expensive faces, sculpted, strong. They didn't know me. All of our dealings had been by correspondence. We never even spoke on the phone. I said, "How do I know you're who you say you are? Put on the light, so I can see you."

She put on the wall lamps. He had his hand on a fusca in his jacket pocket.

"Mr. and Mrs. de Marcos, I'm Bob Martin. The Priest is with me. *They're* with me. It's like he says. There were drifters squatting here. It sometimes happens. That's what insurance is all about." I smiled.

"What are we to do?" Mr. de Marcos asked. He relaxed his hand but kept it on the butt. I held my fusca back.

"We can get a hotel in town," Mrs. de Marcos said. "I'd rather be in LA anyway. This place stinks of tobacco and of unwashed bodies. There's a sweaty alcohol taste in the air. We might have to sell it at a loss. Or live in it." She was whining now, as she free-associated and fell silent, checking out Irmela. He was casing Margaret of all people. He must have been into humiliation. Military punishment type. Dirty rag in the mouth and frequent boot kicking.

"I've been working to show this place. But you know the climate and the pipes need repair. We've had correspondence about this."

"Not working terribly hard I'd say," he said. "By the looks of it." He gave Margaret a once over and said, "You're a sturdy piece of work. The Priest belong to you?"

"He's mine alright, and a life sentence. But I thank you sir. You aren't so bad yourself, even with the suntan. I do prefer my men to have the complexion of veal."

He grinned. It may have been the nastiest thing I'd seen in a decade. "So, back to the city." His hand was tight on the fusca now. He was sweating. His eyes darted from me to Margaret. I didn't know what I knew yet, I was just hopping around. If the guy drew first, I might not be fast enough. He was robust. No Ruler, but closer to that than I am. Mrs. de Marcos stood holding open the left door. He would not turn around and leave, or say anything.

"Are we going?" Mrs. de Marcos asked. I tightened my grip on the butt, waiting for his fire. But he wouldn't go. He had to get it out of his pocket and aim. I only had to raise my arm.

"In a minute. I want to ask Bob a few things."

I smiled again. "How about at the office in the morning?"

"How about now?"

I didn't want to get into it with him. "Mrs. de Marcos is waiting to go." She propped the door open with her foot, and looked at us with her fur-trimmed pissy face.

There came from behind her, downstairs, the loud thump of footsteps and laughter, as Detreuil and Elma burst up from the lower level and staggered up the steps towards the living room. Mrs. de Marcos shrieked and Mr. de Marcos pulled the fusca out of his pocket, turned towards the doorway and fired a single shot. It hit Mrs. de Marcos in the neck and she fell squirting blood. He yelled, "I got one!" And then, when he realized what he had done he turned towards me. I didn't have to see into his eyes to know what was there. His hair was blazing green. I raised my fusca and shot three times. He went down where he stood.

"What did I do? What happened?" Elma asked, looking at the stream of blood meandering towards her foot. Detreuil stood by her, eyes unfocused and face blank, in a white bathrobe that hung off of his shoulders. His head emerged from the top, shrunken, veiny and pale.

"The guy went nuts," I said.

"So you had to kill him?" Elma asked. She moved her foot an inch and the blood raced past it towards the stairs.

"He was going to shoot me! I had to kill him. You would have too. He thanked me with his last breath."

"We have to get rid of the bodies now," Elma said. "I do not want to be the only one to clean this up." She looked calm. Her skin was smooth and her lips were still and her eyes were blue slivers. When she pushed the hair off her forehead it flared.

"Clean up? What's the motivation now?" I asked. "They're never coming home." No one laughed. "Well, how do you get rid of a body? I'm new to this."

Irmela laughed. "With your first, you had no disposal problem."

"We left the trout by the stream," Elma said. They squealed.

"We'll need concrete," said the Priest. His eyes were stricken and he was dark and crumpled up. He looked at no one when he spoke. "We can sink them in the ocean. Who might be looking for them?"

"Yes," said Margaret. "Who are these people anyway, Bob? What do we know about them?"

The blood was slowing down. It stopped before reaching the first step, like an inland river dying in the sand. I said, "They were movie people. They wanted to sell. I never put it on the market. We never spoke, it was all in writing. Frank Orsba got the name from Arphe Lux and passed it along to me. They were in Baguio partying. They were afraid of war. Don't know what the fuck they came home in the wet for. Unless it was Junior who tipped them off."

"Then I'll drive to Santa Monica and pick up some sacks of concrete. If you follow me down Bob, I can take their car and get rid of it. I know just the place," the Priest said. He stood and looked down at the bodies. He kneeled along side each one and blessed it.

"OK," I said.

As we were walking out the door Margaret said, "Priest." He stopped but didn't turn around. "Don't bother about the concrete. We can't do that."

"Why?" I asked. "That's a good plan."

Margaret shook her head no. "The corpses will wash ashore."

"We'll really weight them," the Priest said. "You'll see."

"They'll decompose and bits and pieces of the them will show up on the beach, I guarantee you. Feet are always washing up in Malibu."

"There you go with those feet again."

"I'm telling you, for 500 years now feet have been reported, some with shoes, some without. I can show you. There are places—"

"That's not likely," I said.

"And," she said, after we had shut up, her eyebrows arched, "we haven't got a boat. You can't just throw them in the surf. Not whole, anyway. We need to cut them up and get rid of the pieces."

"We can do it in the porcelain tub," Elma said. "The hinoki tub is no good for this."

The Priest sank down to the floor and moaned softly. Sometimes he was hard to figure. I'd never heard him say a word against Margaret, other than the usual sarcastic shit people who live together say. Harmless crap that really was a measure of how nuts he was about her. Cause that's why he threw it over. Margaret wasn't his first woman but she was the first to make him ditch the church. "I love her more than God, you know?" he said to me once, when we were having a few at Tony's. That was the beginning of them and I was not much older than Irmela. He enjoyed his corruption. Until that night. That was the night he stopped having fun. He was short of breath and faced the floor over his knees. He said, "We canae cut them into pieces."

Margaret chuckled. "Scruples Priest? What is it? You draw a line now? Their bodies are trash. And you know exactly how to do it, *Doc*. As you were once known in some places." The Priest would not look at her.

Elma said, "The Priest is right. We will throw them in the ocean I say."

"My father was a butcher," Margaret said. "I know how it's done. We don't need him."

"And my father will nae let me do it," the Priest said.

Chapter Twelve

Margaret and Elma wrapped the bodies in oilcloth and took them out by the pool to hose them down. When we got back from ditching the car the Priest went down to the guest room to sleep and I cleaned up the hall. There was blood and tissue and hair all over everything, the floor, even in the hinges of the door. I had to scrub hard to get it all out. I poured out bucket after filthy bucket into the toilets, and the drains were starting to cough back in big bloody bubbles streaked with strands of thermo-luminescent hair.

Detreuil was sacked out on the couch in the living room. His breath came in shallow puffs. The only time he was at peace was when he was asleep. I sat down by the window and smoked and took in the view. It was early morning, and clear. In the distance a condor flew across the ocean.

Irmela drifted into the room and stood in the center a moment staring at me. Her lips were trembling and her skin was like moonlight on marble. She didn't say anything. The front of her shirt was wet and clung to her belly. "Aren't you going to sit down?" I asked.

"OK," Irmela said, and she came and sat down on the arm of my chair, the way she did with Elma when she was upset. I put my arm around her and she sank down onto my lap. She put her head back on my shoulder and rested her face against mine. "Hello."

I put my arms across her body and she wiggled her ass and got me hard. "Are you sure this is the time?" I asked.

"I am not afraid." Irmela turned around and faced me, squatting with her feet on the arms of the chair and her hands on my chest. We kissed. It was a kiss I had waited for, imagined, tasted in the dark when I was alone. And it didn't disappoint. I could feel it in my toes. She was lighting me up like a pinball machine.

The floor looked pretty good, no harder than any other floor. It was cold but we could throw the cushions down. Irmela leapt backwards off the chair and lay down, peeling off her green shorts and white tank top. I got up. Her skin was pale; a vein ran up her long leg, and those little tits of hers were perfect. I knelt before her. My lips were not two inches from her pussy when the front door opened and there was the thud of bodies landing in the foyer.

Irmela was right in my face! I was home. It was all right there. The French doors were half open. Elma would be able to see. I stood up and muttered, "Mierda!"

Irmela looked up at me with pity and contempt, her face like a knife, as she made her move to kill. "What are you doing? You are like a clown in one of those TV stage shows you like. The fat one with the sharp eyebrows."

"Put your clothes on and shut up about this, please."

"Oh, but what if I am madly in love with you, Bobbb."

"I'm not that lucky."

"Don't you know Bob, it has always been you."

That voice. Those legs. The face that murders my sleep. Did she even know? I said, "Look, later we'll lose them, and pick up where we left off. Then we can take our time."

"We are in the land of the opportunity. You have had yours."

Irmela pulled her clothes on as Elma entered the room, with blood smudged on her face and tangled, sweaty hair. Her eyes and cheeks sagged like an old woman's, and her arms were limp at her side. She lit a Navy Cut tailor made cigarette. "Is the Priest up yet?"

"No."

Margaret came in behind her in a silent bluster, face pink and creased and lips bulging, as if she were blowing taps on a bugle. "We are not going to weight these. We're going to toss the pieces out in the bush. We'll go at six, as soon as it's dark. To the Los Padres. We'll let the coyotes and vultures eat them."

At five we ate a meal of rice and mangoes and loaded the bodies into the Priest's car, with some camping gear. He refused to look at them, and drove under protest of silence. Irmela, Detreuil and I trailed the Priest, Margaret and Elma. We drove up the coast and camped for the night north of Ventura, keeping well off the road, with a good screen of txaparil. The kiinarabi were in bloom. We found a sturdy tall one on high ground and camped beneath the twisted red branches decked with pink blossoms. The sky was clear. We rolled out blankets and lit a fire. Up the sides of the mountains were other camps, and it was hard not to think of what a fire is like, the rolling ball of flame exploding all that lies before it, and arcs of fire in the sky.

We got up at first light. Margaret had coffee going over kiinarabi wood in an espresso pot. It bubbled out of the top and she poured three coffees and started over again. The Priest passed a jug of water around. It was cold. There was breath in the air. I pulled my sleeves down over my fingers and gripped the hot cup with my hand, feeling the steam on my face before drinking it down.

"When I makes tea I makes tea. And when I makes water I makes water," Margaret said.

The Priest said, "Just don't mix them in one pot," and they laughed to themselves, as they sometimes did.

Elma passed around a bag of pinyons and chocolate. We packed up and hit the road. The road was twisted and bad. We went down over switchbacks towards the coast at 10, 15 miles per hour. It had been wet and there was mud on the road, sometimes under a crust of dirt that looked hard. We came to a good stand of Douglas fir and pulled over.

"Let's walk a ways up and unravel the oil cloth," Margaret said out of the front passenger window. The trunk rose up and I took the legs. She took the arms. We hiked about a mile off the road, to higher land, lugging the pieces up.

"Here," said Margaret. "You're from the desert. What do you say?"

The ground was open but far from the road and shielded by low growing sage and oak and txaparil. It seemed fine to me. "This is fine. They'll be gone before we get home." We put the pieces down and went back for more. It took three trips. Margaret opened them up like roasts wrapped in butcher paper. We tossed Mrs. de Marcos' head and body and then her arms and legs onto a stand of mucitabi oak, her body exposed to the air. The sun was high now and it was heating up. The bugs were thick and the smell was strong of juniper and sage. It was lush, the short wet season and the blossoms were thick and the leaves unfurled.

"Should we move her to the ground?" Margaret asked.

"No need. The coyotes will get her. The birds, the ants and every other thing out here. Their DNA will be scattered. Let's toss him." We headed up a few hundred yards and got rid of Mr. de Marcos above a running wash.

The oilcloth had to be disposed of. We decided to dump it in the morning in Santa Barbara, at the Syukhtun fish markets. We camped a few miles out of town in woods well away from the campground, which was full of the noise of people and smelled like feces.

It was raining, so we set up tents and huddled. We would have to slip in and out of the city early. I doubt I slept at all. We left Detreuil in the car, and I shared a tent with Elma and Irmela, lying between them as usual, and the Priest and Margaret took another tent.

At first sun we pulled out and drove down into a town deep in early morning shadow. The streets were empty and wet. The few mounted police on corners paid us no mind. There weren't any Mexicans here. No convoys, no incursions. And no conflicting checkpoints, with double taxes, and bootlicking of both sides. But try to stay the night in Santa Barbara without ten bucks and the name of a friend?

The Syukhtun Markets are on the south end of town. By now they were closed. There weren't many people around and the dumpsters were full. We pulled up to one behind a fish stall. I went around to the front and found the owner, a man in a sari with gold teeth, bustling around hosing off the pallets and display boxes. It smelled like the sea, with a bit of rot. Blood on melting lumps of ice. Fish scales clung to the worn wooden legs holding up the stalls. His wife was seated under the roof picking through a bushel of crabs, holding them up to watch their legs move and then sorting them into two baskets.

I said hello and when he answered, "Yes," I decided to try Spanish, but that was no go. I tried gutter slang TongvaMex and he wrinkled his brow and looked at his wife. He said something that might have been Russian or Tagalog for all I knew. I was prepared to say Austrian. The fact was, I couldn't even think of much to ask a fishmonger as the market closes. Finally, I asked, "Is road closed?" His wife nodded after the fifth or sixth time. She shook her hand and said to me, very slowly, something I did not recognize and am unable to repeat. By then though they drove up around to the other side of the road and I smiled and backed away saying, "Thank you."

In the car Detreuil said, "Let's get married here."

It was a good idea. We went off in search of City Hall and by noon Detreuil and Elma were married. He was shrunken and pathetic, but sarcastic too. Detreuil may be the meanest person I have ever met. An annoying dying guy you feel sorry for.

Chapter Thirteen

We installed Detreuil with us then. He signed all the papers without reading them, including the life insurance policy. We paid him his silver pesos and got him to sign a payment to the Atlas Insurance Group of Santa Barbara. Our road trip north proved fruitful.

He was sickening slowly. The girls bathed and fed him. The Priest and Margaret moved in with friends in Beverly Hills. Torrance was no good anymore. We settled into a domestic life, drank less, watched more TV.

Irmela slept more and more in the library, which she had fixed up with stuff from around the house, and junk she found on the curbs, so Elma and I slept alone mostly. I had never lived with a woman before or even been with the same one for more than a couple of weeks. I never wanted to be in love and I didn't think I could be. But Elma was different. I did love her. I wanted her to myself. Killing de Marcos changed things in a way killing David didn't. Killing David felt good. I liked smacking his head. As for Detreuil, it was one thing to bet against a guy and another to shoot him. We weren't killing him. He was dying. But I *shot* de Marcos, an asshole who couldn't take a hint. Gunning him down and dumping their cut up bodies in the woods didn't feel good. And we were stuck with it now. It married us. Every time she crawled into bed with me my heart beat a little faster. I lay awake watching her hair in the dark. And I started to notice that stray hairs on her body glowed too. And it made me wonder, how can that be? And if she was a natural, then what does that mean. You burn for fucking a Ruler.

There were days when Detreuil would recover. He was like a fly. It was probably the diet and the babying. And we had gotten to like the guy, so we had a good day when he had a good day. Cause there were other times when we heard him coughing up his lungs. He got a parasite from the water and wasted away with diarrhea. They fed him coconut serum through a tube. The Priest put it down his throat and Irmela and Elma tended to the bags while he gagged and hollered.

The sun was high and it was hot and arid, a perfect day. We drove with Detreuil to Indian Springs, in Kuruvungna. There's a Peyote Church there. The Priest said it might not be a bad idea to whore after alien gods. He took Detreuil into the three-story whitewashed dome to talk to the shaman while we hung out under a eucalyptus tree watching the street go by.

There was a commotion and people started running and screaming, "On Wilshire!" I couldn't tell if they were running away from or towards Wilshire Boulevard. And then I saw. A contingent of Rulers was marching down the street on black horses, in white dress, arms holstered in the saddle. They clopped up the cobblestone street and the crowd stopped running as they approached, invisible behind their visors. It was the Ruler Tobor Ocktomann, and his retinue. First came 16 troops of guard, on black paso fino palfreys, in full grey dress armor with bandoleers of short grenades, batons, bullwhips and assault rifles. Next were the California Rulers, on giant black mares draped in silver mail, with zap guns and vaporounds on their belts. Their masks were of obsidian electraweave edged in titanium, so the light flashed and starred off the visors. They rode on all sides of the Ruler Tobor Ocktomann, the most conceited of the bunch, riding high in state on the largest of the horses, his chest spangled with jewels and medals and his uniform a suit that he had designed himself. It was all white and like the wings to his glowing blond hair, for he wore no helmet into battle. Riding alongside Ocktomann were two young Rulers. One I didn't know of. He was Sargon. But the other of these was Lord Otis. Even behind the shield Lord Otis looked cruel, the hardest of the bunch. The air grew cold around him.

And they were followed by a troop of 16 Rulers on black paso fino palfreys. It was nearly the entire Ruler population of the old province of Sur Califas.

It was too late to run. I stared at the ground as they passed. There wasn't a sound in the air but the creak of saddles, and horseshoes on the cobblestones. Only when they were well out of sight did life drift back to normal.

"Did you see that one? The really scary one?" I asked when we were in the car.

Detreuil said, "I thought it was all a myth."

I said, "No myth man. Where've you been?"

"At sea. I don't believe what people tell me."

The Priest twisted around from the front seat and said to Detreuil, "They're bloody real, don't doubt it. I wonder what they're up to? Bloody avarice writ as moral superiority. Is there an older story? Even Adam and Eve you see, they died for sins imposed upon them by God, their lord, who punishes disobedience like an earthly king, for Adam and Eve were not created by God but conquered by him. It was he who forced them into clothes, and sexual guilt, who made birth, labor and death a punishment, the three things we must assuredly do in this world. And for that, I

could not forgive God, and am damned for it. He'll have nothing to
do with me; he's abandoned me to the devil it seems, to Malebolge
in the City of Dis. And what is the use of being stricken? You
might as well enjoy it now if you're to be damned, for that's all the
pleasure you'll get out of it in this creation." He looked back at the
windshield. I drove us home.

We all felt dirty after the day and each showered in turn,
starting with the Priest. The last one in the shower was Irmela.
It was around midnight. The Priest, Elma, Margaret and I were
seated out on the deck eating fish tacos and drinking white wine.
The Pacific was black and still. Out of that dark came Irmela's
shriek. Were it anyone else's you would think they were being
devoured by ants. But Irmela was liable to shriek like that when
she burned her toast. It could be a scorpion or the wrong color hair
dye. Or it could be the sewer line backing up into the drains. Shit
water rising slowly up into the toilets, sinks, tubs and showers.
Shit water gradually topping the rims and running onto the floor.

"Malebolge!" the Priest thundered. "Dear God, call a plumber."

"Where's the plunger?" I shouted. "Where would they keep a
plunger?"

"A plunger?" Elma asked.

Irmela, who was wrapped in a big terry cloth towel, cried.

"For fucking goddamn," Margaret said to the Priest. "Do
something!"

The Priest got on the phone. Within in an hour a giant rocket
shaped truck with a turning yellow light on the cab arrived and
a man named Carlson was at the door. He was dressed in stained
coveralls and hip waders and smelled like blue cleanser. A mask
dangled around his neck. In his hand was a pink hose and a
ring of brass fittings. "You called a plumbing emergency? Mr. Bob
Martin?"

"Yes, that's me. The problem—"

"I know the problem. Now step aside sir. This is a toxic site."

We sat in the living room. There was a taint of excrement in the air so we moved back out to the deck. It was windy and hard to light a cigarette. I had lost my appetite for fish tacos. There was bacteria swarming all over everything. I could feel them, tiny needles in my eyebrows.

After a few hours of gurgling and gargling in pipes and vacuum hoses and roaring douches, a worn-out, wet Carlson came out onto the deck. It was so windy we had to shout.

"What went wrong?" I asked.

"Well, we sucked out everything up to the obstruction. Then we power washed it, and did a chemical surge, and a typhoon break, but we came up deuces. So, the thing is, I gotta scope her. It's gonna run you some, but without we do that, nothing good here is gonna happen. You're gonna get back-leak, your gonna get pile-up, you're gonna get collar-seepage and unglue. Now if I can scope her, then I can tailor-make you a solution."

"Yeah whatever the fuck!"

"Thanks, Mr. Martin."

"Forget about it. Let me know what you find."

Two hours later Carlson came back, wetter than before, his face flushed and weary but proud. "Well Mr. Martin. The news isn't bad. What you have is a pseudo life living in your pipes."

"A fucking what? A zooto life?"

"A pseudo-life. As in, false."

"A false life? Like a fake life form?"

"No, not fake, but not really alive. Bacteria form dense interrelated colonies built out of genetic material, the secretions and tissues of the people living in a house. Like, finger and toenails, hair follicles, skin. Under normal circumstances it forms a big sticky colony, but sometimes, if there's mutant DNA present, the colony begins to organize itself and behave like a living organism."

"Mutant DNA? What do I look like?"

"Well, you know some well connected people I'd say. But it doesn't take *much* to get it evolving. Once these things fuse with the pipes they're hard to get rid of. Adhesions form, connective tissue. The masses grow organs, skin, hair. I found an optic nerve down there with toenails and hair growing out of it. It looked like it was blinking. They move slowly through the system, digesting and absorbing waste and reproducing, growing."

"Can you get rid of it?"

"Well, you're in luck there." He paused to scratch his head and water beads flew off of his hair. "Sulfuric Acid. It's cheap and it will turn that thing living in your pipes into a sludge you can flush right out of her. Bones, teeth, everything."

"Go ahead then."

It was afternoon. We moved to the garden and watched the hummingbirds. We had been on this thing for over twelve hours. I was hungry and drunk.

"What do you think? Did he find their blood down there?" I asked.

Margaret said, "Just what I was thinking."

"We poured enough of it in. The evidence is there," the Priest said. "Embedded in those adhesions. It's almost as if the corpses had a baby."

"I guess we just have to see what happens," I said. "Go from there."

"What are you saying?" the Priest asked.

"I'm not saying anything."

Carlson, his arm pits stained with sweat, in dirty, squishing hip waders, returned with the pink hose and the ring of brass fittings. "She's all done. I'll be right back with the bill."

Elma and Irmela had been observing this silently as if it were a show they had seen many times. In a crisis they got both calm and serious. Irmela nursed a glass of wine and with each news bulletin shook her head as if to say, *Yeah, right.* Elma was hitting the bottle hard, periodically gagging. "The smell is in my throat. I can't cough it away."

I went into the living room. The air smelled like fresh mint. Detreuil was sitting on the couch reading a magazine. The light shining on his bald skull filled his empty cheeks with shadow. Carlson came in and said, "I cleaned her out. There's not a germ left, not a strand of mutant DNA, hair follicle, nail or blood trace, no reproductive matter or slough, not an RNA implant, she's clean as a whistle." He handed me a bill and smiled.

"You can send that to my office."

"Sure. But I can't leave without settling up."

He handed me the bill. It was for ten grand and change.

"Ten what fuck grand? For what?"

"I burned a mutant pseudo life form from your pipes. I'd think you'd be glad."

"I could pump sulfuric acid down the pipes too!" I yelled. "Ten fucking grand. What if I only have eight?"

"Then I think my boss might have something to say about that."

"And who the hell is he?"

"I work out of Beverly Hills."

"Oh so I get it OK. He wants to shake the last fruit out of the tree. Fine. Tell him I give the fuck up, take it all."

I looked at Detreuil as if he was the prisoner we had brought along to eat.

Chapter Fourteen

"When the fuck is he going to die already?" I asked.

The Priest put his Keane's Cane and tonic down on the flagstone and said, "What's your hurry?"

"Ten grand is my worry."

"We'll have twenty times that soon enough."

"Is that a promise?"

The Priest sipped his drink. The sun flashed off his sunglasses. Palm trees wobbled on the dark blue surface of the pool. The pineapple fountain was splashing. The citrus trees were full leafed with small green fruit. Hummingbirds covered the bougainvillea. The girls were up on the deck and Detreuil was lying in bed, which he rarely got out of now. Elma cleaned him up and Irmela washed the soiled linens. And the Priest was a changed man.

The Priest never lay out in the sun before, no. And he never swam, though he knew well enough how to. "In my early days I taught boys to swim at a church club. I had just come from seminary to the East Coast. I had never seen such wealth. But on weekends I went down to the missions in New York. And I was on the Bowery from 2506 till '11 or '12. Yet I feel like I've been here my whole life."

"Yeah, me too, and I have been. I know people here who couldn't tell you when their people came. I believe what my mother says. This is where god created us. Maybe your god created you somewhere else. I got no problem with that."

"The bards taught that it was at the fall of Babel that the people of the earth dispersed with their confounded languages, and that the first split from the divine word was the Irish, from which all others declined."

"Where's Detreuil from?"

"The sea. A place just as surely as the Mojave is."

"It's a raw deal getting sick and dying before you're thirty."

"There are more of those cards than there are kings and queens," he said.

Irmela came from the house in orange shorts, a cherry red tank top and jellies. Her hair was wet. She looked at the Priest and smiled. "You are dark when you tan, negrito."

"Because my father loves me so."

Irmela sat down at the edge of the pool and put her feet in the water. She wore no sunglasses because the sun didn't bother her. She didn't even break a sweat.

Irmela wore her moods on her face and in her back. When she was restless she could not be still. When she was unhappy, she dragged her knuckles on the ground. When she was angry, she didn't pucker up her lips like Elma did, she was like a knife, her face sharp and eyes glinting like steel.

And sometimes Irmela was completely still.

She didn't twitch. She didn't breathe. The water rippled away from her legs and as she gazed at it her eyes took on the coloration of the pool. Once I saw her eyes turn to flame, staring at a candle, and when we walked to the beach in January, and fog was rolling in, they turned grey, while monkeys screamed in the trees.

Irmela took her feet out of the water and spun around to face us, her legs crossed on the hot flagstones. The Priest grinned and sat up, his stomach slightly rolled and covered in black hair. He asked, "How is he then?"

Irmela put her head against her fist and squeezed her eyes hard. She let go and said, "I don't think he is making out too well. He has the thrush. It starts on the tongue and goes all the way down to the stomach. He cannot have tube, it is too painful, and whatever he swallows he shits out."

"I'll start a line. If he gets any worse, we'll take him up to the Gallows and I'll have him admitted." The Priest stood. "If this keeps up I'll have to lift more supplies from the storeroom."

I said, "Stock up on heroin."

The next day Detreuil took a turn for the worse. He had cloudy liquid stool tinged with blood and his lungs were hemorrhaging. Irmela raced with bloody towels and sheets, stained pale yellow by his shit, down to the laundry. I was worried we'd get another pseudo-life, though it wasn't likely Detreuil had any exotic DNA in him. They carried him down on a stretcher, his naked, emaciated body covered in a sheet and strapped to a board. His bald head peeped out at the top and he appeared to be in great pain but without the energy to express it, except with small grunts when they took him up and when they set him down next to the Priest's car. We had to take him off the stretcher to fit him in. Periodically he would start to gasp for breath. I picked him up under the shoulders. I was afraid his bones would break in my hand. We laid him in the back seat and the Priest left for the hospital. Now all we had to do was wait.

We didn't wait long. Detreuil died that night. The Priest signed the death certificate as *Doctor Steelgate*, stating as cause of death acute diarrhea caused by intestinal parasites. In the morning I drove Elma down to claim the body at the Gallows. She dressed

all in black but wore no veil or hat. It was hot, so I drove fast
with the windows down and the air blew Elma's hair around.
Everything was bleached out white, tinted sun-goggle grey. As we
got closer to LA Yaanga traffic thinned. There were burning barrels
at the exits. A troop of Ruler cops passed by on bikes. Down the
road, maybe a mile, a Mexican armored truck pulled back off the
freeway, and a ball of flame and black smoke boiled up off the road.
I took the next exit and drove the back way into Compton, cursing
a little before I gave up and took random turns. The Gallows was
on Alameda Street. It was the tallest thing around, nine stories
of metal faced with adobe that had not been whitewashed in a
century. Pieces were falling off onto the dirt beneath and it was
pocked with bullet holes.

The street in front was busy with food hawkers and flower
sellers and horses and pedicabs. People came from all over to die
here; it was very popular. Inside was clean enough, but it smelled
like urine and rats. There was a wide admitting desk and a waiting
area it shared with the emergency room. There was a television
making a racket with the news. I sat down while a nurse took
Elma's information. Elma's eyes were red and welled tears as she
spoke, haltingly, about her late husband. I suppose she was tired.
She'd been taking care of him, keeping him alive, and she must
have cared that he had finally died. Even I felt bad and I was
getting ready to give him the needle and be done with it. If it had
been me, I would have shot myself. Better dead than dying.

The nurse sent Elma down to the basement. I sat in the
waiting room and attempted to read, but the people were making
me twitch. They had runny noses and barking coughs, swollen
throats and faces, festering injuries, a gangrenous foot, a brown
recluse bite. The furniture was covered with a film of debris. I
watched the yammering TV. A man with red lips like Margaret's
said, "Today the Ruler Tobor Ocktomann reports that Santa

Barbara police have discovered remains in the Father's Forest. High up in the mountains above the city a hunter's dog found bones and synthetic hair. The Ruler Tobor Ocktomann announced that the Ruler Sargon will investigate. There is a $50,000 reward for information leading to the capture and execution of the murderer." The man, or whatever he was, turned to the woman, or whatever she was, and said, "What about that. A hunter's dog."

"It happens," she said. "And now for the weather. The Ruler Tobor Ocktomann has declared a fire warning. At the first siren, go to your pods and remain there until the all clear sounds."

Now it was certain the de Marcoses would be identified, even if they hadn't been reported missing. I had every right to be in the house, I was the listing agent. Even they didn't believe it was me who had wrecked their house, or rather, they didn't suspect that the guy they found with a half-naked woman and a Priest in their living room was the agent they had hired to sell the house, not at first.

They didn't have a thing on us. The plumber even ripped the drains. They were clean of DNA. And I couldn't see why they would be suspicious anyway, unless Junior had tipped them off. But he wouldn't give a pine nut up for a Ruler. Woe to me if the Mexicans ever came back but as long as the Rulers ruled LA I wouldn't have to worry about Junior ratting me.

It was like I was floating in the room then, with all those sick people below me, because I knew it was all bullshit. With that goddamn fake hair I thought was real and those bones and whatever else they had but didn't talk about, I knew what was coming.

One good thing is Rulers don't know shit about business. An insurance scam, if it's tight enough to pass the company, will pass any Ruler cop. And ours was tight. We were going to collect 250 grand, 50 grand each.

With that kind of money I could afford to rent the house; but who from, that remained to be seen. Their estate was not settled yet. It was not their primary property. If a trust took ownership or a bank, that would be one thing. But even a relative will have to make a sale, and will probably go through the listing agent.

No way was anyone moving into that house; it was cursed as a sale property. Some places are like that. They want to be owned by the right people. They conceal themselves like those girls in glasses with braids and braces on TV, until the person comes along who can see, and has to have it, and will pay. Or like me, not. So no matter what, all the business would go through me. And I would go ahead and not sell it again, see how long that lasts.

Elma walked into the waiting room, past all the injured bodies, without looking at any of them and said, "They will mail the ashes to us. Let's go."

"That only took 12 hours."

In the car, as I tried to follow the dirt and stone streets of South Central, she said, "Let's not meet them right away. Let's go out. Take me to that place in Malibu. Even mee goreng in some tin warung with batik curtains, I don't care." She put her hand on my leg, "I want to hold your hand."

I took my right hand off the wheel and squeezed her hand. There was a loud thud. I jerked my hand away and drove out of the pothole. "It's going to be OK. We'll have money soon. How about we go down to the beach first and look at the water?"

We were past the checkpoints. It was still and dark out there. We were the only car. There hadn't been signs shutting down the road. As we headed into Santa Monica traffic thickened. We crawled through town in a circus of people and every kind of thing that moved. I rolled the windows up and we fogged them with our breath. I held her hand. Elma said, "We need to get out, alone.

Irmela will want you. I have given her everything. I am not giving you to her. No other woman can have you."

"I guess, in fact, if not in principle."

"I don't understand this *not in principle*."

"Well it's like with the law. Precedents. You don't want a precedent like that. Not that I would. I'm faithful to you. I can't be with other women."

"Love is not a lawyer thing. Honor doesn't need the law."

"Yeah well, that ain't my training. Maybe in Austria you can afford that kind of shit but in California it's laughable."

Elma looked down at our hands. Traffic budged. Finally we got free and headed up the coast highway. I pulled off the road. The wind was up, hot. We walked down to the beach. There was a high, rolling surf. The white lights of a nightsurfer flashed into the waves. We sat and kicked sand with our feet. Elma said, with tears in her voice, "It was so sad to see him go like that. I don't care about the money so much. But he was a sweet boy."

"I think he was the most foul mouthed sweet boy I ever met. And when he could eat he really wolfed it down. I guess he shat it all out. He was funny, I'll give him that. He made me laugh. And he went quiet enough, except for the body noises, all the farting and vomiting and coughing. I thought he had cholera. But he was part of us. I'll miss him."

"The peyote really helped. He had a vision of the seagull that talked to the man who was cursed to talk to people at parties about it."

"That's detailed. I just see blobs of color and feel like I'm gonna die."

"Let's dive into the water."

"Surf's very high."

"We won't go out into it. Come on." We stripped down and ran to the water. The moon was low in the sky, about a quarter full, sinking into the ocean while the stars spun around above. I followed Elma into the surf and we plunged forward, till the water was like horses galloping around my thighs. We sank into it side by side and let the beach rush out beneath us. I stood and said, "Now we're all sandy and sticky. How will we go out to eat?"

"Man would not have been civilized if you had been there in the beginning." She ran out of the surf and up the beach to our stuff and let the hot wind dry her off. It carried the smell of fire.

"I wonder what is burning?" she asked.

"Forest. Homes. Kiinarabi. Txaparil "

"I don't understand this kiinarabi."

"In the city they call it manzanita."

"Manzanita. Sounds like a drink."

"Maybe it is, somewhere. Everything is, right?"

"Yeah, sure."

We banged the dried sand off with our pants and dressed. Near the car was a long log on its side. We sat down on it and stared into the sky and watched the nightsurfer's lights go out. The stars were brilliant, like the sky was made of glass that burst long ago and now the bits were caught in time, slowed by my eyes. A boat drove off, three red taillights heading south. The wind blew hot and the moon turned gold and slipped below the waves.

"Let's go," I said. "I'm hungry."

"Let's eat after," Elma said. "And then we can order Manzanitas straight up and dance."

"After what?"

She touched the side of my head. "You do not wish to have sex?"

I put my hand on hers and acted like I had to think about it. "Aren't you afraid of getting caught?"

"The only one who's going to get caught is you, between my legs." She moved our hands behind my head and pulled me to her.

We had it to ourselves, the surf, the stars, the hot wind, and we took it. It was ours. Then we put our clothes on and headed up to The DelBar.

The DelBar had a table in the Candle Room. There was a chanteuse who played piano and a fire going in the glass wall overlooking the ocean. The candles in the room spread out through the windows into the night. The waiter lowered down two long menus and we pretended to look at them.

"Onion rings or fries?" I asked.

"I like the hash browns with mine."

"So we get both then, alright?"

It was the first time I ever talked about the money like it was ours and not mine. But we had just earned the nut together.

We ordered steaks and red wine from the waiter and took our cocktails downstairs to the dance floor. We danced it off a bit and watched the others. For months I had felt like I was sneaking around. I never went to any of the old places. And I spoke about them that way too. Places I had gone to every day just a year ago were old to me. It was the change.

We went into the glass room where the music was filtered to not quite loud. I looked at her hands. They were pale even in the dark. The faint hair on her arms was glowing the same color as the moon had been. I touched her hair and lit it up. I said, "How did you get hair like that? Where are you from?" I saw the look on her face, how it dropped, like I had broken her, and then how she straightened up and puckered her lips. "No," I said. "I'm sorry. I want to know where you're from. Who are you?"

"What do you want to know?"

"Just your hair."

"That is to say everything. You do not want me to say everything?"

"Say something then. One thing."

"You must know then what David thought he knew. But what he knew wasn't true. Our mother was a Ruler in Hungary who got pregnant by her Austrian secretary. If anyone discovers this, I will be killed, and so will you. Understand. I trust you to know this. They fled to Azerbaijan where I was born. We lived there in peace until they came at night and took my father and burned him in the street. My mother was pregnant with Irmela. She was allowed to live, in perpetual exile, and deprived of all wealth. She took us to Jerusalem and there they burned her in the street, when I was ten and Irmela was four. Our father's uncle lived there and took us in. And it was he who betrayed our mother."

"Your mother had the hair?"

"My mother's entire body could light up like the sun. She was seven foot four and had perfect pitch. She ran a mile in 3 minutes and killed with her hands." She put her lips close to my ear and said, "Her name was Phaedra."

Chapter Fifteen

The old lady who inherited the house got in touch with me through the executor of the de Marcos estate, Abby Vonneniu. Vonneniu had offices in Santa Barbara and downtown LA, in one of those fused stone office boxes that have made parts of the city look like Stonehenge. He was on the tenth floor, at the end of a long unlit corridor of stone and plaster. Sun came into the hall from the pebbled glass window and transom of the door to the office. Inside was a black table and three white chairs. Seated in two of them were Mr. Vonneniu and Dr. Oyub, the old lady's lawyer.

"Thank you for coming on such short notice, Mr. Martin," Vonneniu said. He was a tall man, thin, with raw skin and wattles. His hands were older than his face. He had shoulder-length burgundy hair, which was pressed flat against his head.

I said, "Bob is fine. How can I help you?"

Oyub spoke. "I suppose you've been watching the news." He was ovoid, nothing like his buddy Vonneniu. I think he had kidney stones. His eyes were heavy and red with suffering.

I said, "I'm not sure that I follow you."

"The remains found up in the Father's Forest are those of your client, Mr. de Marcos," Vonneniu said.

"I'm sorry to hear that. I'm afraid I don't watch the news. I'm not big on popular culture. Was it an accident?"

"Hard to say," Vonneniu said. "All they found was the hairpiece and a femur."

"The hairpiece is all they need," I said.

"The bone marrow doesn't hurt," said Oyub. They looked at each other knowingly.

I asked, "What do you have in mind for the property?"

"Ah, yes, the property," said Vonneniu.

"The property," said Oyub, "is of interest to my client, the beneficiary. The problem is, she is confined to a home. She instructed me to contact Mr. Vonneniu and set up a meeting. There are forms she needs to sign. She needs to understand clearly what the cost of renting the property would be versus selling it. Since you are the listing agent—"

"We thought perhaps you would go and speak to her."

"What's the old lady's name?"

"She's not actually that old," Oyub said.

"Old by human standards," Vonneniu said, with a raised eyebrow.

"She's eighty. You'll see when you get there."

"Is she wealthy?"

"Good lord no. She has some means but—"

Vonneniu said, "Don't get any ideas here."

"I don't have ideas."

"We're just trying to dispose of a property to close out the estate."

"Then don't talk to me about ideas, OK? Now, if it's her property, and she's a woman of some means, she might as well keep it," I said.

Vonneniu cut in. "Have I misjudged you?"

"You want me to tell her to sell?"

"Precisely."

"Where is she?"

Oyub handed me a card and said, "Santa Monica. The Azodiazadora."

I went to the Azodiazadora, a Spanish Mission palace for old rich people who weren't so rich anymore. The front door had suction seals but after that they all hung on hinges. There was an empty lobby with palm trees and polished stone tables, overstuffed couches and easy chairs, and ceiling fans. The upholstery was stained and faded. The walls were dark green with gold trim and paintings of foxhunts in gilt frames. A crimson sash with gold braid hung down from the ceiling in the corner. There was a black reception desk manned by three humans in red jackets. On it were everflame jack-o-lanterns and candied corn in Siamese fighting fish bowls.

Elma followed me to the desk. Irmela was out in the car with the Priest. I was wearing a business suit, charcoal grey, a tie with holly green-, red-, and moss-colored bars. I put a little polish on my head, just to give it that extra bit of shine. Junior used to like that about me. I nailed the details without sweating. He used to say to me, "Bob, you're the only man around here with a dry shirt." And I'd say, "That's because I wet my pants."

I said to the first clerk, "I have an appointment with Agatha Kennedu."

"And what is your name, sir?"

"Bob Martin."

She checked her book and smiled. "You'll be meeting in the crystal room. Someone will take you in, in a moment. Have a seat please."

We sank into the couch and it was hard not smiling, harder still not touching. I wanted a couch just like it. Under my breath I said, "What do you figure a couch like this goes for?"

"Two thousand at least. Maybe more."

"Why do they waste it in here?"

"You cannot easily buy things this old. This home has been here for a long time. I can feel that many people die here. Over the centuries, many thousands. Have you heard of the moonds?"

"Moonds?

"No, moonds. Like pitcher's mound."

"Mound. Not moond."

"I did not say moond, I said moond."

"Good god. Which ones? There are a lot of moonds out there."

"The ones in Ohio Valley. Around some hotels where many died and were buried the ground is high."

"That's what the earth is made of," I said. "All the dead things that ever were."

A man in casual slacks and a jacket came in with a briefcase. He led us down a dark hallway to a small room so crammed with crystals it felt like a cave. Glass shelves held amethysts, geodes and eruptions of quartz. They were creepier than cactus. The light refracted off the veins and facets. It was a soft and warm light and the longer we sat in it the brighter it became, until it was easy to read the documents. But even so, it felt like the rocks were looking over my shoulder. I started to itch, and I knew I couldn't scratch so I started to cry. Oh no. It was awful. I started to laugh then because of how ridiculous it seemed and that made me cry more. I buried my face in my coat sleeve.

Elma and I sat on one side of a steel stable. On the other were two chairs. Soon the door opened and an orderly led a decrepit old woman in. She looked like she had lost half of herself through attrition. Her hair was unevenly combed, and white. She was heavily made up for the occasion. Bent in half, she shuffled forward. Her light blue eyes didn't focus. Her mouth was slack and crammed with young teeth. She wore a red robe and black pajamas. Expensive fabric. Around her neck were strands of pearls, white and black. These she clutched in one bony, twisted hand while in the other she held a large jeweled purse.

"Are you Mr. Martin?" she asked when she sat down, looking me square in the face. Her voice was strong.

"Yes, Mrs. Kennedu."

"Good. Let's get started. First of all, I'm convinced my nephew was murdered. But I'm also convinced the police will never figure out who did it, not as long as that boob is running this town."

"I'm afraid to mention," I said.

"Don't be. This place is a hotbed of hatred. It seethes in the walls. It doesn't matter who's in charge, we hate them here."

"That would be the same just about everywhere then."

"You see, you get so isolated you forget. I just watch the news. As to the property. I do not wish to sell it."

"All right," I said. "What do you have in mind?"

"What can you get for it as a rental?"

"Oh, in this market, it's hard to say."

"Try hard then."

"Well, there are the costs."

"What are the costs?"

"Considerable. The climate and plumbing systems are superannuated. You might be able to rent it if you go low enough. People expect a certain level of comfort in that market. Old systems are also more expensive to operate. Over the past year there was a ten-thousand-dollar plumbing event. Taxes were twelve thousand. They'll go up. There'll be a war tax, wait and see. The Ruler Tobor Ocktomann will impose it. Anyway, a clean new install would be expensive but necessary for a quick sale. Otherwise you have to discount the house enough to make it worth the buyer's while to do the upgrades herself."

"I don't really care about all of that. Find me a tenant. I'm told market rate is seven thousand a month. I'll take five if you can get a reliable tenant."

"I'm glad you asked. I brought one with me. A client of mine, Elma von Doderer. She suffered a terrible tragedy when her young husband died of an exotic intestinal parasite. She would like to rent the house from you with her younger sister, Irmela. Seven thousand is not exactly market rate for a house in this condition. Shall we settle on three thousand a month?"

Agatha pinched her nose and blew out her cheeks. "I had to clear my ears. I'll take forty-five."

"Elma and her sister would be the kind of reliable tenant you are looking for. Caretakers, really, of an historic property. Selfless stewards of the house."

She looked Elma over. "Is that true dear? Are you an angel?"

"Angel, no. Good tenant, yes. You need not worry about me."

"I like to handle my own affairs. Mr. Martin, do you wish to continue as the agent? I need someone to manage the property."

"I think I can fit it in to my list. About the rent."

"I'll go to four, but that's it. Take it or leave it."

"I can pay four," Elma said.

"What do you do for a living," she asked.

"I am a private care nurse. I trained in Basel at the Hochschule für Soziale Arbeit. I also trained in Ayurvedic in Montreal and did Rolfing in New York."

"Well that's settled then." She pushed a raft of documents at me to sign. It took the better part of two hours to read them over. We had finger sandwiches and coffee. When all was concluded she smiled and said, "I'll see you on the first of the month. That is my one stipulation. Come at five and expect to stay two hours. We'll have martinis with olives."

Chapter Sixteen

With her cut Irmela bought a motorcycle and a leather jacket and pants. Now whenever she wanted to hit LA pinball parlours she could. No more stealing my car and crying when I got mad. The first time she rode up in it the Priest and Margaret were sitting in the living room arguing with me about the take.

Margaret puffed out her eyes, turned a shade of pink darker and said, "You've got three shares and we only got two. It should be 50-50." She let out her breath and her eyes sank back into her head.

The Priest in his priest voice said, "You all live together. We have to make it out there, in the world. Lord Otis has driven everyone out of LA and chased them down to Palos Verdes with his bloody squad of youngsters laying waste to the place. You ought to get out and hear what's happening. You can't live in this house all the time. Death squads are roaming Hollywood and Beverly Hills."

"You owe us Bob. We were in with you before them," Margaret said.

"No deal. You agreed and you know it. And who the fuck do you think took care of that guy while you got shitfaced?"

The Priest said, "We did agree. I'm just registering my protest."

"Well to get the next one up, we'll ante half. The old lady likes to booze. I got her to lower our rent to two thousand a month. We can keep it going on that indefinitely, at least until she croaks. I guess it'll go to probate then. That could be in the courts for years, and we have a signed lease. You should see her. She's decrepit, like one of those adobe shit holes with paint and plaster flaking off. She puts make up on top of it and saws her steak into tiny pieces."

"Some of the most broken birds are fierce in their minds still," the Priest said. "My grandmother was just such a woman. She came from a wealthy family but fell in love with a jewel thief. After breaking her heart for many years he had a stroke and came home, unable to talk or to feed himself, but vigorous. His anger, his constant lacerating anger twisted his features so that his face was purple and the tendons stood out on his neck like cables. Finally, when she was 82 he died. By then she was confined to a wheel chair, but she was a superb card player and made her living as a professional gambler, until she died at the tables just shy of her 96th birthday."

"You're scaring me to death," I said. Elma came up the stairs and stood in the French doors.

"We were just talking about the old lady. What do you give her?"

"Well, sometimes a bath, if she asks me." Elma came in and sat stiffly on the couch.

"I mean months," I said.

"To live you mean? She's very strong. She could be healthy with care. She should quit drinking and smoking and eat more. They allow them to deteriorate. But she is not dying. This kidney cancer, and this chemotherapy, I don't believe them."

"Only the mean live long."

The Priest laughed. "It's said that salt and vinegar preserve."

"Mean? She is not mean. I like her. She is funny. Today she told me about the patients who are having affairs."

"Affairs! That old bat doesn't talk like that with me," I said.

"But this is not necessarily sex. These are affairs of the heart, intrigue. They spy on each other and exchange favors. There is a prostitute who does mamar. She is too dry for fuck."

"Ew," I said.

Margaret looked Elma in the eye and smiled. "She is becoming close to you."

"And I to her."

"That's good. I assume she pays you?"

"Of course she pays me. This money will not last, it must be saved and we must work. I don't care what he does with his, I am going to save mine and make some money from this old lady. I will be her nurse. It will be much more than we pay her back in rent."

The motorcycle idled up, spluttering loudly. Irmela kept it tuned that way so that she could peel out and leave a train of junk behind her. She came in dressed in leather, with her helmet in her hand. Her hair stood off of her head in a hundred directions. She put down the helmet, took off her jacket and threw it on a chair. She had on a T-shirt. She took the water bottle off her belt and glugged it down. Her skin flushed red and faded to white. She peeled off the leather pants and stood in her orange shorts, bare foot. "It's hot in that deer skin. I have never been hot before. I don't like it."

"What do you think of the old lady?" I asked.

"I don't know if she is rich, if that's what you are asking."

"He wants to know how long she will live for," Elma said. They shook their heads and stared at me.

"Same thing," Irmela said.

"I have an idea," the Priest said. "Let's go to a show in Santa Barbara. There's no war up there. We could catch a couple of hours of Lucy. I'd like to laugh."

"Oh you and that Lucy!" Margaret said.

Elma said, "Bob used to fuck the actresses. He fucked the Samantha and the Trixie."

Margaret said, "And then some. I don't want to see Lucy. I'd see Twilight Zone."

"Not the musical one," I said. "In Santa Barbara shows are always musical reviews. That's what those Syukhtun plooks want."

Elma said, "The Priest is right, let's get in the car and go."

"Let's take my car," I said.

We piled into the car and drove up the coast. It was late afternoon. We got steaks and martinis first and rolled into the theater around nine, hot, drunk and flatulent. The place was crowded. The heads showed in the tobacco and marijuana smoke. The stage was lit but empty: the Ricardo's Living Room. Lucy came in with a feather duster and the audience broke out in applause. She looked like the real Lucy. They all do. I love the Lucy shows, they crack me up. I got a thirst on and bought peanuts and beer from the tout. I gave him the change and told him to beat it.

After the show we walked around looking into store windows. There were jewelry shops with windows full of gold and diamonds, rubies and opals and sapphires and pearls. There were fruit and vegetable stands with peppers and artichokes and beets. There were stores that sold beautiful shoes and underwear, stores that sold meat. There were all kinds of stores. And the police rode up the center of the street on armored bikes, with assault rifles, batons and whips.

It was quite late and we got lost in the dark driving on the dirt roads through the Los Padres. For some reason no spot seemed right to camp for the night. I was tired and losing my grip on the road. The Priest was incoherent, swigging from a flask of mescal. Margaret was snoring in back. That left Irmela and Elma. "I don't think I can drive much further. There's a property I showed somewhere around here. It's in the car's memory. And I was IDd so we should be able to clear the entrance, if no one's there, and I can find it. You have to help keep me awake. You have to talk to me."

"About what?" asked Irmela.

"I don't know, anything."

"That is not helpful," Elma said. "That makes no sense."

"It doesn't have to make sense, does it?"

"You can go like that if you want," said Elma. "But if you have no use for honor, but rather for principal, then I have no use for nonsense."

"Now I just flat don't fucking understand! Look at this road. It's like," I tried to find the words for tree limbs slapping the windshield and mud in the tread, of yawning precipices. The car knew where it was going, but I didn't. It was like a dog on a trail. The headlights staggered around turns up switchbacks and then leveled out in deep firs. We came to the corners shaved out in semi-circles and then to the entrance, the long drive under needling sensors up to the stone guard tower. I didn't see lights on. There was no security, no human or Ruler presence at all. The car drove through the gate, through the aisle of redwoods to the Minangkabau portico. Here the car stopped and here we spent the rest of the night, asleep.

In the morning it was foggy. We walked up the gravel drive and gazed at the massive arched windows of the galleries and at the darkness within. The light shined in enough to see the outlines of carved columns, palms and ferns, and parquetry like a Persian carpet.

"This is it?" the Priest asked. "It looks unlived in."

"It's been decorated," I said. "The columns are painted; they were white when we showed it. This house is in the Egyptian style, late colonial. That's the Ruler Tobor Ocktomann all over."

"They say he screws his sister," the Priest said.

"Is that not what they all do?" Elma asked. "The clones pair off each generation exactly as the one before it."

"A lot of rules to produce a crop of feeble idiots," I said.

"So it ever is," the Priest said. "For sheer degeneracy you have to take the English nobleman as number one. He is both a pederast and a conqueror."

"Exterminator!" I added.

"Bugs of the planet getting rich off the discards of others."

"Do you want to see if there are horses?"

We were standing under a sequoia behind a curtain of rain. The air was clean. They stared at me as if the word 'horses' meant something. "I kept a horse when I was a boy," the Priest said.

"Aye, so did I," said Margaret. "Kept her in the yard and used her shyte in the garden. She could pull a wagon full of vegetables to market."

"I hauled scrap with a horse in Long Beach," I said. "After my mother left. Who wants to see Ruler horses? Are you coming?" I asked.

"Well let's go," said Margaret.

The stables were a quarter mile from the house, through landscaped woods, with reflecting pools and streams. There were a couple of black carriages parked out front. Behind that were the reinforced walls of the stable. The doors were double iron barred. We stood by the windows and peered in at the horses, which were on the basement level. They were facing away. Even the swish of their tails was enormous. They smelled like dogs. The Priest took out a flashlight and shined it in. The horses stamped and snorted in the beam. They were eating a wild pig, tearing it apart between them. Blood dripped off their muzzles as they gnawed at the meat. Irmela turned from the window and walked away. Elma went after her. "Will you look at that," the Priest said.

"Let's go," Margaret said.

We turned to go up the path after Irmela and Elma but they were headed back in our direction, followed by a man who at first, from far away, seemed human, but as he got closer, grew larger. It was a Ruler. He was not in uniform but he was seven and a half feet tall and his features, his eyes, his nostrils, his lips, were large and lionlike. He was beautiful to look upon but when he looked at me, I felt myself shrink.

He stood before us now. Elma and Irmela were like children beside him. He looked at me and asked, "Are you the leader here?"

I searched for something to say. "Yes, I brought them here."

"Why did you do that?"

His eyes were blue, dark like first dawn but as we talked they faded to pale blue, a kind color. "To get off the road. We were lost last night coming home. My car knew the way here because I showed this house once to Charlie Gets Along."

He nodded and laughed a little. "So you'd come and stay at a Ruler's palace."

"No one was here. I thought maybe the sale had not gone through."

"That's a lie. Where do you live?"

"Topanga Canyon."

"All of you?"

"No, just me and the girls. The Priest here lives with her in Malibu."

"I'm a doctor of medicine too," the Priest said, hands pressed together, bowing slightly.

"These two, are they citizens? I see one has a scarcode. What is this accent anyway? Are you two from Mars perhaps?" He laughed again. "Well, let me see. The rats have already eaten the cheese. Maybe it's time for the horses to eat the rats, eh? Like in the song. What do you say to that? Shall I have you draw lots?"

We stared at him as his words stood in mid air between us and I tried to fathom what they meant. Would he shoot me first or do they eat live food? "I'm sorry that we came here," I said. "We were only sleeping in the car."

"Those horses," he said. "They disgust me. You can go. Don't come back."

That was the Ruler Sargon.

Chapter Seventeen

Elma was always singing, but she didn't have a guitar. So she took part of her cut and we drove to a guitar shop in Hollywood. Just past Santa Monica, heading east, there was a Mexican toll and the whole way from there the freeway was under the command of the Mexican Army. All that the Ruler Tobor Ocktomann held from south of Long Beach to Hollywood the week before was lost. The Lord Otis was cut off in Palos Verdes, squeezed between the Mexicans to his south, concentrated at the tip of the peninsula, and supplied by boat from Baja, and pressing down from the north.

Blue sensor beams webbed the car at a quarter mile off from the toll. The freeway narrowed to a single lane and we approached the black armored booth. It had a dense glass portal, behind which a soldier took money for the right to drive on the freeway and not get your car impounded and a bullet in your head. We paid her in silver and she waived us through. The air smelled like burning animal fat. Along the sides of the road were burnt cattle and horses covered in flies. A road crew was clearing human bodies from a ditch and piling them into the back of a pick up truck. Up ahead behind a fog of smoke and cinders was a truck dumping rock and a crew raking it level with the roadbed. Beyond that the traffic kicked up dust clouds and a hot wind blew in from the Mojave.

The streets around the guitar store were deserted. Burnt hunks of automobiles and trucks were piled up at the corners waiting to be hauled off. The streets were cratered. There were buildings on the blocks built from the rubble of 40 years ago that were collapsing. The sky was orange and black. The store was in a strip of restaurants and shops that remained open. There were people playing backgammon and drinking tea in the cafe next door. Elma had been there many times when she had no money, to look at guitars. I found the sitting room and joined the other people who didn't give a shit.

There were guitars hanging floor to ceiling, like suits. But she knew what she wanted. She played them, and then a dozen others. I read the automobile magazines, and the tit magazines. We were hours into it. I had filled an ashtray with Kreteks, tailor-made. There were no more TV stars at the beach. She bought a hollow body electric made in Tenocht' by some guy she had heard of. It was 75 years old and cost 2,000 bucks. She counted out rubies and black pearls and silver pesos and they handed over the guitar. It was dark when we headed home. The freeway was lit by pitch torches, swabs of smoking orange dotting the blackness up into the hills where the Mexicans fell back and a line of Ruler troops was spread out over the ridges, behind bales of razor wire. Several times a day they lobbed mortars and shells at each other. The rest of the time they stared at the other side and waited.

"I want to go to Agatha and play. I promised her I would."

"Tomorrow...."

"Take me there now." Elma grasped my leg above the knee and squeezed. "It's not far."

"Alright, we'll go there." We drove to Santa Monica, to the Azodiazadora. Her room was on the fourth floor with a balcony overlooking the ocean. She was seated in the dining room before the open windows. It was scalding hot but she looked comfortable. She smiled, and sat up in her chair.

"Sit down," she said. "What have you got there?"

Elma said, "I bought a guitar today so I could sing to you. Can you tell me what you ate for breakfast first?"

"Never underestimate the savagery of the young. I had grapefruit, eggs and toast."

"No bacon then."

"I'm Jewish. I won't eat it."

"I understand. I lived in Jerusalem as a child."

"Do you speak Hebrew?"

"Only some curses. I can tell you how to fuck yourself with a Russian pig."

"I think the eggs are enough, don't you?"

"Oh yes, you do not need to eat the bacon. You look good."

"Thank you dear. Now play a song, please. Do you know any Austrian songs?"

"Only cheesy ones. That was an act we did, not from our childhood."

"Play something you love then."

Elma strummed a few chords and launched into a long, intricate piece. It seemed as if she were improvising the whole thing, but I don't know. She said she just knew the piece because she had heard it once, but that was hard to believe. She sang a song in the Austrian they spoke to each other. Her songs were sad. They were about work she said. And about lovers who kill each other. She said she learned some from desert nomads.

Elma sang an old drinking song I heard my father and his cronies sing many times, the one that goes, *I was drunk the night my mother got out of prison.* They would sit out nights on chairs watching the dust blow around and the occasional car go by. All those men he hung out with were in and out of jail; the whole neighborhood was when it was Mexican and about half with the Rulers. Chumash, Tongva, are either gonna fine you, kill you, or kick your ass out of their country. Rulers put you in Alcatraz. Or burn you in the street.

What he got pinched on was a robbery, which was really just a burglary gone bad. But it marked him as an incorrigible recidivist. He was spared death because the court dismissed the charge of violence. It was life in Alcatraz, a place we could never visit. I never saw him again. We wrote letters and exchanged pictures. I remember being surprised he could write. That's how well I knew him. But he rotted there. The letters smelled bad. He ate bugs to survive. They fucked him in the ass. They beat him for fun. In letters, he begged me never to go to prison. He was never any good at that. Chiseling's always best. We both knew it.

Agatha watched Elma play. She looked like hell but she was lively. Irmela and Elma cheered her up, visiting every day. She wasn't slumped forward like a dying dog, but held herself up, and her eyes were bright.

They did small things for her and they got paid. The old lady wanted to talk so they sat sometimes for hours together. On the first of every month I showed up alone at 5 and we had martinis with olives and steak and onions with red wine. A couple of months later I was having dinner with her. After a few drinks her skin plumped out and turned pink. She got this eager smile and her eyes were like blue lamps.

"Elma is an angel," Agatha said. "They both are. My life was one of terminal boredom and depression. I have kidney cancer. It's going to kill me. I thought I had been cursed."

"I'd think the same thing," I said.

"Life isn't like that, Bob. There isn't an equation between your suffering and your actions. The two only arbitrarily align sometimes. That's why she is an angel."

There was a knock at the door. We turned to look at it. Agatha's glass berry drop earrings dangled in the air. "Come in," she said. "Oh," she looked at me and raised her finger. "My neighbor. Mrs. Arkady. I call her RK. RK! Come in, come in. You must meet Mr. Martin. I've told you about him."

RK was wizened, wrinkled and thin. She had a frail walk, holding on to the air for support. "Mr. Martin is it? Elma calls you Bob. Irmela sang so beautifully when she was here last. Like an angel."

I said, "Yeah that singing's really something."

"Sit down and pour yourself a martini. They're in the pitcher," Agatha said, pointing at it.

"Let me," I said. I got the chair and sat her in it and got her a drink.

"This isn't quite first rate," RK said taking a sip and raising her eyebrows.

"Next time make it yourself," I said. The air smelled like meat. There was another knock and the door flew open and a man in a chef's toque pushed a steal-domed table into the room.

"Bring a plate for RK. I'll share," the old lady said. He opened the lid. Two rib eyes sizzled on an iron griddle. There were two plates with potatoes and spinach. He laid the steaks down and passed us the plates and cutlery.

"When I first got here, all they let me have was kale and rice," Agatha said. "I was wasting away. Since I started paying off the kitchen, I feel much better." She drank down the wine and poured another glass. "This isn't half bad. Next time you must bring the girls."

Chapter Eighteen

Late one afternoon the Priest and Margaret dropped by. Elma was at the beach and Irmela was out on her bike. It was a windy day so we sat in the living room and watched the sun set over the Pacific Ocean. We were drinking green tea from bowls. The Priest said, "Bob. We need more money. Our part of the take just isn't good enough."

Margaret said, "We've been asking. We've a right to a consideration. When things went south with Junior, we stuck with you."

"That's right," the Priest said. "What's that worth to you?"

"What do you mean?" I asked. "Are you threatening to go to Junior? Now that he's not mixing drinks for Carlos in Tijuana you're going to betray me?"

He gazed at his feet and said, almost whispered, "We don't need Junior's money. We can go for the reward in Santa Barbara. Fifty grand." He looked at Margaret and she looked at me. Their faces were painted with the sun and still their eyes were dark.

"You want fifty grand not to go to the Rulers?" I asked, feeling life slip away, and so fast.

"We just want our share," said Margaret. "That's what our share is worth."

"I thought we were friends," I said. "Without me, what would you two have? Nothing. Sure, you brought me the project, but the project needed the girls. You used them to lure Detreuil in, and Elma married the patsy and nursed him. They earned their nut, just like we agreed."

"I guess you don't have quite everything, Bob," Margaret said.

"So if I don't cough up 50 big ones, you turn me in. I'm dead."

She said, "We wouldn't turn you in, Bob. You know that. But the girls. We can turn in the girls. We'll collect the reward and you go your way. We leave your name out of it."

After all that bullshit about how hard the girls' lives were, how they'd been exploited by pimps, raped and abused, abandoned to drift, when they were just girls, in the sewer of the world? He was going to be the one to kill them? What game was he playing? He couldn't have thought I'd walk away, not even for fifty grand. That was Margaret talking. Well I wasn't doing it.

The only problem was, I didn't have any money. I was down to a bag full of white pearls and some stashed gold ingots. The rest was in silver. Enough for mee goreng, beer and loose Indian tobacco for a while. No, I wasn't gonna pay a dime either. No girls, and no money.

That left one option and I didn't want to think about it. It was paralyzing. I needed a little time. I didn't smile or frown or twitch, I sat there staring at Margaret. A sweat drop welled up off of my head and rolled down my neck. It felt like a tear.

Margaret's face was puffed up and pink, her red lips set. The Priest gazed out the window grinding his teeth. His eyes were bloodshot and the skin around them had dark creases. It was almost like he was mumbling to himself, but the Priest hadn't prayed or said a rosary in a decade. In this his devotion was true, he always said. I pushed my hands into the cushion, leaned forward and cleared my throat. Quietly, I said, "A week from today, come by the house at eleven. You'll get your stones."

Margaret said, "Don't be upset. We need the money to get out and start over. This is your territory, not ours. We belong south of the city. You know that. Now's our time to get out. The Priest can partner up with Junior on some deals."

I was struggling not to blow up and start screaming when there came through the walls the muffled roar of a motorcycle. A minute later Irmela strode in through the French doors and took off her helmet. She was dressed in white: boots, pants and jacket. She licked her lips and asked, "What? What has happened?"

"Nothing. Our friends are going," I said. Margaret stood and smiled. She reached her hand up and said, "Irmela, we'll talk later dear."

"Yes, later." Irmela shrugged and closed the doors. She walked up to the couch, unzipped the jacket and stood, hands on hips, over me. "What is wrong? I have never seen you look at them like that."

My stomach hurt. I gazed up past the curve of her belly and bumps on her chest. Irmela's face was still and remote, but on her lips was the slightest smile. She knew I was down. She was leaning in to strike. But I could not stop the churning in my stomach to play. There was only one thing to do and I didn't want to do it. As I thought about what I didn't want to do, but was forced to do, I watched her face change. It was like she was sailing on my thoughts. I saw the Priest and Margaret dead on the ground, eyes turned to quartz and mouths broken down.

There was no choice. The Priest had to go. I looked into Irmela's eyes trying to find a reason not to. It wasn't there. "They're going to turn you two in for the reward if we don't cough up fifty grand."

Irmela was silent. Her lip trembled and she said, "How can that be? It is the Priest."

Elma came in dressed in a canary yellow caftan. She was barefoot, untying her hair. There was sand on the top of her feet and between her toes. Her hair was tangled. She shook it free and it opened up and brightened along her cheek. "Who must die?" she asked, looking at Irmela. "No, not the Priest."

"How the hell did you figure that out?" I squawked.

"My sister cannot hide the truth from me with a blanket face. I see her thoughts before she even has them."

I said, "I never said he had to die."

Elma sat on the couch and Irmela sat down next to her. They stared at each other, eyes narrowed, pondering the moves. Then they started to talk in Austrian. I had no idea what was going on. I stared out the window. There was still light in the air and the first stars had not come out yet. I picked up my bowl of tea and watched the green ribbons in the bottom stir. I took a sip. It was cold and bitter. I made a face. "What are you doing?" Elma asked.

"What me?" I asked.

"He does not even look at us!" Irmela said.

I put the bowl down and looked at them. "Maybe if I knew what you were talking about."

Elma stood and pointed her finger at me. "Exactly. You are planning to murder the Priest. When were you going to tell me?"

I shook my fists and yelled at the ceiling, "When you got home! Which you just did! And who said we were going to kill the Priest?"

She lifted her chin and glared at me. "Oaschgein! Foitrottl! Hairy asshole!"

"Do you want to hear what happened?" I screamed.

Elma thrust her jaw out but didn't speak a word or budge.

"They want fifty grand by next week or they'll turn you and Irmela in to the Rulers for the reward. You know if he does that they'll get me next. You see what happens. We'll be drowned in butts of water or hanged from a parapet."

Elma blinked and bit her lip. "That can't be. It is all Margaret. Talk to him."

"You won't peel him off her," I said. "Can't be done. The Priest would follow her to hell, he said so himself many times."

"I knew something had to go wrong," Elma said. "We should not have done Detreuil."

Irmela huffed. "You always say to do things then change your mind later. I wish you would make it up when it matters. Detreuil is gone. That is all that matters now. If the Priest wants fifty grand, why not give it to him?"

"You can't let a man who threatens to kill you get away with it," I said. "You lose credibility."

"Credibility? With whom? He is our friend," Irmela said.

"What do you want me to do about it?" I asked. "I don't want to kill the Priest. But there are rules."

Elma said, "We could give him the money and kill him if he asks for more."

"I don't have enough left to kick in a third," I said finally.

"I don't have much after the bike," Irmela admitted.

"What are you two, infant?" Elma asked. "Am I the only one here earning?"

"She earns, I earn," I said. "Who set you up with that old lady? That was me who got the meeting and got you the rent."

"Got yourself the rent. I had the class with nunce. Don't slide bullshit on me."

"You had the what with the who?"

"Nunce!"

"Like church ones?"

"They taught me how to think."

"Yeah, and that the sun goes around the earth. They won't tell you man was a monkey once."

"Why should they do that?" Irmela asked. "They are nunce."

"Nunz, nunz...." I said. "Now. What about the Priest?"

Elma said, "We will do what we must do it."

I said, "I told them to come back a week from today, at eleven in the morning. I said I'd have the money. But instead, we take them in the driveway when they arrive. Shoot them in the back of the head. And this time we're going to dissolve the bodies in acid."

They nodded as one and looked sad. Elma said, "It always turns out like this."

"I didn't think it would be different," Irmela said.

"No mamar."

"For me no. But for you."

Elma became cool and fierce. "It is not mamar for me. It is the oral sex. Those are different things. What do I do?"

"Can you shoot Margaret if I shoot the Priest?"

She stuck her lips out, whistling silently and shook her head imperceptibly. "No."

"I will," Irmela said. "You Elma shall rev up the bike, so the neighbors do not hear the gunshots. Now we all have jobs."

Chapter Nineteen

7:46 in the morning. The light globe was bright and there was the quiet singing of birds. Everything was ready. The black fermentation tub I got from a nam pla plant was out back with carboys of sulfuric acid.

8:15. Very loud chirping of birds. Light globe livid. I got out of bed and headed for the kitchen. Irmela and Elma were crowded around the stove. They were boiling milk and laughing.

"What's funny?"

"We are laughing," Irmela began, but she stopped speaking and covered her mouth and rocked with laughter.

"The xango!" Elma said.

"We are laughing because she called it the pozole xango. Monkey stew."

"I'm still trying to get the smell out of my nose," I said. There was no coffee. I had to make coffee.

"But you hate those monkeys so much."

My arms were scratched up and sore still from going after that ozomatli motherfucker. "Not enough to chase them down and kill them I don't."

"But now we have made our experiment and we know that it works."

"I'm trying to figure out where to dump fifty gallons of pozole ombre."

They snickered and stirred chocolate powder into the hot milk with a whisk and poured it out. Elma said, "In the ocean. We can go to Monterey."

The coffee was ready and we went out in the garden and watched the hummingbirds and parrots and lorikeets and went over it all again, like I had done all week. I wondered why they were destroying me for 50 grand. That was the Priest's price? To do what? Go down to Beverly Hills and start selling houses and throwing parties in North Hollywood? Making me kill them when it would have been easier to just let things lie as they were. Then no one has to die. It was fucking obvious. They were taking us all down with them. But whether it was what they were making me do or what they had done, it didn't matter. Either way it meant the same thing.

Still, I didn't want to kill the Priest. So then what about we kill Margaret and let the Priest go. But he wouldn't be able to bear the grief. He would try to kill me in a rage, and then I'd have to kill him. Sometimes every path leads to the same place.

When I first met the Priest, I was just a kid in LA Yaanga, going to college and working in Long Beach loading ships. He was a priest and a doctor still, working in a church in San Swa'anga, serving a small congregation of Pedro Morons and Tongvas. He worked in different emergency rooms in the city every night, wherever they were short, and ran numbers. The Priest was sharp with money and had a head for details. Soon he was part of Junior's real estate crew, working north and west of the city.

I was at a bar in Torrance, drinking cerveza, trying to talk to some thirty-year-old souse with frosted hair and fingernails, who wouldn't even look at me.

"Bironga!" I cried. The bartender glared at me. He took his time getting out una mas cerveza fucker and put it down. "What's with the attitude?" I asked.

"It's beer here. Fifty cents."

I put down a silver coin. The woman laughed into her phone like a bird. The Priest came in the door and sat next to me. Quietly he said, "She won't go for you. But I'll buy you a drink."

"What are you after," I asked.

"Conversation. I'm a Priest."

"So am I."

"And a Doctor, God bless your soul."

"Go cure yourself, I ain't sick."

He took out a cigarette and laughed coarsely. "What do you do?"

"I load ships and go to school. Insurance and Accounting."

"Accounting! Lowest form of life, the machine of the machine. I'm sorry to hear that my son. But there is accounting and accounting."

"It's all the same to me."

He ordered a drink and we sat in silence. I didn't feel like talking to a priest. I kept looking at the woman. She was two stools down. I could smell her hairspray. Her eyes were like heavy beautiful whale eyes. "Excuse me," I said.

She turned slowly towards me. She was plastered; her gentle whale eyes were bloodshot and belligerent. "Did you say something?"

"Yeah, you got a light?"

"I don't smoke," she said.

"What time is it then?"

"Beats me."

"How will you know when to leave?"

"When the prospect of sitting on this stool is worse than getting off of it."

The Priest said, "What are you drinking? Allow a Priest to buy you a little indulgence on the way to salvation. It soothes the mortifications of the flesh."

"Ha," she said. "Bourbon and Apple."

"And you my son, what can I buy you?"

"Una mas bironga," I snarled.

"Barkeep, a Bourbon and Apple and a beer. For me I'll take a Mekong with a chaser." He raised the glass and said, "Bound to the earth by a tether, of money, sex and the weather, I raise up this glass, to honor your ass, I wonder what it looks like in leather."

We drank. "And what, may I ask, is your name?" he asked.

I waited for her to answer and when she didn't I said, "Bob Martin."

He smiled at her, his cheeks a shade darker than when he came in. Without saying anything, but smiling at the floor now and again, he got her to say, "Stella Lux. I ply IO on the infomercials, if that's where you think you know me from."

"I thought it was Wild Kingdom shows," I said. I had stopped giving a shit about ten seconds ago.

Stella Lux laughed. "So, what do we call you? Priest?"

"As a matter of fact I am known as the Priest. Some people in the city call me Doc. I leave it to you."

"I'll call you Priest," I said. "What's your racket besides god?"

"At the moment most of my income is from real estate."

"You mean *buildings*?" Stella asked. "You don't have a church?"

"I don't at the moment have a single church. I was a priest at St. Andrews down in San Pedro, but now I go where I'm needed, as with the medicine. LA Yaanga is a hard place to work. At the Gallows I knew I would be needed in both capacities. But there are, you understand, unique business opportunities along the way." He smiled and we clinked glasses. "Lechaim," he said.

And I said, "Tolmalok."

The Priest was transfixed by Stella. He didn't take his eyes off of her now. She slapped her cheek gently and asked, "Is it true what they say of priests, that they ward off evil?"

"When they're not courting it, you mean?" he asked. "I was a priest in good faith when I began, but after what I've seen? There's not a believer among them. I believe in God enough to feel the fear but not the love. And I would say that I tend now more towards anger."

"I don't get it, do you or don't you ward off evil?"

"Evil walks with everyone, my child. But yes, I can ward off evil, if that's what you're afraid of."

"When I walk I feel like I'm being followed by aliens. I have a charm but it doesn't work well anymore."

"Then allow me to walk you home." He stood. "Well Bob, I do hope we meet again." I stared at my bironga and nodded.

That was the Priest. But those were different times, and things had changed. I'd like to say that killing the Priest became just another thing to do to stay alive, like eating and sleeping and drinking. But it wasn't like that at all. Sometimes I wasn't sure I could kill him.

David and de Marcos were different. They were self-defense. I didn't have to think. But the Priest? He'd be two feet away and I'd have one second to act, or else he might turn around and beg for his life. And what then? I could still call him and try to talk him out of it. And if they went along, again, what then? If I knew that the Priest and Margaret would never go the Rulers, that would be one thing. But how could I be sure? It would come up again.

Because they wouldn't be able to stop. Once you have fifty, you go for another fifty and claim the reward. And then we're dead. They weren't leaving me a choice. It was all or nothing.

9:00: I was getting Bloody Mary in the kitchen when there was a knock at the door. They were early. I wasn't ready yet. We were still in our morning clothes. Maybe the Priest got suspicious and came to catch us off guard. Maybe he was at the door with guns aimed at us. Another knock. They don't knock, they walk in. Then the door flew open. I reached for my fusca but it wasn't on me, it was lying out with my clothes downstairs. I stepped into the foyer and standing there was the Ruler Sargon in silver armor with a guard of 4 Morons.

"Excuse me," he said. "I thought no one was at home." His voice was deep; it projected into the house and boomed off the walls and windows. The guard stood at attention on either side of him, a foot and a half shorter and in red armor. He filled the entrance. "I'm looking for Bob Martin. Any idea where I might find him?" He had a look of mild surprise. My heart was pounding so hard I couldn't hear. I thought, the Priest betrayed us.

"That's me," I said.

"This is a lovely house. Mind if I have a look around?" He flexed his fleshy nostrils and stretched his lips over two rows of shining perfect teeth.

"Go ahead."

"How long have you lived here?"

"Close to five years."

"What about the de Marcoses? You rented?"

"Not exactly. I was the listing agent on the home. I had a few troubles and they let me stay here while I showed it."

"An unorthodox arrangement."

"Yes that's right."

He nodded slowly and smiled to himself. "Didn't we meet not long ago at the Summer Palace? I recall your face." His eyes widened and he studied me. His breathing was slow, as if he was smelling everything. The features of his face were soft and gentle but because they were so large I saw that they were not just the way he looked but the way he sensed the world. His eyes rested on parts of my face, probing them. He was still, a half smile on his lips. I tried to control my breathing and my heart but I could feel my pores opening.

"Where are the girls?"

"Outside." I looked at the ground.

"It's a terrible thing, what happened to them."

"You mean the girls?"

He looked at me closely again, his face slightly turned. He held up a finger and said, "No. The de Marcoses."

"Oh that, the murder."

"Murders. Has anyone come to interview you?"

"No, as a matter of fact." He wandered upstairs and stood in the living room watching the sea. "I have never been to sea in a boat," he said. "I've been to Mars." He laughed. "But never at sea in a boat." He looked around and surveyed the room, staring at each piece of furniture, at the walls, windows and doors, taking long breaths through his nose and savoring it, like wine. He knelt down by the French doors and examined the floor, holding his face an inch off the ground. From a crouch he asked, "Would you call this place run down?"

"No," I said. "It needs work. But as you see, the floors are good."

He nodded. "Did the de Marcoses come home before they were murdered? They arrived by ship from the Philippines and rented a car. Then there is no trace of them. They were not checked into any hotels. My guess is they were heading here. What do you suppose happened?"

"I don't know, but I never saw them," I said.

"They didn't call? Try to remember. If they were going to be staying here—it was their house—I'm sure they would have called."

"No, I never talked to them and never saw them. We only corresponded. I never heard them on the phone."

"Suppose we say hello to the girls?" He had to duck to get through the door out to the garden and almost topped the wall. The bougainvillea framed his head in crimson. "This is a charming garden. Reminds me of New York. Well girls, you sure do get around, you and your friend Bob." His hair stood on end (it was short) and glowed darkly like the earliest light of dawn. His eyes took on the same color and I felt cold. Elma reached up to her hair, which was dark, but as she did so it glowed so bright you could see the bones of her fingers.

He laughed. "You should get your lights adjusted, or your money back."

Elma looked like she had swallowed a large ice cube.

"What is the word for that?" he asked, pointing to a xango that was sitting on the wall watching us.

"Ozomatli in Mexican," she said.

"But they say xango too," Irmela said. "And monkey everyone knows."

"The Tongva say ozomatli, and in LA Yaanga it's xango or monkey," I said.

"Ozomatli. I like that. I think a Ruler could be called that without indignity, a Lord certainly. Then it would be apt as well." He laughed. "Well, I'll leave you be. I was hoping you could help me out. I'll be back." He walked stiffly out of the house, ducking between rooms, and took his guard.

As soon as he was gone I collapsed on the couch upstairs and hyperventilated. Elma and Irmela stood motionless with eyes fixed and mouths agape. Finally I quit babbling and said, "We have work to do."

Chapter Twenty

There was no time to shower. We dressed and went to our stations: Elma on the motorcycle by the entrance, so the neighbors wouldn't hear; Irmela behind the akuba on one side of the driveway; and me behind the stand of banana trees on the other side.

There was a hot wind. Fire was in the air. Ash drifted high above. By midday it was silent, the ozomatlis and the lizards dozing in the shade. My brain was a stone quarry, cold and still. I stared at things as a man in prison does, minutely. There were long creeping caterpillars on the banana plants and millipedes with black and scarlet bands. A lone monkey dropped to the ground and strolled over to a spot on the driveway. It reached into the bush and pulled out a half-eaten mango, which it sat down to finish. When the mango was done it raced back to the pepper tree.

There was the sound of tires turning on the dirt. The hum of an engine. I gripped the fusca, checked the chamber and turned off the safety. I tried to hold still and rested my face against the cool banana leaves. Elma kicked the bike and it roared open. She let it idle. The car came to a halt. When the car door opened Elma revved the engine.

They got out of the car and walked slowly up the drive. When they passed me by I stepped out from behind the leaves. Irmela fell in next to me, behind Margaret, who was walking with her head down, and wore a blue, knee-length dress. The Priest was all in black, stoop shouldered and slow. I had the back of the Priest's head in sight. All I had to do was pull the trigger and it would be over. They didn't hear us. Their feet broke twigs and crunched stones. Elma waved at them from the bike and they waved back. As they did so Irmela raised her arm. I glanced at her, at Elma on the bike, and aimed again at the center of the back of his head and took my shot. The bullet hit. As he lurched forward Margaret turned her head and her eyes opened wide as he hit the ground and she saw me. At that instant Irmela fired, striking her at the base of the neck. Margaret went down. Irmela hit her again where she lay. There were bloody chunks of head all over the driveway. Elma turned off the bike and sat there for a moment. The air was ringing. And then for a while there was no time, there was nothing.

Elma turned off the bike, went inside and came out with two rolls of oilcloth. We wrapped them up and carried them around by the pool, where I set up the tub.

"Do we have to undress him for the pozole?" Elma asked. The pool water was dark blue, flecked with golden light and her reflection.

"I don't see why," I said.

"So it will dissolve him faster."

"Alright." Getting them undressed was nasty work. I put on elbow length black rubber gloves and a mask and cut the clothes off of them. They were soaked through with blood. We dumped the Priest into the black tub. It was hard to see how there was room for one more. He lay in a fetal position. It was him, and it wasn't. It was early in the day. The shadow on his face was faint.

I lifted a carboy of acid and poured it in, careful not to splash. It was like water washing over his naked body at first, with a rotten egg smell. I poured enough over to cover him and allow room for Margaret. Margaret's face was frozen in a bulge, a look I knew well and that didn't make me sorry for what I had just done. Together Elma and I slowly lowered her into the disintegrating arms of her lover.

I poured the rest of the acid in. Their flesh frayed. The stench was unbearable. My throat burned. It felt like the air was on fire. I looked at the pool and ripped the mask off. A noxious fume flew up my nostrils and filled my chest. I tore my clothes off and jumped into the pool and let the cold water close over me. I wanted to disappear. But I had to come up for air. Finally, a burning ball of food and stomach juices surged up my throat and got out all over the lawn. The Priest was gone. I went inside and stared at the ocean, at the orderly waves of jade beneath a blazing perfect sky of blue.

Later the girls sauntered in with wet hair, chatting in Austrian. Elma said, "That pool is perfect on a day like this. You should not be outside they say if you cannot cool down."

"I wonder if that means he'll cook faster?" I asked.

"Ask someone who knows," Irmela said.

"You," I said. "You were perfect. Why the second shot?"

"I had to be sure," she said. "The first hit the back of her neck. The second was the head shot. What we agreed upon."

Elma said, "They had no idea you were there."

"Margaret knew. She saw the Priest go down, and saw me. She looked me in the eye."

"Still, you were very stealth," she said. Her tone was almost jocular, but her eyes were vacant.

"On the outside," I said. "On the inside my heart was loud and crooked and I stared at bugs."

That afternoon I drove the Priest's car into Mexican territory, just east of Santa Monica, and left it on the side of the freeway. I flattened the front right tire. Elma picked me up in my car. No one saw us. It was out of Ruler jurisdiction. If Junior found out, so what?

It took three days for the bodies to disintegrate into sludge. We threw the clothes in too. It was god awful sharp, the loudest rotten acid stink I've ever smelled. I put the lid on it to keep the stench down. It made no difference. From the minute I poured the acid over them the smell followed me around wherever I went. I tasted it in the water and smelled it in the breeze. My clothes and skin were tainted. I think it soaked into my brain.

The tank was too unmanageable to cart in my car and I was too scared to rent a truck. So it sat out by the pool in the 120-degree sun. On the fifth morning it was worse than the nam pla factory I bought it from. Even the downstairs bedrooms were faintly scented; a few molecules had worked their way through the scrubbers and were diffusing through the ventilators. For a day I stayed in bed trying to sleep. I didn't eat or drink anything but water. At some point I reached a point of clarity. There was no way out of disposing of the sludge on the property. The best thing to do was to empty the pool and pour the sludge down the pool drain. Then refill it. It was at 5AM of day seven that I brought it up with the girls, when they got home from Agatha Kennedu's.

I was sitting in bed watching TV in my underwear. They came in with white wine and brought me a sparkling water with kalamansi. It tasted delicious. My throat was hot and dry and my glands were swollen. I tried not to breathe through my nose. They sat down on either side of me.

Elma said, "Agatha has taken a turn. She is again like she was when we first met her. Bent double, and shuffling."

"That's too bad," I said.

"She is meaner now too," Irmela said.

"What did you expect, she'd get all cuddly when she was dying? There's something we have to talk about. I have a plan to get rid of the sludge. We empty the pool, send the sludge down the drain and fill it up again."

They were silent, staring at their laps and then they turned to look at each other. Elma spoke. "If that is what we must do."

"I think so, don't you? Do you want to rent a truck, with Sargon on our ass?"

Irmela said. "My shoulder felt like a toy in his hand."

"He did that to me too," I said. "With the shoulder. He also noticed Elma's hair."

Irmela shrugged and ruffled her hair up and blew plplplp with her lips. "Who cares about Elma's hair, it is so artificial."

"Unless it's real."

"What are you talking about now, real. What did you tell him? And you didn't tell me?" she asked Elma.

Elma said, "I said nothing."

"What lie has she told you?" she demanded of me, thrusting out her jaw as Elma did but to different effect, there was no menace at all. She dug her skinny fists into her hips and thrust her chest out. "What?" Then her expression changed and she wasn't putting on. Her face became fixed as when she was playing pinball, in a predatory trance. "You will tell me now."

"I told him nothing," Elma said.

Irmela twitched and turned her cat eyes on me. "That's right," I said. "And she doesn't have to."

Irmela spat. "When Sargon comes back, and he will, what will happen then?"

"Let's do that then," I said. "Now, can we focus on the pozole?"

They squealed. Elma said, "Pozole conyo."

"The sangria," I said.

Irmela asked, "How do you drain the pool?"

I didn't know how to drain the pool. "We need a plumber."

Irmela said quietly, her face sad, "The Priest knew the plumber."

"The phone will know. I'll call. Then you two got to help me hide the tub."

There were four handles. We each took a handle and lifted. The liquid sloshed back and forth as we staggered forward and lurched around. The tank started to pull. Even with the lid on I didn't want to pull back. So we half followed the momentum of the tank. It was hard to breath. I took short breaths through my nose. We wobbled over the stone path alongside the house, where it rose to the bluff, behind the tall rhododendrons. "Let's put it down!" I said. We let it down with a jerk. It radiated stink now. My eyes were tearing up. My tongue was thick.

Carlson arrived in his rocket-shaped truck. "You again. More alien DNA?"

"Mutant," I reminded him.

"Same thing. What's it this time? It smells like you've got a bad problem you tried to fix yourself."

"Can you drain the pool?"

The sun was burning overhead. We were sweating and dehydrated, all of us. The air was thick with flies. The plumber laughed to himself, and shook his head. He took off his cap and wiped his brow on his sleeve, then replaced the cap with his thumb and two fingers. "Yeah, sure. But if your idea is you're going to free up a sludge you tried to clear with acid down the line, forget it. It will only mix with the sludge. Do you plan on refilling it?"

"Yes."

"See that's a problem. If you have acid down there and it washes back it will damage the pool lining. It won't hold water."

Was he fucking kidding? We would have to swim in the ocean. No more midnight plunges, no more afternoon dips. Why hadn't I thought of that? The Priest was Margaret now and she was him. And I wasn't thinking straight. "That's not why. We had a monkey die. I disposed of it in acid, as an experiment."

"That's a very interesting experiment," he sneered. "What were your results?"

"About what you'd expect."

"I can drain the pool. I suppose you heard about Junior."

I mumbled something and said, "Is he dead?"

"No, but his wife and kids are. And he's back, working. Not on real estate though." He laughed. "Things are crazy in El Rodeo de las Aguas."

"Just drain the pool. Keep the politics to yourself."

"I have to find the service panel? Usually it's on the side of the house." He headed over towards the side we had put the Priest and Margaret on.

"But not on that side of the house," I yelled.

"If you know where it is, why'd you call me?"

"I know it's not there," I growled. "That's why I fucking called you." I was spitting out my words. In law school they told us never to vent in business, but I already knew that rule from my old man. It's like the first thing you learn and here I was upset about Junior and yelling at some plumber. Really, who the fuck is the plumber?

But what if Junior had sent the plumber to find the Priest? After Margaret put the screws to him to blackmail us he must have gone back to Junior looking for work. He had it all mapped out. Take us for the money, use it to pony up for some house project with Junior, partner on a deal. A no show on a deal would make him suspicious. But he wouldn't necessarily connect it to us, even if he found the car.

Lord Otis put a wolf needle up Junior's ass when he took all that land from Moron Santa Monica to Long Beach. Lord Otis on his march south murdered everyone he saw. His troops raped the boys and press-ganged them. They threw the women and girls into sex tents to be used and discarded when dead. Families deserted their homes as the mortars fell, leaving their animals behind.

The Ruler soldiers shot down stragglers first, then overcame the fleeing mass of people and crushed them beneath the treads of armored back breakers. Blood seeped into the stone streets; flesh was prized apart from bone turning on the wheels of trucks. They drove over the dead till the roads were paved with corpses. To save time they took no prisoners and to save bullets they bayoneted, hanged, burned or beheaded everyone caught behind the advancing line.

Wolves came down out of the hills, coyotes and jaguars prowled the streets of South Central all the way to Long Beach. In every barrio and village from Torrance to Burbank they rammed poles with cross beams into the hard dirt and hanged people day and night until nothing lived and they moved on. The Rulers say that they trace their line back to the first people but I don't believe that and no one else does either. People who oughta know say it's bullshit. Rulers got their DNA in New York 300 years ago and kept it to themselves.

Junior, all the Morons and the Chumash and Tongva who escaped to Mexico were back in LA Yaanga and Beverly Hills, Hollywood and Burbank. They were back in Long Beach and San Pedro, except the small piece at the tip held by Lord Otis. My guess was that Junior wanted more than his business back.

The girls were driving me crazy. The pool stood empty, except for a grey, bubbling, fly covered sludge around the drain. The paint was scarred down to the concrete. We sat inside, prisoners in paradise, afraid to go out and with nothing to do. We hadn't visited Agatha Kennedu in over a week. Irmela didn't speak; she sat flashing her twat in a long shirt reading Thomas Bernhard and Celt Freemason, a Golden Gate writer she liked and the only one who wasn't German or Austrian. I watched TV and slept.

One day on the news there was an update on the de Marcoses. They quoted the Ruler Sargon, who said there were no suspects and very little evidence. We knew that wasn't true. But we were stuck. I don't know why, but that house felt like the safest place on earth. To me. But to Elma? It was an iron lung. The thing she dreaded most was happening, and she lost her breath as she talked too fast, trying to chase down what she was thinking.

Elma didn't think it was a coincidence that he interrogated us on the day we took care of the Priest and Margaret. She turned it over and over. I was blind into TV. She sat half naked with one foot up in the air in front of her face and one on the floor, painting her toenails. "Why? Why did he come that second time? On the very day we are to kill our friends. And all those questions. He is our investigator and he is investigating us! We have Ruler detectives on our ass."

I stared harder at the TV and tried not hear. It was an armored bike race over unbroken terrain. The bikes tore tunnels through kasili sage and txaparil and kiinarabi trees, thickets of wolfberry and boxthorn, and rode down to the coast above Syukhtun. I turned up the sound with my toe.

"I asked you why? Do you think these things happen? He saw my hair."

"So what about that. Lots of girls got hair that lights up."

Elma whispered, "They burned my father and my mother in the street. That's what they will do to me if they find out, and to you and to Irmela. I must not let that happen to her. I made my promises. I will not go back on them." She was panting.

I turned away to watch. The first rider to reach the shore headed out into water and set off charges on the beach. Then the other riders dug in and lobbed exploding balls and short grenades at the lone rider, who far out on the ocean rode a cresting wave down onto a beach in a neighboring cove. He roared up the bluffs and made for the road. I said, "The Ruler Sargon won't do that to you. He's too important."

"The Rulers know everything. And even if they don't, it only takes their accusation. There is no justice. Do you remember that first time we saw him, he joked about Mars? He called me Martian. Do you know what would happen if he believed that? If his joke is not innocent? Do you see what I am saying? He could invent things. He could say I am from Mars, and then how would I prove my case? My lack of DNA? But they will mock that. I know what they can claim. I have read more than magazines. It is written about and we learned from people. And from life!"

"It's your accent. They don't know shit about shit. That's his big ass way of saying you ain't talking like I do. What they grow up in is palaces."

"I have no memories of *palaces*! Only of running. And I think it is time to run."

So, I thought, I need to know what's going on. Being up in that house all the time with those two was making me nuts. I used to go out a lot. Every night in fact. "Look, I'm going down to Tony's to see what's happening. It's been too long since I've been out."

"But what about the road? There is a war."

I wasn't watching the TV anymore, but I tried to follow the race by the sound of the engines. She faced me on the couch, her eyes red and fearful, her toes half done. The smell of solvent was strong in the air. "It's still possible to travel."

"And Junior? You don't think the plumber told Junior? He smelled the pozole."

"We have to hope not."

"How can you live that way? It is to be in shadows."

"Me in shadows? Elma, I was in the sun until I met you." Her face dropped and her eyes were like flames drowned in rain. I felt terrible, seeing her like that. "I'm sorry. We can live the good life again, I know it. This will pass. I'll sell this place when the old lady dies and we'll move on."

At that her eyes opened wide in horror. "I could not bear to lose Agatha now!"

Chapter Twenty-One

The drive to Tony's was terrifying. I came down out of the hills and the entrance to the freeway was a maze of stainless steel bladed walls and blinking yellow eye censors on retractable necks. Troops on either side were digging trenches and laying down defenses. The only open route between downtown and the hills was closing as I drove. By the time I reached Torrance my knuckles had fused for lack of blood and I had cracks in my teeth.

I stood in the parking lot under the blue light poles panting. I had not been at Tony's in a long time. It felt like I was still chasing Irmela out the door. Inside there was a cobweb stockinged girl in Dorothy punks playing pinball. I stared at her, just to see what I would feel. Would I feel like taking her home? But I didn't feel a thing. She was immature, not fully formed. She had no angles and even if she did I wouldn't care. Cause it wasn't how Irmela looked or how young she was, or even how she acted. It was the anger. The anger was the lure. The anger that beat beneath her placid face and days of conversation consisting only of monotone non sequitors. I sat down. The bar smelled of malt and cigars. Tony ambled over and tossed down a coaster.

"Bob. How's it going?"

"Get me a whiskey and a beer and I'll tell you."

"Mekong?"

"Rye if you have it."

Tony raised an eyebrow and left, returning with a dusty bottle of Kentucky Rye. "I hope you have pesos."

I put down two silver pesos. "Let me buy you one too. Sometimes you have to drink the good stuff."

Tony dusted the bottle with a damp bar mop and poured out two shots. He took the pencil out from behind his ear and bounced the eraser on the bar top, catching it between his fingers.

"What's it been, a year?" I asked.

"Time in this place? Who would know," he said, sipping the rye.

"Ya miss me?" I laughed and downed the shot. "I'll take another."

"Everyone is dead. To a child." He shook his head and stared off. "First the Mexicans came and then the goddamn Rulers returned. Back and forth." He pulled over a bowl of roasted pinyons. "Right outside these doors was a gallows. I hid underground, in the supply pod."

"Why didn't they get you?"

His eyes widened and he looked up the bar and rubbed his chin. "Some of us made it. I have provisions. I could stay down for days. They would clear out a barrio and move on. They were an army on the move." He nodded and sucked his teeth and downed the shot. "Don't get me started. It ain't over yet. The Mexicans won't hold this long. They'll relieve Lord Otis. It was the Ruler Tobor Ocktomann who screwed him. Otis would have torn it up all the way to Guatemala. He was amok amok. Why can't they go back to the old way? It makes no fucking sense. LA Yaanga has been free for 40 years."

"It was better before Bard 4. He fucked it up with Mexico and that was it. It hasn't been the same since."

"Ocktomann at least was live and let live. That culero prick who leads his army—"

"I don't like the Vizier of Tenocht any better. And he's Aztlanian; he wants the Indian lands too. My mother will take Ruler over Mexican every time. Me? I don't give a shit. I've been screwed by both."

"I'll never feel like that again. I'm with Junior, Tenocht prick or not. So are the Tongva, to a person. Aztlan is my country now. Angelinos look south. And I'll tell you what. When we go north, people up there are gonna know it."

"What does that mean?"

Tony shrugged and looked at his hands, which were lying out flat on the bar. He picked up the bottle and pulled the cork. He shook his head and poured out two drinks. "These are on me."

"I've got a Ruler on my ass."

He craned his head around to look behind me. "I don't see any Ruler. But if I did, I'd kill him and any other Ruler soldier that walks in. And the humans who work for them are dust in my hands. I will kill them down to my dying breath. If I still had a son I'd pass it on to him and to his son. That's what they took from me, three generations of my family. I'll bloody the walls. I'll mount their heads on poles in the yard and leave them till the crows have pecked them clean."

"And Junior?"

"Junior is running the show. Junior and General Carlos."

The drive home would have been as bad but I was too drunk to notice. Burning vehicles were like candle light. I staggered downstairs to bed. Elma was not asleep but lying in the dark with her eyes open, crying.

"What's wrong?" I asked.

"It is nothing."

"People don't cry for no reason at all." I put my arm around her. Elma was mostly tough so when she cried it hurt. She didn't move.

"We are trapped here. We do nothing but live in fear. It is time to move. To stay still is to die. And I am worried. That you don't love me, and Irmela will steal you and what will I have then? If only I could see Agatha."

"There's no reason we can't go to Santa Monica. The road into LA is closed now but Santa Monica is under Ruler control."

"Precisely. I am not a foitrottl. The Rulers are looking for us."

I kissed the back of her head and inhaled the scent of her unwashed hair. "No, no. The Rulers don't care about a couple of unsolved murders now, with the Lord Otis pinned down in San Pedro and Mexico in control of everything south of the hills. We'll go to Agatha. It will be OK," I promised, stroking her back. Elma turned around and put her face against my bare chest. The tears soaked into the hair and she sniffled. "It's you I love," I said. "Irmela is a girl."

So we visited Agatha. Life in Santa Monica wasn't bad. There were stores to shop from and the beach was crowded on weekends with big hats and bare butts. I ate sausage and chili noodle salad at the cart on Sandero Luminoso Boulevard or else got fish tacos at Sa's truck on 14th Street. The shops and theaters were jammed full of people. All night long drunken groups of friends staggered singing up the streets and boulevards. You wouldn't know that a few miles away total war stood nose to nose over a line of explosives and razor wire, frozen in place, both sides waiting. The whole world balanced on a coin, knowing what was to come but with no way of knowing what it would be like. In every face there was the desperate enforced happiness of fear as they furiously went about their daily business.

The old lady had deteriorated beyond the state I had first seen her in. The desk warned us that she was not very responsive. Orderlies in white wheeled her in from her bedroom and we sat on the balcony overlooking the Pacific. She had a cup of water with ice and a straw which she would periodically grip and bring to her lips, slurping loudly. She was bent over. There were tubes in her nose for oxygen. She craned her face forward like a turtle and tried to stare at us. One eye was drifting and opaque but the other was intense; it glared, like the brightest star in the sky was trapped inside it. She whispered, "I hate this. Please. My lawyer." She wheezed and lowered her head to the table. After a long time she lifted her head again and whispered, this time fixing her eye on Elma, "My angel. Stay. Stay. Have a drink dear." This time she was able to keep her head up for a while. After another rest on the table, her white hair spread in a pool around her, she turned creakily to Irmela and said, "Irmela. Dear. How is your motorcycle?"

"Vroom vroom," Irmela said. She smiled and bent down to look Agatha in the eye, and the old lady emitted several short dry breaths. "More the kicks than the pricks. I miss you. We are sad we did not visit. The roads are so bad. We are haunted by the ride into LA, and what the Rulers have done." The old lady exhaled and flattened her face on the table, her eyes shut. She snored.

Weeks later we arrived earlier than usual, as she wanted us there to talk to her lawyer. Elma poured gin and vinho verde into a chrome pitcher and stirred it languidly. She was wearing a lime green dress the old lady had given her. It had a high collar and a gold chain belt with a scarlet snakeskin purse dangling from it by a tiny fist carved out of bone. She poured out a martini. "The onions or the olives or the twist?"

I was about to answer when Agatha hacked, "Capers dear." Her eyes opened. A hissing breath came out from between her teeth. "Please, don't make me laugh."

"The caper," Elma said and brought it to the table. "How will you drink this?"

"Just throw it in my cup." Agatha clutched the cup and rattled it, and sucked down half the water.

"Make mine onions," I said, a little impatiently. I wanted a drink.

"I know what you want," Elma said.

"I didn't tell you, and you asked."

"But I knew then when she had the capers you would get the onions and not the twist."

"You just reasoned your way there?"

"I do not know what these reasons are that you talk about."

"I'll never get it fucking straight, I know, moyotis, agony in my diaper," I said.

The door knocked. Agatha lifted her finger and said, "Lawyer. Let him in."

In walked Abby Vonneniu dressed in black pinstripe, and Dr. Oyub, in a maroon double breasted suit with a pink vest and red shoes, their shapes cue and cue ball.

"Mr. Martin," said Vonneniu. "Pleased to meet you again. You remember Dr. Oyub I presume?"

"Agatha," Oyub said. "Please tell me you won't do this."

She hissed and shook her head. "Not die alone...please." Her head went down face forward onto the table, resting on the tube protruding from her nostrils. Her hair was white and lustrous, while the rest of her was parched and wasted. Like the stories they told in school of the Nuwu Sybil and her dog, which sat in Old Woman cave weaving a rug and making soup. Every time she got up to stir the soup the dog-chewed part of the rug, which she would fix until it was time to stir the soup again. She never finished weaving the rug, which was just as well, because if she ever did stop weaving it a fire would come down out of the north and destroy the earth. The Nuwu Sybil could never die but was cursed to age forever, and so as she sat weaving and stirring, her flesh got drier and drier until it flaked off and blew around like leaves. And still, even as she turned to dust, she stirred the soup and wove the rug. Some say it was she who prophesied the return of Chingishnish, but this makes no sense, because that happened after the invasion. Before that people didn't need redeemers.

Oyub was reduced to yelling into Agatha's ear, and she lifted one finger for yes and two for no. "So these are your final wishes then?" he shouted, his short fat body bent forward. She raised one finger. "Do you understand what I am saying?" She raised one finger. "Is there any reason to suspect that you are insane or stupefied by illness?" She raised two fingers. "Let it be noted that she is of sound mind and body. Able to assent and dissent." He stood upright and said to Vonneniu, "Very well. Let us proceed."

Vonneniu said, "In essence, because the de Marcoses predeceased Miss Kennedu, ownership of the property reverts to her and she has the right to leave it to whomever she pleases, not being constrained by the prior will in anyway, and there being in addition no claims by descendants of the de Marcoses. Therefore the de Marcos estate now relinquishes any hold or claims on the property." Oyub and Vonneniu shook hands and bowed slightly. Agatha raised one finger.

Oyub said into Agatha's ear, "In consequence of which I move to file the last will and testament of Agatha Moar Kennedu, daughter of the Fifth Lord of Malibu and Hattie Carrol, a maid in the kitchen, her sole inheritance being the house at 459018 Topanga Canyon Spur Remote Plot 57, and the contents therein and precious metal and jewels sufficient for her keep; the terms

204 Gaha: Babes of the Abyss

of said will being modified to make Elma von Doderer of 459018 Topanga Canyon Spur Remote Plot 57 the sole beneficiary of the estate. The executor shall be Dr. Vovim Oyub." He looked at her ear and wet his lips. "Are these the terms we are agreed to?"

Agatha lifted her old chicken bone finger and hissed. Oyub leaned closer, as she attempted to speak while resting face down on the oxygen plug. "Hehhh" she said, and pushed herself upright. "Yes," her voice trembled, "Those are the terms." Down went the face again. She obviously had to have some strength in her. She didn't flop forward but dropped slowly. The old lady was squeezing Oyub's balls.

"Now we have another document here, Elma, which must be signed as a condition of the will. Agatha wishes to go home, to the house the three of you now rent from her. She feels she would be more comfortable there. This is a contract between Elma von Doderer, Irmela von Doderer and Agatha Moar Kennedu. Elma von Doderer and Irmela von Doderer agree to serve as Agatha Moar Kennedu's private nurses. You will be allowed to continue as tenants, the three of you. Is this agreeable as a condition for becoming Miss Kennedu's sole heir?"

Elma looked at Irmela and they flexed nostrils and blinked and bit their tongues. Elma said, "I can do that. I agree."

Irmela said, "Yeah alright. I can do this too. I love you Agatha."

"I think we all love Agatha," I said.

Oyub said, archly, but without humor, "Without doubt." He fixed his tie and gazed at the old lady. She was mouthing the words *fuck you.* "Is that it then?" Agatha lifted two fingers. "What?"

She raised her head laboriously this time and said in a frail whisper, "Proxy."

Oyub stifled a growl and said, "Ahem. The Proxy Document. This document appoints Elma von Doderer medical proxy for Agatha Moar Kennedu. Agatha Moar Kennedu intends to die at home. Hospice care is to be provided there. She wants moderate, not extraordinary measures to be taken in her behalf. What constitutes moderate and extraordinary measures is defined in schedule C of the end of life protocols manual. Do you agree to be medical proxy?"

Elma looked at Agatha's face carefully, her head turned slightly. "Is this what you want?" she asked.

The old lady's finger shot forward emphatically from the knuckle and remained stiff and still. "Then I will do what must be done." Elma's eyes welled up with tears and she dropped to her knees and took the old lady's frail hand in her own. "I don't know what I have done to deserve this. You don't know what a bad person I am." The tears coursed straight down her cheeks and her hair burned a ferocious gold. She lifted her head and said to all of us, "I will allow nothing to happen to her. In my hands she will be safe and comfortable, this I promise." I looked at Irmela. Her face was blank. She looked like she did in the porn movie. I thought, that old lady won't make it a month. In three, four weeks she'll die and I'll own that house. And every inch of it legal, written and sworn to here in front of witnesses. Even with Oyub as executor. I didn't go to law school for nothing. Elma was now my client and no gabacho puta madre lawyer in a motherfucking suit was gonna screw her out of her house and jewels. I was.

Chapter Twenty-Two

Two weeks later Agatha was still alive. She slept in the living room and used a commode, because she couldn't make it to the ground floor toilet. Irmela and Elma gave her sponge baths and massages, changed her catheter and administered her medicine, which was delivered weekly by a kid on a bike with a long pink neck and pimples.

Agatha liked the windows open. All day and night the wind blew in, damp from the clouds piling up overhead. It smelled like fish and fog.

Living with Agatha didn't just come with a payout, it came with an upfront price. I knew the old lady was arrogant and tyrannical, but at the Azodiazadora it was funny. She gave those time serving fuckers constant shit, and they deserved it. God help the swata Moron who talked to her like a child. If she were too weak to curse, a load of applesauce on a spoon would do.

Living with a sick person again was a drag. Elma had all these rules we had to follow. Wash your hands every ten seconds. I do that anyway, I don't need someone telling me when. It's not like I was gonna wipe her ass and if I did I would wash up afterwards! But she made it an announcement. Next comes the sign, I thought.

And if I wanted to smoke I had to go out in the garden. Agatha said smoke irritated her.

The old lady had no right to invade our living room. That wasn't part of the deal. Maybe if they had her stashed away downstairs, like Detreuil. That I could endure. But to be forced to watch her wheeze and snore and fart in that room night after night? Forget about it. I retreated to the lower level TV room.

Elma doted on Agatha. She went to bed late and woke up early. One night I waited for her, not drinking much, hoping to have sex. She climbed into bed and faced away from me. I put my arm around her and she flinched. "What's wrong?" I asked.

"Nothing is wrong. I am very tired. You startled me."

"We haven't fucked in weeks. Not since the old lady came."

"She has not been here weeks. And it is a lot of work caring for her. I must change the diaper linens. I must feed and bathe her. She needs love."

"Long enough for me to have blue balls. How about a blow job or something."

"Ugh. That is too much work." She lay on her back, spread her legs and started to masturbate. "There. I am ready to receive you now. Go ahead."

"Jesus fucking Christ! I don't want it that way."

"That is too bad for you then. Good night." After a while we stopped fighting and I started leering at Irmela, who was looking like a ripe piece fruit.

Elma started to wear an apron around the house, and was barefoot all of the time so her feet were filthy. Then the old lady told her to go out and hire a cleaning service. So a service came in. I took a hike to the beach alone, that's how much I wanted to be there. They steamed the entire house, washed our clothes, changed the linens and made the beds.

When I came home the sun lit up the walls and there were dark shadows in the corners. It felt happy. I had forgotten how much I liked a clean house. The furniture was edged, like in an office and there was a lemon smell. The mold on the floor and carpet was gone. The toilets were not covered in pubic hair and vomit and urine, the bowl no longer spattered with dried shit. The kitchen sparkled; the counters were clean of grease and food splatter and there was no garbage on the floor. No more stale, funky stench of the Priest and Margaret's liquefied bodies. Nothing for the rats to eat.

We were all in the living room. Agatha's hair was tied up in a red scarf and she wore light blue bamboo pajamas. She was playing cards with Elma. Irmela was reading, her legs across the arm of the chair, a book called Iffy Breast. "What about that iffy titty," I said. She ignored me. "Hello," I said. "What about it then."

Irmela lifted her eyes slowly and said, "What are you talking about?"

I said, "That book there. Iffy Breast."

Irmela snorted. "It is the book called Effie Briest, a tragical love story you would not understand even if you could read it properly."

That was shit on my feet. "I read fucking fine! How much college do you have?"

"The school of the hard knocks."

"Hard knockers you mean."

"What on fuck are knockers?"

"They ain't itty bitty titties, conechichihualli." I smiled. I hadn't used that term of endearment in a long time. Not since she found out that it meant baby tits in Nahuatl.

Irmela said, "That is more than you will ever get from me." Elma laid down the cards and twisted around. She wore a green and brown jumpsuit, a mask and gloves. She gazed at me a moment, then pulled the mask down under her chin and wrinkled her nose at Irmela. She turned back to the game.

I said to Irmela, "We'll see about that, one dark and stormy night when you're afraid. I don't cuddle for free. Ask Agatha."

Agatha honked her horn three times. Three times was laughter. Two, no. One, yes. And of course Elma understood a whole fucking lexicon of honks. They spent the first few days honking the horn and compiling a list and a code.

Agatha didn't always use the horn. Sometimes she had the wind to talk. Usually when she got her kidney cancer drip. The drip included a stimulant that perked her up enough to eat ice cream. Then her farts came out in loud sharp cracks instead of long whispers.

Irmela tossed the book down. "I am going to the garden to smoke." She didn't like having to go to the garden. She was used to lighting up wherever whenever and using the floor as an ashtray. I followed her out. We lit up tailor-made Kreteks with filters and watched the parakeets and hummingbirds. "It is too much," she said. "I have not been out in weeks."

"Go play pinball."

Irmela's face turned hard and she said bitterly, "Pinball sucks in Santa Monica, and in Malibu, if you can even find a game. Hollywood, South Central, are the good places. These idiots are so slow and all they want to do is talk and smoke and get drunk. Why would I leave home to do that? Sometimes I feel like pushing her off the cliff." She watched the smoke leave her mouth.

"I thought you loved her."

Irmela turned sideways in her chair and smiled at me. "I do."

"Pushing her off the cliff won't be necessary. She can't live long."

"She is getting stronger. I can feel it." She stared off at the bougainvillea. "Can you massage the foot?" She lifted her leg over the arm of the chair and presented her foot to me. Her leg curved away into a tight pair of white shorts. The door rattled and opened. Elma was standing there, stunned.

"We weren't doing anything!" I said. "She was showing me her toes!"

Elma shook her head and looked like she was going to cry. She gnawed her lower lip. Her hair was dark. The old lady! I thought. I Looked at Irmela and smiled. We'd be smoking inside before dinner. Elma said, "Arphe Lux stopped by to tell us she and Frank are leaving for Vancouver and then Australia. The Ruler Tobor Ocktomann is no more. He has been assassinated by his own guard. Do you know what that means?"

"Besides that he's dead?" I asked. I couldn't get over my disappointment that the old lady was alive. It wasn't the time to think about what it meant that the Ruler Tobor Ocktomann had gone the way of Bard 4.

"It means no one is in control. We have only two guns."

"We don't need guns," I said.

There was a rumble and the lights flickered. At once all three of us huddled low on the ground, thinking it was an earthquake. Ten minutes passed without a jolt or a tremor before we moved. "Agatha!" Elma gasped, and ran inside.

"I'm not going in there," I said.

"I am not either," said Irmela. "Except to get a drink. What are you having?"

"Keane's Cane. Bring the whole bottle and some limes."

At first nothing changed, except that neighbors who could do so fled while others whom we had never met were walking up and down the road chatting out in the open. We were not one of those people. We kept to ourselves, even when the lights on other hills and in other valleys went out and didn't come back on. Even when the ground shook from bombs and arc light flashed up from the coast.

One day Agatha wanted to go for a swim. This was ridiculous. She couldn't get out of her chair without help. "Then get me a gin and tonic," she said. She could sit up now for long periods, as much as an hour, if the girls got her back and shoulders and hips aligned right, so that she was properly stacked. When she drank she toppled over and passed out. Except for the snoring, it was better when she was asleep.

"We don't have gin, but we have Keane's Cane," I said.

"That stuff is vile. What else have you got? Even a blended whiskey will do."

"Mekong?"

"Please. Go out and get some or have it brought it in."

"I told you ten times there's no one delivering. That includes your medicine. Isn't that stuff keeping you alive?"

"Well that's just ridiculous. Not delivering. When I lived at the Azodiazadora I could lift the phone and get a delivery."

"If you were there you'd be dead. They're bombing Santa Monica. They've got snipers all around the city."

The old lady, balanced in place, said, "It's too bad that asshole Ocktomann went and got himself killed. I hate to admit any relation to that line at all."

"I mean, what's that mean?" I asked. Her relations came up, but she wasn't a Ruler, and her father wasn't either, though he was a Minor Lord.

"On my father's side there's a legitimate lateral, heritable graft in the cousin line with Ocktomann, the vainest, stupidest of the first lines. I have seen in my years one other Ocktomann and let me tell you, there's no drift, just drift; they're true to the sire, oafs. Thank god my mother was a kitchen maid. I could not afford to be a brainless boob in braid and brushes. I knew from the time they started marching through Beverly Hills on a palanquin carried by that troop of four elephants, in their silver war suits. People are not children, they're monkeys."

"I've noticed the same thing. So what will you have?" I asked.

"I want gin," she said severely. "Quinine water if they have it."

Elma gave me a long hard look and made an asshole with her lips. She was like the lawman in western shows. "OK, I'll go. But the road is bad. Craters and junk, burning wrecks. Try driving that at night. You have to be an optimist."

The road *was* bad. It was dusk. The cloud cover fused with the washouts and sagebrush to form a featureless fuzzy mass. I slowed down to drive around mortar holes. The fire died in a burning car, charred bodies hanging out of the windows. I stared at the sky, looking for missiles and at the road for debris. There was a whistling rush to my right; I veered left and the road behind me exploded. Up ahead, a mile away, a column of smoke churned against the clouds. The sky darkened and the Pacific came into view. From there I raced into town, to the Peyote Shop.

The smoke was closer. I could smell it with the windows up. I turned off the road and there it was. The shopping center had been bombed. Low flames spit out of the windows and on the sidewalk in front there were smoking bodies blown apart on the ground, which was soaked with blood and strewn with guts and brains. No one was around. I stopped the car and sat there for about an hour, looking in the mirrors, watching a zopilote pick at a corpse. Nobody home, period. I got out. The bodies were blown to pieces and they had been set on fire. I walked around them and up to the buildings. They were scarred adobe shells now, whatever they had been.

Some stores had been spared, and the Peyote Shop was one of them. There was smoke damage, and a lot of broken glass and shelves from the implosion grenades. The owner's daughter lay face down on the counter, her head blown in two, a fusca in each hand. On the floor was a woman with her pants pulled down. She lay where she had been raped, and killed, probably before he was done. The front case was smashed in, but nothing was taken. I took a bag of peyote buttons, a bag of marijuana, and a bag of psilocybin mushrooms, and a couple of litres of gin. There was no Quinine water. That was OK. It would only slow her down.

I got back in the car and started to roll out. A man crawled into the road, dragging his one shattered leg behind him through a puddle of blood. As I drove by he gripped the air with his bloody hands. There wasn't anything I could do for him. I drove away and didn't stop till I got home.

I ran up to the living room. "I hope there are a lot of mangos on those trees."

Agatha pushed herself upright. She wasn't wearing make up. Her skin was like a tomatillo husk. Elma stacked her into place. "Did you get it?"

"Yeah, I got your gin." I was shaking, remembering what I had seen. "It was awful. They had just got done attacking the shopping center. I'd say there were 25 people dead on the sidewalk. They blew up the stores. So I didn't have to pay for this."

Agatha reached across the table, lifted the horn and honked three times. "Let's drink," she said.

"What do you think of taking some of this?" I asked, holding up the peyote.

Irmela became alert. Elma said to Agatha, "This would be very therapeutic for you."

"No thank you dear. Gin is all I'll take. I used to like a touch of absinthe with my gin, when I was young. It was quite fashionable."

"I ain't going out again. Not for something they don't have, anyway."

Agatha put her eye on the bottle and tried to pull the cork. She couldn't do it. She shook her head and said, "I don't know what's wrong with me. It's pathetic." She looked pissed when she handed it Elma.

"Don't worry," Elma said. "Would you like ice?"

"Well, what brand is it?"

"Swata Perrucha, made especially for you, in small bitches," I said.

"I will get the ice," Irmela said, leaping up in white Capri's, a cantaloupe blouse and scarlet handkerchief choker. She trotted off to the kitchen.

"I'll help. What are you having, *dear?*"

Elma said, "A large mug of boiling water and some of those peyote buttons, thank you."

"Somewhere in that kitchen there's a kit, I just know it," I said.

From the hall I heard the old lady say, "Glug some in my glass neat, will you? I'm afraid I'll fall over before getting a proper sip. I don't know what it is, but my throat gets to feeling so *bland*, it just needs a burn. In the old days I'd find me a man who smoked a lot and suck face, but they don't want a piece of this old sack of cancer anymore."

Irmela was filling an ice bucket with her bare hands. When she was done she wiped them on the Capris and took a few glasses down from the cabinet above the sink. I scratched my head and bit my lip trying to remember why I was there. Without turning around Irmela said, "I looked for the brew kit last night but I could not find it."

"That's what I'm looking for."

"Isn't it funny that I thought of that last night?"

"What about right now? That's funnier."

"I overheard you speaking."

"The house has strange acoustics."

"And yet you love it."

"It isn't love. It's that other thing."

"Other thing?"

"That thing you have to have."

"Oh yes, like the pinball."

"Or like you."

Irmela looked over her shoulder at me and smiled. From that angle her face was different. For just a moment, before she turned away to get the glass, it was lined and old, and pale like Agatha's. But we'd never be old together. Not us. "What are you drinking?" she asked the open cabinet.

"I'll have a whatever the fuck it is you're having. I don't have any will tonight," I answered.

"Let's go smoke," she said. "They can wait."

"She's drinking the gin straight up, anyway."

We headed outside. "And Elma should not be taking the peyote tonight alone. If you are the good man you say you are, you will take it with her or forbid her to do it."

"I don't forbid anyone from doing anything. That ain't me. In my world, everyone does as they do."

"Then you will live with the coincequences."

"That's kind of over-dramatic," I said.

"When she must talk to the gods alone you will understand."

"Will you do it with me?" We were almost done smoking. Irmela put her hand on mine and looked into my eyes. I could feel her inside me, the color of candles. She kissed my lower lip with both of hers and squeezed my hand. "It's time to bring them their drinks." Irmela put the cigarette out with her bare foot on the brick and walked into the kitchen.

Chapter Twenty-Three

"I think I'd like to take a plunge in the plunge pool," Agatha said, sipping iced espresso with sweetened condensed milk and green gelatin cubes through a fat straw. "Since coming back I have this flood of primal memory, as if my whole childhood were more alive than the present. I walk these halls and don't see the crummy mess you've made of it but the statuary and vases, with fresh flowers side by side silk ones so real no one can tell the difference. There was a staff of five. How I loved old Gertrude. She swam until she was ninety, in the ocean, no matter how cold. Every morning she was out there. When I was nine my father allowed me to go with her. She must have been like you, Elma, at your age. Anyway, I'm feeling energetic." She shook her white hair out and smiled. The wrinkles had smoothed off of her face as she gained weight. She could pull herself upright and stay that way, although she was still, technically, stacked. Every now and then she just collapsed in a pile on the floor. "So energetic I'm ready for a swim."

We looked at each other. Elma said, "I don't think that is a good idea."

"Why dear?"

Irmela said, "We wouldn't want you to get hurt. What if you unstack in the water and float off in different directions?"

The old lady found that funny. "Oh, Irmela, you are always a breath of air. Wouldn't that be marvelous, to float apart in the water. I think I shall go. I insist on it."

I said, "It's better to stay in the house anyway. Even this time of the year the sun is dangerous."

"The sun is it now?" Agatha asked. "And what is wrong with the earth? Is it about to quake? Or maybe the wind is blowing *dangerously* hard."

"I do not think you are ready," Elma said.

"What happened to the pool?" Agatha asked. "I will see it now." She stood and strode, bent 45 degrees, towards the door, her hand outstretched and hair hanging in her eyes. "Let's go. I can make it down the stairs, on my butt." She pulled open the French doors and, grabbing on to the banister for support, sat down on the top step and rested. Then, step-by-step, she worked her way down and got in the wheelchair. "I'm afraid I'll need a push! I'm winded." She smiled. "Get me my sunglasses and hat." Irmela put a straw hat on her head and tied the purple ribbon under her chin. Elma pushed her into the garden.

The garden was overgrown with weeds and the grass was tall and green with rain. In the center of it lay the abandoned pool. Where once a rectangle of blue stood, set in stone and surrounded by emerald lawn, with the pineapple fountain, was now a scarred pit with green slime at the bottom, a diseased throat into the earth. The sides were blackened and scaled. As it rained, the pool filled, hydrating the sludge clinging to the walls. The deep end amplified the constant buzz of carrion insects.

Agatha stared into it, lifting her head and rolling her eyes up as far as they would go. Her mouth gaped open. She cried, "What did you do to my pool?"

I explained, "It's your damn sewer system that got clogged and the asshole plumber who used sulfuric acid to flush it out. It backed up into the pool and destroyed the liner." I peeled a banana and pretended to enjoy eating it.

"Get this replaced," Agatha said.

"That'll take a lot of scratch and you ain't that rich."

"Rich? You must be joking. You do not have to be rich to fix a pool in California. Find a man, if you can, in Malibu. They must be desperate for work down there."

"What do I pay him with, bananas?"

"You just find a man and get an estimate."

"Strunzo," I said.

"I will go with," Irmela said.

Elma turned her back on us and pushed the old lady around the garden. "I remember these mandarins, and the lemon trees," Agatha said. "We used to wait for the mandarins to ripen and run out in the evening, eating two of every three we picked. And the lemonade! Kieu made it with real sugar. She was not much older than we were, Gertrude took her in when her mother died. She would run barefoot with us across the lawn. The only thing left of that time is the smell. Irmela, come here dear." Irmela stood by her side. The old lady raised a finger and took Irmela's hand. "Use those silver coins I gave you if you have to," she said quietly.

"Be careful," Elma said. And then, to the old lady, "There was a citrus grove where we lived in Jerusalem. When the trees were in bloom..."

"Ah," sighed Agatha.

"There is a famous Palestinian song about this. I will sing it for you, if you like, after they leave." Elma looked at me hard and then smiled. Her hair lit up briefly.

Irmela and I didn't talk till we hit the coast highway and were cruising up to Malibu. The sky clouded over and it started to rain with fat blops every few seconds on the windshield. The wipers weren't working well. The road became wet sheets of headlight. "It's been six weeks almost and Agatha is still alive," Irmela said. "But there is nothing we can do."

There was a lot we could do. "The old lady likes to drink and so does Elma. What if we get them on a bender? Think about it. Agatha has kidney cancer. That kid doesn't deliver her medicine anymore. Let's hit the gas, and get wasted with her every night. We wouldn't be killing her; she'd be killing herself. And Elma can't blame it on us if she's drinking too. You know she can't resist a drink any better than that old lady can."

Irmela looked out her window at the hills. "Elma will know, but I don't care." She put her hand down on my thigh. We drove that way for a while, her looking out the window, me staring at the windshield and the road and the surf, my thigh in her hand.

"Why does it always stop here?" I asked.

Irmela looked at me. "Do you think I would betray my sister?"

"I'd like to think so. I would."

"Well that is you then."

I pushed her hand off my thigh and looked briefly into her eyes, which were like bright cloud. "Then don't pretend that you would."

Irmela put her hand back. "I miss my sister."

"So do I."

"I feel empty. I need to touch someone."

"Look, I haven't fucked her in weeks, OK? So I got just what that empty feeling needs, and if that's what you're looking for, you're getting warmer."

"It doesn't bother you then?"

"When she was around and loving me I never made any moves on you."

Irmela laughed. "How old did you say you were?"

"I don't know, whatever I said last time. That was true. If I said 27."

She laughed even harder. "You are not getting warmer."

"Hey, you knew what that meant?"

"We have the same game in Austria. It is archetypal."

"I played Archetypal in high school. Whoever got the best Archetype opened up all the others, and could do his will with the space minions."

"Oh yes, this game. It is very old. From the space days. It is said the biophysicists played it on Mars."

"I don't know about that."

"It makes you a very old man, at least 45, I would say."

I laughed. "45, huh? What part of me looks 45?"

"Your feet. They are veiny and knobbed. You have cracks in your toenails, and they grow in. Also you have a lot of hair on your shoulders."

"I had that as a boy. Don't talk about it."

"Hairy back and bald head."

"Yeah, it's hereditary from my father's line. Hairy backs and bald heads. Julius Caesar, emperor of the Romans, he was a bald vegetarian with a hairy back. Like the popes of old too."

"They taught us about the popes. They were appointed by Austrians."

"That's a tony history you got there. Popes and Rulers. And porn queens." She flinched. "I'm sorry."

Irmela looked back out the window. "I am trying to laugh."

"Not everything is funny. Now where the fuck are we going to find a pool repair guy? How much money you got?"

"25 pieces of silver and ten pearls."

"Fuck me my friend, where'd you get all that freak from? Agatha?"

"It is not your business how I make my money."

In Malibu it was like the old days, people cooking over packing grates in the yard or out in the road in front of the house. No one drove on the streets of the town. People snuck between destinations, dodging in and out of doorways, taking back alleys and streets, cutting through canyons on switchbacks.

In town you could get supplies at a few stores, or forage on the street for rabbit, lizard, snake and giant grasshopper grilled on skewers. These were sold by hawkers hunched around braziers on obscure blocks, counting their pennies and silver coins into greasy goat hide bags, with bent necks. And then there were the xango eaters, one thing I would never be. I don't care what they say about xangoes eating fruit. And I don't give a shit that they look like little people. No. It's because they're nasty, like bats with arms and legs. And if you look at them long enough you will see; they are never happy. They're either angry or scared. So when they say we come from monkeys I can see why, even if it isn't true. Because I don't think the angels shit on their hands and throw it. So man is much more monkey than angel, in my experience.

There is a commercial strip of offices north of town off the highway, so we drove there and pulled into a parking lot full of entrance domes. There was thunder in the sky but no rain. The palm trees were fat with water. Wind blew the fronds around like hair. It smelled like burnt glass and fire, and decay. But the pods were open. Those without power propped their doors wide with chairs and boards. There was a lawyer, a podiatrist, an insurance agent, and a pool company. Its door was jammed open with a pink rubber pool shoe. The steps down were painted blue, with grit strips. The banisters were iron. Each step down the chemical odor grew stronger until at the bottom entrance I was wheezing.

Irmela said, "This place has an interesting smell."

"Interesting? I'm gasping for life here."

"This chemical smell reminds me of some place I lived in as a child. In Jerusalem."

"Where your mother was burned?" We entered a cramped office, with grey, brown and blue carpeting on the floor, walls and ceiling.

"I will like to have the pool again."

The air was moist; it clung to the skin and there was a constant hum in the background, punctuated by water rushing through pipes. Earwigs swarmed in the corners. There was a glassed-in office facing the entrance with fog in the windows. Off to the right and left were halls with products on display: corrugated hoses, pumps, filters, vacuums and skimmers, brushes and carboys and tanks of chemicals. A guy in a green suit with red suspenders and sandals on his feet and long flashing blond curls, the hair tips in Christmas colors like a net of lights, stood ready to show me the line.

"Where's the boss? I gotta talk to the guy in the office," I said.

He smiled and said, "He'll be back in a while."

"What if I don't have a while?"

He shrugged and looked at the ground, and then at me. "Come back later."

"I drove a long way."

"Bummer man."

"How long is the wait?"

"Probably not long. It could be minutes."

"Don't you know?"

"It depends on where he went."

"You mean like, if he went to the bathroom he's coming back soon, but if he died, then, who knows."

"Exactly. I just don't know where he went."

"Is there a place we can sit?"

"No."

Irmela said, "So then we will stand."

"Cool," the guy said.

About a half hour later, when my skin started to pucker and tears formed in my eyes as they reddened, the guy said, "So what do you want anyway?"

I had to blow my nose. I sniffled, "We have acid damage to our pool lining."

"Fuuuck, man. I can't help you with that at all, that's what the guy in the office does. He's good, man. You won't be disappointed."

A half hour later, I said, "How do you stay open?"

"Uh, we live here now. We have plenty of work. Getting there though. We try not to drive."

"How does that work?"

"We stack the orders, we ride horses and mules on back roads. We walk."

"I took the coast highway."

The door opened and the twin of the guy I was talking to came in wearing a wet black swimsuit, pink rubber pool shoes and goggles around his neck. His hair was wet and his feet squeaked as he walked by, not regarding any of us, not even Irmela. The door to the glassed-in office opened and he sat down in a suit and tie and said through the speaker system, "Dude, how can I help you?"

"We need our pool relined, and maybe re-plumbed. It was damaged by acid."

"Harsh."

"Can you do the work?"

"Under normal circumstances, yeah, but these are challenging times we live in. The 'Eliminate Ruler Lackeys' campaign has us all a little jumpy around here."

"Yeah, I can see how that might be."

"Where are you located?"

"Topanga Canyon."

He rubbed the scruff on his chin then fluffed his hair, which lit up like the valley at night in old pictures. "Look, if I ever can get a crew in and out of there, I'll come. You gotta get on the schedule though. To do that you have to sign a contract. Without coming out there, I can't tell you how much this will cost. And if I do get out there, you will have to pay me no matter what, you know, whether or not I can do the work, etc. A lot of people use their pools since they can't go out."

"You're telling me. I've been swimming in the ocean."

He nodded. "I hear you. Sharks. Jellyfish. Snakes on the trail. I expect payment. How will you pay me?"

"Pearls and silver."

"I think you just went to the top of the list. Suppose you walk me through the drive." He rested his chin on his hand and smiled.

I told him everything I knew about the ride down, where we lived, who lived where.

"Optimistic," he said. "And now a down payment, if you agree to the terms of the contract. What do you have on you?"

"I don't have anything on me," I said.

Now he noticed Irmela, and looked her up and down and nodded. "What about her. She have anything?"

Irmela scrutinized him and then his brother, who was observing everything, standing at-ease by a filtration unit three feet taller than he was, but wafer thin. Her eyes had turned the color of a swimming pool late in the day. She stared at me, her head cocked very slightly. A ripple went through her eyebrows but her face was placid.

"Ask her," I said.

He smiled and asked, "What have you got then?"

"Nothing but silver coins."

The smile became rueful. He said, "If you've got ten you can tell that old lady we'll fix her pool."

The brother smiled and nodded his head. They both flared up and a swarm of sparks raced around their hair ends. Irmela counted out ten coins from a silver pouch with long black handles and slid them through the slot in the window. He scooped them into an armored bag and said, "Now that we have that out of the way, let's do some shots and talk pools."

Chapter Twenty-Four

"I am convinced they were poisoning me with those hideous infusions," Agatha said, as she did most mornings, in a voice stronger than the day before. She sat on the couch facing the sea, sipping a gin and tonic and tapping the ash off the tip of a hashish, tobacco and opium cigarette. Yes, we were allowed to smoke again. I felt like I was back in the saddle, walking around talking and taking drags off a cigarette. "But who was it, was it someone at the Azodiazadora or was it Oyub, or Vonneniu? I even sometimes suspect my niece. I never trusted de Marcos. He had a streak of sadism. I had reason to believe she was his sex slave." She pronounced this while examining her drink, and then looked at each of us. "Anyway, it doesn't matter now."

"Those doctors only make you sick," I observed.

"First, do no harm. Right," she said.

Irmela, who sat cross-legged in the chair across from me reading Young Tortoise said, "I am reading a book about school boys who make a sex slave of the other boy, in the secret room in the attic."

"Exactly dear," the old lady said, nodding her head gravely. "They're Republicans." She took another hit of the cigarette and passed it to me, laughing. "I remember boarding school well, where even normal people are creeps. Everyone was a poor relation or the child of some merchant or military man. It was a testing ground for bastards. Sex slaves had the worst of it. You could tell by the color of the choke collar they wore. Even the teachers loathed them."

Irmela nodded. "I was sex slave for several pimps. I did not like it. But not everyone despised me. There was the worship too. When I was sex slave creeps adored me."

"Dear, I'll have another drink please. It's so early. But I find I don't give a damn. If I want to be drunk half the day, then by god I will be. If I want to get a rub on later, I'll go do that too, in the bath. Now Elma, what have we planned for dinner?"

"I am worried about the finances," Elma said. "We do not know what the pool will cost."

Agatha frowned and took a deep wheeze. "Pshaw, mierda! I've worried myself to death over money, dear. It isn't worth a fart. Let me tell you now, I know where it's hidden. My father never trusted anyone but me. He said Rulers were a bunch of inbred Morons. He was a hybrid too, long life, all of that. But his mother was a merchant. Father got the hard while his sister came out perfect and still as the hills as we used to say of Aunt Chemica. We never met my father's sire, that wasn't possible, but the old man took care of him and us. He made father legitimate, and father made me so too." Her eyes widened and she looked out the window at the clouds. "Soft," she said.

"Let's toast to your pop and your old grand pop then," I said, pouring Elma a shot and raising my glass high. "Tolmalok!"

Elma looked at me and sucked in her nostrils for a second. Irmela held out her glass. I filled it and without lifting her eyes from the book, she said, "May your hands and arms always be healthy."

Elma said, "Prosit."

That was the first day Elma drank with us.

After a few weeks I gave up on the idea of out drinking Agatha. She left me gasping in my chair. I was impotent. The old lady was awake at six every morning, tidying up the crap from the night before. She had a stomach of steel. And she liked to eat almost as much as she liked to drink and talk. Her bottomless pot of silver and pearls (mind, not diamonds and gold) meant we could buy food if I was willing to go out and get it. Then she'd fuss over a menu with Elma, who was an indifferent and bizarre cook, capable of baking turkey in cookie dough. Irmela was worse. When she cooked you were likely to find things like pens and bobby pins in your food, rubber bands, coins and staples. She got a whole desk into her food sometimes.

We ate the steak in the freezer, then the fish. Elma got seeds from the gardener who was living at Frank and Arphe's and planted beets, lettuce and kale.

When the booze ran out I drove down to Malibu to stock up on whatever I could find. It got to be routine almost and I grew lazy and arrogant. I let the quiet go by unnoticed, drinking when I should have been listening to the world. The Mexican Army was shelling Santa Monica day and night. The Rulers provisioned it by sea, from Santa Barbara and as far north as San Francisco. But in the canyons and the hills, tucked up in the Los Padres and all the eastern lands, no one could prevail, and the people kept to themselves.

One day I drove down to the Peyote Shop. Except for a trap parked outside the street was empty. The pavement was shattered and the roadbed cracked and pitted. People darted in and out of doorways, scooting along. Inside, a dozen locals were seated or standing, talking loudly and nodding their heads. A man with white hair peeled an apple and talked to a woman with a face creased like a dried fig. I took down a few two litre bottles of gin and a few more of Mekong and Keane's Cane and packed them into a weathered wooden crate with patches of yellow on the side. I elbowed my way to the register, past surfers and old men from the huts and artists and people who lived outside the law and moved about with the weather and the times.

The man behind the register was called Underbard. I've heard different stories about the name, but most likely it meant simply that in his world, he ruled as Bard did in ours, and it is also an insult, using a Ruler's name. So among people he stood for something. He had muttonchops and baked brick skin and sat like a block on a stool, taking money and chatting. His face was squared off like a shovel. "Bob. Haven't seen you in a while."

I put my box up on the counter. "That's the idea."

"No girls today?" He looked at each item and wrote in a book.

"No girls today. We heard the pool men might come."

"You can wait a long time for the pool men," he said, looking down at the ledger as he wrote.

"What's all the jabbering about?"

He looked up at me. "These people here are going north. No one wants to be around when the Barachas come."

"Barachas?"

"That's what they call themselves. They come up from Beverly Hills, Hollywood and LA Yaanga, out for revenge."

"Revenge? On us?"

"That's what Lord Otis did to them down there. You shall reap what you sow. If they come, don't give 'em a chance to tell you about it. Start shooting and don't stop until you're dead."

The man with white hair who had been peeling the apple sliced off a wedge and offered it to me. He had blue eyes so pale they shaded into white. I took the wedge and he said, "They killed all my animals and burned their carcasses in the road. Then they killed my family before my eyes and left me alive. That was last night. If you're thinking they won't come, that's what I thought too. Now what have I got? Nothing." He sliced off a piece of apple and ate it slowly. "I've had enough. I'm going north."

At the butcher and tea shop the air was dense and foul smelling, of animal fat, blood and sawdust and men and women sweating fear, crowded around the front of the store, smoking and talking. "The Barachas took all of my children, but left me alive."

"I was in the cellar, working on the cistern when the Barachas came. They set fire to my house with everyone in it and shot us when we ran out the doors."

As I pushed by they stopped talking and stared hard at me. Someone said, "It's only Bob."

The shop was run by twin brothers, Hank and Henry Ledel. They stood side-by-side behind the counter cutting fat grisly animal legs and shoulders and dishing out ground goat. They wielded knives like swords. Their arms were thick and veined but moved gracefully, gliding through the joints and the muscle and pairing away fat. As they worked they exchanged looks and carried on a wordless conversation, while also chatting up the customers. They had large heads, round like a soccer ball, fleshy whiskered cheeks and eyes like bulldogs.

"What can I do for you, Bob," Hank said.

"Hi there Bob," said Henry, sharpening his blade on a steel that hung from his belt.

"Do you have any chops? Pork?"

"I'm sorry Bob, all we have left is venison and goat."

"Leg of goat?"

"No, shoulder or neck. I have some ground too, as you can see. But I ground the deer and the goat together with some sage and garlic and made a sausage. I've got a few pounds left. It's yours if you want it."

"Aren't you going north?" I asked.

"That's the Peyote Shop. People here are going to fight. This is a Militia. A Citizen's Militia. We've got some folks here who've read up on it."

Henry, boning out a shoulder, said, "And about little else."

"Henry takes the side of the cowards in this."

"I'm just a butcher, brother and so are you."

"We too are citizens, brother. And we can form our own militias for the defense of our land."

"I'll take the sausage. Throw in 10 pounds of whatever won't kill me, so long as it's a bird or a mammal, and no cabron monkeys."

"You won't be disappointed." Hank's fleshy face smiled and thick creases encased his lips and eyes.

Henry said, "You won't either. I made that batch. There was a little fat back left from that sow we had last week so I threw it in."

"The old lady will be thrilled," I said.

"You be careful up in the hills."

"It's been quiet in Topanga."

"Because the Barachas strike the coast."

"And the Rulers will attack from the hills, once they get their shit together. They aren't idiots."

"Exactly. So the Barachas will move into the hills to get there first, and lay waste to the place. Look what they've done here."

Henry stopped his work and put the knife down. The lady in front of him, in shorts and a T-shirt with a brown winter housecoat that fell open periodically, said, "We're talking about driving into Beverly Hills to get even. Make them think twice before they come here."

I counted out some lake pearls and took the sack of meat and sausages out to the car. I put it in the passenger seat and drove without incident back up to Topanga Canyon. I did see, on the opposite side, fires where there were once houses, visible only by their lights. I pulled into the driveway. There were two broad work horses hitched to a covered wagon loaded with empty cardboard spools and scraps of pool liner, two saddled mules blinking and switching their tails, and a big black sedan, in the driveway. Two men stood on either side of the door with machetes. I had no gun. I didn't think I'd need one. I pulled up next to the black car, got out and asked them, "How's it going with the pool?"

They looked like ordinary guys you see in bars. The one on the right was a tall brown-skinned blond and the one on the left was middle-aged, with grey on his temples and creased eyes that winced in the bright cloudy light. The one on the right said, "They're all done. Get in the house." He raised the machete above his head and said, "Move."

The one on the left stepped aside and pointed his machete at the door. "Go on."

I entered the foyer and headed upstairs to the living room. The French doors were open. There were four men, two with shotguns and two with machetes, pacing back and forth. Lying face down on the ground, their arms bound behind their backs, were the twin brothers and a woman, in bathing suits and tank tops and knee-high black rubber boots. "What the fuck are you doing in my house?" I asked.

"Your house?" a man with a shotgun said. "It's my house, and my house isn't your house."

Elma, Irmela and Agatha were seated together on the couch, their hands, bound in blue twist wire, resting in their laps. Irmela stared at the man with the shotgun. He was dressed in black, with black gloves and a silver snood. He had little eyes and no eyebrows and his lips were meaty. He did all the talking. The other guy with a shotgun, in the same uniform, merely echoed with his movements whatever the man who was speaking said. Irmela never took her eyes off of him, and she didn't blink. Agatha, in the middle, looked like she had washed down the drain. Not two hours ago she was smoking on the deck and nursing a tankard of gin on the rocks, with lemon from the garden. She was like a possum. She had made a fool out of all of us. Elma's eyes darted from face to face, perplexed and terrified.

I said, "What do you want?"

"Your lives. But don't worry; it won't end quickly or soon. Stick out your arms and let Bix tie your wrists."

"Like hell."

"We can get started early if you like. I thought you'd be grateful for the wait."

I held out my hands and Bix, a six-foot idiot with green teeth and bad skin holstered his machete and got out the wire to twist around my wrists. I saw a chance. I could reach the holster and pull the machete. What then? I didn't have long. I couldn't think it out. I reached for the blade and pulled. It slid right out and I stood armed with a machete. No one expected that. I grabbed Bix and pulled him in front of me and put the blade against his throat. It nicked the skin and he flinched. A bead of blood formed and rolled slowly down his neck into his shirt.

The two men with shotguns lowered their barrels level with the couch. The other man with the machete held it high, in striking range of my face. The man in charge wrinkled his forehead and said, "I see you want to pick up the pace. But the Baron wants us to wait."

"We don't have to do that. You fellas can put the weapons down and get out of here. Then your friend walks. Otherwise I start taking him apart an inch at a time. I'll nibble away at his nose first, like a mouse with a chunk of cheese."

"Yeah? We'll start with these three on the floor." He gestured to the other man with the machete and with a flick of his wrist he hacked off the arm of the twin on the left, who howled out with pain. "Shut up." He pointed the shotgun at the pool guy's foot. "You won't walk out of here." He pulled the trigger and the barrel spit fire and roared and the whole lower leg burst into blood and tissue, contained by the black boot. The guy let out a hoarse guttural bark and moaned and cried but didn't have the energy to scream any more as he bled out on the floor. His brother and the woman writhed like worms in the sun and cried. "Whuddya think of that, granny?"

"I haven't long to live one way or the other," Agatha said.

The man with the shotgun laughed. I said, "You don't have to do this. We aren't with the Ruler lackeys. We just live in the hills."

"And what did I have to do with Mexicans when that piece of shit Otis marched in, raped my sons and daughters and burned them before my eyes?" He waved the shotgun around and buried the barrels in Agatha's hair. I pressed the machete closer to Bix's throat. He was sweating. It poured off his forehead and mixed with the blood on his neck, soaking his uniform. The man with the shotgun was not looking at Agatha anymore but at Irmela, who stared into his eyes with cold, analytical indifference. "I'll make sure you die with a smile on your face," he said. Then he looked at Agatha and nudged her head with the shotgun. He said, "You're gonna go first." He took a deep breath. Agatha shrieked and gripped her face and then collapsed to the floor in a heap. His eyes flashed as he lost his target and refocused on the ground, the muzzle pointing briefly at the ceiling. I couldn't do a thing. His partner swung around to aim at me. "What just happened? What was that?" he shouted.

Irmela said, "She has strokes and seizures."

Elma said, "May I go to her?"

He laughed. "Try it. See what happens." Elma rose slowly and crouched down by the old lady and felt her hands and her ribs. She examined her face and neck. A car drove into the driveway. Footsteps approached the door. He said, "Good, the Baron is here."

I said, "I will cut his throat and then yours, if anything happens to her." To prove my point I slid the blade across his neck and sliced a half-inch of flesh. Bix cried out and the wound opened like an eye, blood jetting over the blade.

The door opened. Footsteps ascended the stair, and Junior and Jorge, dressed in black, with boots on their feet, stood inside the French doors with shotguns.

"Frank," Junior said. "Why does Bob Martin have a machete pressed against Bix's throat?"

"Baron, sir. Bix fucked up."

Junior looked at me and smiled. He said, "Hello Bob."

"Pubic ass hair wolf-cunt moron," Jorge said. "It has been an age."

"You too puta madre strap-on son of a bitch," I said. "And Senior *Baron*."

"Bob, what's to stop me from having you hacked to pieces?" Junior asked.

"Not wanting to do it!"

"Ha!" he said.

"Then how about I don't deserve it. I never did a bad thing to you."

"What about the girls? I told you to tell them to scram."

"Nobody tells me who to fuck. That's going too far."

"And then you schtupp David, my porn guy."

"You would have too."

"Why?" he asked, incredulous.

"'Cause what he was doing was wrong. And it ate away at me."

"That's stupid. You didn't used to be so stupid, until you met that conechichihualli."

"Don't tell me that. Look what you got for that Ruler pincushion over there," I pointed my head at Jorge. "Nothing but grief."

He smiled. "Then what do you have to say about the Priest? He disappears, and his car is found on the side of the freeway. Did you think I wouldn't notice?"

"He was blackmailing us."

He stopped smiling and I could see the tick tock behind his eyes go. "For what?"

"Never mind that. We had a project and Margaret wanted a bigger split. They threatened to turn us in for the reward in another piece of business which has nothing to do with any of this. I couldn't let that slide. They were threatening to kill me. Don't you see? It was never going to end. You know how it goes. They broke the rules. They had to go."

"How did you manage to keep this house?"

"The owners, Mrs. Kennedu's niece and husband," I pointed to the old lady with the machete. Bix made a move. I thought it was for a gun and without thinking, brought the machete down on his arm. It lopped off at the elbow and fell to the floor. He started to hop around and shout as the blood shot out from the wound. "Holy fucking shit!" he screamed. "Oh, ah!" The guys with the guns swung around and for a second all of the weapons were leveled at each other as Bix staggered around the room, squirting blood on the floor, his lifeless upper arm dangling from his shoulder. I put the machete on the second guy with the shotgun, the one covering me. The blade was at his throat and the shotgun was pressed against my chest.

"All right," Junior roared. "Everyone puts down his weapon."

Elma stood and said, "Can I help this man?"

Junior looked at Bix and then at Elma. "Sure, why not." She took off her belt and tied off the arm and led him, trembling, downstairs to the kitchen. We laid down our weapons. Junior picked up a machete and pointed to the dead pool guy. "Is he dead?"

Frank nudged him with his foot. "I'd say so, Baron."

"Take the other two out in the yard and shoot them."

"No!" they cried.

"Junior, all they did was fix my pool," I pleaded, over their squirming screams. "They aren't Rulers. They're California Morons like you and me."

He smiled and shook his head. "They're from Malibu, aren't they?" No one answered. He raised the machete and hacked off their heads. The blood poured across the floor. "Take the garbage out, and leave it on the road for all to see. Kill the burros too."

The Barachas set about removing the three bodies, and Bix's arm.

"Bob," he said. "For old times' sake, I'm going to let you slide on that. Think of yourself as owing me an arm, if you like." He looked out the windows and around the room, nodding his head. "I could use someone like you to talk to. Like in the old days. You know the territory. We're moving in. I hope that's OK with you ladies," he said to Agatha, who was passed out, gape-mouthed on the floor, and Irmela, crouched beside her. Irmela turned her head slightly and blinked at him, holding him in a gaze of neutral grey.

Chapter Twenty-Five

It was a warm afternoon. A few of Junior's fighters were turning a goat on a spit over a kiinarabi fire. Agatha and Elma were sprawled out by the pool, Agatha in a straw sun hat, big oval sunglasses with obsidian frames and a lawn green one piece bathing suit that somewhat contained her wrinkled bronze sack. "It's my natural color," she said. "What you saw in the Azodiazadora was a corpse animated by medicine." She sipped her gin on the rocks through a long bent straw and flipped through a magazine. Elma lay back in a lounge chair in a pair of loose plaid shorts, a black bikini top and sun goggles. Irmela lay face down on the small diving board, her arms and feet dangling in the water and her head resting sideways, with wet hair and no sunglasses. She had on orange shorts and a green tank top. Her toenails were painted pink. Junior came out wearing an apron and a silver snood with dark goggles. The goggles made him look like Jason on his first voyage in the Argo, except that Jason was young, and Junior was not, and Jason was thin and Junior was built out of thick blocks, and he wasn't blonde either. Anyway, that's what he looked like. His mouth was set. He picked up a small bucket with a mop baster and slathered marinade over the goat. It hissed and smoked and mixed with melting fat dripping off the carcass into the coals. The goat was impaled from its ass through its mouth, teeth biting the spit and boiled white eyes popping out.

Junior said, putting the bucket down, "Bix!" Bix stood at attention. His half arm dangled at his side, still in bandages. The sun blistered his face. In his other hand was a fusca. He never was without it. He glared at me day and night and gnashed his green teeth. I slept with a fusca and didn't turn my back on him. Junior made it clear there would be no revenge. Which was fine, as long as Junior was around to enforce it. When they went out on raids I made sure he brought Bix along, but Bix couldn't drive and he was a bad shot. Bix was a bag of lead around Junior's neck, but Junior was loyal to anyone who took a shot for him. "Bix!" Bix looked at Junior. "Two beers and a bottle of Mescal." Bix nodded and slouched off, his upper arm bouncing slightly against his body.

Bix returned clutching two bottles between his fingers and carrying one under his arm, which bent his back and made him waddle. "Cheers," Junior said. He handed the mescal to Jorge. "Go ahead." Jorge grinned and drank, holding the bottle upright, his Adam's apple chugging up and down. He smiled and wiped his mouth with the back of his hand. "Thanks, Baron." Jorge's voice had become gravelly. He sounded, at the age of 24, like an old LA Yaanga man selling bus tickets and lottery cards.

The old lady glanced up from her magazine and rattled her ice. "I could use a fresh up."

"You heard her," Junior said.

"Yes Baron," said Bix, who dutifully returned to the house to fetch the gin.

The old lady said gaily, "Let's take peyote tonight, after the goat. We'll have a bonfire."

"We're all out of peyote," Elma said.

"I ate the last of the mushrooms," I said.

"Mierda," Agatha said.

"If you're buying, I'll send Jorge into Malibu," Junior said.

Agatha declared, "It would be nice if you'd bankroll this operation for a change. It's my house."

Junior nodded. "Was, you mean. Put up the pearls and Jorge can pick up whatever we need. Papas too. I like them roasted in the fire."

Agatha stood and clapped her hands over her head, which was thrust forward from her curved spine and humped shoulders. "Papa's got a brand new bag," she sang. "Ooh la la." She made kissing noises. Bix came back with the gin. She held out her glass. "There's a dear. Don't be stingy now." Her ass hung down out of the suit and the skin on her legs was veined and wrinkled. She shook her ass and said, "I'm ready for a rip! Elma, dear, won't you play the guitar?"

Elma said, "Maybe after dinner."

After dinner we drank a brew of peyote and after each of us vomited violently in the grass we sat around with Tiki torches wiping the grease off our fingers and gazing at the sky. A sweet desert wind blew in smelling of wildflowers and fruit trees. Colors creased the skies and I saw what I felt. Elma played the guitar, casually plucking a tune that wandered like mosquitoes. The old lady was talking to Junior, flat out on her lawn chair, with a bottle of gin in her hand. Lately she'd developed a demented cackle.

"For chrissakes Baron, just dive in for once," Agatha said.

"It has to be hotter," Junior said. He was sitting in an iron chair under an umbrella, at a table. He wore a short suit and a big watch. He was the only guy around who had managed to get fat through the war, but he ate when he was nervous, something he never was before, so who knew? "But it sure looks tempting." Irmela rolled off the diving board and into the dark blue water, slowly sinking till she hit the bottom with a slight bounce.

Elma shrieked, "The log roll."

I laughed. "Where do you get stuff like that?" It was funny. I'd been listening to her talk for so long, I had forgotten how nutty she sounded.

"I get it all over," she said, laughing. "I don't know what language I am thinking in sometimes, and then I have to translate."

The old lady said, "I had an ass like yours when I was young, yes I did."

"That must have been some ass you had," I said.

The water wobbled over Irmela. I remember watching the bubbles gently roll to the surface, make a rainbow and pop. She was at the bottom of a blue cube cut out of sky; she was flying there, high above the earth. I said, "The sky."

Elma said, "The stars."

Agatha said, "I remember hearing stories from my mother's father of his grandfather building the new tunnels on Mars, where the Rulers conducted their genetic experiments with Martian DNA. How the dust penetrated everything, and men would choke on silted up hoses. We used to watch through the telescopes and make up stories about the rebel Rulers, and their battles against Earth."

There were no more bubbles. Irmela was bobbing face down on the bottom of the pool, her hair waving, arms outstretched and fingers spread. I started to think something might be wrong. I didn't know how long she'd been down there. I felt cold in my neck and I had to pee. She'd been down there a long time! Ten minutes? Maybe it was five. How long did it take for a brain to die? It was three minutes or five. Five. A person can live with a stopped heart for five minutes. But a stopped heart is different from no oxygen. They were different things. Blood and air.

It was just the peyote. I mean, she couldn't have been down there more than a few seconds. The splash had just hit the pavement. The surface of the water was still agitated. If she'd been down there ten minutes the water would be still.

Everything was still. Still water, still sky, after months of turmoil, of thunderstorms and mudslides and missiles flying out of the hills hitting the coast highway and every town between Santa Monica and Santa Barbara. Then came the strafebots, zipping out of nowhere like a twenty-pound hummingbird spitting lead and glass. And the winds. It started in early December with 105 mile per hour winds. Everything but the surface of the water was still, and the stillness was spreading out from the sky through the leaves and branches, to the xangoes in the shade. Elma stopped playing guitar. I tried to look at the water but my eyes were fixated on the sky. The nights were so black, the sky was dense with stars so bright they lit the ground. Elma's face glowed white and her hair was gold.

I loved Elma. Without her I was nothing, half a man, and it was like she didn't even know it, she was so absorbed in that old lady. And Irmela was always in the bed with us. Just the night before I woke up with a hard on. I kinda had to piss but I knew if I got up I'd never go back to sleep. So I was lying there with my eyes closed, highly aroused, but with a slight piss ache, when I felt her hand on me. Irmela's. I swallowed hard and turned my head to look at Elma. She was snoring drunkenly. I relaxed and didn't let on that anything was happening while Irmela jerked me off. But after the first few incredible seconds, the urge to pee got stronger and stronger. I was not going to get up! I had been waiting almost three years for this to happen. I was so close. She had me spasming. But then I just shot my wad and didn't feel a thing. Nothing. It was the dispelling of fluid, like popping a zit. She took her hand away and continued as she had been, on her back staring at the ceiling.

Irmela was still at the bottom of the pool. How much time had it been? I never wore a watch, never could keep time. I cried out, "Irmela!"

Elma said, "Where?"

I said, "There. In the pool. She rolled off the diving board, I don't know how long ago."

"Irmela can swim," Elma said. "I am sure she is just swimming on the bottom. Doing catfish we call it."

"I can't dive in there!" I said. I stood and pulled off my clothes, running for the pool and diving in. I swam down towards her. The first 6 feet were OK but the last three were murder. The water was like a wall and I pushed through it, ears popping and lungs starting to burn. I reached towards her and grabbed her clothing, letting out bubbles, pulling upwards till I could grasp her about the waist and drag her to the surface. I reached up and kicked as hard as I could, pulling the surface closer with my hand. I gasped at the air and thrashed about trying to get to the wall.

"What are you doing? "Elma asked.

Irmela was limp in my arms. I dropped her and rolled her onto her back. Her lips were blue and her skin was cold. Her eyes were half open. I opened her mouth, cleared her tongue and put my mouth on hers, breathing into her lungs. Then I massaged her heart, thumping a beat back into it. Elma pushed me away. "Please, I will do this."

She touched Irmela's forehead and studied her lips and eyes. Then she bent over her face and breathed into her mouth, feeling her pulse. She pushed her chest three times and paused. Irmela coughed up water and shook her head. "I was catfish," Irmela said.

"You were dead," I said. "She brought you back to life."

Irmela laughed. "No. Not dead." She walked by us and went up to the house.

"What the fuck was that?" Junior asked.

"You will have to ask her," Elma said. "It is not for me to say."

"I don't understand," Junior said.

"And you never will," I said. "Whenever they say shit like that, I don't wanna know. You should hear some of the shit that they talk about."

"We thought you enjoyed our conversations," Elma said. "You complain when we speak Austrian! I did not know we bored you so."

"It's not that."

"I'm waiting for an answer," Junior said. "She was down there for a long time. She was blue."

"And why didn't you rescue her? You saw how long she had been down there," Elma said, pushing her lips out at him.

"I can't swim," he said.

"And you," Elma said, "how long did you stare at her in the water?"

"I could say the same thing to you," I said.

"But I knew there was no danger!"

"That's!" I said.

"Can you explain?" Junior asked me.

"Obviously she can be underwater for 20 minutes or ten minutes or whatever and appear dead and actually be OK. Maybe she's got gills."

Jorge said, "I heardadat. People with gills. Like the flesh eating horses."

"It's not a Ruler thing, gills," I said.

"You are so expert?" asked Elma.

Junior said, "Yeah I heardadat too."

"I saw the flesh eating horses," I said. "We all did."

Junior leaned forward. "You've seen the flesh eating horses?"

"Yes," said Elma, curtly. Irmela came down from the house with a mug of hot lemongrass and mint tea. They were resourceful.

They figured out what the plants were and used them, so we always had herb tea and fruit and greens to eat. But now that there were twelve terrorists living with us, and more arriving by the day, some to stay and some for meetings, the supplies were strained.

"You mean like in a parade?" Junior asked.

"No," I said. "In the stables." I took out a cigarette and leaned back in my chair. "We were in Santa Barbara for a show, and on the way back we got lost in the hills. The car took us to that property you had me show for Charlie Gets Along. You know, Ocktomann 4's summer palace, up in the Los Padres."

Junior nodded and scratched his cheek.

"Well, no one was around, so we drove in and slept in the car. Early next morning we explored the property a bit and checked out the stables. You could smell them from a long way off. Their shit smells like a carnivore's, more like a dog than a horse. The stables are built like a fortress. We went up to the windows. They were barred with iron. Inside, below, in an iron stall, were three horses tearing apart a pig."

"Goat fucker!" Jorge exploded. "That's cool."

"What were you there for?" Junior asked.

"Like I told you. We got lost."

We stared at the stars for a while then, sipping drinks and smelling the night air. The torches flickered. The old lady announced she was going to bed. Elma took her in. Junior's fighters were sacked out on the lawn in two person tents. He, Frank, Jorge and Bix slept in the living room. Junior lit up a hashish and tobacco cigarette and passed it to Irmela.

"I wonder who's living up there now," Junior said. "That place had defenses. You could do a lot of damage from there." He mused the thought over and looked at me. "You had a good idea once. Have a party there."

"You want to have a party there?"

"Not quite. I want to move the operation there. Bring the squads together. We can wipe them out in the hills. Kill every last one of them. I think it could work. Tomorrow we go up to the Los Padres and have a look."

I spluttered awake. "Are you fucking kidding? We? I told you, I don't go out on patrol."

"You're taking me out there."

"Good thing," Jorge said. "I couldn't find my way back there. That place is in a jungle."

Irmela's eyes grew wide and darkened. She grasped the mug of tea in two hands and brought it to her lips.

Chapter Twenty-Six

"We're not taking her!" Junior said, sipping coffee from a demitasse. There was a muffled whistling outside of the window and a few thousand wizz rounds exploded in the air, leaving tracer marks in the sky. *Froomp. Sshhhhwoof.* The windows shook and light flashed in our eyes. "We aren't going to a long term care facility. Jesus. Blood of the Portland cunt!"

Jorge smiled and scratched his cheek. He jerked the barrel of his gun off and said, "Mama, I am the tool for you."

"I told you, respect!" Junior said, glaring at him and smiling.

"Baron, I beg your fucking pardon," Jorge said. He backed off and lowered the gun, retreating a few steps to sulk.

"That's nothing compared to what's there," he said to Agatha, who was staring at him the way a coyote stares at a poodle.

"I will not force Elma to remain here with me and she won't go if I stay. We're coming. I haven't holed up with you for this long just to be left behind."

A crack louder than thunder shook the house. There was the sound of air rushing into a vacuum and all of the trees suddenly turned their leaves and branches up, like in a tornado. But the sky was clear and the sun was out. "You can't possibly expect Irmela to stay," Elma said. "The brush is drying out. If the shells don't get her the fires will. We must all go. We will ride with Bob. You will follow."

"Will I?" He looked at Bix, who was lying on the couch loading and reloading his fusca with one hand. Bix laughed and pointed it at the wall. Junior said, "If you become a problem I will have you shot. That's what I will do. Never forget it. Once we hit the road my word is law."

Elma said, "We will do what we must do. When do we leave?"

"As soon as it gets dark."

We mapped out a route. Going down to the coast highway was too dangerous. It wasn't just Ruler incursions either. The Mexican irregulars and Angelinos were formed into squads, but the squads were as likely to attack each other as the enemy. There were no consistent uniforms. And now that full-scale battle had broken out along the coast, the fight for the interior had begun. Militias that had only fought on the streets of barrios and villages were headed into the hills and mountains.

We decided to go through Simi Valley and into the mountains. We could spend the night at Fort Tejon, in the Chumash Seven Villages. My mother grew up there. I spent my summers there as a child. I had uncles, aunts and cousins all over the place. They would know me. We could rest up safely in the hills. From there it was a day or two drive into the interior on old service roads.

The mountains were steep and the country was wild. Up in the Los Padres it was anyone's land now. The Rulers were just nibbling at the southern edge. That's what we heard, anyway. There was always the possibility that the Ruler Sargon had gone straight to Ocktomann 4's summer palace. It would be a logical move. There was nothing to stop them. The Mexicans were nowhere near there. The Ruler Sargon was alone in southern

California. But I didn't tell Junior that he had caught us there once before or that he was on us for the murder of the de Marcoses. I didn't want to talk about it. The old lady might get suspicious.

We set out in four cars, one for supplies. Three other squads were converging on the summer palace: one each from Redondo Beach, Compton and Yorba Linda. They had no idea what they were doing in the mountains but in the town they were fierce. They were the units that devastated Malibu and joined up with Junior sometimes in the hills and canyons. And there were others coming too, from Torrance, Hollywood, Beverly Hills and Burbank. There was a Barstow gang and troops from Bakersfield. From wherever the Rulers were despised came men and women carrying whatever arms they had.

We kept to small roads in the valleys with heavy tree cover and drove until two or three, when we reached Ft. Tejon. There isn't anything there besides a few historic cabins from the conquest days, and a sign that says Seven Villages. The headlights flashed on a window every mile or so. We went into the hills and pulled into a clearing. There we set up watches by some juniper and spent the night sleeping out in the cold without a fire. Junior passed around a bag of pinyons and chocolate, which we washed down with mescal.

I awoke to two rifle shots at dawn. Jorge and Bix were talking loudly in the bush, out of sight. They came out of the woods laughing and smiling. I stood up on cold aching legs, eyes blistered in my head. The old lady was in the car with Elma. The windows were fogged up. Irmela was lying on the bare ground staring at the sky, still. The door to Junior's car opened and he emerged looking grim and awake. His eyes were black in the shadows.

"Boss, look what they shot for us, dinner. Henry and Monique." Henry and Monique, in black, looking thin and depressed, dragged a 4-point buck into the clearing.

"We don't have time for that," Junior said.

"It won't take long," I said. They looked at each other. I got a knife out of the trunk and dressed it. The gut pile steamed in the red light of cold morning air. I used drinking water to wash off. "You'll have to ride with your feet on it."

Jorge made a face. "That's disgusting."

"Just pretend it's a man," I said.

At the end of the day we parked the cars and posted a guard and hiked into the bush off the road. There was a small gully with running water, and level high ground, where we could put our bedrolls and build a fire. We built another fire between a couple of boulders by the stream, in the shade of a palm. Junior's guys worked silently gathering wood, carrying supplies down from the cars and I skinned and butchered the buck. The Barachas took care of the rest.

Elma said, "I will stay in the car with Agatha."

"I'm not staying in there another night. I wish to sleep out," the old lady said. "It was poisonous, the air of two snoring drunks."

"And farting," said Elma.

"Can't be helped," the old lady said, her face stricken. Then she perked up. "Help me out of the car dear. Bob," she said to me. Elma gave Agatha her arm.

"What?" I asked.

Agatha straightened out her black soft pants and grey smock. "You and I haven't sat down to a martini and steak in an age."

"I don't know how you feel about venison."

"I feel splendid about it. If it's bloody and tender."

"It won't be tender, but it will be bloody."

"Is there any ice?"

"No, not for drinks."

"Then screw it, let's drink gin out of the bottle and sit on the ground." She marched toward the fire.

"You're on," I said.

"Me too," said Elma. "Come on Irmela, we are going to sit upon the ground and drink gin from the bottle."

"My fut hurts," Irmela said.

"You mean fut or cramps?"

Irmela puffed out her eyes.

"It is what Agatha wants."

Irmela sank lower in the car seat and stared at the ceiling.

I said, "Forget about it. Come on."

Agatha stopped and turned around. She said, "Whenever whatever it is that hurts stops hurting, dear, be sure to join us."

Elma stacked Agatha properly on a blanket she had laid out on the ground. I sat on a rock. Elma squatted by the old lady and opened a bottle of gin. The wrens and towhees and sparrows were in and out of the blooming txaparil, lilac manarinimbi, and pink kiinarabi.

"If the guard had not killed Ocktomann, none of this would have happened," Agatha said, tracing on the blanket with her finger.

"I want to know how he died," I said.

The old lady nodded. "I remember when we finally learned of Bard's assassination, how sad we were."

I laughed. "That's not how we felt. His lash was harsh. He earned every inch of his pain."

"I don't mean that imbecile, I mean the third. Bard 3 was stabbed by a farmer while cutting lettuce at dawn. The man saw him in the field and took his chance. That was in the Hudson Valley. Word travelled far."

Irmela joined us. We passed her the bottle. It came to me and I took a swig. "That was a long time ago. The third Bard they say was a good Ruler."

Agatha took the bottle from me and tipped her head back, letting a glug of gin into her mouth. She swallowed and hacked and wiped her lips on the back of her shriveled hand. "When he came to California it was Mexican, all the way up to San Francisco." She pointed north! "He drove the Mexicans down to San Diego and held the line there for 40 years! And he didn't butcher entire towns. Well that makes two killed in a row. An unlucky line."

"They're always knocking each other off," I said.

Agatha shook her head no. "In this generation."

"They have always done this," Elma said. "The knocking off."

Irmela said, "I read the book about the Martian Quarantine knock offs."

Agatha laughed low. "They killed each other in the spaceships going out."

Irmela said, "It was the breathers against the anaerobics. In space and on Mars I know who will win. Ocba. Anaerobics."

"Perhaps," Agatha said. "But Ocba had a purpose. Now they seem frivolous. I remember the old people saying the same thing in those times. Nothing has changed. All princes are imbeciles."

Chapter Twenty-Seven

That night Irmela came to me. Everyone was asleep. The coals of the fire were covered in white ash. I was staring at the sky and smelling the air. It was keeping me awake. Sleeping out always does. I didn't know she was there until she climbed naked into my sleeping bag, or as she would say, bag that sleeps, and wrapped her leg around me. She pulled me to her lips hard and before I knew it we were writhing around in the bag, smothering our cries with kisses.

We lay on our backs staring at the stars, fingers twined and feet touching. An owl hooted and a fox killed a kangaroo rat. When the shrieking was over Irmela stood and walked away, into the crickets.

Sometimes the roads were nothing more than logs thrown across a wash and a path cleared of stones and brush. We changed tires and repaired compressors, patched leaking water tanks with lead seals. We crawled up a gully and then rocked down a sloped clearing into a hole cut in a wall of Douglas fir. By noon the car had gone on scent and was driving itself, Junior and his crew following. By late afternoon we crested a pass and descended over switchback roads to the palace. The back way in was totally different; nothing was familiar until we reached the driveway.

I had no idea what awaited us at the gates. The sun was low. We drove through the silent arrays of sensors to the gatehouse, where the driveway took over, conveying us down the aisle of redwoods and stopping beneath the portico, which was in deep shadow. The house was dark. The car doors opened. A soldier stood behind each door, weapon drawn. Junior approached the front door. "I wonder if it's locked?"

"I wonder if it's provisioned," I said.

Elma said, "I wonder if it's booby-trapped."

"Let's find out," Junior said. He leveled his shotgun at the doorknob and pulled the trigger. The doorknob melted and the door swung open, through bitter metallic smoke and blue flame. We followed the Barachas into the palace. The security lights were just bright enough to reveal shapes, but the distant rooms were black. Junior put on a headlamp and searched the walls for the panel. "Get the lights on," he said quietly. The black shapes of three men approached the wall. The lights came on. They shot through the house. Crystal chandeliers sparked into fountains of light and water. The glass and copper rotunda glowed with evening rays of rose-colored sun. Beyond was the reception hall, ebony columns shaped like palms, with red lotus capitals and gold sheaves of papyrus on the pediment, by potted tree ferns and palms.

Agatha blinked and looked around. "Ocktomann. Tacky to the end."

Elma smiled and sat back on a chair, giggling. She shrieked and ran off through the house.

"What's with her?" I asked.

Irmela said, "She is happy."

Junior said, "Fan out through the house. And try not to kill the moyoti. Bob. What was the security?

"Just the usual."

"What about the missiles?"

"I didn't see them. They were in underground batteries at each corner of the lot with a fifth launch tube in the middle of the southern boundary, connected by a central command unit in a bunker."

"We're going to fire those rockets at Santa Barbara."

"OK Junior, it's your show."

"It's not a show, as you will find out. We are going to destroy the Rulers forever. Ultimately, this is about exterminating Rulers. They are monsters. Self-created to rule us, out of our own flesh and blood. And they are starting to speciate. Some fail to produce offspring with humans. They can only breed with each other. What if a Martian-human hybrid started to breed? What then? This is no show Bob. This is a war that ends when every one of them, or everyone of us is dead."

Junior divided up the house like a barracks. There were a hundred men and women now. More came in daily. Dirty, bloody, exhausted from the field. They came in silent or carousing, but they came and parked their cars up and down the driveway, on the tennis courts. A crew of ten prepared meals in the kitchens.

Squads, units now, were kept together and quartered throughout the palace. Commanders slept in separate quarters, near Junior. The palace had four wings off the central building, like an H, and three levels. Between the legs and arms of the H were formal gardens. In the center were the reception hall, ballrooms, banquet rooms, the grand dining hall, bowling alley, pools and exotic gardens, including a cool-house of alpine plants. There was a small zoo of pygmy animals, lamas and sheep the size of house cats, ostriches no bigger than a canary. They had pachyderms shrunk down to the size of hamsters; elephants picking up crumbs with tiny pink trunks that looked like mouse-tails.

Junior kept his dogs on a short leash and that included us. The four of us shared a single bedroom. There were 12 empty next to us but when I asked about those rooms Junior smiled and fixed his black glaring eyes on me and said nothing.

There were two large beds in the room. Elma didn't want me sleeping with Irmela unless she was in the bed, but the bed wasn't big enough for three, and Elma didn't want to insult the old lady!

"What do you mean?" I asked, next to a potted palm and a marble Corinthian column.

"I don't want to insult her. She must not think you do not want to share her bed."

"But I don't want to sleep with a farting old woman who wheezes and gasps and sounds like she's going to drop dead with snoring when she's drunk. Which is all the time."

"Nevertheless, I think you should reconsider."

"Make Irmela sleep with her."

"I cannot do that. Make her. Can you make her? She will not do it if you ask."

"Not this shit where you wait for her to do what you want her to do because she will whatever it is you say—"

"She will understand that she has to do it."

"But you have to talk to her to do that!"

"What do you know about this?"

"About what?"

"What we are talking about."

"But I don't know what that is! Who is going to sleep with the old lady? Not me."

Elma squeezed her lips into a bud and said, "Then I will do it. You and Irmela can share the other bed." Her lips spread apart. There was love in her eye! Her hair glowed white and pulsed. "But we must meet here when they are doing the drills and do our own drilling. When Agatha drinks, and Junior is not watching. Is this a deal?"

"Deal? I thought you didn't make deals."

"I will give you the deal."

"The deal, OK. I take the deal." I smiled and kissed her. Her cheek gave and our lips touched. I pushed her back against the column. "Here? Now?"

"Shut up." Elma lifted her skirt and I fucked her against the column, the marble cold in my hands.

For weeks Junior drilled his troops in the gardens and the house, as the wind got hotter and drier and the smell of fire was on the air. He took them out on hikes in the forest and then did penetration drills in the house, climbing in through windows, evading safety light. We got drunk with the old lady and smoked cigarettes while Irmela sat on a chair by a window in an obscure telephone room reading a book, L'Assommoir By Zola, which she found in the Palace library. "What's Zola," I asked. I had never heard of Zola of course, who had?

"He is the author," said Irmela, without looking up from the page, her ankle-stockinged feet dangling off the arm of the chair, and her navy blue bamboo shorts crammed into the crack of her ass.

"So Zola wrote the ass book you're reading."

"Or the one you are reading?" Without looking up she reached behind her and pulled the shorts out of her butt, straightening the leg over her thigh. "L'assommoir are the drunks." She looked at me like I was a toilet bug. "Everyone knows this."

"You mean like in Austria."

Irmela shook her head, her hair frozen into place with spray and stopped reading. "Sometimes you seem so stupid to me. I don't mean Austria."

"Then wherever it is you fucking come from. Azer, Azerbaijan!"

There was no TV or radio but there was plenty to eat. There were gardens and greenhouses on the grounds and stores of meat, oil, rice and booze. We broke open cases of Champagne and Bordeaux wines, vintage Napa Valley cabernet sauvignons, cognacs from the old days. And these we drank like Keene's Cane. I guzzled hundred-year-old red wine. I threw down the ancient cognac. I screwed Elma in different rooms of the house, on the lawn beside marble statues of naked Gods, on top of a billiards table, leaving a nearly circular wet spot on the felt. I bent her over antique tables and she tied me to the banisters and left me there for two hours before coming back and blowing me.

Then the patrols and drills ended and the troops came and we rioted with them. I passed around the supply of peyote and mushrooms. We spent days on end hallucinating. They drank until they passed out. The halls were covered in piss and vomit. They shat in the unused rooms. Soon the smell of shit pervaded the walls. I started to sneeze a lot. I vomited. But that was the peyote. Maybe. The old lady was gassed. She didn't speak, she cackled. She cackled at the soldiers, looping her arms across their backs and shaking her head. "Go spill some blood for me!"

Junior finally had had it. His Barachas were getting soft. They needed to fight, to die, to take revenge, to kill. He paced the marble floors, striding behind the black and red columns like a forest of old trees, his shadow casting up the halls, while we unzipped ourselves into that fast silence. The old lady was ranting on the couch with soldiers who had hacked hundreds of people to pieces, some in her sight. She roared out stories of the old days in LA. And Junior, brooding on what had to come next, walked.

One morning he called us all into the great hall. There were now over six hundred soldiers under 20 commanders, organized into units of 5 to 6 fighters each, that could fit into one car. The cars were parked up and down the driveway and in an area by the portico, and on the tennis courts and lawns. Hundreds. The cars were rough, dented, scorched. Wagons arrived from the north, pulled by mulas and oxen, with axles, wheels, compressors, hoses and solar panels. Mechanics worked in the driveway reinforcing the frames and armoring the doors and roofs. Automatic weapons and flamethrowers were mounted on the hoods. Blastglass and solid tires were installed, and the wheel wells extended. The suspension of each car was re-calibrated for driving over dry riverbeds. Some were outfitted with cannon and mortars; others were stripped out to transport gear. Day and night the sound of pneumatic wrenches and hammers filled the air and mingled with the smell of blowtorches and metal.

The soldiers wore black uniforms and berets. They filed into the long hall and stood in straight lines at attention, between the black columns, arms at their side, stinking of sex, champagne and whiskey. Junior stood beneath the dome in a long black cape, tall, a little fat, his face fierce and eyes baleful. The crowd clapped and chanted, "Bar-on. Bar-on."

He raised his hands to quiet them. "Barachas!" Junior said. They fell silent. He saluted them and they saluted back. "Friends, at ease."

"Baron! Bar-on!" they shouted, calling out and wolf whistling until he smiled faintly, and it was dead quiet.

"Friends, Barachas, we grow soft. Although our days are spent in drills, we are still separate bands more dedicated to plunder and drinking than accomplishing the great and difficult task that lies before us. These are not days of pleasure, but of sacrifice. You have worked hard by day and played at night as if tomorrow you would be dead. Now is the time to come together to take back what is ours. We come from all corners of Sur Califas, from the barrios and villages of LA Yaanga, from the Hills, the canyons and the valleys. We are many people. We are Anglos and Angelinos; we are the first people of the Earth and the newly arrived. Friends! We must become a single body, a fist to take back with blood and fire what was ours!

"Tomorrow we strike. At dawn the Torrance, Beverly Hills and Needles units will roll out and go west to hunt down the Rulers in their villages. After that, other units will follow. Starting tomorrow we will roll across the land in waves. There are no innocents in this battle. Who shows mercy is a traitor. Blacken your hearts, be deaf to their cries, let their pain, their agony remind you of all you have lost, and remember the look on the face of your dying child as you take one of theirs. Did Lord Otis show mercy to you in your homes? Did he hold back the machete when it was your mother who lay on the floor in a wallow of blood? We begged their mercy and Lord Otis struck us down where we stood. Nothing in our path shall live. Go now my friends, rest and prepare for victory." All erupted with calls and cheers and cries of "Baron! Baron!"

The next morning I was sleeping soundly, curled half up to Elma, who had crawled into the bed after getting up to pee. Irmela was on my other side, her hand on my shoulder. In the dark I felt Junior's fusca against my ear. And then his voice. "It's time to go, Bob."

"I'm not going," I grumbled, eyes squeezed shut.

"That's not the deal you made. Get up."

"Fuck," I said. My head throbbed, my mouth was sticky and my throat was sore. I stood and puked in the bathroom, brushed my teeth and went out to the cars. The units were half asleep. A few soldiers stood with weapons drawn watching the others slowly load ordinance into the trunks and backseat of the supply vehicle. They loaded rifles and grenade launchers. They laid in flares and concussion mines and vacuum mortars, short grenades. A goggled man with a clipboard checked the cars for water and catalyst. Bix strode about idiotically, his arm swinging. Frank and Jorge flanked Junior, who stood off to the side, his arms folded across his chest, scowling. Five cars, twenty-five Barachas, plus one car for supply. I drove Junior, Bix, Frank and Jorge. We headed down towards Santa Barbara.

The Los Padres forest was crisscrossed by service roads. Systematically we drove these as they wound back and forth, up and down from high to low ground, in search of people to kill. Junior believed there were arms depots and crude factories throughout the hills and the coastal range.

In the hills north of Santa Barbara we came upon signs of a makeshift Ruler village, a camp really, of Morons who had fled the city when it was taken, and lost their Rulers on the drive north. Possibly there were surrogates and Ruler children among them. But they were just humans. If they were making weapons there, I didn't see it. There was a pile of garbage and a few stray dogs milling about it. In the garbage were the bones and pelts of deer and bear. I stopped and all the others behind me halted. Junior got out and smelled the air, then waved out the window to the other cars and we drove along the road till we came to a clearing. There we paused. I looked through binoculars at chickens fluttering by a line of trees. Behind the leaves I could see movement of people, their colorful clothes going by. Children were running into the open, chasing each other, and dogs were chasing the children. Farther off was a small herd of goats in a pen. I handed the binoculars to Junior. "People," I said.

"Are they Chumash?"

"Who could say? I don't see any 'apses."

Junior's expression changed. He engaged. "What's an 'apses look like?"

"'Aps. It's the traditional Chumash home. Like a beehive. They make it out of sea grass and the doorway is made out of a whalebone."

"I promised I wouldn't attack any Chumash villages," he said. "We need them to get supplies in."

We drove closer and could hear the dogs barking and see the kids running back and forth, as if they were playing. But they were screaming. We drove in closer, turned a bend and there was another line of trees, with clothes stretched between some of them and lanterns on the branches. There was a spring and women were filling calabashes with water. They heard us, stood and ran away, leaving the water behind. From the trees came fire. Bullets pinged off the windshield and thudded into the ground. The car behind us stopped and the soldiers piled out, totally disorganized, returning the fire. Everyone else halted. We opened our doors. I stayed behind the wheel. Jorge knelt behind the door and took aim at the trees. Where the puffs of smoke came he laid down a field of fire and men fell out of the branches to the ground in several pieces. Two Barachas dropped to the ground, their heads gone.

The Morons retreated into their camp and shells started to rain down on us. We pushed forward. I got out of the car and crawled on the ground like an ant, trying to avoid fighting, but when the bullets hit the grass near my face I returned fire. We took cover behind the trees. The artillery car rolled forward and unleashed a barrage of shells at goat and chicken pens and huts of lashed timber and palm thatch. An orchard of figs and citrus lay splintered and burning on the ground.

We crouched in the brush taking fire from the huts. Their shells landed wild. Each explosion tore through the air and soon it was blazing hot. Our shells fell on their huts and pens. My face burned from the heat. They fled the fireballs and one-by-one we gunned them down as they ran toward us. Finally, only the weak and unarmed were left standing, and the huts and pens lay in ruins. Slowly we encircled the village. They didn't attempt to run, they were terrified. The old and the young stood weeping and apathetic at the edge of the clearing, knowing it hopeless.

"Round them up," Junior said, his hands on his waist and his face expressionless. There were a couple of dozen people altogether. The air was hazy with smoke. On the ground lay the bloody burned corpses of their fathers, mothers, sons and daughters. The Barachas marched them into the center of the village at gunpoint. We stood in a circle around them, some of the soldiers laughing. Their faces were scorched from battle. Frank lit a cigarette and tossed the pack to Jorge.

"Get in line," Junior said. They stared lifelessly at him, the children clinging to the old, but they did as they were told. They got in line. A kid broke away and ran for the woods. "Get that," Junior said to me. I followed her into the woods but lost sight of her. I was staring off in the direction she had gone, wondering what to do. I didn't want to chase her down, so I wasn't going to do it. The kid gets away.

The people were covered in soot and dirt; their feet were cut and bleeding from running barefoot over hard ground. They cowered behind their hands, shivering and crying softly. Junior walked out and faced them. He looked at each person. They stared at the ground.

"If you tell me where the weapons are, and give up the surviving Rulers you have hidden, I will show mercy."

They said nothing.

"Very well then." Junior nodded his head and Jorge reached out and grabbed the old speckled hand of the bent woman standing next to him, pulled her arm out straight and hacked it off at the shoulder. It came free and he hurled it behind him, spraying blood on the ground. Frank did the same on the other end of the line, to a little girl with glasses. Their cries went up and shattered the air. They brought their machetes down on their necks. They hit randomly into the line of people then, working fast. Off came the heads and arms and legs. They cut them in half at the waist. A flick of their hand and the arm was lopped off and the victim dropped screaming. As panic spread in those first seconds, the people fell to their knees and prayed while others ran about like chickens. The Barachas became frenzied in their pursuit. It was a game, chasing them down in the dirt, swinging their machetes and hacking them to pieces till the blood dripped off of their helmets and gloves and everyone lay dead on the ground.

"Burn the bodies," Junior said. Jorge lugged a can of whale oil out of the car. He poured it over the bodies where they lay mixed up on the ground. Frank lit a flare and tossed it. The flame shot into the sky and spread out over the corpses sending up a black oily smoke that smelled like burning hair and fat. The whole thing took half an hour. When it was over I looked at my hands. They were varnished with soot and blood and grease. My armor was covered in dirt. There were twenty-five of us. Two died and four were injured, lying on the ground. One man had his face blown off. A woman was burned over 90% of her body. They gave her heroin and lay her down on blankets in the supply car. And then there were two men with broken bones. The injured went back in two cars, and we drove on, looking for another village.

Chapter Twenty-Eight

Our activities did not go unnoticed. We were driving back up after sacking a small village not 10 miles from Santa Barbara when our flanks started to buzz. I looked out my window in the side view mirror and there were bikes on our tail and on either side. The mirror shattered and smoke rushed against the side window. Two riders approached my flank from the brush on the bank of the road. I put my helmet on. Up ahead, blocking the way, was a phalanx of obsidian armored Rulers on black warhorses. I hit the brakes. I dove out of the car, under heavy fire. Bullets were zapping by my ear and hitting the dirt not 6 inches from my face. Fire flared against me, singeing my eyelashes. The bikes hissed by. I didn't look; I climbed the bank of the road and took cover behind a stand of young pine.

My fusca was loaded, but I didn't want to give my position away. I looked uphill for an out. The way was steep through heavy brush. Everything had a thorn on it. I couldn't decide what to do. Maybe, I thought, they won't see me. It was a better thought than clawing my way through wolfberry. Anyway, no bike could get to me here, I thought. That was something.

Except I hadn't thought of the horses. One was stepping through the sagebrush. The air smelled like dead animals. I clutched at the soil and ran uphill, into the bush. The thorns and needles tore into my chin and cheek. Sweat ran down into my eyes. I pushed forward helmet first through the wolfberry, the long thorns squeaking and scraping against the visor. They caught in the armor, tearing open burn holes.

I reached a clearing on high ground above the road. Below a firefight was on. Our cars were stopped. The soldiers crouched behind doors, or took positions off the road, in the sagebrush. The horses stamped towards them, snorting and growling and baring their teeth. In rushed about a dozen dogs, swarming between the horses and running ahead, towards the fighters. They shot at the dogs first and the riders gained on them. Batons flashed in the dusk. Five of our soldiers lay smoking out on the ground. The bikes screamed in circles and the Rulers rode into the bullets of our guns and swatted our people down with batons or hit them with short grenades. They hollered as they melted into gravy on the ground. Junior fired back with artillery. Shells wailed and erupted against the black armor of the Ruler horsemen. The horses crashed into each other, or collapsed to the ground. A Ruler rode out and called the retreat. It was Sargon. They vanished down the road.

"Fast," Junior said to Bix.

Bix yelled, "Let's go." I climbed down the path I had beaten with my flesh. No one seemed to notice that I hadn't been there, not with the wounds I had suffered hiding. We bagged our dead and put our wounded into the cars and lumbered up the road for the long ride back to the palace.

When we arrived we walked as one into a plush east wing sitting room with a view of a shade garden, with Greek statuary covered in ivy, and a bronze fountain. There were couches and high-backed sitting chairs arranged around the room, with cherry paneling and floor to ceiling bookcases. Junior walked up to the vaulted windows and stared into the garden, his face set and downcast. When everyone who had been on the raid was seated he faced us and said, "They will be here. Prepare to fire the missiles at Santa Barbara." Bix and Frank left his side. "There is much to do. We'll meet in ten minutes in the main reception hall. You did well today. We suffered losses. And we will honor our fallen when this is done. But now let's get to work." He walked out of the room. I looked at my comrades. Their faces were filthy, blistered, pitted with shrapnel. Their armor was stained and pocked. They stood and I followed them to the reception hall, thinking, I've had it. I'm not doing this again.

Soldiers packed into the hall, facing the rotunda. There stood the Mexican intelligence team that had arrived one day on foot from the north, and moved into the rooms next to Junior's, hardly to be seen again; Bix, his sleeve knotted at the stump; Frank, rubbing his nose and winking at the ground; and Jorge, at attention, off to the right of the others, facing the crowd. Anyone stepping up to the rotunda would have to go by him first.

I took my place behind a fern, by a pillar, where I had a view of the room and the exits. The soldiers were still mismatched. Some had armor and some didn't. There were no consistent uniforms. Some were dressed in dirty street clothes. Their hair was long. The men were bearded. They carried an assortment of weapons, some light, some heavy. There were units with heavy assault weapons and there was one unit of assassins and another of snipers. All had killed, but only some had fought.

We stood at attention. As Junior walked into the center of the rotunda they started to chant, "Ba-ron! Ba-ron!" until it filled the room. "Ba! Ron! Ba! Ron!"

"Friends!" He raised his hands to quiet the army, not exactly smiling, but looking pleased. "Friends, thank you. Now, thank you now. Thank you. Please." They were stomping their boots in rhythm, shouting out, "BA! RON! BA! RON!" The hall shook. Junior smiled and then the hall hushed. The smell of bodies was heavy on the air, sweat and the shit piling up in the rooms, and dirty injuries. "Friends, the Rulers have discovered our location. I am ordering the missiles to be fired at Santa Barbara. We will break them there and they will have to abandon Santa Barbara. Then we will march with General Carlos and the Mexican Army. Together we will seize Monterey and blockade San Francisco. But for now we must prepare for their attack. You will each of you go to your battle stations.

"They will come at us with machines that break you into pieces. They will burn and melt us with their batons and short grenades. Their horses will devour our heads as a reward for killing in battle. You will take them off their motorbikes and break them with your bare hands. You will mow them down like grass. They will know what it is to die because of you. We must burn them off the face of the earth. Ours are the hands that have taken up this task and now to the finish. Go. Prepare to die for victory."

The room exploded with "BA! RON! BA! RON!" Then three trumpets blew and all fell silent as they marched to their stations. Well, that sealed it. I was getting out. Junior had crossed beyond obsession. He strode by wearing green goggles on his head.

I went straight to our rooms. I needed Elma to bandage my face. She had gifted hands and could soothe and heal with them. She would know what to do. The cuts were like welts now, as tiny fibres lodged in the skin. The room was dark. Agatha lay with her mouth open upon the pillow. Elma was applying a compress to her forehead, which she dipped in a metal basin and squeezed out with both hands. Irmela was singing softly and strumming the guitar. She looked at me and stopped singing. "What happened to you?"

"We were in a firefight."

"You fought with fire?" she asked, looking horrified.

I laughed. "Fire, yeah. Explosions and shrapnel and implosions, and melting, and sound shattering. All kinds of shit."

Elma dropped the compress into the basin and wrung it out. She looked at me and blinked. "You are hurt?"

"Yeah," I said.

Irmela stood up and took the compress from Elma and sat next to Agatha on the bed. "It is OK," she said. "Elma will be back. Bob has been hurt. She must help him."

We went to the bathroom. It was a small gymnasium built of rocksalt slabs, wood and stone with walls of glass facing the crowns of trees.

"How did this happen?"

"There was a firefight."

"These are caused by thorns."

"I was cut off, on the side of the road. I had to run up through heavy bush, wolfberry and peachthorn." She looked sad as she worked bathing the cuts on my face and legs in warm seawater, tweezing out needles, thorns and burs. "What's wrong?" I asked.

"You saw! Agatha."

"Did she finally drink too much?"

Elma frowned at her lap. "Do not joke now. She has had a relapse. I have no medicine."

"Have you searched the place?"

"There are antibiotics and antivirals. There is barely any soap. You must bathe now, in the hot tub. Then you must sit in the cold seawater pool."

I got in the hot tub, and the cuts felt like they were tearing open. "Ah!" I yelled.

"I don't know what to do for Agatha."

"Well, we're getting out of here, that's what. He's gone nuts and wants to take us all down with him. What we faced today was the tip of the spear. Sargon."

She hugged herself and said, "Agatha cannot travel now. Here at least we have an army to protect us."

"You don't know what's about to happen. I told you he's crazy. He's going to shell Santa Barbara. How many missiles can he have? Then what? He and his band of 900 descend on Santa Barbara? They'll be all over this place. It will be Armageddon."

I looked at the bath water and there was Junior's face looking up at me, saying, "No Bob, we're meeting the Mexican army there in two weeks. We are going to draw the Rulers east with those missiles and hold them off until Carlos can attack from the south."

"Do you mind, Junior? I'd like my privacy."

"You have no privacy here. I am always in the room."

"OK *Baron.*" I stood. Elma trembled as she wrapped me in a towel and sat me at the mirror and applied salve and bandages to my face, all around the mouth and chin, and a long one on the jaw, and up and down both legs. Junior stood watching from the doorway silently, a dark brooding frown on his face, his black eyebrows furrowed.

He did not follow us back to our room. It was dark except for one light against the wall that that was like the sun setting behind the bed. I paced back and forth and said, "The fact that he has a plan changes nothing. Crazy people make detailed plans all the time."

Elma bathed Agatha's forehead, her face turned slightly towards the wall. "He listens!" she said. "We must be respectful and obey the law."

From the other bed Irmela said, "I am for leaving. This place is no good. We can take care of her on the road."

"It is too dangerous."

I blew up. "You don't know what it's like! It's fucking terrifying. Bullets and blood everywhere, flying through the air, your face burning, and the stench. I want out of it."

Irmela said, "We must listen to him."

"You always look for the pimp, and then blame me. I am done listening," Elma said. "You must be quiet now, you are disturbing Agatha."

"Then we are going to the Mink Room," Irmela said. We liked to drink in the Mink Room. It was a room with images and statues of minks and mink fur pillows and upholstery. There was a short wall covered in mink.

The chairs were especially comfortable. I screwed Elma in them more than once. They were so big we could curl up on one chair and go down on each other. It had a view of a miniature Zen monastery with trees and streams and cliffs, to scale.

Irmela lit a cigarette and lay down in a chair, her feet a foot off the floor, skin glowing pale white on the black fur and her eyes dark. "Why do you want to go?"

I opened a bottle of wine and handed it to her, and then another, which I drank from.

"Because I'm scared. I don't want to run into a troop of Rulers on those man-eating horses. And I certainly don't want to be caught on the losing side."

Irmela flinched and drank. "Then we must go."

"You have to talk Elma into it."

"Agatha is very ill. We are going to go, soon. I can feel it."

"I can't feel that yet."

"If you see it my way, it will not be difficult. You are very smart for a plan. I just do things."

I thought about that. "That's part of your plan, saying things like that. So what's the plan?"

"It is not plan. I will give her medication for pain. There is heroin in the house; I have found it."

"Elma will never let us do that."

"She trusts me to do the injections. I do not know how to make the heroin powder so you can inject it."

"I might know something about that, in theory," I said. "We need a spoon and a candle and a syringe. Oh yeah, and something to tie her arm off with. One of Elma's belts will do."

"Ew. That is barbaric."

"Whatever it is, that's how you do it."

"We must do something else."

"You could put it in her cigarettes. But that won't kill her."

"I will find my method and opportunity," she said. "And then we will go?"

I guzzled some red wine. "We'll go." I opened another bottle and sat on the floor in front of her chair, my head back on the seat cushion, between her legs.

"Where?"

"Topanga. We've got to go find the old lady's silver and pearls."

"And if that's no good?"

"We can go to my pod."

"Goyaałé Street." She put her hand on my face and stroked my temples. I stretched out my legs. She put her feet on my chest and squeezed my ears between her thighs. I wanted to turn around and do something, but it was so comfortable, I couldn't move.

Chapter Twenty-Nine

Junior walked into the reception hall just as I was heading out to the car. "Bob," he said. He was dressed in his black uniform with green goggles. The glass magnified and obscured his eyes. It was hard to gauge his mood but he wasn't smiling. High sun filtered in through the redwoods. "Come, we are firing the missiles now!" He seized my elbow in excitement. "We've been together a long time Bob. Do you realize that?"

"I do realize that."

"Since you were a young man. Since I was a young man." He laughed gently, leading me away from the door and down the reception hall. "When they chant *Bar-on, Bar-on!* I feel that I ought to be doing something, and I don't know what it is. But now I know. This, this here, these missiles, this time, this is what it has been about all along." Junior bustled along. The Mexican long ops fell in next to Junior and then, on the other side, Jorge and Bix and Frank. The top dogs from each unit joined us as we headed down the iron stairs, underground, to the utility floors and from there out to the command and control center for security systems, in the armory. We walked tubes and tiled rooms and concrete tanks and glass alleyways and light walls until we reached the room. It was not large enough for the dozens of people squeezing into the corridor, so they spread out and watched through the thick curved glass walls.

Junior stared into a depth monitor, the green goggles glowing as the images passed by. His mouth was set. Bix, Frank and Jorge, also in green goggles, crowded around him. He raised his hand and said, "On a count of five." A giant screen came to life: a picture of green leaves shaking in the breeze and blue sky. "Five, four, three," the room grew quiet. We were watching the green leaves. "Two, one, blast off!" The green leaves shook and a geyser of gas engulfed the screen. It cleared and there was only blue sky. We watched the blue sky for a while. There was some coughing, scattered at first, spreading from person to person and becoming continuous. And then, on the bottom of the screen, an arc of color appeared, and it grew and grew until it filled the entire screen. Buildings. Buildings hurtled into view and then flame consumed everything. There was loud steady applause, whistles and cheers of "BA-RON! BA-RON!"

"Commence firing multiple salvos. I want ten rounds altogether. Friends, it has begun! Now, to your stations. I want heavy artillery in position. Send out probes. Scout two miles beyond the periphery."

Now the screen divided into four, and ten times we watched the missiles launch, fly and hit. The crowd in the corridor pressed into the room. The glass was fogging up. All came in to embrace Junior. They shook his hand. They kissed his cheeks. They knelt and kissed his ring. He knew what to do with everyone.

I squirmed out, gasping for air when finally released into an empty hall. Somehow I got into a wing of the house I knew. It was near the zoo but I didn't want to go there, no. I ran back to the room. Agatha was sitting up in bed, taking some soup.

"It's time," I said. "She's better. We can go."

"No," Elma said. "I won't discuss this here, it is upsetting. Anger is upsetting. I feel sick to my stomach. I want to vomit."

Agatha made a face and waved her hand. "He's right," she muttered. "I don't care anymore. I'm tired of this."

"You mustn't say that," Elma said.

"I'm beginning to feel pain again," she said.

"There's heroin here," I said.

Agatha raised her eyebrows. "I used to like a bit of heroin now and again in my day. We smoked it in college."

Elma said, "It is very addictive."

The old lady laughed. "My health is in danger." She laughed so hard it became a gargle. She started to gasp, came undone and collapsed, making sucking noises with her mouth, her eyes bulging. Elma fell on her and cried out. She gently shifted her around on the bed so that she was laid out correctly for later stacking. Her breathing eased.

"She needs oxygen sometimes, if she gets too excited. But it is the incontinence that will be a problem. We must have linens."

"Oh why not," I said. "Every other room is full of shit."

"I will look for the linens tomorrow."

"There won't be a tomorrow. Tomorrow you'll only need those bed sheets to hang yourself with."

Elma said, "Why did I ever love you?"

My heart constricted. "Why did you ever what?" There was a thud and a muffled explosion. Plaster fell from the ceiling. "Shit."

"I am staying."

I grabbed both of her hands. "You loved me because you knew it was us all along. There wasn't any other way." She smiled at me and then her face soured. She burped and ran out of the room.

278 Gaha: Babes of the Abyss

A few minutes later Irmela came in. "She won't tell me what's wrong. Did you see?"

"See what?"

"That there is something wrong. She is in the bathroom. Again. That makes three times since the morning."

"She said she needed to puke. I thought it was more of her mishegas."

"What was that boom?"

"Retribution."

"So now is the time." Irmela went over to Agatha and placed her cheek above her nose. She touched her mouth and felt her skin and listened to her chest. She placed her hand over Agatha's face and squeezed her nostrils shut and covered her mouth. The old lady started to squirm but she had no strength and her limbs didn't respond. She held her like that until she was still. When she was done Irmela adjusted the old lady's head on the pillow, so it was turned slightly away and said, "Now we can leave."

"Fuck," I said. "Yeah, I guess we can."

Elma came in wiping her mouth with a washcloth. "That's the third time today I threw up." She rubbed her breasts and made a stink face. The walls shook and there was a thudding in the corridor. She looked around and then over at Agatha and her eyes wilted with weariness. She sat down and when the mattress sank, Agatha's head rolled over. Elma touched her cheek. "Huh! What happened? Why didn't you get me?"

I asked, "What's wrong?"

"Look." She cried out and beat her thighs. She wept and wailed, as if her body had been ripped open. I tried to calm her down. "Leave me alone!" she cried. She screamed and cried out and fell down next to Agatha. "What happened? Why didn't you get me?"

Irmela said nothing. I said, "We didn't know anything was wrong. Let's go. Do you want to take her with us?"

Elma stared at me, her whole body trembling and her face red. She tried to speak but nothing came out. It was like she was all knotted around in herself, strangled on thoughts. And I thought, I don't know what I am doing. And I thought, where am I. What is this place? The car. I had to get the car. The windows were vibrating and turning colors as the heavy ordinance fell. A siren went off. There was a distant swooshing of rockets leaving tubes, and then frump, frump, frump. An odor passed through the building on a puff of air. And then the suction. I looked out the windows through the bent blue glass at the trees and waited for the roar of the air sucking skyward.

Irmela took Elma's elbow and said into her face something I didn't understand. Elma said, "If we must do that." Light concussed in the air and the windows vibrated and stretched thin, bulging before they blew out. The blankets on the beds, empty wine bottles, Irmela's book, everything was sucked out through the jagged edges of the glass and disappeared into the sky. Then all was still and quiet and the light was yellow. The air pouring in from outside was hot. Isolated dots of flame broke out across the ceiling.

"Let's go," I said. They followed me out into the hallway. It was empty. Everyone had taken up positions or was in the bunkers beneath the armory. The ceiling lights were out, only the emergency lights along the floor were on. I passed through doors and looked back to see holographic soldiers in black berets standing guard.

The reception hall was as dark as it was on our arrival. We ran between the black columns and palms till we reached the rotunda, which was weakly lit by filtered sun. Smoke wisped over the dome. I pulled the brass ring of the door with two hands. Shells screamed down a short distance away. The driveway was pounded into rubble. The towers were smoking piles of rock. But all the cars were parked as usual, to the right of the portico, out in the open. I ran. I ran out and ran zigzag as hard as I could to the car, opened the door and started it up. I pulled under the portico and Elma got in front and Irmela got in back. I jerked out and drove over the flowerbeds and green lawns, onto an access road that went out of the property through dense wood. Now the air was lit up by explosions, and there was the sound of soldiers getting knocked to pieces. It was dark with smoke and dusk. An explosion to the right rocked the car, shrapnel ripping through the side and missing us. I drove my foot forward and thought, I'm fucking dead. And then I didn't think at all, I was a ball of fear that could drive. I drove into explosions and ripping flame bomblets and spitting metal. It kadanked off the car but I drove. I drove through it.

The sound was less furious, it wumped and thumped. The ground was higher and the forest gave way to scrub oak and boxthorn. We drove down to low ground and made our way out towards the Seven Villages. By nightfall we were in the wilderness, not a soldier in sight. We pulled well off the road and slept out on the ground behind some kiinarabi. Before dawn Irmela heard a bear so we got up and were on the road again, driving on baked mud.

That afternoon we made the Seven Villages. On the main road, in the middle of hills of txaparil and stone was a roadblock. The car was rattling and clanking along, coughing steam, the windows starred and chipped. I came to a halt and a man on a horse rode up alongside the door and motioned for me to roll down the window, which I did. He held a rifle across the saddle. His face was brown and wrinkled. He wore black goggles and silver wrap. He said, "Good afternoon sir."

I nodded

"What's your business here?"

"I'm trying to get home, that's all."

"And where's home?"

"Topanga Canyon."

He looked at me closely. "And uh, where are you coming from?"

"From in there."

"In there?"

"Right. The forest. We were in the forest and fighting broke out and we got out of there."

"By the looks of your car, you were in a battle."

"Trying not to be."

He looked at Elma and then motioned to Irmela to roll down her window. It cracked into three pieces and fell on the ground as she lowered it. Now the car would be as hot as the road.

"Around here," he said, "we don't take sides in it. This doesn't concern us. So if you're thinking of bringing those troubles into this country, I'm going to have to tell you to leave."

"Well I got plenty of family around. Growing up I spent summers here. I still have cousins, aunts, uncles."

"What's your name?"

"Bob Martin."

He glanced the car over. "What's your mother's name?"

"They called her Maria. She married my father, Rock Martin, from LA Yaanga, and took his name. Her mother was Etta Hernandez and her father was Ralph, I never knew another name for him. Maybe Lost Bear. That was a long time ago. That's who I used to stay with."

"Didn't she move down to Long Beach?"

"A long time ago. She lives in Barstow now."

"I don't know about Barstow. They might kill you there. On the other hand, I wouldn't want to drive into Topanga either, not anywhere near it."

"Is there fighting still? That's what we came up here to get away from."

"You're lucky nothing ate you in there. As for fighting, it never stops. The Mexican army came in behind the Barachas and blew the place to hell. There are refugee camps in the Hollywood Hills. But the battle you ran away from was the Rulers against the Barachas. That's what they said on the news anyway."

"This is in the news?"

"Yeah. All day long."

"I haven't been around TV or radio or anything."

"You're not the only one. You can camp here overnight. There's water nearby. I'll see you off in the morning."

We put up the tent and walked the short trail into a gully with a clear running stream. I washed and brought water up to boil for the next day, and to have tea. In the morning I would take on water for the car. Elma had a fire going. We ate chocolate, dates and pinyons and some rice cakes Elma had in her bag. It was chilly when the sun went down. We huddled together on the ground in front of the fire.

"Tomorrow we are going to Topanga," I said. "I have no idea what to expect."

"Then let's not go," Elma said. "Let's stay here."

"We weren't invited."

"But you have a right. Your people live in these villages."

"That got us a night. Look, everyone going in or out of there came through these passes. Not only us, but those long ops. The oxcarts of weapons. They know who we are, or suspect it. They're afraid the Rulers will come in next, and kill them all for harboring an outlaw. So we gotta beat it fast and get out of Indian country. There's also the house and the money to think about."

"What house and what money?" Elma asked. "All we have is the clothes on our backs."

Irmela rolled her eyes and said, "The house we now own. And the jewels he thinks she stashed there."

Elma turned to Irmela and squinted.

"She's right," I said. "Soon as Mexico takes Santa Monica we have to go to court with that will."

Elma said nothing. She pulled her knees to her chest and rested her head on them.

Chapter Thirty

Simi Valley was quiet. There was no visible damage although the road down had the occasional burnt-out wreck and pieces of bodies not yet eaten. The Vietnamese Catholic villages were empty and the rice paddies were dried patches of bleached stubble. The vines and orchards weren't pruned, picked or tended. The lawns were dry meadows. Up ahead something that looked like a human disappeared into the brush on the roadside. The roads into the canyons were dark. A few trucks raced by with escorts. I drove off the road to let them pass. Elma said, "Please, I have to stop."

"OK." I slowed down and she opened her window, her hand on her mouth. "Hold on." Dust was swirling around us and up into the hot empty sky. She pushed open the door and half fell out, vomiting on the ground. She staggered away from the car and bent over and puked again.

Elma got into the car and said, "I'm going to get good at this I guess."

Irmela said, "Like the Romans with the feathers."

"But they were the gluttons," Elma said.

"I only make myself puke when I get too fat," Irmela said.

"I used to puke for revenge," I said.

Irmela laughed and lay her head down on the back of the front seat. "How do you do that?"

"Well, like the first time was a bet. Some guy bet me I couldn't make myself puke. I said sure and stuck my finger down my throat and heaved on the guy. It was easy to do and it came in handy. If I didn't like someone, I'd puke on them. Or if someone is trying to rob you, start puking, they'll run off. I got out of a lot beatings that way."

Elma said, "There are no people anywhere."

"No people," I said. "I wonder what that means."

In Topanga Canyon every house we passed was a pile of bricks and beams. The hillsides were cratered and none of the tall trees had leaves. There were a couple of cars on the road driven by people with black rings around their eyes and thin faces. Here and there stood a house or a dome completely intact. Cars in the driveway, horses in the barn.

As we drove up to the house the xangoes panicked in the leafless trees and raced screaming back and forth, throwing shit down at the car. The house looked normal at first. The wood and stone were intact and aside from a few tiles blown off the roof it was fine. Only the low lying shrubs, and trees, the bananas and young mangoes and papaya, and a few lemons, were in full leaf. All the other trees were skeletal against the blue sky. The gardens were overgrown and brown.

On close inspection things were not right. There was no glass in the windows and the window paint was peeling and charred. There were cracks in the foundation. I ran up to the front door and pushed it open. The old brass knob was wrinkled and black. It smelled like the gasses and broken air of battle, the grit of burning metal, of vaporized glass and bodies, fat, bone and gristle cooking in the road. Inside was dark and the air was strong with the scent of dried mold and animal piss. I tried the switches but there was no power. Irmela and Elma came inside.

Elma said, "So it is still here."

"Yeah, and it's ours now," I said.

Elma put her blue eyes on mine and said nothing.

"Where will we sleep?" Irmela asked. "I do not like these animals."

We went down to the bedrooms. Someone had been sleeping in my room and had used the guest room as a toilet. Their shit formed a perfect pile in the exact center of the room. I don't know how he did it without a stool, unless his legs were very long.

"Ew," Irmela said. "Why do they do that?"

"Same reason the Barachas did it in the Summer Palace," I said. "Power. Territory."

Elma said, "Oh yes. The monkeys. It is not necessary to live like that."

Irmela said, "The people and the monkeys are the same."

"You mean like me?" I said. "Cause I'm not a Ruler?"

Irmela laughed and said, "No you are just monkey because that's what you are."

Elma laughed and said something fast in Austrian and then, "He is more dog than monkey, and still is the ass violin. Scheisse!"

"You know, I want one day to know what the fuck it is you two are talking about."

We went up to the living room. Animals had chewed holes into the upholstery of the couches and chairs. Agatha's mattress was eaten down to the springs. Leaves and sticks were strewn about the room. There were yellow stains on the walls where wind had blown the rain in. The curtains were gone.

"This is where we sleep then?" Elma asked. She sat down on the couch and lay down sideways, asleep.

"I do not want to sleep on the couch. Help me to clear a space on the floor? Will you?" Irmela asked.

"The air in here is bad," I said. "Spores. Bats. Roof rats." At least it was a stone floor.

There were clean blankets in the cedar chest in the corner, still dry. I swept as much of the floor as I could, but even the broom was dirty. It needed to be scrubbed. We laid the blankets out and lay down. A hot wind blew through the dark. There wasn't a light on anywhere, no glow from Malibu. Not even Santa Monica or LA Yaanga colored the sky, which was black, with a swirling blaze of stars.

Elma couldn't get off the couch. She had not kept food down since the day we left the palace. She was gaunt. I stood with my back to the empty window, hot air blowing on my neck. I was sweating. It broke out on my head and ran down my back in a stream. There was a gourd bowl by the side of the couch in case she got sick. Elma covered her eyes with her hand and said, "I can't look at the light." The room was in blue shadow.

Irmela said, "We need to find a doctor."

I said, "I guess we should just call one up."

"No doctor," Elma whispered. She hiccupped and sat up, then stumbled through the French doors. She crawled down the stairs. The front door opened and closed.

Irmela's hair had grown since she last had hair dye and it glowed, every follicle of it lit up all the time, but at a nearly frigid frequency, so the glow was like the light in ice at the Winter Museum. And her eyes were the color of water at the bottom of a drain. "I am worried. It is because of Agatha that she is sick."

"What the fuck does that mean?"

"When she feels grief it makes her sick. She has lost some of her heart when Agatha died."

"If a doctor can't help, then why I should get one?"

"Because I know she must see a doctor."

The land all about was dry. The lawns and gardens were dead without water. The hills were brown. Up north the sky was grey with smoke. There was a column of fire below that smoke, out of sight. The ocean was still. "I don't know how to find a doctor."

"In Malibu there must be a doctor."

"We don't know what's down there. We don't know what's going on."

"I will go out walking and find the people and ask them for the doctor," she said. "And you must come with me to ask."

I laughed. "You're a pisser. OK. Let's go." I took the fusca. We walked up the driveway, past Elma who was puking in the banana trees, the xango motherfuckers yacking overhead.

The next lot was the Spanish colonial owned by Frank Orsba and Arphe Lux. It was a nice place. I sold it twice. And lived in it between sales. It was a pile of sticks and plaster topped with broken roof tiles. Something darted out of the pile and I pulled the fusca. Whatever it was ran off.

"It was a dog," Irmela said.

"No, it was smaller than a dog."

"It was a dog. I can smell it."

"What else do you smell?"

She sniffed the air. "Dead people are inside." She pointed at the rubble with her nose. Her eyes briefly looked like the sky and then darkened.

"Squatters."

Every house was the same story. The road was dusty and hot without the shade of the cottonwood, eucalyptus and pepper trees. I was thirsty. After an hour or so we came to a house that was standing. It was a split-level ranch. It had power and the lawn was green. There was water in the fountain in the formal garden on the side, and in the driveway rills threaded the entrance.

The door had a Medusa head knocker. I lifted it and let it smack a few times against the striker. Footsteps approached and a voice said, "What do you want?"

I said, "A doctor."

"What for?"

"A sick woman," Irmela said. "She has some parasite."

"Just a minute." There were steps away from the door. A moment later the locks opened and the door swung in. A man in a red Oxford shirt and white slacks was standing there with an outrageous blunderbuss, an old war weapon that fires an exploding vacuum shell. He had short hair, a young, healthy face, clean shaven, with a straight nose and grassy blue eyes. "I'm a chiropractor. I think I can at least take a look at her. If I can trust you. So you should know, I've fired this thing off. I know exactly what it can do. And I will fire it. Is that clear?"

"Yessir that's clear," I said. Irmela took my arm.

He smiled, wary but not murderous and said, "My name's Pyotr."

"Bob, and this here's Irmela."

"Bob. And Irmela. That's an unusual name. Where are you from?"

Irmela said, "Austria mostly. And Montreal. And where is *Pyotr* from? Mars perhaps?" She smiled the way she smiled at a ball headed for her flipper.

"Maybe, I'm an Ares. Did you come up the road or down the road?"

"Up the road," I said.

"How is it down there?"

"Not good. There's not a leaf left on the big trees," I answered. Irmela looked at him with sad pale eyes.

"Where've you been?"

I said, "Kidnapped by Barachas and taken to a fortress in the Los Padres."

Pyotr locked his door and we headed out to the road, he with his blaster on his shoulder and I with Irmela on my arm. He said, "The Barachas drove out most everyone they didn't maim or kill. Then the Mexican army came in with heavy weapons and destroyed as much as possible before moving up to Santa Barbara. Two weeks ago wrecking operations were still going on."

Irmela said, "We saw the battle of the Rulers and the Barachas."

He paused and nodded. "Really. Well you must tell me about it. The few of us left here don't get any news, unless a stranger comes by. I'm sure you know what that means."

"I can't tell you any news," I said. "But we saw the Rulers take down a division of Barachas. When we left, their fortress was burning and their lines were in disarray."

"That must mean the battle for Santa Barbara is on. It will be decided there. The Ruler Sargon and General Carlos. The Ruler Sargon is untested."

"I have seen the Ruler Sargon," I said. "I've talked to him."

"Really? He has a presence on a horse marching through a square. But they all look good doing that."

"Ocktomann 4 knew how to ride a horse and wear braid. But he wasn't any better than Bard 3."

"Well, I suppose we'll find out. If they've defeated the Barachas they may have the upper hand. The whole Mexican strategy hung on the Barachas taking the interior and attacking from behind."

"Junior, Baron—"

"Baron! The butcher. Was he your captor?"

"Yes, it was the Baron who took us. We were forced to march through the forest and imprisoned most brutally. They sodomized my wife and her sister."

"Had it been Rulers they would have sodomized you."

"Maybe so. Why is your house standing? What did you do?"

He shrugged and put his hands in his pockets. "I didn't do a thing. I was too afraid to leave. I should have been one of the people who died shivering in their houses. When the shelling was done my house was unharmed. My power and climate systems were functional. I kept things off at first, but when everyone was dead or gone I figured, what the hell."

"How's Malibu?"

"Occupied by the Mexican Army. You can travel all the way to Long Beach again if you want. Unless they suspect you're a Ruler." He stared at Irmela's hair.

"It's fake," I said. "Painted. She's good at it."

"I don't care either way. Now your wife—"

"Elma." We approached the driveway.

"How old is she?"

"She is twenty seven," Irmela said.

"What are her symptoms?"

"Vomiting. Fatigue. Dehydration," Irmela said.

We entered the house. He winced from the stench and the heat. "You live here?"

"Upstairs it's not as bad."

"Can she move?"

"Mostly."

"Then bring her down here. I'll examine her on the ground. Lay out a bamboo matt." I got a bamboo matt out of the cedar chest and a light blanket and a pillow. Irmela helped Elma down the stairs. She lay down and squeezed her eyes shut. "Can you leave us alone for a bit while I examine her?"

We went out in the garden and drank water. There were no hummingbirds. Irmela put her head in my lap and I stroked her hair. The sun was just peaking overhead and shined down on the edge of the garden. A strong smell of smoke was in the air. I felt lethargic and nauseous, sweating out the water as fast as I could drink it. Irmela was dry and cool. Her long legs were tucked up to her chest. I touched her thighs. They were strong and smooth and eggshell white. A vein was visible. I traced it on her inner leg, the part exposed. She put her arms around my waist. The sweat soaked my shirt. I took it off and she didn't move, but placed her hand flat against my chest and then traced circles around my left and then my right nipple.

There was noise in the house. Running water, a glass being washed. She sat up and I caught my breath, covered my hard on before they came out. Elma was drawn and emaciated, her eyes circled in brown and bloodshot from vomiting. Now she looked depressed too. There were tears in her eyes. He handed Irmela a glass of water and said, "Can you show me round to the garden? Elma says you have botanicals."

Irmela said, "Everything is dead. We don't even have tea except for lemongrass."

He massaged his jaw and leaned the blunderbuss against the table. "I have ginger and peppermint growing at home. Have you tried ginkgo nut?"

Elma grunted.

"Ginkgo is a specific against vomiting. We could also try tincture of *arsenicum* or *gelsemium.*"

Elma frowned.

Irmela looked at her intently and said, "You must do as he says. He is like doctor."

Elma said, "He is back cracker."

"That's true," Pyotr said gently, with a smile. He was attentive of Elma. He looked at her with kind and concerned eyes. He didn't check her out. There was something wrong with him. I wondered what he was after, why he was trying so hard to make her trust him. "And I gave you an adjustment that's very good for your situation. But I had four years of medical training first, and I worked in an integrated practice. If we could get to my office in Malibu I could confirm the diagnoses with a test. But I fear my partners are all dead or gone. At least, I haven't seen any."

"What's she got, amoebas?" I asked.

"Not without bloody stools she doesn't."

Elma gripped her stomach and leaned forward over her lap and groaned. She mumbled, "Why now?"

Irmela's eyes turned to blue flame and widened into circles. "No," she said. "It cannot be."

Pyotr looked at them, puzzled, and I said, "They'll go on like that. So it's a virus then? Or cancer. Maybe she caught cancer off the old lady. Did you tell him about the old lady?"

"Hardly," he said. "Though it is a growth of sorts." Pyotr smiled. "Congratulations, Bob. Elma is pregnant."

Chapter Thirty-One

"I'm going to be a father?" I screamed. I never wanted to have children. They fuck things up. My brother and I almost killed our mother with our appetites and later, my brother's insane war on teachers, police and bosses. When he was found beaten to death and dismembered in a dumpster in San Pedro we weren't surprised, but my mother cried for years and never got over it. It struck her down. It struck me down with anger. I was angry he'd made her cry, that we wouldn't have his paycheck, that I would have to go to work as a longshoreman. I was angry that he put a pain in my heart that didn't go away. I was angry that I had to write the letter to my father. It took a month for the response to make it down from Alcatraz. It had five words. Better off dead. Love Pop. I could stay angry at the world, or say fuck it. Get mine back. Which is what I did. But if there's a baby, that changes everything. You have to protect the baby and the mother. If you don't do that, who are you? Some chump god left out on the road to mark low ground.

Pyotr said, "Take time to let it settle in. Can I borrow a bike?"

"Yeah, why not."

296 Gaha: Babes of the Abyss

"Thank you. I'll just be off then. I'll come by later with herbs and ginger, for medicine."

Irmela stood and walked into the house without a word. The motorcycle roared in the driveway. I heard it fade towards the Pacific Coast Highway. Elma sat up and looked at me, her face wretched, her hair lifeless and dark. The blue of her eyes made my heart beat faster. She looked so weak, so sad, like a baby herself but with an old face, the kind of face you see in soup kitchens in LA Yaanga, where the Indian priests dish out tortillas, beans and fry bread. She took my hands, trembling, and began to cry. "We are in trouble."

I said. "I don't know about babies."

"We must run, go far away where no one will ever find us." She sobbed against my chest. As I held her to me her hair warmed and turned gold. "Who will care for Irmela? She will die without me!" She stood and glared at me. "Don't think I don't know what's going on, what you are planning!"

"I'm not planning anything!"

"I can tell what she feels around you. Ever since we left, since Agatha died."

This was crazy. Nothing had changed. The only thing that had changed was her. Her eyes became angry and wild. "Sit down," I said. She grabbed the side of her head and snarled. "Sit down."

"I am too weak to sit. Dr. Pyotr says I must eat, that soon the vomiting will stop. If you abandon me and go off with her, because she is afraid, and you have seduced her, your intention—"

"Way way way, my intention—"

"It has always been for her. I don't care when she makes the paja with you, because I can't, we are too busy. That is OK. I am not jealous. But do not put your mouth on her and do not fuck her. I will feed you to the rat!"

I laughed. The rat? "*The rat?*"

"Oh shut up." She smiled and sniffled and sat back down. "I am not joking about danger."

There was a rumbling. We had gotten used to sounds and rumbles. We figured they weren't earthquakes, and so far there had been nothing but the occasional truck carrying supplies north. But this was deeper, longer, farther away and it shook the ground. Then more sounds, closer. There was a whistling followed by a loud crack. Elma jumped. "Does it start again?"

"I don't know." I looked around at the naked trees, the still cobalt sky. The heat was enough to peel paint. Nothing stirred. The lizards were hiding in the shade. Only the flies were out.

"We need to clean the house," she said.

"You have more energy?"

"I know what my fate is now. I can do things. It will happen now what they said. I too will end in a bonfire on the street."

"Don't be ridiculous. We don't have much but we have this house. It's fucked up, sure, but we can clean it like you say. And while we're at it, search for the jewels. And I'll get mesh and we'll have screens. We don't need a climate system, do we? It's been OK. I've slept. With the house in our name we can borrow some money, or I'll throw parties again. It doesn't matter who's in charge. The Mexicans had been half running things anyway before all this started."

"Junior has gone too far, General Carlos, all of them. The Rulers will get revenge."

"That may be but we'll be on the winning side, you'll see, I promise."

In the shed there were tools, shovels and trowels for the garden, a lawn mower. I got a big shovel and a garbage bin and dragged it into the house. I wasn't used to work and the sweat poured off of me. I felt like vomiting but I kept at it. I shoveled the perfect pile of shit up and threw out the stuffing from the couches

on the floor, the broken glass and shattered wood and debris.
I threw out the mildewed and dried clothes, stripped the beds.
Sirens screamed up the road, followed by light-armored vehicles.
Elma came into the downstairs bathroom, where I was scrubbing
out the hinoki ofuro and the shower. "There are armed vehicles on
the road. I am worried about Irmela!"

"Relax."

"Relax?"

"Look, she left!"

"Pyotr says it isn't safe. These are Mexican vehicles and they
are headed towards LA, away from the hills."

"Hopefully she's headed in the opposite direction."

"She must have gone to Beverly Hills to play pinball, or
Hollywood."

I put down the sponge and wiped my forehead. "Can you get
me some clean water to drink?"

I sat against the wall panting. It was dark. The air smelled
of cleanser and sweat and mold. My energy was flagging but
something kept me going. The house must be clean, that was the
thing. Elma needed a place to sleep. And I couldn't search it filthy.
In the old days the smell alone would have made me sick. We had
become animals, the months of killing, of blood and travel. Sweat
stung the eye. I went upstairs to the kitchen. Elma was standing at
the front door, listening, my glass of water dripping in her hand. I
drank it down and stood with her. Pyotr rode up the driveway. He
was relaxed, in sun goggles with a silver snood and cape, carrying
a leather shoulder bag.

He smiled. "How's it going?" he asked. When we didn't
respond he nodded. "It's frightening, to be pregnant, I know. But
this is a good thing. The world goes on. Babies make us human."

"Her sister's gone. Rode off on a motorcycle."

"Oh dear," he said. After a while he smiled again. "I brought you some things."

"Come on in," I said.

He looked dubious but entered the house. "Good. You're cleaning up."

"Yeah, I think we were in shock at first."

"Yes, certainly, and you were caring for Elma."

There was the distant sound of a motorcycle approaching. Elma ran back to the door. It got louder and louder, passed the house and faded up the road.

We went out to the garden and sat down in the shade of the awning. He opened the bag. "This is stuff to make tea from, chamomile, sage, peppermint, lemongrass and some fresh ginger. Grate the ginger into hot water. I also brought you honey, the last of it. I don't really need it. After all, the stores will be open soon."

"You think so?" I asked.

"There's also some pills. Dissolve one of each on your tongue morning, noon and night. And you need protein."

"We have tinned fish," I said.

Another motorcycle approached and passed. This time Elma didn't run, she just sat upright and flared her nostrils.

"That's good. What else?"

"Rice and figs. There are some pinyons left."

"That's all fine. Well, I'll check in tomorrow if you like. I'll bring you some eggs. The bantams lay more than I can eat and there's no one left to barter with."

"Please don't go yet," Elma said, not looking at him but in the direction of the road.

He looked at me. The guy wasn't an idiot. I nodded. What did I have to worry about? "OK," he said.

"I'm gonna get back to work," I said.

My fingernails were filthy and chipped and my muscles were sore but the house didn't look half bad. There was a lot left to do, but we would sleep better and the bathrooms were clean enough to use. The smell in the lower rooms was still nasty. I decided to make the living room really nice. It would be fine for a few months without windows, though the bats were making me crazy. I hung up the blankets and linens and washed the walls and floors down. It didn't sparkle exactly. With Pyotr's help I gathered wood from the road and the property and we built a fire by the pool to make rice. The pool water was green, full of mosquito larvae.

"You've got to drain that," he said.

"Easier said than done," I replied. I smoked cheap desert tobacco rolled in newspaper and drank from a bottle of Mekong, which I passed to Pyotr. "The last time we had pool work done it was murder."

"No thank you," Pyotr said. "Then put some fish in there. I'll bring ten over if you like. That's a breeding population I'd say."

In the distance came another motorcycle. Now all three of us were on the alert but didn't dare show it. The buzz got nearer and nearer. It was definitely on the road, then outside the house. It roared into the driveway and putted off. Irmela came into the backyard, in her leather riding suit, and pulled off the helmet. Her head was shaved completely bald. "The news is quite shitty," she said. "But I got some supplies."

Elma glared at her and made an asshole with her lips. "I did not tell you to go to Beverly Hills."

"It does not matter anymore. The road is open. You would not believe what I saw. Trucks full of people." She didn't exactly look sad, but her eyes were grey circles. "I did not know death had undone so many."

"They were dead?" Pyotr asked. Tears rushed into his eyes.

"Yes," she mumbled.

"Where did you go?" he asked.

"Torrance to play pinball, at Tony's." He squinted at her.

"She does this," Elma explained. "How do you think we ended up here?" She wasn't smiling or anything, but she touched my arm.

"I seem to recognize you two," he said, almost to himself.

"Maybe you caught their Austrian folk song act," I said. Elma smacked my arm and smiled.

"He is joking. We worked as nurses."

He nodded. "My mother was Mrs. Arkady. RK. At the Azodiazadora! She loved you."

"Isn't that funny," I said.

"Whatever happened to Agatha Kennedu?" he asked. "That old lady was a kick."

Elma said, "She died."

"I'm sorry," he said. "It's just as well. See, the home was bombed early in the siege. Everyone was killed."

"You're mother too?" Elma asked.

"Yes." He fell silent and stared at the ground.

"Agatha was a mother to me," Elma said.

Chapter Thirty-Two

Elma fell asleep outside in the lounge chair to the sound of shells and explosions raining down on Santa Monica, Malibu, and all the other towns to Santa Barbara. We didn't even know whose shells they were. She wouldn't come in. The smell of fire was strong on the air now and the wind was starting to blow. There were thick clouds of smoke to the north and east.

"I am afraid," Irmela said to her. She didn't move or talk.

"Elma, please come in," I said.

Pyotr had given her an adjustment and left long ago, but not without having a few drinks and singing a few songs. We shared our rice with him, for which he was grateful. "I've been living on toasted wheat germ and oat bran," he explained. "I'll bring dried beans tomorrow, if you like."

It was past 3 AM. The moon had sunk behind the bluff. I tried to make her stand up. "She won't budge," I said.

"Come in," Irmela said. "We cannot stay out here."

Irmela and I staggered up to the house, brushed our teeth and crawled into bed. I needed to sleep, I ached from cleaning and my lungs burned from the chemicals. I grabbed the pillow and shut my eyes and started to fantasize about Elma. I wanted to get up and go outside to her. So I tossed about, eyes squeezed shut and arms folded like a mummy across my chest, not sleeping. Finally I stood.

"Where are you going?" asked Irmela.

"Out to pee."

"Don't stay long."

I grunted and went outside. Mosquitoes bit my ass. The bites swelled up and itched. I didn't care. The stars were intense but vanished under the cool white flashes of exploding ordinance on the horizon. I stood by the chaise. Elma's mouth was half open and she was snoring. I shook her shoulder.

"Don't do that," she murmured.

"I need you."

Elma grunted and didn't move. I swiped at the mosquitoes buzzing in my ear, biting the back of my head. She looked so good lying there but she was inert. I could not rouse her. I went back upstairs completely lit up by lust. Irmela was lying there. Her head was a dull bald ball in the dark. Her eyes were open. I lay down next to her and she said, "I can't sleep, it is no good."

"Neither can I."

Irmela put her arm across my chest and then climbed on top of me. We kissed. We kissed and brought the world down around us. And then we fucked like gods do and made a new one.

In the morning I went out to the pool. It was cool with dew on the dead grass and covering the furniture. Elma sat up. "I will have rice and coffee." She smiled but it was like I didn't see her, she was a bunch of clothes going by. I said, "Me too," and trudged back to the house. We kept the rice in a calabash bowl in a cabinet that would at least be cool and keep rats out. I brought water and a pot and cups for coffee. Elma lit the fire.

"I don't want his fucking fish," I said. "Fuck his fucking fish."

"You would rather have malaria? Think of your child."

"I don't give a shit. I don't want his fucking fish. What kind of a putz offers fish to people?"

"He is not a putz, whatever this putz is."

"It's Austrian!" I said. "If you really spoke Austrian you would know that."

"No, this word putz is not an Austrian word. This is not possible."

"Well, whatever Yiddish is then, and it means an asshole."

"Which asshole is this, the one that is our anus, or the one who is the donkey?"

"That one, the donkey one."

She laughed. "The donkey is a fool with a very large penis."

Irmela drifted down in a white wrap with a brooch. She had found a box of Mrs. De Marcos' clothes in a closet, undamaged, and she was trying different things on. "I could smell the coffee. There are no more books left to read, only the bible in the King James translation, and Goethe. I will read Goethe."

"Gur?"

"*Goethe. Die Leiden des jungen Werthers* in the modern Englische. It is, *The Sorrows of Young Werther.*"

Elma made a face of disgust. "It is so bad that one. In the modern Englische. It is a noise in my ear."

"Then read the bible," I said. "That's what you read in prison and hotel rooms. On rocket ships and submarines. To repent."

"Goethe is more exciting, even in the barbaric translation of some stupid American who did not know German at all, it seems to me."

"No," Elma shook her head in agreement. "There is no question. And the bible has been nothing but trouble. I know. I have been where it began. There is nothing there that is any different now. All the world's the same and people aren't chosen."

The sunrise soaked the air in orange and red and pink. When the sun crested the sky, it was a molten red through a haze of ash and smoke. We fell silent and listened to the wind pick up and drop, and blow across the leafless crowns of the trees.

Pyotr showed up carrying two buckets, one in each hand. His car was out in the driveway. He walked in smiling, cool, with his snood flashing and goggles swallowing glare. "I brought the fish. I had to drive." He set the buckets down. "These won't take any time at all. I've turned mine into a pond."

"How do you cool down?"

"In the mandi."

I laughed. "Of course." A mandi feels cooler than an ofuro or a shower. A mandi is about the coolest thing you can do in the heat. The tiles keep the water cold.

We walked up to the pool. "The road is busy now," he said. "And the sky is not encouraging. What's your plan?"

"Besides staying here?" I asked. Elma was reading an old magazine. She looked up at Pyotr and smiled.

"In case of fire," he said.

I had been thinking about it. "Well, make for LA Yaanga, right?"

"By what road?"

"Topanga to the coast."

"You would go by Santa Monica?"

"If what you say is true, about the route to downtown—"

"I didn't mean that route."

"How would you go then?"

"North. We go up the canyon to the head, to Anza's Road. It threads its way east all the way to the Hollywood Hills."

"That's how I went to Tony's," Irmela said. "And when I came back I did something different, but I don't remember what. There are many roads in there."

"Would you like some figs?" Elma asked. "It is good that I like them. There is nothing else but rice."

"It's a healthy way to eat," he said.

"Bloody, and a lot of it, is how I like to eat," I said.

"You can hunt a monkey. They eat fruit mostly. Their flesh is supposed to be nutty and sweet."

"You eat the xango motherfuckers!" I said.

"No thank you. I don't eat things with human faces."

"That's not it at all. They're dirty and they're mean, that's why they're like people. Their faces don't mean shit."

He gave Elma an adjustment and left. I said to Elma, "I don't like him. Why's he got to hang around here?"

"Because we are the only ones," Elma said. "And he's worried about me. I am his patient."

The pool cleared up. Pyotr brought over some plants and frogs. "Put these in," he said. The sky was dark and hazy with ash. He was wearing a respirator, but not the goggles and snood. He stooped by the pool and did all the work himself.

"The fish are great," Elma said. "With the fish and the bats there are no mosquitoes."

I said, "I wouldn't say no mosquitoes, and I also wouldn't say sleeping with bats is much fun. I spend my days thinking I have rabies. Ain't rabies worse than malaria?"

Pyotr was taken aback. "I keep hitting nerves," he said. "Interesting. No, I would say that the probability of one of these bats having rabies is low, whereas the mosquitoes are definitely malarial now. We've been 24 months without eradication."

"Is that right?"

"How long have you lived here?"

"Oh, for years."

"Since the de Marcoses died?"

"No, before that. While they were in Baguio I rented from them. I was the listing agent."

"So you are in real estate?"

"Yes, but it's been a while since I carried a card."

"Real estate's a hard business during war," he observed.

"It's hard all the time. But I could sell snow to a moose."

"Ha ha, how colorful. Yes, I imagine you would, that is, could, do that."

"What time is it?" I asked.

"Ten."

"Day or night?"

"Day."

"I'm going to go get totally drunk and come back later."

One night I asked Elma, "Does he have to always be here? Do you really need an adjustment every day?" She stared at me. "And how long are you going to sleep outside?"

"The inside freaks me out." I looked off in the distance and there was an orange glow in the night sky. It was hard to breathe for the smoke.

"This freaks me out," I said. "And what about him?"

"Pyotr is a good man, he does stuff for us."

"He's suspicious. You heard him talking about how long have I lived here. Am I in real estate."

"You are paranoid. We are in constant danger. Without him, we would not even know that I am pregnant."

"How do we know? What if he's lying? What if he has no idea? He isn't a real doctor, he's a back cracker."

"He isn't lying. And he knows."

"How does he know? He didn't show you a picture, you didn't see it, and it's too small to feel."

"He can feel it. He examined me."

"What?"

She looked at me indignantly. "He examined me!"

"With what?"

She laughed. "His hands. What did you think, his donkey dick?"

"No, I didn't think that. I mean did he put his finger in you?"

"The first man ever to do that!" she scowled. "No. With his hands. He felt my abdomen. He knows, from my symptoms and that my period stopped."

"Like I would notice these days."

"I thought it was grief and stress. I did not think it would happen. At the palace. Like we were under a spell."

I said nothing, knowing that I was under a different spell. While Elma slept on the lounge chair by the pool, I was screwing Irmela and it was getting louder, harder, more desperate as the sky darkened. The air was infernal, hot and thick with soot. The wind blew the fires around us; but if the wind turned, if an ember were to land in the right place, how would we know? The fire would be upon us without warning. There was a silence in our days. Unless Pyotr came, I searched the house. I turned it upside down. I pushed into cavities and crawl spaces. I tapped floors and walls. They sat reading and staring at the sky and the road until night.

I said to Elma, "If you're not coming in, I am going to bed. If the fire comes—"

"I will go in the pool. This is why I sleep here. I am not going to die in a burning house."

I went upstairs to Irmela and asked, "Did you get the car ready today, in case we have to leave?"

"I don't want to talk about that." Irmela pushed me down on the floor. We started to roll around. Soon she was sitting on my face and then I took her from behind and then she got on top. All along I felt possessed by the sweat pouring off my head, the sound of our wet skin slapping... it made me want to howl. And then I howled, "Irmela!" More than once. I crowed it out, and as I did so, as Irmela's tiny tits jiggled over my eyes, and she pushed down and up, our hands locked overhead, the French doors opened and Elma stood over us holding a sheet to her bare breasts.

"Schlampn! Bitch! Oaschloch!" Elma dropped the sheet and pounded her chest with her fists. She let out a wail and sobbed and then stared at Irmela, who sat cross-legged on the floor, gazing back indifferently. "So."

I tried to speak but I couldn't. What was there to say? I had to wait for her to get over it before explaining.

"For how long have you betrayed me?"

Irmela shrugged. "Not long. Except for bricolage."

"Bricolage! Pugh! I do not care about your stupid bricolage. And you." Her eyes narrowed and she looked like a rattlesnake. "Have you nothing to say?" Tears brimmed her eyes.

I shrugged. "Ever since you took care of that old lady it hasn't been right."

Elma said, "That old lady? You mean Agatha. What has she to do with us? Who do you think supported us? And why do you think she would give me money, to ignore her? She made me her heir!" She looked at me and stopped crying. "Of course. Why didn't I know it? You killed her! For the house."

Irmela said quietly, "She did not want to live."

"And we would have been killed," I said. "I would have taken her with us but you wouldn't go and we wouldn't leave you."

"That's right," Irmela said. "We did not betray you then."

Elma turned on her. "My sister. Liar. To protect that man, that killer. God damn you both. I despise you. You are dead to me." She picked up the sheet and said, her chin raised and jaw thrust out, "Good bye." Then she turned her beautiful ass on me and walked out the door. A minute later the motorcycle coughed and roared down the driveway.

Chapter Thirty-Three

It looked like snow in black and white movies, drifting down through the haze of smoke, covering the dead grass and walkways, the trees and shrubs, and the roof of the house with ash. Irmela sat before the empty window watching it build up on the sill and floor, reading the bible.

"We have to go get her," I said.

"What would be the point?"

"I'm just saying. That fucking asshole she's with? That's one person I would kill if I saw him. And I'd be right too. He seduced her away from us with those adjustments."

"I don't think that's what happened," she said. "He talked to her about things."

"You can't have everything in one man. I hope you aren't planning on joining her."

"You heard what she said." Irmela turned a page. "There is not much point in smoking," she sighed. "But it tastes better than this fire. When do you think it will come?"

"Any time now."

"When are we leaving?"

"Just as soon as we find the silver and pearls and whatever else the old lady had stashed."

"She had no stash."

"She said so, right in front of us."

Irmela put the bible down on the windowsill and looked at me with her pinball eyes, not the daggers she had for pimps, or the asterisks when she didn't want to do something. She said, "Now that you are done ripping apart the house, you should dig up the yard."

That was just what I was thinking, all morning, when I wasn't chasing Elma down and killing, or forgiving her. "I was hoping you would help."

Irmela laughed. "Can we go sledding later? And drink hot cocoa? The one with the marshmallows?"

"What's a sled and what's cocoa with the marshmallows?"

"Xocltl," she said.

"Oh, like to drink, with the white spray?"

"No these were the lumps. And the sled is when you go on the snow in the cart with skis. I saw snow many times," Irmela said. "In the alps. And in the Caucasus. The high passes were covered in snow. We took horse sleighs out into the country and hunted bighorn sheep. We slept with bear rugs."

"Was that in Azerbaijan?" I asked. "Or Austria?"

"In Montreal too, at Christmas it snowed and there were yaks. The pork butchers were very happy. And there were men in fur coats selling reindeer meat. That is what I called it. And I pronounced it like, 'renn deeuh'. I didn't want to eat the renn deeuh meat."

"It snowed in LA when my old man was a boy. First time in hundreds of years. He said he still had a snowball saved in his aunt's freezer, but whenever he would tell the story, my mother always said it was a lie. 'Your aunt didn't have no freezer,' she would say. 'She didn't even have an *icebox!*'"

Irmela followed me as I worked the yard with a spade and pick axe. She pushed the wagon with the tools. The ash settled on our hair and shoulders. It clogged the filters of the ventilator. We stopped by the tangerine tree the old lady loved. I said, "She went to this tree every day, once she could get around. Let's try here."

Irmela said nothing.

"Give me that spade," I said. She handed it to me and I put the shovel to the dirt and pushed with my foot. It went in half an inch and stopped. The earth was like a brick with a thin layer of crusted earth on top. I eyed the pickaxe in the wagon and looked at the sky. The sky was blackening, with washes of red and orange and yellow. "You hung out with her. You must remember something."

"Agatha had that purse, and bags on the wheelchair of coins. She wore many necklaces of precious stones, but you would not notice so much unless you undressed her. And then she had little sacks of jewels, and stamps, and rare coins in her clothes and around."

"So where is that stuff then?" I asked.

"At the summer palace."

"Scheisse! You didn't take it? And why did Elma go with that nudlaug? Ugh. I'm talking like you now. Elma's going to be so fucking bored with that pussy doctor of hers!"

"He is not the pussy doctor, he is the chiropractor. And he has movies and TV and radio and food."

"Maybe we should move in with them. That would be funny, huh?"

We moved to the lemon tree. Same story. The soil was baked hard. I asked her for the pickaxe. I hate pickaxes. I never wanted to swing one again. I swung it into the dirt and it clanged, sending shock waves up my arms into my neck and head. A sharp burning pain shot through my neck. "Ahh ahh!" I screamed, throwing it down.

The heat from the fires was spreading and it was pushing 140 degrees. I couldn't breathe. "We have to get out of this," I said. The sky reddened and broke out in lightning forks followed by craterous thunder. The wind was steady at 30 miles per hour, blowing towards the coast. I ran into the house expecting it to be cooler but it wasn't. The paint was pealing and the wood looked like it could combust at any second. The kitchen was dark. The courtyard was caked in ash, the bougainvillea and jacaranda like grey sacks. I soaked towels in water and wrapped my head. I thought I needed to save something, but I couldn't imagine what. The sweat dried on my skin. I took shallow blistering breaths. Ridges of flame licked the windowsills of the house. I ran outside and yelled, "Irmela!"

"Bob," she cried. "In the pool!"

I looked at her. She was up to her neck in the water. I looked out at the tree line. The crowns were haloed with fire. A burning eucalyptus ejected a geyser of flame that raced through the air towards the house. I ran to the pool and dove in next to Irmela, going under as a wave of fire rolled over us and poured over the bluff, burning down to the highway.

I raised my head and gasped and went under again. Irmela was near the bottom, in the murk, with the fish, lying dead still. I decided to see how long she would stay there, if I lived. I came up for air sooner than before. Patches of fire remained but the fire had consumed all the fuel in a matter of minutes and moved on, except for the house. The house was engulfed in a swirl of flame that seemed all one from bottom to top. It swept around and through the windows so fast all within exploded. A single flame stood high in the sky and gloated before dying down into the heap of burning timbers and exploding stone and mortar

It was hot, but not as hot as before. Everything in sight, in all directions, was blackened, including myself.

I sat on the edge of the pool, my feet in the water, staring at the house. I had no thoughts or sensations.

There was not enough light to see Irmela at the bottom of the pool. The water was green, but dark with the sky overhead. I had no desire to get back in, but it was making me nervous, her being down there so long. Elma had said she knew what she was doing. Unless she killed herself out of guilt for betraying Elma.

If she was dead, I'd bury her in the yard and say a rite later at the Peyote Church in Beverly Hills, the place that the Priest took Detreuil to. Those were good days, I thought, when it was me and the girls, with the Priest, Margaret and Detreuil. We had food to eat and clothes on our backs. Now we had nothing.

I walked to the driveway, dripping wet, feet squishing in my shoes, to look at the car. The tires had melted. The paint was scorched off. The interior was charred with soot. I tried to open the trunk. It was stuck. I gave it a couple of kicks and the hood eased up. Within were 4 two-litre containers of water and a bag of chocolate melted all over roasted, salted pinyons. I drank a little of the water and went back to the pool, where I laid my wet clothes and shoes out and waited for Irmela to rise up out of the water. The hot air bit my bared skin.

After a while there was a break in the clouds. Sun struck the water. Irmela stirred. She swam slowly to the surface. "It is gone," she said, climbing out of the pool.

I stood and asked her, "How do you do that?"

"It's just some trick I was born with." She coughed up spoonfuls of water. Her skin was blue and her eyes were like black opals.

"Do you want to dry your clothes before we get Elma?" I asked.

Irmela rolled her eyes and said, "No." She had on white shorts and a clementine-colored tank top that clung to her nipples. She was barefoot. "We cannot go get her. You do not understand."

I sat down on the hot stones and said, "Explain what I don't understand. Because you're right. I don't. I don't understand. Every time this happens one of you feeds me some line and I get so screwed up I don't care."

"You made a Ruler's daughter pregnant. You cannot mingle your line with hers; they will kill you both for that. That is why she ran. She was angry, but she would have run off with him anyway. To save you and to save me."

"But you aren't pregnant."

"No. Because of what our mother did. Elma's father is not my father. My father is from a different place, where our mother went."

"Jerusalem."

"No," she shook her head and stared at the green water. The fire had passed. The frogs and the fish came up and stared at us from among the plants. "Our mother was allowed to go to Mars Quarantine, rather than to die, when they discovered she was pregnant with Elma. And when she went there, she had a child by a Quarantined Ruler, one of the Rebel Rulers of Mars, and that was me."

"You're a Martian Princesse?"

"Phaedra, our mother, was not a Ruler, but she was a Ruler bastard. My father was an outlaw. His line is banished from the Earth. He has the DNA from Mars, and so do I. I was bred to break the quarantine. That is why I can breathe underwater, and why I don't get so hot or so cold. I am a chameleon. I am here to contaminate the Earth." She smiled. "We have not used any birth control ever. Have you not noticed?"

"Why didn't you tell me? Did you think I didn't need to know that? And what about Elma's father? Who is he?"

"No one must know. The man who is Elma's father loved our mother; he lost everything to save her. We must not know who he is or he will destroy us to protect his secret. This is what we are told."

"I'm in love with a Ruler's daughter and I'm fucking a Martian. Right. You've made up so much stuff there's no way to know what to believe!"

"Now you know what the problem is, you see?"

I was dumbfounded. "No. What?"

"Confusion. You are mad who would make sense."

"How long were you on Mars for?"

"Until I was five and Elma was eleven. We left our mother behind. A man smuggled us to Earth, where he was to raise us in secret. I was supposed to marry into a Ruler family, but the man betrayed us and used us for controlled breeding. He harvested eggs. He had stem cells. He was a pimp. They all were. Jedidiah. That is what people called him." She spat.

"Where did you go then?"

"Our rocket landed in Azerbaijan. He took us to our mother's people in the east of Europe. Sofia, Wiener, Pest, Prague, all over. At first it was OK. Our mother's people were Rulers in Donau and they treated us well. Elma knew no one must know who I am, so she said my father was an office clerk in Jerusalem, which is where Jedidiah was from. We went to school in Austria and lived sometimes in Jerusalem with Jedidiah. Immediately he started to rape Elma. And then he got her pregnant as often as possible to harvest the embryos. And they were sold on the black market. He was the first. The night he came for me, Elma killed him with a brick. He was not tall. It was easy. We ran away. Now we always run. You know the rest."

"Why doesn't she get an abortion? Then we could disappear together."

"No! You are an idiot. They will kill us for that too. And for us, to pass the line on is everything. This is what they tell you each day, in their schools, and in their libraries. The story of the old ones goes on. But it is forbidden to talk of things. We have to go. Come."

I looked at her white naked feet. They touched the black ground like hands. I said, "You can't walk barefoot."

"Yes I can. I have done it." She walked away across the smoldering lawn leaving smoking footprints behind.

"Wait for me to get my clothes on!" I shouted.

Chapter Thirty-Four

The road north and south was crowded with refugees, mostly on foot, and in rags, moving past each other in a daze. Irmela and I trudged up north. We passed Pyotr's house. It was burnt to the ground. Everything had been destroyed by fire. Irmela's feet were filthy now, worse than Elma's. The dust blew in our faces. The sun was slanting across the blackened hills, shining into the cloud of smoke boiling out of the fire.

By sunset hundreds were walking the road. We kept to ourselves. Along the way people had set up camps for the night. It was quiet, peaceful. People were sharing food and water. We kept going silently, till late in the night when we sat down by the side of the road and slept until first sun. Then we walked again. We still had not reached the end of fire. We were walking into it. The ground grew hot. Smoke rose from the charcoal spires of fir trees and houses were ablaze. We walked into the hills. There the earth was bulldozed, blasted and bleached, and covered in rolls of razor wire. Trenches lay further back, and behind them pillboxes and abandoned missile batteries.

We walked down through the Hollywood Hills and into West Hollywood where we found ourselves on an interminable line, the end of which we couldn't see. Every few minutes everyone picked their things up and advanced a couple yards forward. If you carried anything you could not simply take it off and relax. The line required constant advancement and vigilance. The road was blasted to pieces; the buildings and bridges and underpasses damaged or destroyed. We squatted by hunks of concrete and rebar waiting for the line to move. I draped the towel over my head.

Hours later, I could see a Ruler checkpoint at the village entrance. Later, obsidian-visored Rulers on battle horses. Then the detachment of bikers behind electric roadblocks. Then, when the sun was low, the batons, dogs and vacuum grenades.

"What are you going to say?" Irmela asked. It was what everyone was asking. The older people ahead of us, with button down shirts and canteens, and the artist family from Topanga behind us, who had followed us all the way.

"I'll say our house was destroyed by fire," I answered.

"But who are you?"

"I'm Bob Martin. I haven't done anything wrong, have I?"

"Well. I can say that I am Irmela von Doderer. I have to. I have scarcode. They will see. I must have hat. Give me your towel please."

I handed it to her. "The hair isn't that visible yet. You only have fuzz."

She wrapped it around her head in a turban. "At night it will be like a torch soon. What if I am standing there when it happens?"

The Rulers on the horses were looking at each person and talking to them, through that fucking black visor they have, what I had bad dreams about as a kid. My heart beat faster. I wanted it to slow down. I thought of being in the ocean with Elma, of the waves and her body pulsing. Irmela looked out through eyes of green tinged sapphire.

The Ruler sat upright on his horse, in silver armor, with black gloves. "Who are you?" he asked.

I could see myself reflected in the beehive mesh beneath the polished black surface of the visor. I said, "Bob Martin, sir."

"And you?"

Irmela stuttered, "Irmela von Doderer, sir."

"Hold out your arm," he said. Irmela stretched her arm towards him slowly. The horse snorted, its nose above her head dripping blood. He, high in the saddle, examined the scarcode without bending forward. "That must have hurt. You're tough? Where from?"

"Topanga."

"Where are you going?"

"With him." Irmela nodded in my direction.

The Ruler asked me, "And where are you going? Why are you coming south?"

"I own a pod on Goyaałé Street, in Puvungna."

"Pu-wha?"

"Long Beach. I own a pod in Long Beach."

"You have some sort of deed?"

"No. Look at me."

"I've been looking at you all day. Well, I'll let them sort you out down there. Go on."

There was a park beyond the checkpoint surrounded with palms and full of dead plants where people were resting. We sat on the ground and I said, "So we need to walk a ways."

Irmela looked at her feet. She had cuts oozing into crusted over blood. It was getting dark. We slept on the ground, curled around each other like dogs and got up at first light. The park was packed cheek to jowl.

We headed south to Torrance, through the barrios and villages. Not a building stood. There were thousands of people milling the streets in rags. As far as I could see in any direction the buildings and domes were reduced to piles of adobe, whitewashed plaster and roof tiles. There were no animals, no dogs, no donkeys or mules; there was not a horse or a goat or a chicken in sight. Just white rubble and people wandering silently, with unfocused eyes, trying to avoid each other. There was no one I could see who wasn't afraid.

In Torrance we headed east to Long Beach and there some buildings were left standing. I didn't know what I would do if the pod was destroyed. But I figured it was underground, we'd at least be able to sleep there. Hoped, anyway. Puvungna is a small village of adobe domes with underground quarters. Each one the same, each with a place to park a bike and a basketball hoop.

"So this is Goyaałé Street?" she asked. Up and down the line the domes were cracked in three pieces. The palm trees didn't give any shade and everything else was dead without water. Out front were my old neighbors sweeping their entrances as if it were any other day, except they were scrawny and had the same dead eyes everyone else had.

"This is the place." The door opened and the pod exhaled a dank odor. The way down was dark. I felt for the light and it went on. The stairs were dirty with debris from the cracked walls, and with trash. I hadn't been there in years. The lower doorseal was good though. It hissed open and the smell wasn't bad, just a little musty, like an old box of stuff.

I put on the lights. People joke about the Jeannie bottle, but it is true, they designed it based on that. The walls were covered in parachute cloth and there was circular seating around a sleeping area. The lamps came on amber soft at first, like last light. It was a little small, but a lot better than a chunk of concrete. The bathroom and kitchen were satellite Jeannie bottles, or what the manufacturer called Little Bellies. We sat down.

"I wonder if there is water?" Irmela asked.

We took the short tunnel to the kitchen pod. There was a vented burner, an oven and water kettle and an icebox. I turned on the spigot. It coughed dust and a thin drizzle of brown sludge fell in the sink. "No showers I guess. The desalination plant must be closed."

"What if Lord Otis comes?" Irmela asked.

"We'll say we live here and this is where we've lived for years. Who's gonna say different?"

We sat down and drank water from our bottles and fell asleep. I slept for a day, maybe more, and woke up in the dark. Irmela wasn't there. I staggered up the stairs, needing to piss. She was squatting in the gutter taking a leak, her head wrapped in a towel.

She stood and said, "I'm going. See you later."

"Wait. I'm going too. I'm hungry. I can't eat more chocolate and pinyons."

We walked into Long Beach. Irmela headed towards the water, hoping to find an open bar with pinball. I went looking for a soup kitchen. There were buildings left standing; plenty of them, but without water, there was not much food around and I had no money. I roamed the streets, back and forth. There was a bookstall, and there were people selling water out of giant cow skins, a buck a shot. There was also booze for sale, two bucks a bottle. I didn't have any silver in my pocket.

I was feeling faint but pressed on to the waterfront. Maybe a hawker would be there, with a tangerine or a papaya. The entire waterfront was under armored guard; tanks wheeled by, their gun turrets turning back and forth, blue current arcing in the muzzles.

I didn't know how late it was. Lanterns went up around the booths on Fremont Street. I walked, lurching about. There was no food anywhere. Just coffee and tea and water, and dried buffalo meat. After passing the yellow lights swaying in front of pieces of jerky, dried squid and sausage several times I stopped to beg a piece of buffalo from the hawker.

"Please," I said. "I've only eaten pinyons and water. I have no money...."

The hawker took down a piece of dried meat, wrapped it in paper and handed it to me. "Don't come back."

"Thank you sir," I said, gnawing the meat as I backed away and headed toward the Chingishnish Church. It was lit up, a white adobe dome three stories high in the center. In the back was a line half a mile long of people waiting for food. I sat down behind a man with a greasy tangle of long blond hair, dressed in a filthy white polo shirt and tomato-colored deck pants. He said, "Is that dried beef you've got?" His lips were cracked and scabbed over. He hadn't shaved but his beard didn't grow so his skin was tanned black and held his green eyes like Venus in the dark.

"Buffalo," I said.

"That's better than beef. And I've got a bottle of bourbon." He pulled a bottle of Heaven Hill out of a wicker backpack stained mahogany by smoke and fat. "I found it."

"Let's eat this and drink that you mean?" I asked.

"Yeah why not. There's got to be more food up there, at the end of the line, don't you think?" He pulled the cork and took a long pull, coughed and handed me the bottle.

"It could be the killing stick," I said. I drank some down, gasped a little and handed him the bottle back. I chewed on the jerky.

"You think?" He took a glug and looked at the jerky. I handed him a hunk and took the bottle.

"I hope not," I said. "But you never know when the killing stick will come."

"That's right," he said. "You don't know that. It's like the Gris Stick."

"The Gris Stick is a *kind* of killing stick." I gave him the whiskey.

He set the bottle down in the road and said, gesturing with his two index fingers, "But with a killing stick you don't get your face stuck in the wood."

"Face? No! The soul, man. That's why it's twisted up. That's a reflection of you in hell."

He tipped the bottle back and swallowed. "I thought all along it wasn't supposed to be a picture. Like your whole face is just froze there, and you are imprisoned in that stick. Like Ariel in the tree."

He handed me the bottle. I glugged some down and wiped my lips with the back of my hand. I could feel the dirt smear in the whiskey and the film of sweat on my lip. "No," I said. "That's you frozen somewhere else that appears here simultaneously as an image. It is like a portal."

"That's right! A portal between worlds," he said. He leaned back on his calves and stirred the dirt with his finger while I drank. I handed him the bottle.

"I've read about that anyway," I said.

"A cunt is a portal between two worlds. On one end is a pointless existence and on the other is everything right with the world. One door, two places. You go in and come out a different man. A man with a soul."

"After I fuck, I don't feel like doing shit," I said. "It's like there's nothing left to do, except maybe get fucked up."

He shook his head and passed the bottle. "I know what you mean."

I looked towards the church. We were 10 blocks away still. People were sprawled out, their feet in the road, lying in the dust with whatever bag of belongings they had. "I wonder if this line's going anywhere?" I asked.

"Every few hours it moves forward. See, they seat a hundred people and feed them. If there are ten thousand, it takes a while. I wish they would dish out some white mush from a big pot over there in the dirt. Just pull up a truck and start feeding us. It's not asking a lot."

I said, "They aren't that fucking organized. These people are chumps."

"Then why are they there and not here?" he asked.

"Why? Because over there are the ones who are even worse than we are. You can be so bad but eventually, if you want to be really *bad,* you have to be in charge."

"This jerky is good man."

"So is this bourbon."

For the first time in a while my stomach felt full and my throat was warm. I took a deep breath and almost wretched from the smell of burning and rotting corpses, of maggoty wounds wrapped in dirty cloth, peed on twice a day, until you have to drink your urine.

"Do you have anything to smoke?" he asked.

"No! And you know, when the war began I got a load of peyote and psilocybin and marijuana. We had tobacco and opium; we had everything you could want. And I had a girl to fuck who was the most beautiful woman in the world. Two of them. Sisters." I sat down in the road, too drunk to squat on my heels. "One them is from Mars."

He looked at the ground and said, "I don't fuck beautiful women. They're not worth the trouble. I like the ugly ones. And a Martian woman? That sounds like a whole lot of trouble. I'm not looking for trouble in a woman."

"Well who the fuck is? I didn't go looking for this, no. But I sure found it. And then, she walks out on me!" I stood up and could feel my lower jaw thrusting forward.

"You are disappointed in romance?"

"Aren't you?" I scratched my belly and belched.

His face fell and he stared at the ground. "I don't remember. I had children. I was married to a woman I loved and liked." He shrugged.

"This buffalo meat is good. I want to go get some more, but I haven't got any money."

"You can get a job rebuilding the desalination plant, if you can do that kind of work."

"I'm looking for a fucking handout," I said. "I'm not working for no pendejo motherfucking Rulers."

"I wouldn't use those Mexican words if I were you."

"No?"

We passed the bottle back and forth and chewed on the smoky buffalo meat. We ate all the jerky, and finished the bourbon. He was going to toss the bottle.

"What are you doing?" I asked.

"Throwing it out."

"Give it to me. We can put water in it. We might need it as a weapon."

I passed out on my hands and awoke two hours later. It was cold. The night sky was sharp with stars. There were scattered yellow lantern lights up and down the road to the church. People all around us were standing up stiffly, shaking off sleep and facing the white dome, where the line had started to advance. We walked forward a block and sat down on some large rubble extending across the sidewalk into the street. There was a flat piece pitched at a low angle and large enough for two to comfortably sit or lie flat on. I stretched out on the concrete and tried to sleep. But

I couldn't stop thinking about the girls. The thoughts danced in tight circles. They came around and around. I wondered where Irmela was and what she was doing. Was she playing pinball or was she slinging her ass on Sunset Strip? Was she someone's slave? And Elma, alone and pregnant surrounded by boy soldiers, who use bayonets to save ammo. They were alone. I was alone. I never used to think about that. Being alone was great, it was the best thing in the world. Before I met them I was always out in the world, with people. But they didn't mean a thing. It was all about a good time. Except for the Priest and maybe Junior, I didn't have a friend. And when I was at home I was alone, and glad of it. No one told me what to do. But now, without them, it was awful. I felt like nothing, like I was the nothing man. Just a big empty middle where the girls used to be. Always laughing and talking in Austrian.

In two hours we advanced another block.

They were in trouble. I could feel it. There were Rulers out there rounding people up and driving them off in trucks. The roadsides were scattered with the burned and drowned and hanged and shot. A lake of blood drying in the sun scattered with hacked off limbs and heads under a veil of black flies. They would be safer in the pod. But I had to stay on the line. I couldn't go out looking for them. They would have to come to me. And I could be on that line for days. If they went to the pod and I wasn't there, and didn't come back, they'd think I'd abandoned them.

Those same thoughts never stopped all that night and into the morning. Around and around they went. I hated it. I never wanted to feel them chase each other like cats. You create a world for yourself so that won't happen. And here it was happening. That meant my world was gone.

Chapter Thirty-Five

It was Irmela who rescued me with two pearls she had won at pinball. Like on that first day we met, she wore them around her neck on two gold chains.

Most days I spent lying on the church food line with my friend. He was clean now; we all were, not dusty for more than a few days. His hair was lemon yellow, and lay down his back in a thick braid. The patches and swirls of white hair were gone from his face and I couldn't smell his decaying teeth in a light breeze anymore.

The line structured my life. It took about 36 hours to get fed, so I was always hungry, always on the line. I can't complain about the amount or the quality of the food. There was meat, buffalo, venison, goat or whale and rice or bread, and fresh fruit and salad. You had two hours to eat all you wanted, and use the showers and baths. Then it was back to the end of the line, unless I had something to do.

Once you start eating, things start to make sense. I knew I could get on the line anytime and eat in 36 hours, so even if I was hungry, I sometimes went to the pod to sleep on foam and cloth, instead of concrete slabs or, worse, bare ground. The bare ground was embedded with glass fibres and metal filings. The pressure blasts drove the fragments into the concrete and, now, when you slept on the ground they got into your skin and festered if you couldn't tweeze them out somehow.

I woke up early one morning, no longer feeling hunger, insensate but well, on the bed, not wishing to be disturbed in any way. Actually, almost hoping to die. Another day without the girls, sitting on a hot road, blasted by the sun, talking to the blond haired man, scratching sores. But lying there in the pod on the foam, the world outside ceased to matter. Soon, it didn't exist. I had no needs or wants. Everything had stopped. The world left me, then I left the world.

Into that void came Irmela, dressed in a knee length black skirt and white collared shirt turned brown by dust, the sleeves rolled up. On her feet were green jellies. Irmela's hair was black and her eyes were like red rocks at dawn. "I'm looking for Elma. I want to tell you that. So you won't worry. And here." She reached behind her neck and unhasped first the one chain and then the other, and held out the two black pearls that had just lain on her pale, dusty chest. I put out my hand and she lowered the pearls until they just touched the palm. The chains dropped and she closed my fingers over them and held me, before pulling away. Then, without a word or change in expression she turned her back and walked out the door.

That was it. She was gone for good. My stupor grew numb, and my brain felt like it was on the ceiling, dazed eyes attached to straws. What had I done wrong? I couldn't figure out why they would both leave me like that, after everything I had done for them. They bring love into it and I go for it and this is what they do? But of the millions of things I considered there was one that could stand for all the others: Time to go. Staying was dangerous. Dangerous for them and for me.

I thought, this is all of love I know, two bodies and no soul.

I dwelled in silence.

Many hours later, out of the extinction I had become, a question formed. Somewhere in the void a spark of myself persisted, blinking on and off. And now it asked, what are you going to do with the pearls? I smiled and looked around the pod, restored to myself and the world. There were pillows thrown against the wall, all the way around. I shook two pillows out of their cases and had sacks for the silver a single pearl would get. With that I would buy water, tobacco, food, and a case of Mekong Whiskey, which I would sell out on the corner for twice whatever I paid. For food there was buffalo jerky and soup. Soup had come back.

Most scheisse oaschgein motherfuckers selling bottles on the street sell food dye and solvent. But I knew from the line about a guy down by the docks who sold cases out the back of real booze. They would sell to me and even if mine cost more, it was real and it didn't kill you. The problem was carrying it. I was weak and it was heavy. Nevertheless I found an exchange operating out of the intact security pod of a bombed out building. The composite shell was exposed and scarred but they dissolved a wall into glass and installed a woman to make change and do wires and all of that. When I got up to the window and deposited the pearl, she looked familiar. When she told me the exchange rate I recognized her voice. She was from Malibu. She looked at me and smiled.

"That's a beautiful pearl," she said, sliding the silver into the sacks. "How did you get it?"

"Playing pinball right here in Long Beach."

"It's a tough pinball town. You must be good."

"I didn't learn playing in Malibu."

"We all know Malibu sucks for pinball. Thank you."

I walked to the buffalo jerky guy. "I told you never to come back," he said, looking at me over his glasses, and hanging a rope of sausage on a hook.

"I have money. I'll pay you for what you gave me and buy an assortment. Who around here has rice?"

"Sometimes there's a guy two blocks down. He cooks it in a barrel. You'll need your own tin."

The pillowcase was no good for that. I'd have to eat rice later. He handed me a paper bag of buffalo sausage, jerky, dried squid, and dried baby sardines. I chewed on the sardines walking towards the warehouse. I needed to rest. I sat under a palm tree and ate jerky and drank water. No one was about so I took a nap.

When I awoke I walked down to the docks. There was frantic activity all about, trucks hauling concrete, cranes, bulldozers, excavators. Surveying bugs crawled on graphite legs beneath the rubble, sending data back to the tower crew. Rolling over this was the Lord Otis's army, the child soldiers on fast bikes with pistols, machetes and whips, tearing between the work crews after outlaws and Mexicans trapped behind lines. Cruising behind them on larger bikes were the Ruler biker patrols. Nothing else could fit between the machines and trucks hauling rubble away.

With the roads in and out of the docks impassable by larger vehicles, a certain trade took root between the biker patrols. I found the metal warehouse on a dirt road with two drainage ditches full of dust and the only shade beneath the roofs, along the walls of buildings. The front half of the warehouse was crushed flat but the back was open. I walked down a narrow alley and up to the truck bays, climbed up and rang the bell. A man opened the door and stuck his face out. He had a full white beard, which flowed out of a thin face of caramel skin. "Where you from?"

"Puvungna, born and raised."

"Who do you know?"

"I don't know no one. My people come from up north in the mountains. Tehachapi."

"You said you was born and raised."

"Practically."

"Then why ain't you know no one"

"I've been away and my mother lives in Barstow now."

"Barstow, eh?"

"Yeah. She lives in a hole in the ground, just like me."

"Watch you want?"

"I hear I can buy a case of clean liquor from you for a fair price. Is that true?"

"If you know no one, where'd you hear that one?"

"Just on the food line. People say."

He stared me in the eyes and shook his head. "OK. Watch you want? I got but one or too."

"Mekong's good."

"I can give you," he stroked his beard, "up to ten cases."

"I can't but carry one."

"You don't look like you can even do that. All right, one it is. That'll be 24 dollars, not pesos. I ain't about to lose my head to one of them monsters they created." I counted out the silver and hefted the box.

It was hot but I was used to it. I didn't even sweat anymore. I didn't think. I subsisted. I walked on, head wrapped in a towel, with my sack of silver and dried meat tied around my waist and the case balanced on my head, which after a while was the only comfortable way of carrying it. I wasn't the only one. Everyone carried their life in their hands or on the their heads and about their belts. The only talk was of food. The man on line said there were reports of cannibals attacking people and eating them. They found the butchered bodies of refugees from the hills, stripped of their edible flesh and organs. That's what he said. Everything was a rumor.

By the time I got home I was so exhausted I couldn't go out and sell the whiskey. I needed to rest, eat and build up my strength. I lay in the pod drinking whiskey and eating the meat. It was hot but not as hot as outside. The system puttered along. Eventually a water truck came once a day. I drank a lot of boiled water.

Nevertheless, a diet of dried fish and meat took its toll. I became constipated and couldn't shit at all. Part was shame of course, squatting alongside the pod, trying to do it at night so no one will see, which was when everyone else was crapping too. The ground was too hard to dig and so it sat there, piles of shit and newspaper in the dead weed patches between pods, urine running in the street gutter. The sun blazed all day baking it into rocks. Then the water truck came and I could use the toilet and flush once a day but there was nothing to flush.

I decided I had to consume something other than dried meat and whiskey. I went in search of rice and fruit, waddling along lugging my intestinal knot of smoked sausage and dried squid. The whiskey was merely rinsing it.

Soon I reached the streets I played on as a kid. There was the strip of takeout food shops, single-story whitewashed adobe cubes with three evenly spaced palm trees per block. And the lot where the food hawkers used to park, empty now except for Frank the Noodle guy. His truck, strung across the side with red lanterns, three stools and a counter, had a line. Everyone with a job had some money now cause everything had to be rebuilt. It wasn't worse than an earthquake, it just lasted longer. And earthquakes are good for guys in the construction business.

I felt like a stranger, yet I had lived there longer than anywhere else. I was a kid when we got kicked out of Seven

Villages and moved to Long Beach. I didn't leave until I was 19. And I always kept the pod in Puvungna. The first property I ever bought, and I'd make a lot on it even now if I sold it.

There was a bar called Thirst that I had drunk in many times nearby. It was a Spanish colonial dome on a deserted, dusty street. The other bars and dance halls on the strip were closed. The hibiscus trees were dead. I took my sack of silver in and sat down at a stool. A fan spun overhead. The walls were dark green. The front window faced the harbour. The water was turquoise and flat and the sun was starting to shine low on it. Out the back windows I could see heaps of fly covered garbage. I had drunk in this bar many times, but it was always packed.

"Bironga, please." I said.

The bartender had a baldhead with a blond comb over, and a potbelly hanging in a T-shirt against black suspenders, holding up the pants, which were cut for a much fatter man. "I only got one kind, Tijuana bock."

"That'll do it."

He walked over to the taps, got out a pint and started to pull the draft. "You got any news?" he asked. "I ain't seen you before."

"I'm looking for some rice. I can't shit."

"No one can. That's why there's no rice." He finished drawing the draft and handed it to me. I paid him and as he went to make change I noticed a slight painful waddle in his gait.

"Any idea when we might get water?" I asked.

"Some fellas in here last week said they was days away from turning it on. The problem is all the broken pipe."

I sipped the beer and looked at the garbage. I said, "It was different before, right? They did pick up the garbage. I'm not imagining that."

"I don't know what's real anymore," the bartender said, rolling a cigarette from a red and black tin with a parrot on the lid.

"Can I buy a cigarette?"

He pushed the tin across the table. "Turkish tobacco."

I rolled up a cigarette. "I was in Topanga and the Los Padres when all this happened."

"You ain't missed much. It was OK when Otis was pinned down in San Pedro and Sargon was up in Santa Barbara, Ocktomann dead. Things got back to normal then. But Sargon defeated the Barachas and chased the Mexicans all the way to San Diego. When he relieved Otis, Otis marched his army on LA. Sargon took his army north. So who do you think is gonna rule Long Beach? It ain't gonna be Sargon. His rule ends in Santa Monica."

"What difference does it make? They're all the same."

"Did you see the city?"

I smoked the cigarette and drank the beer. "Everything between Hollywood and Torrance."

"All that, the work of Otis, against his own people, because they rebelled. Sargon they say don't destroy everything, and he don't rape. Otis rapes whatever moves. And cuts to pieces. He tortures parents in front of their children and impresses them into his army. His troops carry machetes, and they use them from their horses. And the horses eat the bodies of the dead. Sargon don't do all that."

"How about a bottle of whiskey, on the bar, you and me." I stacked the coins and pushed them towards him. The sun was low.

"Yeah, why not. No one's coming in."

I woke up on the food line lying next to the blond man, by the side of the road. It was dawn. I was covered in a damp sweat and chilled. The shadows were long and lavender and the light was apricot. "When did I," I asked the blond man.

"I don't know. I was asleep."

I staggered away and lurched about, falling down and vomiting, until I found my pod and somehow got to bed. I sat in the Jeannie bottle drinking and eating. My stomach throbbed. My eyes were blurry. I really had to find some rice. But I couldn't get up. I drank some more Mekong and fell into a long semi-sleep that lasted for days or weeks. I'll never know. But I knew I had to get up and eat something besides dried beef.

It was morning, the sun was already hot and people were out doing normal things, at least, whatever is normal in a city just after a war. I blinked in the bright light, wrapped the towel around my head and looked at the white ground, shielding my eyes with my hands. Women were sweeping in front of the pods. On Therese Street there was a bustle of workers pushing wheelbarrows of rubble to bulldozer sites, and of couriers, and people walking purposefully by. I sweated and could smell the smoked fat and old turds coming out of my pores. They looked at me and veered away. I wasn't steady on my feet. I was wearing a blue bathrobe over the filthy street clothes I had arrived in.

On a side street I had never been on, in the nice part of town, by the water, past the desalination plant, I found a man selling fruit: figs, dates, plums, grapes, lemons, mandarin oranges. I filled my pillowcase with fruit and waddled home, sweating grease, bloated with stones. In the Jeannie bottle I laid the fruit out on the black, pink and yellow silk coverlet. They were so plump! There were two kinds of figs, green and purple, three kinds of plums, black, yellow and ruby, some mandarins and dates. I pushed a whole plum into my mouth and crushed down to the pit. The sour skin gave way to sweet pulp; I chewed in rapture and ate as much as I could cram into my stomach without rupturing it. I ate so many figs and plums I was panting. Then I drank as much water as I could stand each hour and waited. The stabbing pain and bloat began to change. It mutated, and kicked like a baby going down.

When the time came I didn't dare go outside. The purging lasted days. It was disgusting. My life was disgusting. The pod stank, like the stalls of the flesh eating horses. When I was done I felt ashamed but much better.

No longer pregnant with shit I sauntered over to the line to say hello to my friend, the blond man. I wrapped my head with the towel, took a few silver coins and a bottle of water. Halfway there I had to slow down as the sun was high and the whitewashed buildings blinded me. The blond man was near the entrance to the church. I was filthy, not having bathed in weeks, but I couldn't get on the line with him, the others would kill me.

"I'm glad you came by," the blond man said. He sported a towel around his head and sun goggles. "There were some men asking about you."

"What men?"

"They didn't say. They wore goggles and snoods and suits. They drove up in a black car and they sounded like Santa Barbara Morons."

"When was this?" I looked around. "Do you see them now?"

"No."

There was a commotion up the road, around the block. The corner building was in several pieces. The crowd was visible through cracks in the masonry. They were running towards us; they rounded the corner, came up the block and stopped, turning to face the cross street. There followed three bikers escorting a half dozen prisoners in neck irons, chained together at the waist and hands, shuffling forward, heads bowed, bruised and bloodied from beatings. Following up the rear, two Rulers in silver armor with holstered machetes at their side, whips in hand.

"What the fuck is that?" I asked.

"Otis is in Long Beach rooting out rebels." He spat. "I've been watching them from the line for days now. Some they hang, some they drown, some they shoot, but most they burn. Haven't you smelled it?"

"I've been in my pod."

"The Jeannie bottle, dude. You have to watch out for that. Did you finally shit then?"

"Yeah yeah. I found a guy selling figs and plums."

"The food here doesn't bind you."

"I know, but I couldn't stand being hungry."

He laughed. "What are you going to do?"

"I don't know. When were they here?"

"Just a couple of hours ago."

"Mierda. What did you tell them?"

"I don't even know your name, dude. They said do you know this guy Bob Martin and I said no, cause I don't. Then they showed me the picture. It was you."

I had to think. They were letting people into the church. The line ahead was rustling. Families of eight stood shaking out, rolling and tying their bedrolls. A grandmother brushed her granddaughter's hair and braided it into pigtails, two faces fretting. The little girl wanted her hair wild. She kicked her legs out and made fists with her hands.

"I'm going," I said.

"Where to?" We didn't stand. Not until they were walking. Two guys behind us started to speak in Spanish. I looked at them and raised my eyebrow. Another group of prisoners was marched by. The crowd that followed, or fled, the first, remained, booing and cheering. The Rulers on the horses lifted their black whips and lashed the captives forward. Their backs opened into bloody welts. The crowd cheered and booed even louder. Someone threw a chunk of adobe. It struck the near Ruler's horse on the ass, and the horse missed stride. The Ruler turned his black-mirrored face on the crowd and holstered the whip. The other Ruler stopped but the bikers continued on. He drew out the baton and struck the first Moron he saw across the chest. A puff of smoke rose past his face and the man burst into flames and burned. Others in the crowd threw more chunks of adobe and the Ruler swung his baton, but the crowd surged away and broke up. People ran down the street towards us while the ones throwing the rocks took up positions on the roofs and started shooting at the two Rulers. They reeled around on their horses. The line broke up. I was swirled by people crashing through us to get away. The Rulers holstered their batons and took out concussion guns. A bullet from the top layer of rubble of a collapsed office building struck one of the horses. It surged forward. The Ruler aimed his gun and there was a loud whistle. A shell erupted against the Ruler. He and his horse exploded into pieces. Then two more struck the other Ruler and his horse.

"Fuck!" I said.

The line reassembled and it was quiet, except the sound of the red flames ripping off the body of the man the Ruler had burned.

"Where are you going?"

"How do I know you won't say something?"

"Fair enough. I know your name now," he laughed.

"Well, take care of yourself, man. Here, take these." I handed him a few hand rolled cigarettes and some matches.

"Dude, thank you."

I ran away, clutching my bathrobe. I had the pearl on me, and a little water, but that was it. Back at the pod I had all my food, water and silver, and my goggles. I had to go back there.

I walked east on Grant Street and stopped to buy bag of tobacco and a bottle of whiskey from a woman sitting on a wooden box. I rolled up a cigarette and slowed down, swigging the whiskey as I went. The only thing to do was go to my mother's. It was a risk, but she'd know what to do. She always did. Trouble was her element. The sun pulsed. I came to a water pump and joined the line; washed my head and neck and drank my fill. I wrapped my head with the wet towel and walked on.

I gazed about searching for a sign of the Rulers. There were no black cars that I could see or streets to drive on. As I got closer to the pod I started to circle around. I crossed Goyaałé Street and looked up at the pod. The street was empty. Nothing moved. Dust blew across the dirt yards. I turned and approached slowly, looking this way and that, smelling the air. My mouth was dry and I was sweating through the towel. I came to the pod and checked out the door. I turned the handle and pushed. The stink of mold and garbage grew heavy. I looked into the stairwell, descended into the dark, and listened at the door. It was sealed tight. No use putting it off, I had to open it. I pressed my thumb to the knob and it hissed open. The light was amberglow and as I entered the sun rose on the walls. The Jeannie bottle was empty.

I pulled cotton fabric off the pillows for a cloak. Put all the silver into the bag. Pocketed the pearl. Took two litres of water and two litres of Mekong and strapped them to my waist. I packed the last of the fruit and jerky, and made to go. But I was hungry. So I sat down and ate some jerky and dried sardines and washed them down with the water. Then I remembered the constipation and wolfed down a plum and a fig and an orange. I had to piss. I went to the toilet and peed on a hunk of dried meat shit.

I sat down and started drinking, thinking about how much I missed Elma. I should have stuck by her side. I shouldn't have ever followed Irmela. But Elma didn't give me a choice. She was with that old lady all the time. And before that, Detreuil. There was always someone more important than me. I got bored. Of course I wandered. And it wasn't just for anyone. It wasn't for Betty or Veronica or Lucy in Santa Monica, it was for Irmela, the one who started it all. Because from day one I would have died to have her. So what was I supposed to do? I couldn't figure it out. I drank more and smoked a cigarette. I wanted to smoke some marijuana or opium. I was tired of Mekong. It was time to go. I checked everything and corked the bottle and headed for the door feeling pretty good. I had enough food and money to make it to Barstow. For the first time since the fire I had a plan and a destination. A way out of drift.

There was a knock at the door and nowhere to run.

The blood thumped in my throat. "Come in," I said. The door popped open and two large men in suits entered. They wore silver snoods and green goggles.

"Are you Bob Martin?" the one on the left asked while the one on the right looked around at the parachute cloth walls and the torn up cushions. He sniffed the air and his face twitched.

I was still. I looked each in the eye and said, "Yes sir. That's me. How can I help you?"

"We have a warrant to arrest you on charges of murder and terrorism, and return you to Santa Barbara for trial and execution. Come along."

Chapter Thirty-Six

They bound my wrists behind my back with twist wire, pulled a hood over my head, fastened a choke chain about my neck, and carried me up the stairs. I was thrown into a compartment of some sort. They locked the chain to the lid. Then the doors slammed and we drove off. Every bump we hit tightened the chain against my throat. I had to piss. It was so hot I passed out and only awoke to the feeling of urine running down my leg. Hours later the car stopped and they opened the doors, undid the chain and yanked me out of the compartment. I was marched forward over hard ground and into a building, which was cooler and smelled of polished marble. Next I entered a stifling room that suddenly dropped through the air.

The elevator sank so fast my stomach leapt. It clunked to a stop and they pulled me by the choke collar chain into an even hotter place. We walked for a while. My wet pants were cold and the legs scraped against each other. The air became thick and sour. I could taste blood and sweat. We stopped. They stripped me and yanked the hood off. It was no longer the two men with chiseled faces but two schlubbs with big fuscas on their hips and short batons. The guy on the left was tall. He had a young neck and face red from shaving and a bald head tattooed with spiders. His partner was a toad-shaped man with black hair and dark, warty skin. He had stubby fat fingers with dirty nails. We were in an unlit stone hallway except for a bear-oil lantern hanging from a rusted hook embedded in the wall. It was hot and the air was close as if it were the air originally enclosed by the walls two hundred years ago. They were an arm's length away, batons raised.

The toad said, "You lie face down on that board and we push you in."

I looked down on the ground and there was a filthy board, wet and gritty.

"Go on, lie on it," the tall young one said. He raised his chin slightly. I lay face down on the board, naked, my hands bound behind me. It smelled like raw sewage. It was cold.

Along the wall opposite to the lantern were pressure seal doors a yard high and a yard wide. The door in front of me was open and I could see into the dark cell, which was not much wider than the board and not high enough to stand in. A foul odor emanated from it like bad breath. I shut my eyes as they slid the board with their feet into the hole and the door hissed shut. The cell was 8 feet long, a yard high and 4 feet wide. It was hotter than the hall. I could kneel; I could lie on my stomach, or side. As the board warmed the smell grew stronger. Dangling from the ceiling was a thin clear tube with a drop of water at the end. I immediately got the tube in my mouth and drank until it wouldn't give.

After a while I became comfortable and could lie in a position floating in and out of consciousness, until the pain became unbearable and I would shift. My eyes adjusted to the total absence of light. I entered into nothingness and seemed to float out into space, where I drifted, able to breathe in the absolute silence and dark. Where were the stars and planets? What spur was this? The desert skies of my childhood flashed across my eyes. The owls were hooting. My father put a knot of greasewood on the fire, sparks blooming in the night. He passed the pipe to my mother, who puffed quietly on the Indian tobacco, pulling the serape closer around her shoulders. My brother smoked a cigarette and whittled a stick. I poured coffee into a tin cup and listened to the night singing. Everything became indistinct in my mind as time raced and slowed and the day and night coiled about each other. There were rattlesnakes in the rocks, scorpions in the shoes. Morning never came. The stars faded and the fire died and I was dark, forever dark, in a black, warm beyond, which didn't curve or dance but lay flat and black from one end of time to the other.

That was when they turned the lights and music on.

The light radiated off the walls. It was like living in the sun. It shined through my eyelids and I couldn't block it with my hands. And the music! They played one song that never ended, not for one second:

Irene Goodnight

Irene Goodnight

Goodnight Irene

I'll see you in my dreams

I started to scream. "Please, help! Get me out of here! I'll talk. What do you want to know? I did it all, everything, just please stop!"

I screamed and started to cry and babble. The only thing that silenced me was rage, when I flopped about trying to hit something, until the twist wire cut into my wrists. The wounds festered and got infected from the board and I felt nauseous. Waves of cold and heat surged over me beneath the ceaseless glare of the light and the music, the voice croaking, *Irene goodnight Irene goodnight goodnight Irene.*

Then I lost control of my body. I shit and peed and vomited. The board became slimy and sticky with filth, and all the filth deposited by the people before me. The lights blazed and there was no night, no silence. The music ceaselessly played. I went mad. I exploded inside and my thoughts rioted into incoherence. But my mind would not go, it just crumbled into smaller and smaller pieces and each piece felt all the pain and there was never any relief.

Then I lost track of the outside and entered a place where I understood that I was nothing, that I had never been anything. That when I thought I was on top of the world, that day I first met Irmela, I was not. I had never done anything for anyone. No one knew or cared that I was where I was. I was alone in a world of pain without end and it did not matter. Because I am nothing, not even a speck on the wall. Because I have no thoughts, but thoughts of my own nothingness. *I want to live. If I live, I will be different.* And then the outside world blazes in and I am back on the board.

I can't say if it was more than a couple of days, weeks, hours, months. At random times the tube with water was lowered in for a few minutes. I drank it dry. I don't remember how many times I got the tube.

Finally I disintegrated into the elements of light, music and pain. By the time the door opened and I was slid out into the hall, I was beyond confession, beyond resistance. I wasn't human anymore. I wasn't even an animal. I was fungus.

I couldn't move, so they undid the wire, and lifted me onto a gurney. I was given an injection and pushed down the hall to the elevator by the bald guy while the toad man led the way with a lantern.

The injection aroused me and I became lucid, aware of the pain and of my surroundings. I watched the lantern light bounce off the stone walls and then stared at the ceiling of the elevator, so happy not to be hearing Goodnight Irene. But I was afraid to look at my wrists and ashamed by how filthy I was.

We got off on a floor with offices and lights. There was the sound of typing and of dictation. I was wheeled into a room with a metal door and no windows. The bald one said, "Sit up."

My eyes were focused on the two men. I tried to sit up, but it was too difficult. They each took hold of my arms and lifted me upright and I was able to sit, my legs hanging off the gurney. But my hands were black and bloated with puss and fluid. I couldn't flex my fingers.

"You won't be able to eat," the toad man said.

"What a fucking shame," said the bald man. "That means we might have to feed him."

"If he talks we might." They left and locked the door behind them.

There was a grey metal desk and a chair. A light shined down on the room from the ceiling. The door opened and the men who had arrested me came in. I swung my legs back and forth, hoping to get feeling back. My hands were resting in my lap. One sat down in the chair and the other stood in front of me and said, "Those hands look pretty bad. I could have someone look at them. They'll regenerate if we treat them in time."

The one in the chair looked at me with brittle blue eyes and said, "Let's have it then."

"What?" I asked.

"It," the man in the chair said.

"That's right," the man standing said. "It."

The seated man said, "I think we've demonstrated that we are serious people. Now let's have it."

"I can't if I don't know what *it* is."

The man standing said, "That's just it. We know you know what *it* is."

"But I don't know what it is you want."

"All of it."

"The whole thing. Don't leave anything out."

I asked, "What do you think I know?"

The man in the chair tented his hands and said, "Let's have it." He blinked a few times, leaned back in the chair and took a pack of cigarettes from his coat pocket. "Here," he said. "It will jog your memory. Of course, I know what a fan you are of *Goodnight Irene*."

I couldn't pick up the cigarette so I got one out with my mouth and said, "Will you light it? Please?" They looked at each other. The man standing shrugged and the seated man struck a match with his finger and held the flame to the cigarette. I puffed and inhaled and felt good for a second.

He shook the match out and said, "Would it help if I said the Baron gave you up in return for life in Alcatraz?"

I smoked hard. Junior had to do that. Give me up. Of course he did. Like I was about to do to him. But they got to him first. "So what do you want from me? You got Junior. He's the Baracha, not me. He kidnapped me."

"Why did the Baron kidnap you?"

"Because my car had been to the Summer Palace. When I was an agent working for Junior I showed the place to a guy named Charlie Gets Along who worked for the Ruler Tobor Ocktomann's business agent. So Junior knew my car knew the way in and had cleared once. I was his key, that's all."

The man standing approached me and looked into my eyes. "So, other than those two times, have you ever been to the Summer Palace?"

I knew I had to be strong and not twitch or look away or swallow. I had to be still. If I couldn't be still, and started to tell them things they couldn't possibly know, it would come out, I would talk about the girls, and that I mustn't do. So I froze my heart and said, "No."

"I can take the cigarette if we're done here," the man in the chair said.

"You know we have the story from Junior. In fact Junior knows a lot about your life, Bob. Now you might wonder why, with all this carnage, we'd be busting your balls. Because you were part of a terror gang. Because you harbored the enemy in your house. You didn't report the murder of three Malibu pool workers."

"Report? To who? There was no law. You abandoned us." The standing man placed a hand on my head and with the other squeezed my right hand. The pain burst in all directions. I roared out, "Stop!"

He let go and seized my other hand and said, "Tell us about Agatha Kennedu."

"What's there to tell? The—" I fell silent. I couldn't speak. He squeezed until the tears poured down my face and I gasped.

"The what?" He let go of my hand and the pain and throbbing slowly subsided.

"She owned the house I rented, where the pool people were killed."

"The what? What were you going to say when you cut yourself off?"

"I don't remember." I must not say.

"Remember."

"No, I can't." There was a black hole where the memory was. The standing man reached for my left hand and I jerked it away, which sent a flame up my arm. "I don't know what I meant by The— maybe it was, *the* girls."

He stood upright and I thought I saw a smile pass over his lips like vapour off an ice cube. "The girls? Why won't you talk about the girls? What are you afraid of?"

"Nothing. Junior must have told you about the girls."

"You tell me."

"What's in it for me?" He looked at my hand and gazed into my eyes, his lips still. "Elma was my girlfriend. She has a kid sister, Irmela."

"Yes," the seated man said. "You were very fond of them, weren't you? You protected them. You're protecting them now."

"They had a bad time growing up."

"What kind of a bad time?" he asked, his hands folded on the desk.

"You don't need to know that."

"I'm interested in the full story."

"Junior's got his side of things. I'm not moving against him though, if that's what you want."

"Now you're protecting the Baron? You were ready to give him up two seconds ago."

"This guy's not very smart," the standing one said.

"I'm smart enough to know a thing or two."

The seated man nodded. "Then why don't you tell me about Irmela and Elma. Why did you need to protect them?"

I put up a black wall in my mind, between me and what I knew about the girls. "Like I said, they had a hard time growing up."

"What kind of a hard time?"

"They were orphans, raised by an Austrian uncle who took them to Jerusalem and Azerbaijan to pimp them out. They escaped but everywhere they went some man took them in and enslaved them. The last was this guy David, who owned a sex club off of Sunset Strip."

"So how did you help them with that situation?"

"I guess you could say I helped them get out of it. The man was a pig."

"Tell me about it," said the standing man. "When you say he was a prick, how do you mean?"

"I said he was a pig."

The seated man said, "Describe a pig for us."

"He was fat and smelled bad, but that doesn't make you a pig. He sat in a chair watching movies of women fucking. That doesn't really make you a pig either. But chaining the girls to the bed, forcing them to fuck each other, and fuck clients for no pay, that makes him a pig."

"He tortured them. They were his sex slaves."

I blurted out, without intending to, "He blackmailed them."

"With what?" asked the man standing, leaning his face closer to mine.

I tried to make my heart still, and put a stone up in my mind, grey and featureless, like an asteroid in space drifting. "I don't know. Maybe something happened in Jerusalem, or Azerbaijan that David knew about. They never told me."

"They are Austrians, orphaned at a young age, who lived in Jerusalem and Azerbaijan. How did they come to California?"

"Their uncle brought them to Montreal and they ran away from him and went to New York, where they started a musical act called Gaha: Babes of the Abyss. A producer took them to Vegas, promising to make them rich, but he made them do porn films between bookings. David bought their contract and brought them to LA."

"How old were they?"

"Seventeen and twenty-three when we met."

"And how long have you known them?"

"Why is this all about them? I thought you wanted to know about the time with the Barachas, and Agatha Kennedu."

"We want all of it," the standing man said.

The seated man said, "If you want us to help you, you must tell us everything."

"How long have you known them?"

"I don't know. Say three years. It's a good guess."

"You don't know."

"We were fucked up a lot of the time."

"Where did you say the girls were from?"

"Jerusalem. Or Austria. It was Austria."

"And what about David, the pimp. What happened to him?"

"You know what happened, he got shot."

"Who shot him?"

"I'd rather not say."

"Why?"

"For obvious fucking reasons. It was self-defense. That man had a shotgun on me, and Irmela, who had stolen my fusca, shot at him but missed. I hit him in the head with a baseball bat. Then she gunned him down to be sure."

"I see. What happened next?"

"We went to live at my house."

The man seated at the desk held a cigarette up and I leaned over and grabbed it with my lips. He stood and lit a match. "It wasn't your house. It never was. You stole it from the de Marcoses to use as a terror base, to make war against the Rulers. We'll be back." The two men left the room, and a minute later one of them brought me a bottle of water and a stick of sugarcane. I picked it up with my teeth off of the gurney, which had an ammonia and onions smell and chewed out the juice until my molars hurt. I drank the water but I didn't want to be lucid. I wanted to be nothing again. I wanted to walk around the room but was scared my legs wouldn't work. I swung them back and forth and somehow hopped down off the gurney onto unsteady feet. I took a few steps and then paced the office. After the drawer it felt like infinite space.

Chapter Thirty-Seven

Hours later the door opened and the man who had been seated came in with a Ruler who ducked in the doorway and filled the room, which had seemed so large to me earlier. The man who had been seated sat and the Ruler stood in front of me. I looked up at his face from the gurney and saw that it was Sargon. "So. Bob. We meet again. Let me see your hands." I held them up. They were black, yellow and purple, swollen with bloody cracks weeping clear fluid. The fingers were like chorizos and the nails blackened and soft, about to fall off. "Who put you in the drawer?"

"A couple of guards."

"Did you order that?" Sargon asked the man who was seated.

"Yes, sir."

"Why?"

"Because he is a Baracha, a war criminal and terrorist."

Sargon chuckled. "He is a murderer, not a terrorist. If he were a terrorist, and honorable, I would have him shot or sent to prison. The Baron I sent to prison. He is a principled man. His revenge was just. But you are a psychopathic killer. I have been following you since you killed the de Marcos's to gain ownership of their house. I could smell their blood on your floor. But I didn't know about Detreuil and the Priest and Margaret until I interrogated the man who calls himself the Baron and he gave them up. I could have you burnt for these crimes tomorrow. Is there any reason I shouldn't?"

I said nothing.

"Let's go over it again."

"I already told them what happened."

"I want to hear it from you."

"I never murdered anyone. If I killed it was in self-defense."

"You mean David? The pig who deserved to die? The younger woman, Irmela, shot him?"

"But she missed. He turned to shoot at her and I hit him across the head with the baseball bat. So maybe I killed him, maybe I didn't. But either way it was self-defense. He was gonna kill us all with that shotgun of his."

"I suppose the de Marcoses were self-defense too?"

"Absolutely. We were clearing out of there. If they'd arrived two hours later nothing would have happened. And the way it was I tried to get them out without a fight. But the guy was an idiot. Wanted to be a hero. He pulled a fusca out and accidently shot and killed his wife. Then he turns on me, so I shot him."

"Why didn't you call the police to explain yourself?"

"They would never have believed me. Just like you don't."

Sargon nodded and smiled. "I'm trying to believe you Bob, but you don't tell the truth. Tell the truth and I'll believe you. Tell me about Detreuil."

"Detreuil was a poor dying marica, a sailor the Priest and Margaret found. He needed someone to take care of him and my friend Elma needed residency papers. So she married him and he made her his life insurance beneficiary. She took good care of him, and when he died Elma got the insurance money."

He nodded. "Things have a way of working out that way for you. I pulled the paperwork in Santa Barbara. Seems you sold him the life insurance policy."

"I'm licensed. It was legal."

"So you lived at the house with the von Doderer sisters and Detreuil."

"That's right. Taking care of him. They trained as nurses in Switzerland."

He turned his head slightly and blinked. "Switzerland? Montreal? New York, Vegas and LA. Interesting. Did Detreuil know about the life insurance policy?"

"He signed it, didn't he?"

"Did he?"

"You saw the form."

"I'm not asking you that. Did he know what he was signing?"

"Yes."

Sargon looked at the seated man, wet his thick lips and stroked his chin with his index finger. The room was silent. "Agatha Kennedu. Why did she make Elma her heir?"

"Elma was her nurse. She wished to die at home. She had a little cash and wanted to reward her."

"How did you meet her?"

"She inherited the house after the de Marcoses disappeared."

"You mean after you murdered them."

"I told you, he killed his wife and tried to kill me."

"Let's get back to Agatha Kennedu."

"The old lady leased the house to us and the girls started to visit her at the Azodiazadora."

"Yes, we have witnesses."

"Impossible, it was destroyed during the siege."

"How do you know that?"

"A person hears things."

"Who told you?"

"A neighbor."

"Give us his name."

"What difference does it make? He's nobody."

"You should have no problem with the name then."

"Pyotr Arkady? That's all I know. A chiropractor whose mother was at the Azodiazadora too."

"Where is he now? How can we find him?"

"How should I know? When Topanga burned he either died in his house or fled like we did."

"We."

"Yeah, me and the girls."

"Where are the girls now?"

"I don't know. We got separated walking into LA."

"And Agatha Kennedu? What happened to her?"

"Ask Junior! We left her with him, when you attacked the Barachas."

"I'm asking you."

"I told you."

"Tell me again."

"We left her when you attacked."

"And what was her condition?"

"Bad. The kidney cancer had come back and she was dying."

"Not dead."

"I left her alive in the bed. But the Summer Palace was under attack. I doubt she survived."

"Why did you lie about the Summer Palace?"

"I didn't. No one ever asked me about it."

"Earlier they asked you how many times you had been there. You didn't mention the time I found you there."

"I forgot."

"Really? Interesting." He said to the seated man, "It seems I am forgettable!" He laughed and turned back towards me. "Why were you there that day?"

"Which day?"

"The day I found you."

"We were with the Priest and Margaret seeing a show in Syukhtun and got lost in the Los Padres. The car took us to the Palace. I figured with no one there, what could be the harm?"

"Ocktomann 4 didn't worry you?"

"Like I said, he wasn't there."

"So what happened to the man you call the Priest and his wife Margaret?"

"Everyone called him that and I have no idea. When the Mexicans overran Ocktomann 4 they went down to San Pedro to start over. Maybe Lord Otis knows where they are."

He slapped my face so hard I fell off the gurney to the floor, striking my hands. I pissed and cried out. "Get up."

I stood, afraid to look at him, and sat naked on the gurney, staring at the puddle of urine on the floor.

"Now tell me what happened to the Priest and Margaret. Why did you kill them?"

"I didn't kill them. I told you, they disappeared."

"I thought we had a deal here Bob."

"What kind of deal was that?" My cheek throbbed. I was starting to get tired. The stimulant was wearing off. My hands trembled.

"Maybe you are as stupid as they say." He shook his head and looked sad. "I don't believe in the drawer. I think torture is wrong. But I am determined to find out the truth. In war, truth is destroyed for the short-term gain of victory. But after war, the first act of recovery is the restoration of justice and truth, so the people will know that they are safe, and that their Rulers are just. So if you can convince me that your crimes were justified and not for money, then I might consider not burning you. There are other destinies even for the damned."

"What am I bargaining for?"

"You aren't bargaining Bob. You're confessing. Now what happened with the Priest and Margaret?" The man seated at the desk whistled a few bars of *Goodnight Irene*.

"I'm getting tired. I can't really think straight." Voices in my head, thoughts, memories, were running together. The stones were crumbling into sand that oceans carried off to different shores.

"Would you like to lie down on a soft bed and sleep for a while?" he asked in a slow, gentle voice, as if he were calling me into bed, a beautiful young woman beckoning with her open mouth and breasts.

"Yes." I felt small. I wanted that bed so badly, I could feel the sheets fresh from the wash against my cheek.

"It would be lovely, wouldn't it? In a room cool enough for a blanket, your hands soaking in ReGeneGel." I stared at the floor. The air swarmed with phosphorescent gnats. "Tell me about the Priest and Margaret."

"What do you want to know?" I mumbled.

"How did you kill them?"

"It wasn't my fault. They were going to turn us in for the de Marcos killing to collect the reward. There are rules. I would have burned for it."

"So what did you do?"

"Irmela and I shot them in the driveway."

"Irmela again. She's quite the little murderer isn't she?"

"It was self-defense, like I said. He worked for me. Do you think I wanted to kill him? It was Margaret who put him up to it. I should have just gotten rid of her."

"So you regret killing the Priest."

"I don't regret anything. I did nothing wrong. If you don't do anything wrong, you can't have regrets."

"How did you dispose of their bodies?"

"I had a much better idea this time. I dissolved them in acid and poured it down the pool drain. But it fucked up the pool. That's why the pool guys were there when the Barachas came. They were working for me. I didn't kill them. I tried to save their lives."

"You're a good man, you're trying to say?"

"Yeah. I wouldn't just kill anyone. Even if it wasn't stupid I wouldn't do it. When Junior made me go out on patrol, I didn't kill anyone."

"Why?"

"Why? I had no reason to."

"Weren't they shooting at you? It would have been self-defense."

"Not at me, no. At Junior and his gang."

"Gang? Weren't they an army?"

"Not at first. They holed up at my house and they had a couple of cars that's it. But Junior was full of hate. He wanted to exterminate the Rulers so he brought all of the militias from LA to the Summer Palace, and trained them to be an army. He didn't tell you that, did he?"

"What happened to Agatha Kennedu?"

"I told you already. She died in her sleep on the bed and we left her."

"You said she was alive and well."

"When was that?"

"A moment ago. Now you say she was dead?"

"I don't know. I haven't eaten. I can't remember what I just said."

The light grew bright. I looked at the floor and the bulb glowed on the puddle of piss. "What happened to Agatha Kennedu?"

"We left her!" I screamed.

"Alive or dead?"

"Dead! Irmela suffocated her so we could leave. We would have been killed if we had stayed."

"Irmela."

"Yes Irmela."

"So where are Irmela and Elma? Hmm?"

"I don't know. I told you, we became separated."

"Separated where?"

"In the Hollywood Hills. We walked out of Topanga after the fire and at the checkpoint entering LA there were crowds everywhere. It was impossible to stay together."

The Ruler Sargon looked at the man seated at the desk and said, "Don't bother cleaning him up. We'll burn him in the courtyard in the morning."

The man who was seated at the desk stood. I panicked and shouted out, "Wait. There's one more thing I didn't tell you."

The Ruler Sargon said, "What's that?"

"I don't want to die. I didn't murder those people, not in cold blood."

"Where can I find the sisters? Are they together?"

"I don't know. Irmela plays pinball for pearls."

"Where?"

"I don't know the places, but I know she likes LA Yaanga, I know she likes Hollywood and Beverly Hills. Maybe Torrance."

"I can arrest the von Doderers on your confession. And after I arrest them, I can execute you on theirs," the Ruler Sargon said.

"What if I knew something about them you don't know. Would that be worth something?"

Sargon looked at me strangely and smiled. "It depends on what that is."

"You don't just have a killer on your hands, you've got a Martian Princesse." His eyes opened wide and became dark blue. The man seated at the desk sat up straight. "Her father was a Quarantined Martian Ruler, a rebel, and her mother was the woman they called Phaedra."

He grabbed my throat and threw me to the floor. "You are a liar! A murderer!"

I gasped. "Elma is Phaedra's daughter by a Ruler! They have been on the run their entire lives. And she's pregnant!" He let go and narrowed his eyes. I tried to breathe but my windpipe felt like a crushed can.

"Guard!" he called out. The door opened. He said, restraining his voice, his eyes blackening and hair taking on a malevolent glow, "Throw it in the drawer."

Chapter Thirty-Eight

They dragged me into the elevator and forced my screaming head into a hood. It was only the pain of my throat being strangled by the choke chain that made me quiet down. When they bound my hands again I started to whimper and beg. My knees gave out. They raised me by my hands and pulled the chain and I gave in to the fire shooting up my arms. I begged until my voice was dead and then they forced me down and held me to the board. The door closed and the lights and music came on. *Goodnight Irene, Goodnight Irene, Irene Goodnight, I'll see you in my dreams....*

There was no sleep and no dreams. I had betrayed Irmela and Elma. And I betrayed myself when I broke the promise I had made in the drawer, when I found the hidden place where things were clear. The path was set. Now we shared the same fate. Maybe we had all along. From the day of my birth I knew I had entered a whirlpool. Elma and Irmela were in it too and it was taking us into darkness and death where we belonged.

For my people death is no dishonor. But we were not warriors. We would fight and die, but our life was one of peace, as was our neighbors'. What came after was part of the fall, but it was not the whole fall, or so they tell us. There is an old English

song that Elma sometimes sang. It is the one called *Katie Cruel.*
She whistled between the verses.

I wish I was where I would be

Then I'd be where I am not

Here I am where I must be

Where I'd be I cannot

I don't know how I lived but I did. I lay in the jaws of that
sarcophagus for hours that felt like days, listening to *Goodnight
Irene, Goodnight Irene, Irene Goodnight, I'll see you in my dreams.*
Where no dreams are possible and the only darkness is within. I
am nothing.

The door opened. The board rolled out into the corridor. A
woman's voice asked, "Can you move?"

"I don't know," I said.

"Try."

I was lying on my stomach, my head propped up on my chin,
facing the open door. I tried to get up but I couldn't manage it.
I was like a fish in a net. She bent forward and cut the cord. My
hands fell free and struck the floor and I rolled up into a ball like
a bug and screamed. The hall was dark except the circle of amber
light thrown by the lantern. As the pain subsided the white lights
faded from my eye and I saw the dark, and then the walls and
finally boots casting shadows on the floor. I got to my feet. A Ruler
woman, a head taller than me, was standing there in black armor.
Her face was framed entirely in shadow, floating in the air above
her body.

"Come with me. Don't give me a reason to kill you." Her voice
was void-like but not unkind. She took me down the passage to a
back stair that I took a step at a time down three flights to a door
that led into another unlit stone passageway and to another door,
which hissed open. We went into a bare office with baize walls.

There was a steel desk in the center of the room and two chairs, one on either side.

She said, "Sit down."

The Ruler Sargon came in and sat down opposite me. He was in a plain black collared shirt. The Ruler woman stood by staring into the middle distance.

"I want to know everything you know about the von Doderers. And start with the so-called Martian Princesse. Where did you hear that phrase?"

His face swam in and out of focus. I tried to remember where I had gotten the phrase because I wanted to be good. But I couldn't. "I just made it up on the spot. I knew she was from Mars."

"How did you know this?"

"I didn't at first. I thought they were Austrians. And they turn out to be incestuous lesbian porn stars from Mars. Go figure that happening to you. But all I can say is it made sense as I went along. You know, one foot in front of the other, following the scent. And then you look around one day and go, what the fuck happened? Where am I? How did I get here? Anyway, Irmela told me because when the hills burned we were caught in a wildfire, and had to hide in the pool. I went under three, four minutes. It was terrifying. But she went down for a half hour and comes up with blue skin and lips, alive. And that wasn't the first time. The first time we were on peyote, so I didn't know how long she was really down for."

His face died as I talked; the cheeks dropped, the eyes welled up with tears. He was leaning against the desk, gripping his arms to his chest. He took a breath and did nothing to hide his grief. He said, "I was following them not you. Since they lived in Montreal, where they killed the man you call their uncle. I followed them to New York, but they had moved on to Vegas. I was always a step behind, and I didn't know what they looked like. In every city their pimp turns up dead and they disappear. When I learned of David's murder I was suspicious.

"I suppose something about them always disturbed me. I felt uneasy both times I met them. It was always a possibility. More than once I had the absurd idea that I was chasing the Martian Princesse. Still, it had more the quality of a tabloid myth than reality. Our intelligence is not good. We only knew that a forbidden hybrid was reported to have escaped the quarantine. In some versions it was two young women, children of the Ruler Ocba, a Martian/human hybrid. No one believed it. But I knew. And I used to wonder, what if it was my daughter? Would I blame her for killing these men, or for being born of the mother and father who made her?

"Elma is my daughter. Her mother, Phaedra, was my wife and I loved her. Her children are my children, whoever their father might be. But you must understand, if Irmela is a hybrid, what this means. No one must ever know who she is. If they do she dies. I trust no one but the Ruler Renee. Do you understand? The man who was in the room when you blurted out that she was a Martian Princesse is suspicious. My reaction alerted him certainly, but he heard what you said, and he's trained to listen for things like that. He won't forget. He has already made inquiries. You and I have no reason to trust each other, but I can offer you a deal."

"What's that?"

"My troops searched the city for the von Doderers. They were too late. Lord Otis has seized them. They're in the holding cell of the city jail. So far he doesn't seem to know who they are. But word will leak out. We have to move fast. Go to the Lord Otis's prison in Ruler uniform, assigned to my staff as a sergeant and bring Elma and Irmela to me."

"For what?"

"You may go free, if you can. You will be an outlaw. I will not pursue you, but others will. You have to leave my jurisdiction. Go where you like, but never return to LA, or anywhere south of San Francisco."

"I've never been anywhere else. If you won't go after me, who will? Can't you fix that?"

"What you have heard of Otis is true. I tell you this now because I must know that I have your loyalty. If he or anyone should find out who Irmela and Elma are, they will be killed and then they will kill me, and they will hunt you down and kill you too. You mustn't tell anyone, here or there what you are doing. I will kill you myself if you do. No one."

I looked at my hands and then at him and saw the lights in my eyes and heard the song. I said, "It depends on what they do to me."

"You'll be safe in that uniform. There's a badge that checks out. We'll clean you up, heal your hands, make you strong again. You are under the jurisdiction of the Ruler Renee. She, and only she, will see you from now on. We've never talked."

"OK, yes sir," I said, sitting up as straight as I could.

Sargon's face lightened and he asked, "Is she really pregnant? Is the child yours?"

"I've said all I have to say."

"I regret putting you back in the drawer." His hair glowed and he walked away.

The Ruler Renee had black hair and daisy white skin. She wheeled me to a small room with a high, barred window, a bed, a toilet and a shower. On the bed were white cotton shorts and a shirt.

The Ruler Renee brought in a basin of ReGeneGel and sat down on the toilet. It looked so small beneath her. She put the basin on my lap and said, "Soak your hands in this for two hours, then take them out and rest. I'll come later and replace it. We must do this several times, until the tissues grow back."

I lowered them into the warm blue liquid and feeling returned to my hands. They gave me something to drink, ground up bananas and oatmeal, with yogurt and honey. Then I drank bitter tea. When it was time to rest, the Ruler Renee helped me bathe, stood at the shower door and used a soft brush to scrub my legs, chest and back. I couldn't hold a toothbrush so I washed my mouth out with AgitRinse, and put on the pajamas and fell into a deep sleep.

When I awoke I didn't open my eyes, I curled up into the sheets and blanket and tried to forget where I was. The light came on and the Ruler Renee, dressed in black, brought me a tray of grapefruit, coffee, lemonade, a banana and cold rice cereal with coconut milk.

I said, "I can't use utensils."

"Have you tried?"

I looked at my hands. They were lobster red. But I could touch my fingertips and hold a spoon. I ate everything. Later she came back with a basin of ReGeneGel. I sat mindlessly soaking my hands, watching them recover. Soon I could flex all of my fingers and the skin was a normal color. And she sat there with me, so big and beautiful. She reminded me of Elma. Her lips were strong; her eyes were dark and sparking. And her skin. It was unreal, a white I had never seen in humans.

I started to pace the cell. I ate thin strips of venison and boar with sprout salads, rice and fruit. I took a honey drink. They brought sashimi, seaweed and a bowl of vinegared rice. The next day I was ready. The Ruler Renee brought me my uniform, a soft inner garment with black armor and a helmet. The sergeant stripes were frayed. The armor was dented and scarred. The boots had worn down heels. It smelled of smoke.

"Couldn't spring for a new one?" I asked.

"It would stand out. You must listen now. There is bad blood between them. The cities stand poised to war, which we would prevent. But if Lord Otis should prevail, we both know what is coming. Otis could seize us without firing a shot if it were known that the Martian Princesse exists, and is alive on earth. I remind you of this to protect you from being stupid. Much more hangs on what you do today than you can imagine."

She opened a bag and laid out two fuscas and a baton, ID, short grenades and a curved battle knife. "While you were sleeping we placed a bomb in your heart that will go off if you try to run away."

"Thanks for letting me know."

"Your position will be known at all times."

"What do I do?" I put the grenade belt on and holstered the baton, the fusca and the knife.

"No one here will go with you, but if you don't know what you're doing, that won't tip them off. No one knows what's going on there. The headquarters is on South Alameda Street. Go into the 6th Street entrance. You'll have to sign-in as Gus Holloran. Can you do that?"

"If I practice."

"Scribble it out. Every transaction is a signature and a thumbprint. They'll let you into the general jail and you'll have a paper remanding them to your custody. There shouldn't be a problem. Put the wire on their wrists and drive them to the Summer Palace. Sargon will meet you there and then you can go. Do that and you will not be burned. If you try to run off or are captured, we will blow you up."

Chapter Thirty-Nine

The city jail was a broken white tower of 25 stories. Many floors had collapsed; others would support weight, and some were precarious. I stood on the sidewalk, the cruiser parked by a hunk of upended roadbed, and gazed up at the facade. It was blasted hot, late afternoon. A windless, polluted day, thick with the smell of burning human flesh and the gunfire of mass executions.

The door lintel had a giant crack in it, but officious looking men in suits and troops in armor marched in and out so I figured, it must be OK.

The tall metal doors entered into a green and pink marble lobby with a five-story atrium lurching at an angle over itself. Every few seconds a piece of the ceiling, small, the size of a silver coin, spun to the floor. The back wall of the lobby was a bank of brass-framed, bulletproof windows, like the train depot, with doors to the elevator lobbies under heavy guard. A sensing unit sat in the middle of the room in a dried-up fountain. It made inscrutable noises and blinked, the scout of people hidden behind steel blast walls. I hadn't thought there would be one. And what it could read off me, I didn't know. I felt the grenade belt and the baton, to be sure where they were, and touched the fuscas. Then

I walked into the bustle of military brass going back and forth in the lobby. There was a sign with a picture of a helmet with a red line through it. I took mine off and carried it under my arm like everyone else.

Behind the glass, heavy-lidded Morons checked credentials, which had to be hand written and embossed by the sender, and embossed by each recipient. I stood on the information line. A man with a crew cut and warts on his neck, one eye a little lower than the other, reviewed my papers and directed me on to a short line at the last window.

The only light in the room came in through the information windows, the color of suncups. Ahead of me were two soldiers with papers for prisoners. They had the same uniform and equipment I had. For a moment I thought they might be the guards who put me on the board. I felt hot and awhirl then, my heart thumped. I told myself to calm down. I smelled the marble. It was clean. The lobby was soothing and clean and polished. People dressed in uniforms and suits. They weren't wolfish. They were relaxed. I could be relaxed too.

The soldiers took back their papers and went through the door next to the window marked 1. I stepped up to the window and handed a red-headed man with pink skin and bloodshot green eyes the papers. He examined them through half-framed reading glasses. "We transferred 59 and 60 to the common holding cell. You can pick 'em up there. Just put your thumb down and sign here, and here. OK, go through door one and take the first elevator to the fifth floor. You're going to take them out the back way. That will be via the rear elevator on that floor, marked EXITS."

"I parked out front. Can't I bring them through here?"

"No prisoners transfer through the lobby," he said, as if he'd said it 20 times that hour.

"Should I move the car then?"

"Just walk them out the tunnel and go around the building."

"Thanks." I went through door 1 and pushed the up button on the first elevator. It was a stone hallway painted in butter yellows. The elevator creaked into place and I listened to its Marley chains jangle in the shaft. I got off on five, walked down a greenlit hall and into a cavernous room in which the entire perimeter was jail cells. The room smelled like the human tide at its lowest ebb. People packed the cells. They gripped the bars with bony hands. They squatted haunch-to-haunch and stared. They were pressed up against the walls. There was a low, constant murmur punctuated by hysterical cries, piercing wails of grief, sobbing. Coughs and angry argument erupted and spread and faded when a guard stepped towards the cage and raised his baton.

In the center of the room were desks and armed guards. Guards stood before each cage and before each desk. They stood two to an exit. I recognized people in the cages from the line and the neighborhood. But they were unfamiliar, pressed together like that inside. I handed my papers to the Ruler seated at the desk, pondering a crossword puzzle. He was older, with bushy eyebrows and glowing grey hair, but his face was still strong and angry and his eyes seemed to stare down at me, even looking up from the desk chair. I handed him the papers. There was a loud man talking in one of the cells closest to us pointing hysterically out of it. A guard pushed him back from the bars with a nightstick and he yelled louder. I searched for the girls.

The Ruler said, "They are at the far end with transfer cases. Go to the last desk and they'll direct you." He signed and pressed his finger on the papers and said, looking at the guard, "What's he on about? Doesn't he ever stop?" I embossed and signed and headed to the last desk.

The Lord at that desk was a mere pup compared to the other, probably a motorbike failure. He glared at me too and his size made me think of a giant toddler, and I was scared. "Guard?" he called, holding up the paper. "He's here for 59 and 60. It's a remand."

The guard nodded and took his time walking to the cage. There they were standing, Irmela in her black skirt and stained and torn white shirt and jellies, Elma in a grey tunic over black drawstring pants and flip-flops. Elma looked terrified as I approached. Irmela stared at me with blank grey eyes. The guard opened the door and Elma looked into my eyes and recognized me. She blinked and her hair glowed. Everyone stared at it as it pulsed dully. Irmela betrayed nothing. She stared at me with curiosity. The guard moved them out and I said, "Turn around. Put your hands behind your back." I took out the twist wire and saw the guard watching me work. I had never put twist wire on, only had it put on me. It wasn't that hard. I wrapped her wrists and twisted it three times. She opened and closed her hands. Then I did Irmela. Her hands were cold. Her hair was glowing in the roots.

The Lord said, "Where'd you girls get your hair? It looks real."

"We had wealthy relations in Austria," Elma said. "This was a gift of our family."

He nodded. "Oh yeah, Austria."

"Thank you, sir," I said. I signed and put my thumb on the paper, as did the guard. I walked behind them three steps and we advanced down the room between the cages and the desk. The guards turned their heads to watch us pass. The front line of the cages erupted in hooting as the girls went by. Men yelled out.

As I passed the cage where the commotion had been a man reached for the bars and I recognized him. It was the blond haired man from the food line. He yelled, "That's him! I'm telling you, the man who had the Martian girlfriend! I told you it was real, but you wouldn't stop, you kept pouring the water! That's him. Bob Martin! And that must be them! Look! I'm telling you, she's a

Martian. Bob Martin told me so. Get me out of here! I don't wanna die."

"Shut, the, fuck, up!" the guard said. He smacked at his head with the baton and sparks flew off the bars. The man from the line continued pointing at me. I had to keep going as if I didn't know him. And we had to get the fuck out of there. But I didn't want to blow it by moving too fast. No one there was in any kind of a hurry. And in the cells, you did what you were told.

I marched them towards the elevator at the far end marked *Exits* and passed the two men who had arrested and interrogated me. I couldn't put on the helmet, so I looked straight ahead. On the elevator Elma started to say something and I blinked and she fell silent. At the door to the tunnel I presented the paper and the guard examined it slowly, as the light was dim and he didn't read well. "All right. Take the tunnel out. Don't talk to anyone in there. Don't engage your helmet until you hit the street."

He signed and embossed the papers. The door seal hissed open. I marched the girls forward into the tunnel, a stone tube leading to the street. There were many entering and leaving the tube at different points. We walked silently by them towards the light and then, into the dusty broken whitewashed glare of the afternoon. I had to get my bearings straight. There was a desperate throng that circled the building, of people released, of those awaiting news, and prisoners being delivered in the back, by the wagonload.

Out there we were just more of the same. I breathed a little easier. We turned the corner and got to 6th Street. I cut the wire to free their hands. "Get in front, Elma," I said. "Irmela sit in back and shoot from the windows if you have to." I tossed her a fusca and kept the other one, the grenades and the baton for myself. Elma kissed my lips. I started the cruiser up and rolled out. There was a noise, a siren, and I looked in the rearview. Bikes were headed our

376 Gaha: Babes of the Abyss

way, and a guard group came out of the lobby doors, training their fuscas on the car. I hit it and drove out fast. Bullets whipped off the armored glass and doors.

As long as I had road I could beat the bikes. Alameda to the Freeway to Santa Monica had to be open. But that was where they'd go so I took backstreets to Wilshire Boulevard, the bikes on my tail, sometimes gaining, sometime falling back.

I came to a cross road blocked with a pile of construction debris and drove up over it and down the other side. But it didn't slow them down at all. Every wreck, every pile of rock I lost ground to them. Their sound was sawing into range. In the mirrors they were blurs of red and black. Irmela looked out the back window.

"Who are they now?" Elma asked. "Why were we in that place?"

I gripped the wheel and tried to breathe. "What do you mean why?"

"They did not say why. They asked many questions about you."

Irmela said, "They put the water down my throat. I betrayed you. I was afraid they would discover that I cannot be drowned."

I said, "Either way you're dead."

"And this way? Are we not dead also?" Elma asked. She was indignant. "Always it is death with us. It never ends."

The road was thick with bicyclists and people on foot. They fled to the side of the road as we tore by. There were no cars except official ones, and no livestock. I couldn't see then how all of this would end. It would just go on, a war that outlasts generations.

The motorbikes were gaining on us. Two more joined at an entrance and I saw ahead, coming from a hotel parking lot, another two. They came upon us like a swarm. I knew what I was going to do. The girls had to make it to Sargon. He would protect them better than I ever could. I said, "I'm going to pull off in the service lane and get out of the car. Drive to the Summer Palace, Elma. If you can make it to Santa Monica you'll be all right. The car will drive you there."

"I won't do it. I'm not leaving you. We will do what we must do Bob. Keep going."

"I'm done for," I said. "You have to get away now, or die on this road. You see Sargon, he's your father."

Elma made a noise I didn't understand.

Irmela said, "It can't be."

"It's true. The point is he'll protect you. But you have to drive ahead. I can hold them off." I drove into the service lane and got out of the car and Elma yelled out, "Bob!"

I looked at her and smiled. I said, "I told him about the baby. It makes him happy." A shell exploded and shrapnel ripped into my helmet.

Irmela opened the door and took aim at the riders. I turned around. The bikers were almost upon us buzzing in a haze beside the old palm trees, fuscas drawn. The first approached. Irmela fired on him and I tossed a grenade. The driver exploded into tiny pieces and slicked the road with a bloody grease that combusted into dark red flame and chugged black smoke. Yes, I thought, and threw another, and another at the riders, who erupted across the road, their bikes whipping out from under the falling gel. I hit a bike and it melted beneath the rider, who clattered across the hard dirt. I hit the rider behind him and his bike skidded into the rider on the ground.

A round knocked me across the road, away from the car. The bikers swarmed towards me. Irmela kept up fire but fell silent, and the car pulled out. A biker flew in from ahead and lobbed a grenade at it but missed and hit another biker who was engulfed in flame. I turned and threw at him and missed. It was close; the rider had his gun on me. He fired and my leg gave out. Another ripped across my back. Then I was hit in the head. The helmet took most of it. Then the chest. I couldn't breathe and fell. I tossed a grenade at him and it hit his helmet, only partially melting his body, which rode straight on for 500 hundred feet, headless. A biker chased up the road, after the cruiser and threw. That time the grenade exploded on top of the car and a ball of flame opened around it. But the car kept going. I fell to the dirt.

I was down to two grenades, lying senseless on the ground with breached armor. I had broken ribs, a broken leg, I was bleeding from shrapnel that found my neck, and I could feel blood trickling in my helmet. I sat up and turned my head in all directions, waiting to throw. But there were no other riders. The road was empty.

There were bikes and smoking grease spots all over the road. I crawled on the ground towards a bike, dragging my leg behind me. I didn't want to end my life like that, on the road, or tortured by Otis. I didn't care how far I'd get, that's how far I'd go. I didn't care if they set it off. Let them do it. I lay beside a bike until I had the strength to stand. The sky pulsed above me and swam around. I stood and took the bike and sat down on it. It glided forward. It obeyed my hands. I rode it into the Hollywood Hills, waiting for the bomb to go off in my heart.

THE END